THE GENEVA PROJECT

SECRETS

To Emma,
Can you keep a SECRET?

To Emma,
Can you keep a secret?
Olli

THE GENEVA PROJECT
SECRETS

CHRISTINA
BENJAMIN

For information regarding permission, write to:
Attention: Crown Atlantic Publishing
136 ML King Ave., St. Augustine, FL 32084

Published in the United States by Crown Atlantic Publishing

ISBN 978-0-9883375-2-7

Text set in Adobe Garamond
Designed by Philip Benjamin

Printed in the United States of America
First edition paperback printed, September 2014

This book is dedicated to,

Dalton, for being a continued source of light and inspiration in my life. The sun will shine, for you alone have the power to bring light to the darkness.

And to Philip, whose unconditional love and support continues to astound me. You are my anchor, without you I would be lost at sea.

Special thanks to my helpers, who cheer me on and encourage me. I'm so grateful for you all.

And to my Fairchildren who remind me that the future is bright.

PROLOGUE

Some people come into your life by choice, some by chance, but others come in like a freight train, with certain uncontrollable force. Sometimes you can feel them coming, sometimes you are completely blindsided. Under either circumstance, you know your life will never be the same again. But don't waste time fretting in despair. You were on this collision course long before you knew it, before you had a choice or a chance to change it. Your only choice now, is what to do when that time comes. What will you do when these two worlds collide?

CHAPTER I

I squeezed my eyes shut and counted silently to ten. Maybe this was all a dream, a vivid and horrible dream. I mean honestly, when I thought about it, that almost seemed more plausible than the events of today being real. Isn't it possible I dreamt the whole thing up? I've always had an active imagination. Or maybe this was some new kind of magic power I'd just developed and it had me trapped in one of my daydreams. Perhaps when I opened my eyes I would wake up behind my favorite palm, in my secret hiding place in the Troian Center courtyard. Our headmistress Greeley would still be alive, the rainforest wouldn't be smoldering around me, my friends and I wouldn't be homeless and most importantly, Jemma would NOT be my sister.

I took a few more deep breaths and slowly opened my eyes. Then panic set in. It was all still there, all still in front of me, just as it had been before I closed my eyes. Jemma was staring at me and she seemed closer than before. Her face was twisted in some sort of quivering frown while tears created tiny winding rivers down her sooty cheeks.

Not possible, I thought to myself. *Jemma doesn't cry.*

I could feel my mind getting fuzzy and there was a dull buzzing in my ears that seemed to be making it really hard for me to connect my thoughts. I looked around to see where it was coming from and my eyes took in the devastating scenery surrounding me once more.

"This can't be real," I whispered, more to myself than anyone in particular, but it seemed Jemma thought I was talking to her because she launched herself towards me and crushed me in a desperate hug.

"It is! It is real!" she squeezed tighter and sobbed harder. "It's you! I can't believe this either, but it's you! You're my sister! I thought you were dead. They told me you died in the Flood."

It was all too much for me to take. I pushed her off of me, quickly wiping my eyes to hide my emotions, which were dangerously close to brimming over.

"I can't do this," was all I managed to squeak out before my voice betrayed me with a sob, so I turned on my heels and ran away.

"Wait! Eva!" Jemma called after me, but I didn't stop. I kept going, quickening my stride. I willed my legs to carry me far enough away, so I could have some privacy when I broke down.

"Let me talk to her," I heard Remi say. "You're overwhelming her Jemma."

I tried to tune them out but my telepathy fed me a steady stream of their voices. I hurried my pace, sprinting away from their voices.

"I think she's probably in shock. She just needs some space to come to terms with all of this new information the Book of Secrets has just dumped on her," Nova said, putting his arm up to stop Remi.

"Are you some sort of Geneva expert all of a sudden? You've known her for a second compared to me, so stop acting like you're the only one that knows what's best for her. I know her too and I think she needs someone to talk her through all of this," Remi challenged as he tried to push past Nova.

"She wants to be left alone," Nova said, stepping into Remi's path.

This time his tone was final and I didn't hear any more arguments from Remi. Maybe they'd stopped fighting or I was too far away to connect to them anymore. Either way, Nova was right. I know he only knew I wanted to be left alone because he was reading my thoughts again even though I'd asked him not to a million times. He probably couldn't help himself right now because my mind was practically screaming 'back off!' And honestly I was glad for Nova's mind reading abilities at the moment, because I truly did just want to be alone. I'm sure this probably hurt my best friend's feelings a bit, but right now, Remi's feelings weren't my focus. I was trying desperately not to freak out. I needed to keep breathing and calm myself down so I didn't lose control of my powers and so I could think of a solution.

CHAPTER II

"It's happening master. I can feel it. The Eva has taken possession of the book!"

"The Book of Secrets? You're sure?"

"Yes, very sure master. No one other than the Eva would be able to open it."

"How do you know it's been opened?"

"Look here master," the old man said, pointing to an open book in his lap. "The legend continues."

The tall man watched in wonder, as scrawling script inked its way across the brittle parchment of the open manuscript. The words formed slowly, darkly, like blood seeping through the ancient pages.

The two men stood, watching the words spread. One man short, crippled by age and the other, tall and menacing. A slow, wicked smile spread across the face of the tall man. It was obvious that he was the one in charge. He wore a black robe that billowed as he moved, gracefully skimming across the spotless, stone floor. Even beneath his robes, it was easy to see he was muscularly built. His hair was glossy black, and shimmered iridescently like obsidian feathers. It was pulled back so tightly, that it gave his angular features an even more severe shape. His eyes were dark and keen. He narrowed them in a sinister way, as he threw his head back, releasing his intimidating laughter.

"Excellent work Kobel. I think it's time I meet our Eva, don't you? Get me her location."

"Each time she uses the Book of Secrets, I can try to zero in on her location master."

"Good. In the meantime, send a search party out. Scour the island. I want that book and I want the Eva!" he bellowed.

CHAPTER III

My lungs burned as I sucked in ragged breaths of smoky air. I was far enough away from my friends now that I could let my composure slip even more than it already had, and I launched into a full blown conversation with myself.

"How can Jemma be my sister!? She's the most awful person I've ever met!" I wailed.

Well that's not true, I argued with myself.

My mind snapped back to our Headmistress Greeley. She was much more awful than Jemma. She killed Niv, or at least she thought she had. She tried to kill all of us and she would have if I didn't stop her. I shuttered at the thought of it and suddenly the reality of what I'd done unexpectedly gripped my stomach! I found myself lurching over a bush nearby, heaving up guilt and bile.

Finally unable to fight my exhaustion, I collapsed to the ground and gave in to the river of tears that were battering the dam of my eyelids. I shook and gasped for air as I let the events of the past few days wash over me. It was almost too awful to bear.

There were so many highs and lows. We had found the Book of Secrets, but what had it cost us? Greeley had caught and cornered us.

She tortured my beloved marmouse, while I stood helplessly by, frozen by one of her spells. Then she let her tarcats tear him to pieces before my very eyes. I had foolishly tethered my soul to his and instantly expected to extinguish with him. But, when I didn't, I used every ounce of my love for Niv to fight back against Greeley and save my friends. We escaped to the forest, and Remi, my incredible best friend, shocked us all by leading us to a perfectly happy and healthy Niv! He had foreseen the dangers of my soul being tethered to Niv's and used shadow magic to create an imposter Niv, while protecting me and the real Niv all the while. I didn't think I could ever be as happy as when I was reunited with Niv. I owed Remi my life and so much more.

But my happiness was short lived, because Greeley and the Grifts from the Troian Center had followed us to the forest and set it ablaze in their search for us. I knew I had to face Greeley, but I had to protect my friends as well. I couldn't bear the thought of losing any of them after coming so close to losing Niv. I trapped them with a fissure and confronted Greeley myself. All my training in the forest had paid off because I was able to stay calm enough to realize that I could beat Greeley with her own tools by turning her vicious tarcats against her. But now, I was left with that final image of her, writhing under their blood stained fur, and I knew it would haunt me forever.

I started heaving again, even though there was nothing left in my stomach. I didn't know how to move on from this.

"I killed someone," I whispered the words out loud to help them sink in.

Yes, she was evil and trying to kill me and my friends, but I still took a life. It seemed like my only option and the right thing to do, but "If it was right, why do I feel so horrible?" I asked myself.

"I wish I could take it back," I sobbed.

I didn't regret that we were all safe now, but I just didn't know how to live with this awful feeling. I let myself cry shamefully on the damp forest floor. It was covered in soft moss that comforted me more than I deserved. I felt something touch my leg and I immediately stopped crying and held my breath. Then, I felt it climb upon me as I stiffened until I saw Niv's twitchy little nose creep into view.

"Niv," I sighed as I sat up and scooped him into my lap. "You scared me half-to-death!"

He twitched his nose at me and I smiled as he rapidly combed at his whiskers with his agile, black paws.

"Well, I guess if you found me I'm not as far from the others as I hoped," I said to him.

I stood, dusting off my badly torn and tattered Troian Center uniform. The tan, thread bare material was scorched where I had come too close to the fire and one sleeve was torn, flapping sadly each time I moved. Looking at the dark stains on the rest of my uniform, I shrugged and gave up trying to brush away the moss that was still clinging to me. I lifted Niv up to let him perch on my shoulder as I continued my trek deeper into the forest. I still wasn't ready to face my friends. I needed to sort out my thoughts and I preferred to do that without Nova listening in on them.

My legs felt sore, but steadier and my chest felt lighter.

"A good cry always leaves my head clearer," I said to Niv as he watched the forest scenery float by from my shoulders. His ears pricked up and down, tickling my neck as he took in the forest sounds.

I was wandering aimlessly, trying to organize my thoughts. Somehow walking was helping. I felt that each footstep was taking me a step closer to coming to terms with this new role that had been thrust upon me.

"You wanted to know the truth Tippy," I said to myself.

When I heard the name Tippy come out of my mouth I smiled. It was the nickname Nova had given me and I'd grown fond of it. It seemed my real name was Geneva, though.

"Geneva," I whispered trying it out. "Geneva," I said again, this time with more confidence.

It felt so foreign rolling off my tongue, but it's what I had wanted more than anything; to know my real name. It's what started this whole crazy quest. I met a boy who knew his name and I couldn't stop thinking about him and about what my name might be. I wanted to know my name and now I did, so I guess I had better start going by it.

I was sad to let go of Tippy though. It was so endearing to me now because I felt like it connected me to Nova. My cheeks flushed at the thought of him. The events of the past year had brought me closer than I ever could have dreamed to Nova, yet somehow I still didn't know where we stood. He opened my eyes to a whole new world of magic and secrets and we solved them together to find out my true identity. It was a rough road, but I knew I would do it all again because I was addicted to him. When he kissed me, it unlocked a part of my heart that I didn't know I had. I sighed as I remembered our perfect kiss in the Locker. I shook myself quickly from the reverie of that blissful memory because it was too easy for me to get caught up dreaming about Nova. I really needed to have a talk with him to find out where we stood, but now wasn't the time.

I reminded myself I was out here, wandering around the forest, because I needed to figure out what to do next. Now that I knew who I was, I had to figure out what it all meant.

My name is Geneva Sommers. I'm the Eva, the chosen one who will lead Hullabee Island back to peace and equality. It sounded like a tall order for a teenage orphan girl and I felt like I was being swallowed whole by the idea. I wished there was some kind of guide as to how I was supposed to accomplish this task, because I had no idea.

"What do you think Niv?" I asked as I scratched him between his ears. He cooed and chattered in response and I laughed. "Well I was actually looking for a more specific answer, but thank you," I said to him.

Suddenly, his little body tensed up and his ears flew to attention. I stopped walking and tried to train my eyes to where he was looking.

He was spooked and looking around wildly, while his hair was bristled with agitation.

"What is it buddy?" I whispered to him.

I used the hunter powers that I'd acquired from Journey to get a better sense of my surroundings. Niv was right. Something was off here, but I couldn't put my finger on what it was. It was quiet, too quiet actually. I looked around and for the first time, took in the oddness of the forest around me. It didn't look much like the rainforest at all. I'd been walking for a while and the majority of my surroundings were blurred away by the haze that the forest fire had left behind, but ahead of me, I saw an eerie clearing. It was devoid of trees or vegetation of any kind. It looked like the surface of the moon. Everything was ashy and grey, and there was a light mist of something white falling around me. I took another step forward to get a better look and Niv went into a frenzy.

"Niv! What is it?"

"It's me," came a sheepish voice behind me that just about made me jump out of my skin.

For the split second, before I recognized the voice, I was ready to fight. Blue orbs glowing in my hands at the ready.

I turned around just in time to see Remi materialize in front of me.

"REMI!" I scolded.

"Sorry! I'm sorry 65, I mean Geneva? Eva? What am I supposed to call you now?"

I couldn't be mad at him. We burst into a comfortable laughter as only best friends can.

"Geneva will be fine," I smiled at him. "You nearly gave us a heart attack you know?"

Niv chattered his disapproval from behind an ashy boulder.

"I know, I'm sorry. I know you want to be alone, but…"

"It's okay. I'm feeling a little better … I think. I'm glad you're here Remi."

And I really meant it, I realized, as I gave him a long overdue hug.

"Where are we exactly?" he asked.

"I'm not sure. It's what I was trying to figure out when you snuck up on us. I thought there was something spooking Niv, but it must've just been you."

"I don't know," Remi said, "this place is pretty spooky if you ask me."

"I think it's kind of pretty," I said. "It almost looks like it's snowing."

"That's not snow, Geneva. It's ash."

"Ash? But we're so far from where the fire broke out. Could the ash really have traveled this far?" I asked.

"I don't think it's ash from the fire," Remi said warily. "I think it's from the volcano."

"What?! It can't be. I didn't run that far! Did I?" I asked with a bit of panic in my voice.

But, I knew he was right. We had to be near the base of the volcano. That would explain the different terrain, the lack of vegetation, and the clouds of ash that frequently spewed from our very active volcano. I'd never actually seen the volcano up close before. I'd only read about it, but the reading didn't do it justice. I craned my neck to look up through the thick clouds, trying to catch a glimpse of the legendary peaks. The flurry of ash raining downs seemed so surreal. I took a few more steps into the clearing and reached out my hands, letting the ash land weightlessly on my palms. It made me smile and I was lost in thought for a moment before Remi called me back to reality.

I turned to look at him when he called my name and he opened his mouth to say something, but stopped himself.

"What?" I asked.

He had such a peculiar look on his face.

"Nothing," he said shyly.

"Remi, what were you going to say?"

He looked around for a moment, like he was expecting someone else to be nearby. When he turned back to me he looked more confident. He took three quick strides and closed the gap between us. He reached out his hands and placed them under mine as I continued to catch the silent ashes. We smiled at each other, spellbound by this dreamlike moment.

Remi broke the silence and said, "I was going to say how beautiful you look."

And then my world caved in.

There was a deafening, splitting sound and the ground beneath our feet moaned and exploded to life! Remi was pitched away from me. I lost my grip on his hands as my footing crumbled away. It happened so fast. One moment I was staring into my best friend's eyes and the next I was swimming though the air, clawing at clumps of dirt and stone as I desperately fought a losing battle with gravity. I tried to keep my eyes open, but fear clamped them shut and all I could hear were my own screams echoing around me. It felt like a bad dream that wakes you in a cold sweat. The kind where you thought you were falling only to awake to the relief that you're in your bed. But, there was no waking. No bed. No solid ground. I just kept falling until an ice cold pain shocked and strangled me all at once!

I choked and my lungs burned. It felt like my chest was about to explode. I tried to open my eyes but they stung and I only saw a blurry blackness around me. I fought hard against the unknown source that was smothering me, but I couldn't strike anything, no matter how hard I tried. I kicked and clawed, but each of my furious movements felt heavy and sluggish, yet they took every ounce of strength I had left. I felt my struggling slow as I fought the pounding resistance in my lungs for a few moments more, before letting go. My last breath slowly escaped in a long, hopeless bubble that lazily climbed away from me. As I watched it rise bleakly away, toward a distant light, it finally clicked. I realized I was underwater. The sad reality that I was drowning washed over me as I sunk helplessly away from the light. There was something peaceful about it now that I'd stopped fighting. It was cool and quiet as I let my life drift away from me.

CHAPTER IV

"Master! Master! Come quick!"

The tall man with the dark hair was suddenly and soundlessly at Kobel's side.

"What is it Kobel?" he asked, unable to hide the hint of distress in his normally calm voice.

"The book . . ." he said, pointing to the Book of Gods that lay open on the marble pulpit before them.

The color drained from both men's faces as they watched water seeping from the ancient book. The ink that had magically been scrawling out the prophecy of the Eva as it unfolded was now mixing with the cold, clear liquid, as if blotting out her existence.

CHAPTER V

It seems what they say is true; your life does sort of flash before your eyes when you're dying. At least it did for me. Everything slowed down, as bits of memories flickered into view.

I thought of my friends and how unfair it was that I wouldn't get to say goodbye. I was saddened by the bittersweet last memories I had of them. I didn't want to remember them the way I had left them in the forest after unlocking the Book of Secrets. They had all looked so defeated. I frowned as I pictured Journey, resting on a mossy boulder when I'd stormed away from everyone. I hadn't noticed it then, but in my memory, he looked tired which struck me as odd. Journey always looked as though he was ready to fight the world at a moment's notice and he had the physique to make you think he would win. It frightened me to see him look so subdued and wounded. Who would fight to save the island if Journey wasn't there to lead the charge? I struggled to think of another time when he might have looked this exhausted and hopeless but I came up empty.

Hopeless? Journey? I resisted the thought, not being able to make my brain fit the two words together.

Maybe it was this darn buzzing in my ears. It was getting louder.

I tried to shake it from my mind and when I refocused, I was startled to see Sparrow's image floating in front of me. She was curled up next to Journey. *Had she been there a moment ago*? She looked so sad and dirty, her usual perkiness was missing and something else too. What was it? She looked small and frail sitting next to Journey's feet. She had one arm clutched around his earth caked leg, with her head leaning against his knee. Her soft brown hair was dull and matted with twigs and leaves. It was partially covering her face in an unruly way that made it impossible to see if she was crying, but there seemed to be some sort of noise coming from her. Sparrow's slender legs were folded under her as delicately as butterfly wings. They appeared to be shimmering too. *Is that what made me think of butterfly wings*? No it was that noise. That buzzing, it was growing louder and it had a faint flapping beat to it now, like something was fluttering inside my ear drums. I thought the flapping was coming from Sparrow but it was so close, too close. And Sparrow was just a memory. *Wasn't she?*

Sparrow? Wings? My mind shuttered; nothing was making sense.

I wanted to comfort her. To thank her for being such a great friend to me. Her image glowed before me and she seemed so close, so real. I tried to reach out to her but her features evaporated from my view as I extended my arms. All that was left, was a glowing shadow that was moving towards me.

As it advanced and enveloped me in light, I suddenly felt cradled and safe. I was surprised I didn't instinctively jerk away. The pounding in my head escalated to a powerful new decibel the closer the glowing being came, but I floated in place, paralyzed and placid. The shadow slowly approached and I closed my eyes when the light it emitted overpowered me.

Remi and Nova flashed into my mind, as if they were burned into the back of my eyelids. They were so vivid, so bright and so painfully handsome. There was so much left unsaid between us. The final beats of my dying heart ached for them. I think they were trying to say something to me, but I couldn't make out their words and it frustrated me. I could see their lips moving and hear their different tones vibrating, but it was drowned out by the buzzing inside my head.

My failing mind agitated me. I was anxious to hear from them. They could be trying to send me a message and this was my last chance to see them. I focused hard, but suddenly something caught hold of my hand and I jerked my eyes open. To my surprise the glowing shadow hovering before me took on the face of Remi. I reached out my other hand to him and when he took it, I felt a strange sensation take hold of me, pulling me forward.

But to where? I wondered.

I felt like I was floating and I smiled as a glowing Remi tugged at my limp hands. The soft lines of Remi's face seemed deeper, more ridged with maturity or maybe it was worry. His large, chocolate brown eyes were determined and his forehead wrinkled where his dark eyebrows met. He was frowning as he ran his hand through his thick messy hair. He had patches of ash peppered through his locks and it looked like he was going gray. I smiled as I took in my best friend's appearance. His clothes flowed effortlessly from his pale, strong limbs in the water. His stern expression amused me.

Oh Remi, always worrying. I laughed to myself. *Things aren't always as bad as you think. I know I'm dying, but I'll never leave you Remi. You're a part of me and I'm a part of you.*

I grinned ruefully as I closed my eyes and let some of my favorite memories of Remi fill my sleepy mind. When I reopened them, I gasped and felt my lethargic heart skip a beat. The glowing figure guiding my suspended hands now, was Nova!

I felt his intoxicating aura envelop me and I let out a soft sigh and felt myself slipping into that all too frequent Nova-daze. Lovely Nova. Since I had surrendered to the idea of dying, I was glad I was getting to spend my final moments with him. Even if this was just in my mind or some Utopian pre-death state, or maybe it was magic. Whatever it was, I wasn't wasting any time thinking about how it was happening. I wanted to be greedy with my last seconds with Nova. How was it that he still looked so dreamy even as I was dying? The dirt smudged on his face looked as though it had been expertly shaded by the keen hands of a talented artist, accentuating his ruggedly chiseled face. His green eyes were angled into Emerald slivers as he scrutinized me. His blonde hair was as messy as ever, yet on him it looked good, textured and shiny even; casting a golden glow in the rippling water surrounding him. It almost looked like a halo!

Saint Nova, I sighed.

I pulled back against his hand. I wanted to stop him from taking me wherever I was going. I wanted more time with him. I needed more time. I wanted him to hold me again. To kiss me again. I wanted to know he felt the same way I did. I wanted so much more. Suddenly I wasn't okay with parting this world anymore. I fought against the pulling sensation and lost hold of his hand. I reached for him again and his image rippled away, dissipating like the reflection of the moon on the ocean waves.

For a flash of an instant, the glowing light took a shape that looked familiar; like a beautiful angel, with long flowing blonde hair like mine. She reached out to me with fear in her wide blue eyes. It was like looking at a frightened reflection of myself. I felt her take hold of me, but then everything seemed to flash forward at warp speed and I was engulfed in panic and pain. I was swallowed up in the bright light that had been shaped into my beautiful memories. It was too bright, blinding me with searing, white agony.

This must be it. The end. So it wouldn't be peaceful and painless after all. I felt burning in my lungs again and I was cold, shivering and coughing up something that tasted horrible. It stung my nose and throat and the ringing in my ears was so loud it was blinding me. A hard, cold surface pressed against my face and my hammering heart protested as I tried to move.

My heart! It was still beating. And my lungs; they ached as I fought to rake small shallow gulps of air through them. I was still alive!

I was too fatigued to move, but I concentrated on catching my breath and trying to open my eyes. I lay on the sandy shore and stared up at the bright light above me, counting my blessings with each breath I raked through my aching lungs.

CHAPTER VI

The men stood silently by, holding their breath and counting the seconds since the water had stopped leaking from the pages of the Book of Gods. It had gone from a rush of water, to a steady stream, then to a slow drip and now nothing.

Kobel was the first to move. He walked up to the water logged book and touched its soggy pages.

"What do we do now Kobel?" the tall man asked.

"We wait."

CHAPTER VII

At first, the bright, blurry light just aggravated the ringing in my ears, but I found if I opened my eyes just a tiny sliver at a time I could start to make out shapes.

I was laying on the shore of a black sandy cave lagoon. The ground was wet and cold. It smelled like damp soil and sulfur. With a great deal of effort and pain, I rolled from my belly to my back and looked up at the hole above me, bathing my cavernous surroundings with light. It must have given way under the weight of Remi and I.

Remi!

Where was he? I tried to call him, but my throat was in no shape to speak. I sputtered and coughed as I tried to say his name. Finally, I heard an answer.

"Geneva."

It was faint, but real. It echoed slightly off the cavern walls. I slowly raised myself to my elbows and looked around. The cave was dark, but enough light bounced off the endless expanse of black lagoon water to illuminate the world in front of me. I marveled at all the different shades of black. The cave walls glistened like black glass as the water reflected light off of them. It was hard to tell if the walls were actually wet, or if their black, inky, shimmer was just an illusion from the water. The black sand was cold and coarse under my waterlogged flesh. It was hard packed and didn't give my aching body any sympathy. I inspected the flecks of it that clung to my skin and dotted my palms as I pulled myself up into a sitting position. Some of the pieces were actually clear and they reflected the light in a way that made them shine like precious gems. I held a small grain up to the hole above me that was spilling light into the cave and it sparkled so bright that I felt like I was holding a tiny star in my hand. I smiled as the light shined brighter still and I heard my name again.

"Geneva."

I strained my eyes and looked out over the water, following the strange sound of my new name. I was stunned when my eyes landed on an unexpected image. It made the barely regained air rush from my tired lungs again.

"Mom?" I whispered in a hoarse voice.

The words felt so fragile and foreign crossing my lips, but there shimmering on the water's surface, was my mother, Nesia. I crawled quickly to the water's edge, careful not to touch it for fear that the ripples would carry her away from me. I called out to her more desperately this time.

"Mom!?"

"Geneva, my darling. It's all right dear one. Please don't cry."

I hadn't even realized I was crying. I uselessly swiped at my eyes and looked at my tear stained reflection in the water. Nesia's reflection glided closer to mine and gracefully cupped my face in her alabaster hands. I felt her! It felt so real, like she was actually there comforting me, holding me. It was the same familiar comforting pull I felt when I was drowning. Then it dawned on me; she was the one who had pulled me from the water. She was the glowing shape I had seen guiding me, luring me towards the light. She had been my guardian angel. I dissolved into a sobbing puddle as I let my mother cradle my reflection with hers.

"Mom. Oh mom, you saved me didn't you? You were the light!"

She nodded. "I wanted to reach out to you, but it's not safe. I tried to use the love you have for your friends to get you to fight... but there wasn't enough time darling. I had to pull you out. You were too far gone."

I didn't know what she meant, but I didn't care either. Suddenly I was just a child who wanted her mother more desperately than anything else in the world.

"Please stay with me Mom. I need you," I whimpered breathlessly.

"Darling, I'm always with you. You know that don't you? You are a part of me and I am a part of you. We will never leave each other. I am always where you need me."

It was like déjà vu. I spoke some of those same words to Remi when I was drowning. Or had I? Perhaps I was hearing my mother's words in my mind. I had so many questions for her, but I didn't know where to start. I wanted to stay here with her forever.

"Mom, so much is changing. My life is so, so…" I struggled to find the right words, "much bigger than I am. I don't know if I can be the Eva."

"Geneva, you already are and you always were."

"But I don't know how to do all of this? I don't know how to save an island and free its people. I'm just an orphan…" I trailed off, feeling guilty for saying I was an orphan in front of my mother. It wasn't her fault I was alone.

"Darling, your destiny has already been written. You are the Eva because of who you already are, not who you will become. You were born into this role. You just need to be yourself. That's why you were chosen. Believe in yourself and your choices and the rest will fall into place."

She was right, that was my biggest problem. I always doubted myself. I let doubt, fear and guilt slip in too easily. I was doing so much better recently, since Nova, Journey and Sparrow came into my life. They taught me so much. They believed in me and their feelings were infectious. They gave me enough courage to seek the truth and fight for it, and that had led me here.

Now that I was here, at the edge of my true identity, I needed to have the courage to continue my journey. I don't know whether it was the comfort from my mother or my new zest for life after narrowly escaping drowning in this cave, but I could feel my strength and steadiness returning.

"Your right mom. I wanted the truth and now I have it. I guess it's just not what I expected."

Nesia smiled at me, that wise, kind, motherly smile that I'd been craving my whole life. "It never is darling. There is so much greatness inside of you."

"I wish I could see it," I whispered more to myself than to her, but she'd heard me and replied.

"You can..."

The cave around me unexpectedly came to life. The walls lit up and danced with dozens of colors that reflected gracefully off the water's surface, unfolding the scenes of my life before me.

There were whirling visions of battles, victories, tragedies, betrayals, love and loss. Images of me, leading my friends, some of whom I didn't know yet, into an uncertain future. I saw Remi and Nova, both by my side, yet I looked in turmoil as they tugged me in different directions. I saw Jemma and I embracing, we looked happy, like true sisters. Images blurred together and became one clear image of me; older and wiser. I was alone, but I was looking down at a peaceful Lux under a new, united flag. I seemed content that peace had been restored to Hullabee Island.

Could these visualizations be real? I wondered.

"They are all possible Geneva. You will have many paths to choose from. Just know that none of them are wrong, because you were meant to lead your people on this quest. Only you can choose its course, my darling daughter."

She had such love and confidence in her eyes when she spoke to me. We stared at each other in quiet solitude for a moment and I let my mother's love wash over and through me. Filling me up, refueling my soul. She renewed my optimism. What was just a ray of hope, began to swell through me, washing away my fear of what was to come.

"Will you do something for me darling?" Nesia asked.

"Yes, anything mom."

"Give Jemma a chance Geneva, you'll need each other. And give her my love," my mother said breaking my reverie.

She was no longer holding me. She started to back away and I reached for her.

"Please don't go yet. I have so many more questions to ask."

But she didn't stop. She kept on drifting away from me. I rose to my feet and took a step towards her into the cold water that stifled my breath. The shivering ripples from my feet sent her drifting faster.

"No! Mom! Wait, please! What about Nova? And Remi?" I called out to her, still reaching.

Then I felt a warm, hand squeeze mine in return.

"I'm right here," Remi's reflection said to mine.

I turned to see Remi in front of me. He had no shirt on and his wet skin looked paler than ever as he glistened in the cave light. He looked so ethereal I was terrified he might be an illusion. I put my hand to his chest timidly at first. It felt warm. I pushed both hands into his skin and felt his blood pulsing hot beneath it. He was real. It was really Remi! I had never been so happy to see him and feel the realness of his soaking wet, flesh and blood. I threw my arms around him and sobbed.

"Are you hurt?" Remi asked me, holding me at arm's length to look me over.

"I'm fine," I said, pulling myself back into his arms. "Just cold."

He tightened his arms around me and whispered, "It's okay. We're going to be okay."

We held each other like this for a while until the shivering stopped.

"Where's Niv?" I asked when my teeth stopped chattering.

"I haven't seen him," Remi replied. "But I'm sure he's fine," he added when he saw the worried look on my face.

"Niv!" I called. "Niv! Where are you?"

I pulled away from Remi's embrace. "We have to find him," I pleaded.

"The benefits of being dumb enough to tether your soul to a rodent comes in handy sometimes," he joked. "Niv probably saved you from drowning. He has to be alive if you're alive."

Remi continued talking when I didn't respond to him.

"I saw you go under," he said sounding haunted. "You didn't come up for a really long time. I tried to get to you, but I ended up on the other side of the lagoon," Remi said motioning to a part of the water that extended past the light.

"My mother saved me," I said casually as I walked the shoreline looking for Niv and calling his name.

"What?" Remi said. "Your mother? Are you sure you're okay?" he asked.

"Shhh!" I hissed. "I hear him."

Sure enough we looked up to the mouth of the hole above the lagoon and saw Niv peering down at us. He was making all kinds of racket.

"Niv, it's okay buddy. We're okay, but we need you to go get help. Can you go tell the others where we are? Go get Nova okay?"

Niv twitched his nose in response and with a final squeak he retreated from the mouth of the hole to go get help for us. Remi was staring at me with a look of amusement on his face.

"Geneva, I know that you think the world of Niv, but he's a marmouse, he doesn't know how to go get help. We need to come up with a real plan to get out of here, because I don't think Nova is coming to our rescue this time," he said, unable to hide his bitterness when he said Nova's name.

"Listen Remi, we'll be fine. Niv is on his way to tell the others right now."

His blank stare reminded me that I had never shared that I possessed a certain power with him.

"Oh yeah, I'm an animyth."

Remi just blinked, staring back at me blankly.

"It means I can talk to animals. It's one of my powers. Nova knows that and he'll follow Niv. We'll be okay."

"Um, alright. I guess that's just one more secret you forgot to share with me, but it's not the craziest thing I've heard lately so sure, I'll go with it."

I found a dry spot to sit and settled down to wait. I patted the sand next to me, motioning for Remi to join me.

"So, anything else you need to fill me in on?" Remi asked.

"Yes, actually a lot…" I said.

I spent the next few hours filling Remi in on all he'd missed. We started at the very beginning and talked about everything. I told him how I'd first learned I had powers when Nova took me to the forest, and about our crazy training practices, some of which led to scuffles between Journey and I. We talked about how I learned I could talk to animals, and how I defeated Greeley by releasing her tarcats and turning them against her. And finally, we were caught up when I told him how I had seen Nesia in the mirror at the New Year Gala, and now again in this cave, where she had just saved me from drowning.

It felt really good to have my best friend back. Being trapped in a cave wasn't the ideal day, but at least I was with Remi and it finally gave us some much needed time to catch up. Remi and I had been through a lot together. He'd been my one and only friend my whole life, up until my whole life started changing. I'd always been able to count on him, but when I had to exclude him from my new secret life of magic and powers, it created a rift in our friendship. Since he managed to uncover our secrets and had a few of his own, we'd been working on patching our friendship back up and I really felt like for the first time, things were going back to normal. Well, as normal as things can be for an orphan with magical powers I guess…

I hadn't realized how much I really missed having Remi's support. He truly understood me. I always felt comfortable enough to be myself around him. His friendship sustained me and it was exactly what I needed right now. Little by little, I was starting to feel whole again. My conversations today with my mother and Remi were a big part of that. I leaned into him and he hugged me. I sighed and looked up at him. Into those big brown eyes that knew me so well.

"Thank you Remi," I whispered to him. "You're m-"

Before I knew what was happening, Remi's hand was on my chin, pulling my lips to his. His kiss caught me completely off guard and my instinct was to pull away!

"REMI!" I shouted as I scrambled to my feet. "What was that?!"

"I thought…" He stammered as he stood as well. "You were… We…"

My face burned bright red and neither of us could look at each other. Remi paced back and forth sputtering words and I was staring at my feet trying to come up with an excuse to change the subject.

"Um, I think I'm going to go look for some firewood or something we can burn. It'll be night soon and it's probably going to get really cold down here." I said, trailing off as I walked away from Remi.

"Oh, good idea," he said. "I'll go this way."

We walked off in different directions and I kept trying to catch inconspicuous glimpses of him. Remi was muttering under his breath to himself, which he always did when he was frustrated. I sighed and tried to focus on finding some roots or wood to keep my mind occupied. It was no use though, beside the fact that there wasn't anything to burn, I couldn't stop glancing at Remi and thinking about his kiss. Why had he done that?! I wasn't sending him mixed signals. At least I didn't think I was. I was just about to tell him he was 'my best friend' when he kissed me! It was so out of the blue and so surprisingly ... good! Nova was the only boy I had kissed until just now and he wasn't my boyfriend, but I still felt guilty, because I wanted him to be, and I hadn't wanted to kiss Remi. Except, now I couldn't stop thinking about kissing Remi!

"Ugh! Maybe we can just forget this ever happened," I muttered to myself.

Not much chance of that happening my heart replied to my head.

I wandered aimlessly along the black sand shore, deep in thought with myself.

Why can't things just go back to how they were? Remi is supposed to be my best friend and Nova is supposed to be... well I don't know what Nova's supposed to be yet either. But, now everything is so, so... blurry. Oh Remi, we were just starting to get back to how it was too!

I felt so confused. Remi and Nova were both so different, yet I needed them both equally. My mind instantly snapped back to the visions my mother had shown me of being torn between them. I tried to shake them off, but they stuck in a haunting way; like the afterglow of staring at the sun.

I was still stewing over the unexpected kiss when I heard Remi calling me.

"Geneva! I think I may have found a way out of here."

Perfect! All I want to do right now is escape!

That thought motivated me to jog over to where Remi was standing. He'd found a small opening above the steep, glistening walls. You had to look at just the right angle to see where the fading light was sneaking in among the vines and rotting roots. It didn't look promising, but we were out of options.

Maybe, if I could get out of this stupid cave, I could clear my head. Maybe the cave was making us both a little crazy. I was starting to feel claustrophobic down here and that can make people do strange things. I got to Remi as he was winding some vines around his wrists.

"Remi, those won't hold you," I said cautiously.

He wouldn't meet my eyes, but the tone of his voice said he was as desperate as I was to get out of the awkward air that was suffocating us in the cave.

"I think it might. I've got to at least try."

"Why don't you let me try? I really don't think - Oh Remi!"

I didn't even get to finish my sentence before one of the vines snapped, sending Remi skidding down the short distance he had managed to climb.

"Are you okay?" I asked.

"I'm fine," he sighed. "It was worth a try."

I had a feeling he'd bruised his ego, more than his backside.

"Let me try, I'm lighter than you."

"No, I don't think it's a good idea. They're not as strong as I'd hoped and I already broke a few of them."

"It's worth a try," I said, mimicking him while trying to lighten the mood. It didn't seem to work though. Remi just stepped aside so I could access the vines.

"Well, here goes nothing," I said.

CHAPTER VIII

Niv scurried breathlessly back into the make shift camp that Nova and the others had set up. Journey and Sparrow were busying themselves collecting wood for a fire, while Eja sat nearby continuing to translate the Book of Secrets. Niv ran past them and headed straight to where Nova was comforting a distraught Jemma.

"She hates me. My own sister hates me!" Jemma sobbed.

"She doesn't hate you Jemma, you just need to give her some time. This is a lot of change for her, and for you."

Jemma continued her self-absorbed crying, ignoring Nova's efforts to calm her down.

"I can't really blame her, can I? I've been awful to her. Just awful. And for years! My own sister!" she wailed as she paced anxiously past Nova.

Nova ran his hands through his golden hair in frustration. He felt bad for Jemma and could actually relate to how shell-shocked she must be, having lost his own little sister in the Flood, but he was about at his wit's end with Jemma's inconsolable weeping. He finally grabbed her shoulders and hugged her tightly, pinning her flapping arms to her side. This only made her break down further. If Nova thought she had been crying before, now the flood gates were really open. She shuttered and gulped in high pitched breaths.

"She... hates... me!" Jemma sniveled into Nova's taut shoulder.

"Take deep breaths Jemma, deep breaths. I know you think she hates you, and maybe she does, but all this crying isn't helping. You need to just take a step back and think of it from Geneva's point of view. Then maybe you'll see how you can mend things with her."

"I just wish I could tell her how much I loved her - still love her. I know I was awful to her, but I think it was because something about her always reminded me of my lost baby sister and it was too painful to face. I used mean remarks and teased her to shield myself from facing the pain of missing my family."

Nova was stunned by her moment of clarity. He leaned back and looked down at the raven haired girl that was staining his chest with tears. He smiled at her with his dazzling grin and she obediently fell under his spell and smiled back, but only for a moment. She somehow broke through his trance and pulled away from him.

"Why are you smiling at me like that?" she demanded defensively.

"Jemma, you nailed it. You just need to tell Geneva what you told me. Just tell her the truth. That's all she's ever wanted. No more secrets and lies. Just the truth. That you love her, you miss her and you're sorry. She'll have to appreciate that."

Jemma smiled back at him again, and this time it was of her own free will.

"Thanks Nova, you're right. You really do want to help me don't you?" she asked timidly.

"Yes, Jemma, of course I do. I – hey! What the heck?!"

Nova's thoughts were interrupted by a furry intruder. Niv launched himself between Jemma and Nova and was chattering angrily and showing his teeth at Jemma. She squealed and tried to take shelter behind Nova but that only angered Niv further. He snarled and spat at her until Nova motioned for her to take a few steps back. He crouched down to Niv's level, trying to calm him down.

"Niv! Buddy, it's okay. What's wrong with you? Where's Tippy?"

Niv chattered rapidly to Nova and nipped at his hands as he ran a few feet away from him and twitched impatiently, waiting for him to follow.

"Jemma, something's wrong with Tippy. She needs our help. Go get the others."

I grabbed hold of the few scraggly vines that were left and tried to wind them together to make them stronger. Then, I wrapped them around my wrists like Remi had done and tried to pull myself up the slick cavernous wall.

"A little help here?" I asked Remi. "I could use a boost."

He quietly hoisted me up and once I got a good foot hold, I was on my way. Remi was straining below me, trying to point out good hold positions for me. I was half way up now and it was the darkest part of the cave. The light at the narrow mouth was still far away and the light reflecting from the water below did nothing to illuminate the walls at this elevation.

"Remi, I can't see anything up here. I think I need to cast an orb to light my way."

"Okay, be careful," he called.

I took a few deep breaths and concentrated hard. I usually drew my orbs into my hands. I hadn't ever just cast one out of thin air purely by thinking about it. But it seemed like I should be able to. I remembered what Nova had told me when we were in the Locker. It was how he'd first discovered he had powers. His light was born out of desperation. He just kept thinking all he needed was light. He repeated that mantra over and over until it became a reality.

Okay, I can do this I said to myself. *Light, Light, Light, LIGHT!* And there was light! It burst forth so fast and bright that it temporarily blinded me. I had to close my eyes and let them slowly adjust to the bright orb that was radiating light through the cave.

"You did it!" Remi cheered from below.

I made my way up further and the route was much easier now that my path was illuminated. I was making progress when I hit a snag.

"Uh… Remi? The vine ends."

"What?"

"There's no more vine. It stops here."

"Come back down. It's too dangerous without the vines. It was a good try."

I was so close. I didn't want to turn back now. I could see the fading sunlight above. I could feel the warmth of it bathing me as it filtered in from the overgrown opening above my head. There was no way I was going back down now. I was too close. I steadied myself and looked for an alternate route. There seemed to be some good hand holds a few feet above my head and then there was a ledge that was wide enough for me to stand on. Once I reached it, I should be able to grab onto the roots and climb out easily.

"I can do this Remi," I called to him as I made up my mind to keep moving upward.

"No! Geneva! Just come back down. It's not worth it. I don't want you to get hurt."

I tried to tune Remi's calls out of my head as I kept ascending the slick, earthen wall. Now that I didn't have the luxury of using the vines as a ladder, I was having to press my face into the wall to stay as close to it as possible. The smell was not enticing. The walls were covered in musty dirt that reminded me of the mildewed potatoes I used to peel back at the Troian Center. I pressed on, but soon found myself stuck again. I had misjudged the ledge. It was too high for me to reach. It was too late to turn back now. Despite Remi's pleading, I knew my only option was to keep going up. I mustered up all of the strength I had left and pulled from a reserve of courage I didn't even know I had. I channeled Sparrow, when she taught me how to bound through the tree tops. It was her way of 'flying' and I had been able to do it when I fought Greeley. I was praying I still possessed Sparrow's power now.

I pushed off the stale, crumbling wall and stretched my limbs to their limit. I shrieked with glee when my hands connected with a root on the ledge I had been aiming for!

"I did it!" I called to Remi.

"Woo-hoo!!!!" he hollered from below.

I turned to grin at him when I heard the heart stopping sound of splintering wood. The root I was dangling from had long been dead and it cracked, snapping under my weight as it pulled away from the wall, taking me with it.

For the second time today I found myself falling uncontrollably through the air, into the earthen cavern. This time I fought the urge to close my eyes and scream. I knew I was not over the lagoon this time, so I needed to keep my eyes open as I scrambled for anything to latch onto that might delay my fall as I bounced and tumbled down the walls, back into the cave. I clawed at the vines on my plummet, and they managed to help slow me a bit. But, they also spun me wildly out of control and possibly dislocated my shoulder. I felt searing pain as I careened down the cave walls, connecting various parts of my body with unyielding rock faces. One struck me so hard on the side of my head that I tasted blood.

For a brief moment, I thought I heard Nova call my name. *Was I dying again* I wondered? Then, the lights went out.

Blackness.

"Tippy!" Nova screamed.

He had arrived at the mouth of the cavernous hole in the earth right as Geneva was falling. He and the others were following Niv through the forest when they came to the disheveled clearing. He heard the splintering of wood and then Geneva's scream. Nova rushed to the opening just in time to see her land with a thud on the sandy shore near Remi's feet. All the breath left his body as he was consumed by fear. His panic only lasted a moment before he sprang into action.

"Remi! Is she breathing?" Nova shouted down into the cave.

"I can't tell," Remi called back frantically.

"Check! And if she's not, you need to breathe for her. I'll be right back."

"Where are you going?" Remi called as Nova disappeared from his view. "Don't leave us!"

Remi leaned in and listened for breath sounds. When he was answered with silence he was frozen with fear. The girl he'd known his whole life, lay motionless before him! He reached out gingerly touching her cool lips, remembering how warm they'd been moments ago when he kissed them. That thought fueled him forward.

Remembering what he'd learned in Plants and Poisons, he leaned over her and tilted her head back and then gently pressed his lips to hers, breathing into her lungs. At first, his hands trembled as he regarded her delicate jaw line with fragility, but when she didn't respond, he breathed deeper and more desperately this time.

"Geneva, we need you," Remi said between breaths.

"I need you," he pleaded.

He put all his love and want for her into his next breath and something finally caught!

Geneva sputtered and coughed weakly. Her eyes didn't open, but her chest maintained a ragged rise and fall and Remi collapsed next to her in tears as he gripped her hand and kissed it.

Within moments of Geneva catching her breath, Nova was back at the mouth of the cave, tossing a length of heavy vine down. It landed in a coiled thud next to Remi and an unconscious Geneva. Nova repelled quickly and gracefully down the vine into the cave. He landed with cat-like ease on the black sand and rushed to Geneva's side, edging Remi out of his way so he could cradle her head.

"Tippy! Tippy… can you hear me?" he said, with a hint of un-Nova-like fear.

He leaned in to listen to her ragged breathing.

"It's okay Tippy. You're going to be okay. I'm gonna get you out of here," Nova whispered tenderly into her ear. He lightly stroked her temple and kept murmuring to her. "Journey is helping Sparrow down here and she's going to heal you. You're going to be alright. Eja went to get more help so we can get you out of here. Just hang on for me Tippy. You're going to be just fine, love," he said as he kissed her forehead.

Remi couldn't watch Nova dote on her any longer. It was making him nauseous and angry. He cleared his throat and interrupted their tender moment. "How exactly are we going to get out?"

Nova looked up startled for a moment, almost as though he'd forgotten Remi was still sitting there. When he focused on him, he narrowed his eyes and almost growled, "You had to go after her, didn't you?"

"What? This isn't my fault!" Remi said defensively.

"Really Remi? How'd she end up down here? And why was she the one climbing out of this cave? You thought it was a good idea for her to risk her life climbing up some dead vines to save your hide?" Nova accused through gritted teeth.

"I asked her not to. You know how she is." Remi replied indignantly, getting to his feet. "Besides, she was being unreasonable. I think she just really wanted to get away from me," he muttered to himself more than to Nova.

"What?!" Nova said incredulously, getting to his feet too. "Why was she trying to get away from you? What did you do?"

"Nothing, geez Nova get off my back alright," Remi shouted. "Maybe you should be thanking me for saving your precious *Tippy*. She wasn't breathing you know? I had to give her life's breath."

"Yeah and I'm sure you thoroughly enjoyed that Remi. Do you think I don't see the way you look at her? But it's never going to happen. She's with me, so go ahead and enjoy your mouth to mouth moment, because it's the closest you'll ever come to kissing her," Nova hissed.

He stood still, clenching and unclenching his fists as he took in deep breaths, trying to keep his cool. His eyes momentarily left Remi as he watched Journey and Sparrow landing smoothly on the cavern shore. Sparrow immediately scrambled over to Geneva and went to work on healing her while Journey stood over her shoulder anxiously watching. Nova gave Remi a disparaging look and started to turn away from him to go back to tending to Geneva, but Remi couldn't let it go. He should have known better but his emotions were raw and he was taking them out on Nova.

"You don't know that. You don't know I haven't kissed her," Remi barked defiantly at Nova's back, stopping him in his tracks.

Nova whirled around and before Remi knew how it happened, Nova had a vice grip hold of his shoulder. Remi tried to squirm away but Nova had gone right for the nerve slightly above the collarbone and it just about immobilized him.

"Nice try Remi. I know you haven't. You don't have the nerve. She would have told me if you had, because she knows she can tell me things. But, I do know she won't like you talking about her like this."

"I don't know what she sees in you, but I can only hope it wears off in time. All you care about is yourself. I'm the one that's always been here for her. I'm the one that saved her just now and you can't even thank me. I'm fine by the way. Thanks for asking."

Nova pulled Remi close and whispered into his ear in a calm, quiet voice through gritted teeth, "Thank you for saving her life and I'm glad you're feeling well Remi, because this is gonna hurt."

He drew back and punched Remi square in the jaw, dropping him in one strike. Remi landed in a sprawling heap a few feet away from Geneva.

"Remi!" Sparrow cried! "Nova, what the heck was that for!?"

She scrambled from Geneva to Remi. Cradling his head and calling his name. She snapped her fingers until he came to.

While she stroked his dark hair, Sparrow hissed at Nova, "I don't know what that was all about, but it was uncalled for Nova! We're all on the same team here, so quit whatever this is so I can concentrate on healing Geneva please."

"Sorry Sparrow. It won't happen again," Nova politely apologized.

"Sure it won't mate," Journey laughed.

Nova shrugged at him and then pointed to the opening above them. "Looks like Eja's back with reinforcements."

A vaguely familiar shadow danced before me. It was slim and brown and moved calmly and gracefully about. It was a man, no, a boy. He was taking me in, studying me, poking at me, but in a gentle way. He was talking to me, but I couldn't hear him over the pounding in my head. I tried hard to focus on him and it finally registered; it was Eja, my Beto friend. He was whispering something to me. I could feel his voice faintly reverberating off my ear drums. I squinted as if that would help me hear better. Something wasn't right. I tried concentrating harder and I felt the tiny beads of sweat that had been forming on my forehead finally swell past their limit and begin their uncharted voyage down my face. For some reason this made me think of tears, and that made me think of Jemma. I imagined my beads of sweat were leaving the same unattractive streaks as Jemma's tears had on her face when she found out I was her sister.

"Jemma," I muttered bitterly. But it didn't come out right. My tongue felt too fat for my mouth and I tasted blood.

Slurp. Finally something broke through my trance, I looked down and focused on the dark, furry rodent shaped creature by my side. How long had it been there? It softly nuzzled my limp palm and licked me again. *Slurp.* It licked my hand. *Slurp, slurp.* It licked my wrist and then my arm and tickled me with its coarse whiskers. Then, it looked up at me with those large dark brown eyes. Those eyes that could see into the deepest part of my soul. I locked eyes with him and watched as the long, silver wisps of his ear hair floated, like strands of silk in the wind. They hung in the air, momentarily frozen, as though time had stopped. And perhaps it had, because suddenly the hammering in my ears had stopped and I was blanketed in an eerie quiet, allowing my mind a moment of clarity.

I lifted my hand with tremendous, trembling effort and laid it softly on the marmouse in my lap and let his name escape my lips in a whispery exhale, as the searing pain in my arm took over. "Niv..."

Blackness.

CHAPTER IX

Kobel fondly stroked the leather cover of the Book of Gods. He'd been tasked with babysitting it since it had unexpected spewed water. He took pride in caring for the Ravinori's most prized possession.

The Book of Gods had first been discovered by Ravin, himself. He had built his life around the lessons in its pages, convinced that if he followed them just so, that he could achieve perfection and that would lead him to greatness and godliness.

Ravin had gathered supporters during his reign. They agreed with his goals of elitist perfection for Lux and would meet in secret to come up with ways to help him rid the city of the lowly locals and natives. This group became known as the Ravinori; a powerful secret society, set on total rule and domination.

After the Flood, the Ravinori held fast to Ravin's beliefs and made it their goal to find him. There had been many rumors regarding his whereabouts. Some said he was hiding on the island, some said he'd fled, some said only pieces of his soul remained, waiting to be gathered by his supporters. There was even a rumor that he had perished. But, once his book, the Book of Gods, was discovered, the doubt about his survival was made clear.

The book possessed a magic about it. It was somehow able to predict the future, thus writing legends before they came to be. This made the book widely coveted and bound the Ravinori together, sworn to protect it, because in the final passage of the book, it said;

"*he has fallen, but is not forgotten, he will rise again and he will not forget who served his side in his absence. Seek the bringer of light, for after light comes the darkness...*"

That ominous statement had kept the Ravinori going for years, convinced that their master, Ravin was somewhere watching, waiting for them to bring him back.

Kobel carefully flipped through the pages until he came to a map of the island. He closed his eyes and concentrated on one thought and one thought only.

The bringer of light; the Eva.

CHAPTER X

I awoke with a start. It took a moment for my eyes to adjust to the warm soft glow of firelight. I was resting comfortably on a soft, cocoon-like surface. I was elevated and when I moved the whole room swayed. I closed my eyes and waited for the spinning to stop. I felt dizzy, but it passed after a moment and I tried to sit up again. The swaying returned with a vengeance. I teetered wildly, as I uselessly tried to steady myself with my arms, and then I lost all control. Before I knew what happened, I was lying in a heap on the ground. I looked over my shoulder for the culprit that had landed me on my aching back, but all I saw was a tan, woven hammock, swaying peacefully behind me. I glared at it as I stood.

"Stupid hammock," I muttered as I surveyed myself.

I was noticeably worse for wear. I was covered in cuts and bruises and my uniform was unrecognizable; completely tattered and torn. I was wrapped in bandages that had strange smelling tinctures on them and there was a sling on my left arm, but as I timidly tested it out, I was pleased to find that it didn't hurt. I slid it off my arm and winced as it brushed past my forehead. The worst pain was coming from my head. I felt the bump protruding under the thick bandage and flinched.

I looked around me as I gingerly stood, peeling off a few flapping bandages. It appeared that I was alone and in a primitive tent, lit by rustic candles, leaving haphazard wax puddles upon the old tree stump they occupied. They made the tent feel warm and inviting and filled the air inside with the sweet aroma of honey. There wasn't much else in the tent. A water canteen that I was happy to find, and my shoulder bag; but Niv wasn't in it.

Niv! Where was he? He was the last thing I remembered before, before… Strange memories flashed through my mind. *Oh yeah, How could I forget? We found the Book of Secrets and all hell broke loose.*

The last place I remembered being, was in that stupid cave with Remi. Well, actually falling into the cave for a second time, to be more exact. I shook away the queasy feeling that started to creep up my spine from the pit of my stomach. Whether it was from my throbbing head or from the events of the past few days, I decided these bad feelings would still be here later. Right now, my heart was driving me to find Niv and my friends.

I pushed the tent flaps open and was shocked by the sight that greeted me in the inky darkness outside. It was night, yet it wasn't all that dark and I wasn't alone. Dozens of little glowing tents like mine dotted the forest in front of me. There were tiny fires crackling here and there, illuminating the heavily tattooed tribal people that casually milled about the thick rainforest landscape.

I rubbed my eyes. I had encountered some strange things in the past year, some magical and some not, yet nothing prepared me for this. I felt like I had walked into a page torn straight out of one of my History & Trade text books. The scene before me looked exactly like every painting I'd ever seen depicting the Beto tribes of Hullabee Island. But it couldn't be real, could it?

"How hard did I hit my head?" I murmured rubbing the goose egg again.

I had a strange feeling of déjà vu. My mind returned to the cave and the visions of my future that my mother had painted on the water for me. This was one of them. At the time I had thought it was nothing more than a memory, rather than a history lesson come to life! I immediately thought of Eja. He had said that he wasn't the only Beto still remaining on the island, but somehow this wasn't what I'd envisioned. Why had he been so elusive? I had assumed he was referring to his family or something normal like that, because he was just a kid like me, so I was sure he was living with a parent or sibling at least. Even with his magical powers, I would have found it hard to believe he could survive out here on his own. The rainforest wasn't a safe place to live after the Flood.

I rubbed my eyes to make sure this wasn't some type of illusion, but the images stuck. Bewildered, I scratched my head as I scanned the horizon searching for any signs of Niv and my friends. I didn't see anything to tip me off on where to start my hunt and I was still a bit uncertain of how I got here and if my friends were even here at all. I backed my way into the tent and let the flaps close silently in front of me. I felt a little safer in the confines of the tent, but was still on edge. What if the Beto people weren't happy that I was here? What if I was a captive? I couldn't just go traipsing around camp like I belonged here. Even if my tattered Troian Center uniform didn't give me away, my shocking blonde mane certainly would. And my clear blue eyes and pale freckled skin didn't fit in among the tan, painted skin of the Beto natives.

I tried combing my fingers through my hair, but it was no use. The best I could do was a quick messy braid that I tied with a fraying scrap of string I tore from my shoulder bag.

Well here goes nothing I thought as I engaged my hunter skills, courtesy of Journey. I steadied my mind and slowed my breathing and focused in on the sounds surrounding me. The soft percussion of tribal music floated pleasantly to my ears, but I listened past it. Past the quiet campfire conversations, past the rustling of the forest leaves, past the gentle cooing of the night birds, all the way down to the march of the insects that dwelled on the forest floor. That would be what interested Niv. He was always on the hunt for something to eat. I listened carefully, but no matter how I strained I didn't hear anything out of the ordinary.

"This is going to be more difficult than I thought," I said out loud with a sigh.

I suspiciously eyed the hammock, but set out to conquer it, so I would have somewhere to sit and think. It was surprisingly cooperative this time and I settled in to come up with a plan. I didn't know if I should try to telepath to my friends or Niv because the Beto tribes were known to be home to Truiets; enlightened people with magical powers, like myself. If I could telepath, maybe they could too and I would end up giving myself away.

"How am I going to get out of here? I've got to get out of this tent and find Niv and my friends."

I started thinking about each of them and what they would be doing if they were trapped inside a tent in a Beto tribal camp. Journey would be pacing and probably want to just fight his way out. Sparrow would be scolding him for his destructive ways and giving us all a pep talk on how to befriend the Betos. Nova would take charge with some risky scheme that I would tell him would never work, while Remi sat silently in the corner looking nervous and like he wished he could just disappear.

"That's it! Disappear! Thank you Remi!" I said as I swung out of the hammock.

I grabbed my bag and concentrated on my new power that I'd acquired from Remi. Soon, I felt light and knew it must be working. It was always a tricky power to navigate, because other than a feeling of lightness, nothing really changed to indicate that you were actually invisible. I could still see myself. I waved my hands in front of my face and they were still there, just as true as they'd been a minute ago. I walked over to the cluster of candles that were almost entirely melted now. I smiled when I noticed my shadow was missing from the tent wall. I felt safe now and I slipped out of the flaps and into unknown territory.

The Beto camp was the most wonderful place I'd ever encountered. Barefoot children were merrily running about, filling the warm air with their carefree laughter. My stomach growled as I passed by tribe members preparing delicious smelling meals over their fires and conversing with their families. It was so simple, yet so perfect. I was in awe as I slowly made my way unnoticed through their camp. The glowing ashes from the fires danced like lava pixies on the barely present breeze and guided my way, winding deeper into the forest. The sights and sounds of camp life lifted my spirits and I felt a familiar longing to be a part of something like this. A cheerful melody caught my attention and I felt drawn towards it as I followed the notes to its source.

I came upon a small group gathered around a fire at the edge of camp. I stood mesmerized by the beautiful music being strummed expertly on the strings of a gourd guitar. I was spell bound as I stood behind the musician, his silhouette framed by glowing orange firelight. The song he sang was so soft and sweet and it spoke to my heart in a way I'd never felt before.

"...you are the light that guides me, you are my dream's sweetest delight..."

The words disarmed me. I didn't feel my invisibility slip away, but it must have, because the beautiful ballad ended abruptly, leaving me desperate for more. I looked around to see what had stolen the song from me and was shocked to see everyone around the fire staring back at me. They were all suddenly on their feet and I held my breath, finally realizing I must have let my invisible power slip. I was frozen with fear, not knowing what to do next when the musician turned around to stare at me as well.

"Geneva?" said his familiar voice.

Everyone simultaneously kneeled and bowed their heads. Everyone except for the boy who had been playing the gourd guitar. He put it down and rushed over to me.

"Tippy! You're awake!" he said cheerfully as he hugged me.

"Nova?" I whispered. *How did he never cease to amaze me?*

"Oh, you better bow to them," he said gesturing over his shoulder to the Betos who were still kneeling.

"What?"

"You're their Eva," he said with a smile. "Get used to it."

I gave an awkward curtsy and they all rose.

"That was weird," I whispered to Nova. "What do we do now?"

He laughed and then addressed the crowd of spellbound Betos.

"We'll have time for formal introductions later, but right now I have a pressing matter for our Eva."

They all nodded.

"Come on Tippy, I've got something to show you."

Nova grabbed my hand and slung his arm over my shoulder. My body involuntarily flinched and I cursed my wimpy muscles when Nova retracted his arm.

"Tippy, I'm sorry. Did I hurt you?"

"No," I said trying to shrug it off. "Just a little sore from my fall I guess."

"I'll bet. Are you okay walking?" he asked, pausing next to me.

"Why are you going to carry me?" I asked half joking, half wishing he actually would, so I could be in his arms again.

"Do you want me to Tippy?" he asked softly.

My attempt at being funny seemed lost on him, as he just stared deep into my eyes. I felt like he was searching my mind for something and my cheeks burned red at the feelings that instantly crept up to the surface. I didn't want him reading these embarrassing thoughts!

Ugh, why did I always feel so nervous and flustered around Nova?

I was squirming in my skin so I laughed, and started walking again. The laugh was forced and came out too shrill and almost sounded like a snort.

Smooth Geneva! I scolded myself.

In an effort to change the subject I said, "I didn't know you played the guitar. Where did you learn?"

He just smiled and winked at me. "I'm full of secrets Tippy."

I was about to challenge him, when I heard someone calling me. I turned towards the familiar voice, unable to place it at first and I barely caught sight of her long, raven mane before I was engulfed by her arms, choking on her long black hair.

"Eva! I'm so glad to see you're alright," gushed Jemma. It was no wonder I couldn't place her voice, I'd never heard her sound happy before. I balked at first, but my mother's words floated in my ears, like they were being whispered on the wind, *'give Jemma a chance.'*

"Okay," I sighed reluctantly.

"What? Were you saying something Eva?" Jemma asked releasing me from her awkward embrace.

"Uh, I was just saying I'm okay, is all," I said as she stepped back to examine me.

"I'm so glad," she said, pulling me into another hug. "I've just found you, I'm not ready to lose you again," she said, her voice threatening to crack.

It was so strange to see Jemma this way. She seemed so genuine and vulnerable. Not at all like the mean older girl that had spent years bullying me at the orphanage. I was struggling with my own emotions as my newly found sister continued to hug me. I felt an undeniable connection to her. It felt so comforting, like pulling on a familiar shirt, yet so strange at the same time. I couldn't put my finger on it, but being this close to Jemma made me feel like there was an electric pulse running through my veins. My mind told me to pull away, but my mother persuaded me to give my sister a chance.

I couldn't help thinking that a few weeks ago I would have been beyond excited to find out that I had a loving sister who would hug me close and worry for my safety. I just never could have imagined that Jemma would be that sister. If only she'd been nice to me, decent even, this would be so much easier. It was going to take some time to erase all of the spiteful thoughts I had of her. I vowed to try though. I had promised my mother I would.

"I hate to break this up you two, but I think you might be smothering our Eva," Nova said to Jemma.

"Oh! I'm sorry, I didn't mean to. It's hard not to get carried away I guess," she said shyly.

"Remember what we talked about?" Nova asked Jemma.

She nodded obediently. "That's right, I remember. Small steps."

I shot Nova a questioning look, wondering when they'd been talking about me. He just smiled and changed the subject.

"Is everyone still playing?" he asked Jemma.

She nodded mischievously.

"Good," he said before returning his gaze to me. "Do you still want to see what I was on my way to show you?"

"What is it?" I asked.

"It's a secret."

I nodded but didn't have time to ask any more questions before Nova gave me a playful look and turned to jog away. I looked at Jemma, who just shrugged. So with a sigh, I jogged after Nova. I was beginning to hate secrets I thought to myself as I chased him into the twilight.

CHAPTER XI

A short distance ahead of me, I heard Nova give a whistle. I shook myself, thinking my eyes had momentarily deceived me, because I saw Nova running towards a gigantic Bellamorf tree. I'd never seen one in person, but had read about them in our Plants and Poisons lessons. They were very rare and extremely poisonous. Even our teacher, Miss Banna hadn't seen one before. She said she thought they were extinct and in her opinion, we were all better off that way on account of how dangerous they were. According to her, one nick from a Bellamorf leaf and you'd have horrible hallucinations. The delusions wouldn't quit until they drove you completely mad. The worst part was, that there was no known cure for the delirium the Bellamorf poison induced. Death was the only way to end it.

But here it was, looming in front of me, larger than I'd ever imagined it could be. It had to be fifty yards wide and it was twice that in height. Its thick winding trunk seemed to be shimmering, which was odd, because I didn't remember reading anything about that in lessons! And there was Nova, steadily running towards it.

"Nova?" I called.

What is he doing? Surely he knows this is a Bellamorf tree, right?

"Nova! Stop!" I shouted, but I was too late!

Nova leapt onto the trunk and up into the boughs of thick branches, whose leaves swallowed him whole, blocking him from my view!

"Nova!" I screamed as I reached the trunk breathlessly.

There was all kinds of commotion coming from the tree. It seemed to be humming with life. I shifted my weight from one foot to the other, impatiently trying to get a glimpse of Nova and whatever was causing all the noise above my head.

"Nova!" I called again. "Nova, are you okay? This is a Bellamorf tree! Please answer me!"

Nothing.

Jemma caught up to me and saw the panic in my eyes. She grabbed my hand and tried to tell me it was alright, but I was beyond reason, staring into the tree, calling for Nova.

"It's okay Eva. Eva! He's okay I promise."

"No he's not! This is a Bellamorf tree! Did none of you pay any attention to Miss Banna?"

The tree suddenly went still and silent.

"Ahhh!" I shrieked and jumped backwards, tripping over the large protruding roots behind me.

Something furry had jumped out of the tree and knocked me to the ground. I was shielding my face and shrieking, when I heard giggles above me.

I opened my eyes to more eyes peering out of the tree limbs, grinning down at me.

"Is someone going to tell me what's going on?" I yelled.

"This tree isn't dangerous," Jemma said crouching next to me. "And, I think someone is excited to see you," she said pointing to the base of the thick trunk.

I spotted Niv, peaking around the bark at me. He must have been the fur ball that launched out of the tree at me. He looked sad and shy as he crept towards my feet, looking up apologetically at me. I couldn't help but smile at him. That was all the encouragement Niv needed. He raced into my arms and showered me with wiggly, tickly kisses.

"I missed you too buddy," I crooned into Niv's scraggly fur. I hugged him tightly, burying my face into his coat as he nuzzled my neck. I drank in his familiar scent of sweet hay. Oddly enough that smell always conjured up a fond memory, reminding me of walking through the fields to Flood work at the Troian Center. Holding Niv in my arms always felt like the closest thing to home I'd ever known.

"I love you Niv," I whispered to him. "I knew you'd find the others and tell them Remi and I needed help. You saved us didn't you little buddy? You're the best marmouse in the whole wide world."

Niv chattered with delight and twitched his whiskers in agreement.

"Hey, we helped too," called Journey from above.

"Hi Geneva! Welcome back!" Sparrow said, swinging down a few branches until she could gracefully drop out of the Bellamorf tree. She ran over and gave me a big hug. "I missed you!" she beamed.

"We all did," said another voice. I looked up to see Eja smiling at me.

"Thanks," I called, "but what are you all doing in that tree? Isn't it a Bellamorf tree? Aren't they poisonous?"

"Ha-ha-ha" rained giggles from above.

I looked to Sparrow for answers but she just smiled and shrugged.

"Yes, it is a Bellamorf tree and we're playing morf tag" called a voice I didn't recognize, "and you're IT!"

I strained to look up and see who the voice belonged to, but a strong gust of wind picked up and the tree instantly shook to life, sending leaves spiraling down around us. I flinched as one grazed my arm.

"It's okay," Sparrow called to me over the falling leaves. "I guess the whole poisonous tree thing was a bit of a legend that the Betos cooked up to keep locals and citizens away from their Bellamorf trees."

"Why would they need to protect a tree?" I asked.

"Well it may not be poisonous, but it's still pretty special," Sparrow said. "Come see."

Sparrow caught my hand and pulled me with her towards the massive shimmering tree trunk. We picked up our pace and stepped up and onto the solid bark, propelling ourselves upwards, just as she had taught me to when we first started coming to the forest to practice using our powers.

It felt great to be soaring up among the branches, reunited with my friends again. It let me forget about the burden of my role as the Eva for a moment and I lost myself in the fun of being young and carefree. I was giggling and breathless when Sparrow and I came to a stop on a sturdy branch in the center of the tree.

"So how does morf tag work?" I asked.

"It's an ingenious game really! Jovi taught us how to play."

"Jovi?"

"Yes, she's Eja's friend. She's the one who told you that you were 'it.' She's a Truiet like us and she can control the tree, which is what makes the game possible!"

"Okay…" I said taking in all of what Sparrow was saying. "So how do we play?"

"Well, it's simple. When Jovi says 'launch' the person who's 'it' has to count to 10 while everyone else hides. Then Jovi will get the wind going in the tree and the 'it' person has to come find us!"

"That just sounds like hide and seek in a windy old tree." I said.

"Wait, I'm not done yet," Sparrow reprimanded.

"Alright, alright," I sighed, "get on with it! I want to play!"

The laughter and calls from my friends above were making me itch to join them. I loved games, especially hide and seek!

"So it *is* like hide and seek, but the Bellamorf tree along with

Jovi's powers adds a twist. "

I nodded for her to continue.

"If you can catch a falling leaf from the Bellamorf tree, you can morf away!"

"Morf away?"

"You just have to see it to believe it," she smiled.

"Are you Janes ready yet?" Journey called clearly impatient.

"Bring it on Journey!" I called back to him.

"This is going to be fun!" Sparrow squealed and her excitement was infectious.

"Remember, you're 'it'," called a bright eyed girl from above me.

Something about her looked familiar to me; like maybe we had met before. She had the biggest smile I'd ever seen. It lit up her whole, heart-shaped face and it was impossible not to smile back at her. *Jovi*, what an appropriate name I thought, remembering it meant joy in Beto.

"You're on!" I called.

"LAUNCH!" Jovi yelled and the tree exploded to life once more.

My friends all took off, bounding from branch to branch as I closed my eyes and counted to ten. I couldn't help cheating though, because with my eyes closed, my hunter powers kicked into overdrive as I listened intently to their footsteps, trying to pinpoint their positions around me. Just as I smirked to myself, thinking, *this is going to be a piece of cake,* the wind picked up and howled in my ears, drowning out the sounds of my friends. Next, the air around me was filled with the powerful rustling of falling leaves.

"10!" I yelled. "Here I come!"

I opened my eyes and was amazed at the breathtaking sights surrounding me. There were millions of leaves, spinning like pinwheels in the wind. As they were cascading down, they rapidly reflected the light bouncing off the moon, making them shimmer and light up, the way bellies of silver fish did in the ocean. It was beautiful. I was caught up in the majestic view, when someone whizzed past me.

"You have to chase us you know?" the tiny, brown eyed girl called from a branch above my head.

"Oh, Jovi right?" I asked coyly, as I poised myself to pounce at her when she paused to answer me.

She just smiled back at me, white teeth lighting up her face. "That's right!" she said as I made my move and just as I was about to land on her branch she reached out and closed her tiny palm around a rotating leaf and *poof*, she vanished!

She left me grasping at the air and I nearly lost my balance. I was stunned. I spun around looking confused.

"What? Where...?"

"Over here," came Jovi's sing-songy voice, followed by a fit of giggles.

I looked up to see her doubled over, laughing at me.

"Okay, I get it now," I smiled up at her.

I reached out and grabbed a leaf myself, morfing and landed on the branch just below her. I saw the shock wash over her face for a moment, before it was replaced by a big grin as she grabbed a passing leaf and vanished again, leaving a trail of laughter behind her.

And just like that, the game was on!

We played for hours. It was so much fun. Everyone took a turn at being 'it'. I don't know which I liked more, hiding or seeking! Journey complained that there was never a winner. Sparrow and Jovi were so fast and light on their feet that Eja exclaimed they would be the winners if we had one. This just fueled Journey's desire for a rematch. Nova and I morfed together for a while and gave each other sly smiles between the falling leaves. This always ended up distracting me and getting me caught, but I didn't mind. I collided with Remi at one point and instantly felt awkward. I had hoped we'd left that mistaken kiss in the cave where it belonged, but it had apparently followed us here. I even found myself watching Jemma in awe at one point in the game. She was having fun, and laughing. She seemed so different. So normal. Almost like we could actually have a chance at getting along. My mother's words echoed in my head. *'Give Jemma a chance.'*

"Okay, Mom. I'll try," I said to myself gathering up the courage to morf over to Jemma.

When I landed, Jemma wasn't where I'd last seen her. I looked around, thinking I must have miscalculated, but then I spotted her below me. She must have morfed away when I was morfing towards her. I was about to call to her, but then I noticed that she was on the same branch as someone else. Nova. She snuck up on him and grabbed him from behind. The two of them laughed and playfully knocked at each other and I felt my jealous heart ice over!

The sounds of their laughter made me want to vomit! I'd seen Jemma look at boys that way before and I didn't like it. One thing I knew about her, was that she always got what she wanted.

"NO!" I cried involuntarily, and they both looked up.

"Hey Tippy!" Nova called to me. "Come over here! We're - "

But I didn't wait to hear the rest of his sentence. I wanted to get away from them. I couldn't look at Jemma and Nova for another second. I grabbed a leaf and just wished it to carry me away. When I landed, I found I was on the highest reaching branches of the tree. The view from up here was astonishing, but it did little to diminish the image of Nova and Jemma flirting. It had been burned into my brain.

CHAPTER XII

My mind and my heart began an internal battle with each other.

How could he? How could he betray me like that? With Jemma!

He didn't do anything. He was just talking to her, just having fun playing a game like everyone else.

But he knows how I feel about her.

She's your sister and Nova didn't do anything wrong.

That's right, Jemma's the one who was chasing after him! I can't trust her! I'll never trust her!

But your mother asked you too. You should give her a chance! She was being so nice to you. She probably doesn't even know you like Nova.

"Ahhh!" I screamed in frustration. "Why does she have to like the same boy as me?"

"Tippy! There you are!" came Nova's voice.

I whirled around ready to rip into him, but I lost my footing and nearly fell. But, Nova's strong arms came to my rescue again!

"Whoa! Tippy! Take it easy. You okay? Are you still feeling a little woozy from your fall?" Nova asked with genuine concern, nodding to the bandage on my head.

I had forgotten it was still there and felt instantly self-conscious of it as I reached up to tear it off furiously.

"No, I'm fine," I said indignantly. "You just startled me."

"Good," he said and he let go of my shoulders, but surprised me when he slipped his hand around mine.

Nova is holding my hand! It made my mind go a bit fuzzy, but then I remembered I was mad at him.

Not his fault, echoed the voice in my head. "Shut up!" I muttered.

"What?" Nova asked.

"Nothing. I'm just deciding whether or not I'm mad at you."

"Mad at *me*?" he asked sounding incredulous. "I should be the one who's mad at *you*!"

"What!!?" I exclaimed. Now he was just fueling the fire. *What could he possibly be mad at me for!?*

"Plenty of reasons!"

"Name one! And get out of my head Nova! I hate when you read my thoughts."

"I'm trying not to but your mind is practically screaming at me!"

"Ah, you make me crazy!" I yelled.

"Ditto!" he said but the corners of his mouth were turned up slightly, threatening to dazzle me with his gorgeous smile and I knew his heart wasn't really in this fight.

"Don't smile at me!" I scolded, losing steam for the fight myself.

"Why?" he asked with his full, dazzling smile taunting me now.

"Because, you just drive me crazy sometimes."

"Ditto," he said with a smirk.

"And stop saying 'ditto'."

He just nodded and smiled at me. I sighed. It was useless to fight with him. His charm always flustered me and my pounding heart always drowned out whatever nonsense my brain was cooking up as an argument.

Nova was still holding my hand too, which didn't make it any easier to stay mad at him.

"Why are you mad at me?" I asked him in a calmer voice.

"Because you drive *me* crazy."

"How?" I demanded, realizing I sounded childish as soon as the words passed my lips.

"Because I'm always worried sick about you! You storm off, you fall into caves! Twice! You almost drown and then almost break your neck trying to climb out of the cave! You need to be careful Tippy. A lot of people are depending on you. We can't have our Eva maimed or worse."

I sighed, it was true. I seemed to be a magnet for trouble lately.

"Ok, I'll try to be more careful. But, I guess we'll just have to agree to live with driving each other crazy every once in a while, because I don't set out to do foolish things you know? "

Nova laughed and looked into my eyes, my pale skin reflecting brightly off his deep green irises.

"Tippy, I think it's pretty obvious that you drive me crazy in a good way." He pulled me closer and whispered into my ear. "I'm crazy about you."

I closed my eyes as his lips closed on mine, losing myself in the perfectness of his kiss.

Meanwhile, below us, Jemma was 'it'. She was cheerfully morfing from branch to branch, chasing after the others. She smiled to herself when she landed silently below Remi. He had his back to her and hadn't heard her approach. She narrowed her eyes and artfully coiled her muscles, reading herself like a tarcat about to pounce on her unsuspecting prey. She was just reaching out to grab a leaf when something peculiar caught her eye; a single glistening tear on Remi's cheek reflected the moonlight from the flurry of falling leaves. Jemma paused, watching him intently. He was looking up and when she followed his gaze, she saw what had upset him. Two figures, barely visible among the swirling leaves, were entwined in an intimate kiss.

She looked back at Remi just in time to see him morf off of his perch and disappear from sight.

Jemma gazed back up at Nova and her sister, lost in their embrace. A tiny seed began to take root in the pit of her stomach. She tried to choke it back, but it burned hot and jealous nonetheless. Having lost her appetite for morf tag, she closed her slender fingers tightly around a spinning leaf, pulverizing it in her palm, as she disappeared from the tree as well.

CHAPTER XIII

My heart swelled as Nova embraced me atop the Bellamorf tree. I could barely tear my eyes from his to soak up the breathtaking view of the rising sun he pointed out. Dawn was breaking, illuminating the forest, bathing it in light and warmth. From this height, I could just make out the glistening shoreline of the surrounding sea, revealing how far inland we truly were. I was happy to stay like this forever, oblivious to the rest of the world, wrapped in Nova's arms. It seemed my problems couldn't follow me when I was perched so high. I wasn't the Eva, I wasn't an orphan, I wasn't a long-lost sister, I wasn't a fugitive … I was just a girl, as close to heaven as she'd ever felt. I nestled in closer to Nova, wanting to hang onto this feeling forever. But as the clouds evaporated in the hot sunlight, so did my reverie. I could feel the perfect moment slipping away and I think Nova could too. He pulled away from me ever so slightly, so he could look down at me with his dazzling smile.

"What?" I asked.

"It's a new day Tippy, we have lots to do."

"We do?" I questioned. "Like what?"

"Well for starters, I think we need to get you cleaned up," he smirked.

I instantly remembered how tattered my uniform looked and laughed. "Didn't you know this is the new look? All the orphans are dressing this way now," I said holding out a shredded shirt tail.

Nova laughed whole heartedly and said sarcastically, "Well, who am I to object to the Eva." He tore his shirt to match mine and we both laughed, joking as we started to make our way out of the tree.

Our journey down the tree was a bit slower now that morf tag was over. Without the magic leaves to transport us we had to climb down the old fashion way. I could have used my powers and bounded down like Sparrow had taught me to, but Nova didn't share that power so I hung back with him. Truthfully, I was enjoying the extra time with him as we climbed down the tree.

"So, how did you end up in this tree anyway?" I asked.

"We met Jovi the first day we got here and she said she had a secret for us. She brought us out here and showed us how to play morf tag. She's a sweet kid. I think she was trying to impress us. Apparently she plays with a few of the other younger Betos, but she said they're not supposed to. These trees are sacred."

"So they're not poisonous?"

"No. Their leaves have magical powers that the Betos use to transport themselves throughout the forest. That thing about them being poisonous was just a myth they created to protect the trees so that they wouldn't get cut down and harvested by the locals."

I was about to ask another question when we were interrupted by a shrill cry, followed by two streaking balls of fur.

"What was that!?" I said, jumping out of their path in surprise.

"Quin," replied Nova with a smile.

"What's a Quin?!" I asked.

"She's my wex," Jovi called breathlessly, as she vaulted past me, hot on their trail.

I turned to Nova in confusion and he smiled and grabbed my

hand, "Come on," he said "Niv will appreciate you coming to his rescue."

We followed the chattering commotion down the tree to the forest floor where the others had gathered. I dropped to the ground just in time to get caught between Niv, Quin and the tree. They circled each other furiously around and around the massive trunk. I couldn't tell who was chasing who, but they were darting between my legs and making enough noise to wake up the whole forest.

"Niv!" I shouted. "NIV! Come here!"

He jumped into my arms and unfortunately so did Quin, introducing me firsthand to what a wex was. I landed sprawled out on the ground again. I was being showered in sloppy kisses that were occasionally mixed with a nip.

"Hey!" I howled. "Stop! Quin! Someone call her off of me," I laughed.

Although she was small, she was strong, and so wiggly that I couldn't properly grab a hold of her. I finally lifted her off my chest and held her away from my face to get a better look at her. Her tongue lolled out and she panted, out of breath but clearly not out of energy as she squirmed in my grip. Niv squeaked his protest from below.

"Shhh, Niv. It's okay."

I turned my attention back to Quin. Her black eyes sparkled with mischief as she tried to nip at me when my face got close to hers. I swallowed warily when I got a closer look at her wickedly sharp teeth. They were white and delicate, but they could have torn my skin easily. I stared at her as she wagged her tail merrily, still squirming her long body and stretching out her tongue, from her elongated, narrow snout to try to reach me. She was a conundrum: her sinister teeth didn't seem to fit her playful personality. I surveyed the rest of her as I put her down. She was covered in curly chestnut and black fur. It was soft and gave a deceptively large appearance to her light frame. She was still raring to go when her paws made contact with the earth.

She went straight to Niv, who backed away from her, bristling his fur, clearly done with their game of chase. I scooped him up just as Jovi grabbed the wex.

"Quin!" she squealed as she caught her breath. "Bad Quin! I told you to leave Niv alone."

She turned to me. "I'm really sorry Geneva. I told Quin to stop bothering Niv, but she's so playful, she can't help herself. Every time he runs, she thinks he's playing. I'm still training her," she beamed proudly.

"Oh, that's okay," I stammered. "She's yours?" I asked.

"Yes! She's the fastest in the whole litter and she's so pretty, isn't she?" Jovi crooned as Quin wiggled out of her grasp again.

Quin obviously wanted to play, because she shook the small girl's grasp and darted to the side, crouched down on her front paws, rear haunches coiled and ready to pounce at a moment's notice. She bobbed and weaved a few times before Jovi was able to leap onto her wily wex, spoiling Quin's fun.

Jovi snuggled Quin tightly to her chest and was showered with a frenzy of nips and sloppy kisses. I couldn't help but smile at them. Jovi's zest was contagious. Her smile lit up her whole face as she came closer to let me get a better look at Quin.

"Want to hold her?" Jovi asked.

"Oh, no thanks. She looks happy with you. Besides, I've got my hands full with Niv here."

Niv snorted his disapproval when Quin came closer before departing to the safety of my shoulder bag.

"So, she's a wex?" I questioned.

"That's right. She's my very own wex. Pretty great, huh?"

"I've never seen one before," I admitted to the barefoot, brown eyed girl.

"You haven't!?" she exclaimed, her earnest eyes growing even larger with disbelief. "Why not?"

"Well, I don't know. I guess because I grew up in an orphanage and we weren't allowed to have pets."

"That sounds horrible," she frowned.

Jovi's eyes welled up like chocolate saucers ready to overflow. I was afraid the petite Beto girl would start to cry.

"It wasn't all bad," I quickly reassured her. "I got to have Niv. I just had to keep him a secret."

She didn't look convinced, so I asked her to tell me more about Quin and wexes to change the subject. That instantly perked her up.

"My family breeds them. They're distant relatives of the canidae family. Us Betos use them to help us hunt. They're very fast and cunning. Quin is one of four kits from our last litter. She's the only girl and no one wanted her. Can you believe that?!" Jovi asked looking shocked. "Everyone always wants the boys," she said, shaking her head. "Anyway, I knew Quin was the one for me. She's so fast and brave and has no trouble bossing the other kits around. She's going to be a pack leader when I get her all trained!" she boasted proudly.

I smiled down at Jovi as she rambled on about Quin and the history of wexes. Her big brown eyes brightly sparkled as she crooned on about Quin. She stroked the jittery wex in her tiny arms as she spoke, occasionally pausing to scold her and pull strands of her tangled brown hair out of Quin's mouth. She sure knew a lot for such a youngster. She was a bright, confident young girl, full of enthusiasm. I liked her instantly.

Jovi was just starting another Quin story, when Sparrow walked over to me.

"Hey Sparrow," I beamed when she walked up. "You've met Jovi and Quin I presume?"

"I have," she said, smiling at Jovi. "How's Quin today? Staying out of trouble?"

"Sort of..." Jovi replied shyly.

"Do you mind if I talk to Geneva for a moment?" she asked Jovi.

"Oh sure, I'm going to go find Quin some water. I'll see you back at camp."

We watched Jovi skip away from us and I couldn't help but smile. Sparrow pulled my attention back to her, "Geneva, I have something of yours," she said.

"What is it?" I asked.

"Here, I kept this safe for you," she said, pulling my magic journal from her shoulder bag and handing it to me.

"Thanks Sparrow."

I was glad to have it back. It held all the details of the amazing events that had changed my life over the past year. Sparrow had taught me a charm to make the pages blank to anyone but myself. I felt instant relief having it back in my hands.

"I knew you'd want it. I took care of Niv too while you were recovering. It mostly consisted of keeping Quin from chasing him and eating all his food."

"Ha-ha. Well thank you for taking care of him. That Quin seems like a handful."

We both laughed.

"She is a handful," Sparrow said grinning, "but she's sweet."

"So, how long was I out?" I asked Sparrow.

"Not too long… about a week?"

"A *WEEK*?!" I shouted.

"Well yes, you were pretty banged up you know?" Sparrow said bossily.

Then she proceeded to fill me in on what had happened and how we'd ended up at the Beto camp.

"I had my hands full trying to heal you in the cave. Luckily I think your echo power kicked in and started magnifying my healing powers. Eja got word to the Betos and they sent help to get us all out of the cave. Once we brought you back to their camp, the chief came and he and Vida, his top Truiet medicine woman, worked on healing you. They dressed your wounds and gave you a potion to help you sleep so that your body would have time to heal."

"Wow, that sounds pretty serious," I said with concern.

"It was! You almost died Geneva. From what Remi said, you probably got hit by the falling debris when you initially fell into the cavern and that's why you almost drown. Then when you fell trying to climb out, Vida said you broke your arm and your collar bone. Vida is amazing though. She's been teaching me a lot about healing and different potions that can help heal without using powers. She set your bones and healed them, and knew just what herbs to mix to help relieve your pain."

"I wish she could do something to help the bump on my head heal faster," I said massaging it.

"Oh, Vida said she doesn't mess with the mind. She said it's best to let the mind heal itself. You had a concussion Geneva, it's going to take a little time to feel right again. I'm just really glad Remi was with you. I'd hate to think what would have happened if he hadn't been there."

"Uh, Remi," I muttered, feeling shame flush my cheeks as our awkward kiss came rushing back to my mind.

"Geneva!" Sparrow scolded, sounding appalled. "Remi saved your life! If he hadn't given you life's breath…" she trailed off, but her eyes said the rest.

She looked genuinely frightened. I hated seeing her look this way so I threw my arms around her neck.

"I'm okay Sparrow. I promise, I'm okay. I'm going to be more careful. I already promised Nova that I'd try not to be so foolish and…. Wait…did you say Remi gave me life's breath?" I asked, as her words finally registered. I stared into her earnest amber eyes.

"Yes," she said, but then looked away distractedly.

"What else aren't you telling me?" I asked.

"I had to heal Remi too."

"What? Why? He seemed fine when I was climbing..."

"Nova punched him."

"What!? Oh no ... does he ...?"

"Know about the kiss? No and you're lucky he doesn't or it would have been a lot worse than some bruises for Remi. But, *I* do know about the kiss. Remi told me what happened."

"He told you!?" I hissed. "What was he thinking?"

"Don't worry, he told me not to mention it to anyone and I won't, but I don't like to be involved in these sort of secrets. They never end well."

"Sparrow it's not what you think. I mean, I don't think it is. I don't know why he even kissed me!"

"I do. He has a crush on you Geneva. He's had a crush on you forever," Sparrow said sounding slightly annoyed. "Do you like him?" she asked.

"Yes! I mean no, not like that. I like him as a friend. He's my best friend! Why did he have to complicate this? Ugh, I just wish it never happened!" I whined.

"Wish what never happened?" asked Nova as he slung his arm over my surprised shoulders.

"Nova! Oh, hey, what's up?" I asked, trying to sound as even as possible.

"Nothing much, just came to check on my girl. Gotta make sure you're not falling into anymore holes. What were you two talking about?" he asked with his devilish smirk.

My girl? My cheeks flushed and my heart leapt!

"Nothing," I stammered.

"She was just saying how she wished she hadn't fallen into that cavern and how she's going to be more careful from now on," Sparrow said, coming to my rescue.

"You got that right!" said Nova with a laugh. "Well, you ready to go babe? Eja said the chief heard you're awake and wants to talk to you."

"Oh, okay," I said, doubly stunned by the fact that Nova had just called me 'babe' and that the chief wanted to see me.

"*BABE*?!" Sparrow silently mouthed to me as Nova steered me away from the others and over to a group of Beto horses that were busily nuzzling their way around the mossy forest floor. I turned to look back at Sparrow over my shoulder. I raised my eyebrows to try to convey to her that I was as shocked as she was that Nova was calling me babe. I turned back to look at Nova, who had swiftly mounted a horse and was smiling down at me with his arm outstretched.

"What's this?" I asked Nova.

"Tippy, it's a horse. How hard did you hit your head again?" he joked.

"I know it's a horse! I meant what's going on? You just called me babe. Are we… is this…?" I stammered. "What I'm trying to say, is that we should probably talk if you want to officially call me babe."

"Oh we're definitely going to talk babe, but I know that we're *officially* going to be late to meet with the chief if we don't get going."

"Fine," I sighed. "What am I supposed to ride?"

"I figured you'd ride with me," he said with a wink.

Oh that smile! It made me want to melt into him and agree to anything he said. I shook myself from his spell and said, "Well, you figured wrong. I know how to ride a horse on my own, thank you very much."

It took all my will power to turn down his outstretched hand, but I needed some time to think and if I was clinging to Nova's waist, I know I would only be thinking about him. I needed to sort out what Sparrow just told me about Remi. I needed to talk to him. I didn't want to hurt him by gallivanting around with Nova right in front of him. Especially if the two of them were already fighting. He deserved to hear it from me, if Nova and I were going to be an item. But I didn't even know if we were! Nova can be so cryptic. One minute he's calling me babe, kissing me atop a tree and the next he's flirting with my sister! It still felt so weird to be calling Jemma my sister. Sparrow was more of a sister to me than Jemma had ever been.

I shook all these mind bogging thoughts from my aching head and marched past Nova to another horse, lazily basking in the shade of the rainforest trees. He was a small dabbled grey with long whiskers and bright Beto symbols painted on his hindquarters in yellow and red. I grabbed a tuft of his coarse charcoal mane at the height of his withers, expertly vaulting myself up onto his back. He lifted his head in surprise and I nudged him forward softly with my heels.

Nova looked on, his blonde eyebrows raised in amazement. His mouth curved up into a grin, highlighting his chiseled cheekbones as I rode up next to him.

"Ready?" I asked.

"Where'd you learn to ride a horse?" he asked.

"I'm full of secrets," I said quoting him, with a wink.

Before wheeling my horse around and digging my heels in, I flashed Sparrow a smile over my shoulder, as she and my friends looked on. I couldn't help being amused by their bewildered looks as Nova and I galloped back towards camp. It was nice having some secrets of my own I thought to myself.

CHAPTER XIV

The wind licked my hair as I prodded my horse alongside of Nova's. The feeling of being on a horse, flooded me with memories of how I'd learned to ride.

. . .

It was a few summers ago. Remi and I had the misfortune of being sentenced to work as stable hands at the Troian Center. The Grifts usually did this job on their own, but they were shorthanded, so a few of us ended up assigned to the stables. At first, I was excited to ditch boring laundry duty, thinking I'd get to groom the horses and maybe even ride them, but I had been wrong. They saved the really awful jobs for us, which mostly consisted of mucking out the stalls in the hundred degree weather.

I was determined to make the most of working in the stables though. I talked to the horses as I fed them and cleaned their stalls, and whenever no one was supervising me, I'd sneak them treats that I'd smuggled from the dining hall. I couldn't help it. I'd always shared an affinity with animals. Looking back now, perhaps my animyth powers were serving me before I even knew it.

The horses at the Center were as thin and malnourished as us orphans were. I felt it was my duty to make their day a little better whenever I could. They came to trust me after a few weeks and I worked my way up to climbing onto their backs. It was an exhilarating feeling, being on a horse's back. I have fond memories of wrapping my arms around their long necks and winding my fingers through their coarse manes, whispering imaginary adventures into their telescoping ears, listening to them rhythmically chew their sweet hay.

One afternoon, while Remi and I were mucking stalls, I heard the Grifts yelling in alarm. We poked our heads out to see what was going on and almost got plowed over by a stampede of panicked horses. Someone had left the paddock gate open and a tarcat had sauntered in, causing chaos as the horses reared up in fear, calling warnings to each other. The Grifts were doing their best to corral the horses towards the stables, but a few slipped out and made for the open fields. Remi and I stood by, flattening ourselves against the warm stable walls, trying to stay out of everyone's way.

Once the Grifts got the tarcat out of the paddock and stabled the rest of the horses, Jest, the Grift in charge, ordered us to go back to the Center. "What about the horses that got loose?" I asked. "They're lost to the island now," had been the answer. I was appalled and about to say that we should go find them when another Grift spoke up as if reading my mind. "I can retrieve them, sir." It was Sabine, she was one of my favorite Grifts. She was younger than most of the Grifts at the Center and very kind. She would often look the other way if it meant not making life worse for us orphans. There weren't enough Grifts like Sabine if you asked me.

"I think you're wasting your time, but suit yourself. If you're going after them, take these two with you to help wrangle them in," spat Jest, pointing to Remi and I with distain.

I perked up, blue eyes twinkling, ready for adventure and flashed Remi my "can you believe we get to do this" smile. He answered with a gulp and a feeble nod. Poor Remi, always so timid, I thought as I looked back at this memory. I remember trekking through the sun baked fields for quite a while before we found the loose horses. They were grazing peacefully, as if they'd already forgotten the ordeal that had caused them to flee. They looked up when they saw us approach, but continued grazing and swishing their tails complacently. Before I knew what was happening, Sabine was hoisting me onto the back of one of them.

"What are you doing?" I squealed.

"You know how to ride, right?" she asked with a wink.

When I didn't reply she said, "Oh, come on, I've seen you on their backs in the stalls."

"I'm sorry," I whispered shamefully with my eyes averted from hers.

"It's okay, I ride them when no one's looking too," she said with a grin.

"Oh!" I smiled, my kinship for her immediately growing. "But, I've never actually ridden one anywhere," I said.

"Well, this is Bastian and he knows the way home," Sabine said and with a hard smack on my horse's haunches we were off!

I didn't know what I was doing, but every instinct told me to hold on and let the horse take control. Bastian seemed to be on track, because I knew we were heading back towards the Troian Center when I felt the salty headwind fighting me. After I realized we were traveling in the right direction, I decided to stop being afraid and take it all in. The warm, velvety fur bouncing beneath me to a rhythmic gate, the coarse, dark mane lashing at me in the wind, the sun on my back, the breeze lapping at my hair and grazing my cheeks. I sat up straighter and soaked in the moment. It was so wild and freeing to be riding this beautiful creature. I felt like I was soaring above the world on the broad shoulders of this horse. I let go of Bastian's mane and held on with my legs, lifting my arms up over my head and howling into the wind! It was the most liberating moment I'd ever felt and after that I was hooked.

I couldn't wait for Remi to get back so I could tell him how amazing my ride was and to hear about how much he'd enjoyed riding as well. I was already busy coming up with plans for how we could do it again. I was the first one to return and decided to wait for Sabine and Remi in Bastian's stall while I groomed him, slowly detangling burs from his long tail, while he munched on hay. I heard Sabine return and was about to go greet her and thank her for letting me ride, but I stopped short when I heard Jest yelling at her.

"Real convenient how you found all those horses Sabine. Are you trying to make me look bad? Did you think you could return and be the hero? How do I know you weren't the one to leave the gate open?"

"No! Jest, you know I didn't!"

"Well, if I tell the headmistress you did, then you did! There ain't no one here to say any different. Don't think I don't notice how soft you are on these horses and orphans. You probably let them out on purpose so you could go for a joyride. The headmistress will hear about this! I think I'll tell her that your behavior is irresponsible and unacceptable."

"Wait, please don't Sir," Sabine pleaded. "Headmistress Greeley will fire me and I have a family, I need this job to provide for them. Please!" she begged.

I couldn't stand to let her lose her job. She'd told me of her family before. She'd lost her mother in the Flood and her father had been badly injured, losing his leg. That left Sabine to care for him and her younger sister all on her own. I didn't know what would happen to them if she lost her job at the Troian Center, but I didn't want to wait to find out. I ran out of the stall and skidded to a halt, blocking Jest's path.

"It was me! Sir, it was me. I left the gate open. I'm really sorry," I said.

"Ah, so you have an accomplice," he said as a slow, wicked smile spread across his rotten face.

. . .

Sabine still lost her job even though I'd said I was the one at fault. Greeley decided that Sabine had put us in danger by allowing us to ride the horses and that she would have to be dismissed for endangering us. I was so mad! We were orphans, no one ever put our safety first. Especially not our Headmistress Greeley; not unless it was of benefit to her anyway. I knew Greeley was gone, but I still shuttered when I thought of her.

I never saw Sabine after that and I never got to ride a horse again. That's just how things worked at the Troian Center. Nothing was ever fair.

That was how I earned my third trip to the Locker. Or, perhaps it was my fourth? It was hard to say. I guess I had lost track, surprisingly. Each visit to the Locker was terrifying. While I was there, I felt like I'd never be able to shake the feeling, yet as soon as I left, my mind thankfully had a strange way of blocking out such horrible experiences. The only time from the Locker that I could truly remember with vivid clarity, was when I'd been locked down there with Nova. When I thought he might be dead, when I saved his life, when he kissed me…

Oh that kiss! Just the thought of it brought all my feelings for Nova rushing back to the surface. I glanced over at him riding next to me. He looked like he was having fun and it was nice to see him smile. The handsome cheekbones of his tan face weren't stretched with worry for a change, they looked rounder, and full when he smiled like this. He looked younger, more his age, like Remi did … Oh I had gotten way off track. I was supposed to be figuring out my feelings and what to do about Nova and Remi. I sighed, hoping I could procrastinate these decisions a bit longer.

I could have ridden alongside Nova for hours, but our ride ended abruptly when the path we were on narrowed and the Beto campsite came into view. I followed Nova's lead, slowing my horse and dismounting. I patted my horse thankfully as I left him to nose around for something to graze on.

I noticed that all the tents I'd seen last night were gone and the few Beto people that remained were hurriedly breaking down what was left of their campsites.

"What's going on?" I asked Nova.

"They do this every morning. They break everything down and travel by Bellamorf trees to a new area. They don't like to stay in one place too long. It helps them stay hidden."

"What about that tent?" I said gesturing to the large tawny structure that loomed in front of us.

"That's the chief's tent!" came a voice from behind me.

I jumped and glared at Eja when he popped up next to me.

"Eja! How'd you get here? Why do you always sneak up on me?" I scolded.

"Sorry Geneva. Perhaps you should pay closer attention?"

I rolled my eyes and looked past him to the intimidating tent, made of skinned and stretched animal hides. Beams of light softly filtered out of the spaces where the hides had been seamed together with some sort of primitive twine. I took a deep breath trying to steady my nerves.

"Do you know what the chief wants with me?" I asked Eja, trying not to sound nervous.

"He wants to talk to you about the Book of Secrets."

"Oh" I said. I felt my stomach flip flop. I felt unprepared and underdressed to be meeting the mystical leader of the supposedly extinct Beto tribe.

"*Do you want me to come with you?*" telepathed Nova.

"*For once I'm glad you're reading my mind,*" I telepathed back to him. "*Yes, please.*"

"Um, I know you're going with this new rebel chic look, but you may

want to change before presenting yourself to the chief," Nova telepathed to me with a smirk.

"*I know,"* I replied taking in how ragged I looked. I looked down at my dirty hands and tattered uniform and suddenly felt very young and vulnerable. I was definitely not fit to be meeting with the chief of the Betos. I doubted even my healing charm could fix the thread bare garment I was wearing that barely resembled a shirt anymore.

"Is there anywhere I can clean up?" I asked Eja timidly.

He pointed to a nearby tree. It had a large knot that had sunken in, giving access to the cool rain water that collected in the center of its trunk. I walked over and shrugged off my shoulder bag, letting a sleepy Niv wobble out. I smiled at him and scratched his head affectionately and then began running cups of cool water over my face and hands and arms. The water was refreshing, but it was doing little to improve my overall appearance. I was trying to comb my hair into submission by raking water through it with my fingers, when Niv came flying up the tree and leapt onto my shoulder, angrily chattering.

"Niv! What are you doing!?"

But, I knew the answer to that question instantly, because two seconds later I was sitting on my rear end again thanks to Quin. She had followed Niv's path up the tree and unfortunately also thought she could land on my shoulder. She was much bigger than Niv and caught me off guard, sending me sprawling. To make matters worse, I had landed in the tiny puddle that had been forming under me as I washed myself off. I looked down at the spattering of mud that Quin and Niv sprayed all over me, as they chased each other in circles around me.

"That's enough!" I scolded and scooped up the wiggling wex. Quin covered me in excited kisses, making it hard for me to stay mad at her.

"Quin! There you are," came a familiar voice.

Jovi came panting into view and stifled a tiny shriek, her hand flying to her open mouth when she caught sight of me.

"Geneva! I'm so sorry! Did Quin do this? Quin! Bad Quin!"

"It's okay Jovi," I said handing Quin to her. "It was an accident," I added when I saw the mortified look on the little girl's face.

"Is there anything I can do to help," she asked with her big doe eyes blinking up at me.

"Well, not unless you have any clean clothes that would fit me." I said half joking, knowing I couldn't wear any of the pint-sized girl's clothing.

"I do! I'll be right back!" she said, and was gone before I could stop her.

She returned in a flash, padding barefoot up to me. She pulled open a sack that she began rummaging through.

"I knew these would come in handy! I always keep the things I find along the way. Clothes, gems, tools, shoes… Everyone calls me a pack-rat, but I always say 'it'll have a purpose someday.' Today's that day!" she said excitedly as she pulled a pile of material out, handing it to me.

I smiled at her contagious enthusiasm and pawed through what she'd given me. I held up a sage green, linen shirt. It was oversized, with a soft collar and wooden buttons down the front. It was too large for me and obviously meant for a man, but I pulled a sash from the heap and used it to cinch in the waist. I inspected myself, running my hands over the fabric, trying to smooth the wrinkles. I didn't look half bad. It was a definite improvement from my tattered uniform, which lay in tragic pieces at my feet.

"What do you think?" I asked playfully, twirling dramatically for Jovi, who squealed in delight!

"It's perfect!" she said, clapping her hands with glee.

"Now for my face…" I said, going back to the watering hole in the tree.

"Here! Try this," Jovi said, coming up beside me.

She dipped a piece of moss that she pulled from the bark into the water and handed it to me. "It helps scrub off the thick stuff."

I tried it and she was right. It was a vast improvement.

I smiled at her, "Thanks."

I took one more look at my reflection in the watering hole and sighed deeply. It was the best I could do and I couldn't come up with any more reasons to delay meeting the chief. I had to stop procrastinating and do my duties as the Eva.

"Okay," I said as I returned to where Nova and Eja were standing outside the chief's tent. "I'm ready."

"Wait, one more thing," called Jovi, running up behind me.

"What is it?" I asked.

"Bend down," she said.

As I complied, she tucked a bright ruby red flower behind my ear. "Perfect!" she said. "Good luck!"

"Thank you Jovi," I smiled at the young girl.

"You ready?" Nova asked as he reached for my hand.

I nodded nervously and Eja held the tent flap open for me.

CHAPTER XV

It was humid and fragrant inside the tent. It took a second for my eyes to adjust to the dim light. When I was able to focus, I saw that the tent seemed somehow larger inside than I had expected. The light from outside painted everything inside with a glowing orange hue. I noticed it was similar to the one I'd awoken in, but with more candles and incense burning. Instead of a hammock, there was woven grass mat with a large man sitting upon it, in the center of the tent. My breath caught at the sight of him. He was sitting with his legs crossed, yet I could tell he was tall. He was lean, yet muscular and he had dark skin and long, raven black hair collected in a series of braids down his back. His weathered hands were resting upon his knees, palms upward and open. His eyes were closed and he was breathing slowly and deeply.

I studied the barely present lines in his face. They started between his dark, bold eyebrows and continued around his almond shaped eyelids, where they fanned out, connecting to the dimples that creased his cheeks. The faintness of them made it impossible to guess his age. He was definitely younger than I'd expected. I guess when I heard the word chief, I had expected an old and sage leader.

We stood before him for what seemed like an eternity. Neither of us spoke, and the chief continued to sit, quietly breathing, in and out, in and out. I gave Nova a questioning glance. *"Do you think he's sleeping?"* I telepathed.

"I am not asleep my Eva, I am meditating," replied a low, smooth voice.

"Oh, I'm sorry, Chief, I … I didn't mean to interrupt you." I stammered, mentally kicking myself for flubbing up my first impression with the Beto chief.

"Don't despair young one. I was meditating on you, and here you are. You're interruption is welcomed," the chief said, bowing his head to me.

I glanced nervously at Nova. I didn't know if I was supposed to bow back or curtsey or say something special. This whole chosen one role was still new to me. Nova smiled reassuringly at me and after a moment, the chief motioned for us to join him on the floor, as two men moved swiftly and silently from the wings of the tent, to roll out grass mats for us as well. They startled me when they emerged from the shadows. Their faces were painted with dark ash, depicting sinister skeletal masks. I hadn't noticed them when we came in. How was it, that everyone around here was able to catch me off guard? The Betos just moved so much more gracefully and silently than I was used to.

"Don't be alarmed Eva. These are Beto shadow scouts. I always have a few of them with me, working as body guards. They are good at seeing the things that I can't always see. They paint masks of death on their faces to scare away the evil spirits they may encounter, for they can see the dangers present in all realms that may wish to harm us."

I didn't really understand what the chief meant, but I nodded anyway, trying to regain my composure. Perhaps Eja was right, I needed to pay attention more, I thought to myself as I sat down in front of the chief, folding my legs to mirror his.

"Eja is very wise, he will serve you well my Eva," the chief said.

"You can read minds?" I asked forgetting myself for a moment. "Oh sorry, am I allowed to ask you that?"

He chuckled softly. "Yes, I can tune into the minds of those around me and hear their thoughts. Yours are very clear to me. That is proof of your strength. And you are our Eva, we are here for you. We have been waiting for you for a very long time, so please hold nothing back. We want to help you in every way we can. If you have questions, by all means, ask them and we shall do our best to answer."

"Thank you," I said, feeling more at ease.

Nova, cleared his throat and I suddenly remembered my manners. "This is my friend, Nova," I said.

The chief nodded to Nova and I felt silly. Surely, if he could read our minds he knew who Nova was.

"What's your name?" I asked before I could stop myself.

Again, I felt like the words just slipped out of my mouth. I felt so open and unguarded around the Beto chief. I wondered if he had some sort of power that disarmed my thoughts.

He smiled ruefully. "No one has asked me my real name in a long time. You are refreshing my Eva. My given name is Koele, but my people call me Jaka. You may call me Jaka as well, if you like."

"Like the first chief?" I questioned.

"Yes. Do you know the story?"

"Yes, I know the Legend of Lux and how the Beto chief Jaka sacrificed himself into the volcano to stop the war and cleanse the island. I never dreamt it could be true, or that I could be part of it."

"I know the feeling young one. I too was thrust into the role to lead my people at a young age. Take comfort in knowing that these roles are only bestowed upon those who are meant for them. It may feel overwhelming at times, but always remember you are never given more than you have the means to bear. My people and I will be here to help you along your journey."

"Do you know why I was chosen to be the Eva?" I asked.

"Your destiny was written in the stars. You weren't chosen out of many to be the Eva, you just are and you being who you are, is why you are who we need."

"Okay, you kind of lost me," I said apologetically.

The chief smiled warmly, "Maybe that is because you are asking the wrong questions. We already know you are the Eva and the time for you is now. We need you and you have come. Do not waste time questioning what is."

Jaka's words were so simple, yet so powerful. They could be applied to everything I was dealing with right now. I needed to stop questioning how it was possible that Jemma was my sister and just appreciate her. I needed to stop wondering what to do about my feelings for Nova and just welcome the moments we were spending together. I had to stop questioning my relationship with Remi, we were best friends and that would never change, no matter what happened between us. I had to stop wondering if I could fulfill my duty of being the Eva and just be myself. None of what was happening to me lately seemed to be in my control, but I could control how I reacted to it and to stop questioning it all. To just embrace it, seemed like the best idea I'd ever heard. It instantly took a weight I didn't even know I was shouldering, off of me. I hadn't realized I was wasting so much energy worrying and questioning my future, but now that I had, it was liberating. I took a freeing, deep breath and cleared my mind.

"So, what do I do next?" I asked calmly. "We have the Book of Secrets, but I don't know what to do with it."

"I think you do Eva. You just need to do what you feel is right and it will be so."

I looked at Nova, who with a simple smile, encouraged a confidence in me that allowed me to speak my mind.

"Well, I haven't been able to really study the Book of Secrets, but from what I do know, I've been thinking... I feel like I need to go back to the Troian Center."

"What?" Nova whispered. The approving smile on his face had vanished and was now replaced with a startled expression.

"Nova, you know how horrible that place is. And now without Greeley there, who knows what's happening. What if no one is taking care of the other Johns and Janes? And I was thinking, I didn't get to really read much of the Book of Secrets, but Jemma and I were in it. What if there are other orphans in that book. What if it can help explain who they are or who their family is? I can't keep that from them. It's my duty to help them if I can."

As I said the words out loud, I realized I truly meant them. It was more than that. I felt them in my bones, like something underlying that had always been there. But, now suddenly, I was able to put my finger on that feeling. I needed to free the other orphans, the way the book had freed me.

Nova must have felt my conviction, because although he didn't look enthusiastic about the idea of returning to the Troian Center, he didn't look like he was going to resist it either.

"You are very wise indeed my Eva. The Book of Secrets tells of many others."

"You've read it?"

"Eja and I have been interpreting it since you arrived. I trust that's alright with you my Eva?"

I nodded.

"Can you tell me what it says?"

CHAPTER XVI

"Master, look! Something is happening with the Book of Gods again. The Eva must be accessing the Book of Secrets."

The brittle pages of the Book of Gods had since dried out. And now, once again the men watched in awe as large, looping script bled across the barren parchment landscape, causing a smile to curl the edges of the tall man's lips.

"She lives! The Eva lives! And she's in the forest master. I think she's with the Betos."

"Where in the forest Kobel?"

"I need more time to narrow it down master."

"I'm not a patient man Kobel. I want the Eva and the book!"

"I'll find them master, I won't stop until I find them."

"Redirect the search to the forest."

"Yes master."

"And Kobel? Don't let me down."

"Yes master."

CHAPTER XVII

My mind was whirling as Jaka filled my head with what he knew of the Book of Secrets. The Legend of Lux was just the beginning. There was so much more. He said the book reiterated that nature requires a balance; for every good there is an evil, for every birth there is a death, for every light there is a darkness.

He told us of a dark book, the Book of Gods. It was the balance to the Book of Secrets and it was believed to be possessed by the Ravinori. They were a secret society of Ravin supporters. Their sole purpose was to consume power, until they had enough to resurrect Ravin.

"My Eva, you must be very cautious of them. They will lay waste to those who opposed their views. They will be your biggest opponents."

"Do you know who they are?"

"No, they are very secretive and keep their identities hidden. I only know their beliefs and that I can feel their power growing. They are preparing for you my Eva. They are very powerful. If I can feel their presence we must assume they can feel yours."

"What can you tell us about the Book of Gods?" Nova asked.

"I have never seen the Book of Gods, as the Ravinori guard it heavily. I do know that it was never intended to be a dark book, but as with any literature, it can be misinterpreted. The Legend of Lux begins with the Book of Gods. It is said, that when Ravin read the Book of Gods, he was reborn. He believed it was a manifesto to create gods and he dedicated his life to becoming one. The book supposedly tells the story of the first war that took place among the immortals long ago. The results of this war were said to have divided the world into realms and given birth to mortals and gods and demons."

"So it's true? There were really immortals? Gods?"

A warm smile slowly spread across Jaka's face. "Yes Geneva, all the legends are real. You of all people should believe this to be true."

I was almost afraid to ask, but I couldn't stop the word from escaping my mouth.

"Why?"

"Because you are a direct descendant of them."

Nova reached out to steady me before I even realized I was shaking. I didn't know why I felt so shocked. I had already accepted that I had magical powers, a long lost sister and that our parents were part of an ancient legend. I guess hearing confirmation from a respected source just made it more real. I was so used to letting my imagination carry me away, but this was far more than I could have ever dreamed. My mind was buzzing with fear and questions. I felt the weight of expectation heavy on my shoulders and I was having a hard time knowing what to do or say next. I was grateful that Nova could read my mind.

"Can you tell us about this war among the immortals?" Nova asked Jaka. "I've never heard of it."

"Ah, I suppose that is the way the Ravinori prefer it. They don't want to draw attention to the secrets they've learned from the Book of Gods. There will be time for all of that, but for now, I think I've filled young Geneva's head with enough to ponder. Why don't you take some time getting her acquainted with the tribe and our ways," Jaka said to Nova.

He turned to me and smiled warmly, "Tomorrow we would like to welcome you formally with a celebration in your honor."

My eyes bulged and I was sure Jaka could sense my panic over the idea of a party, where I was the center of attention. This sort of thing would have suited Jemma perfectly, but I was never comfortable in the spotlight.

I tripped over my tongue, sputtering any excuse I could think of to get me out of an awkward party, where I'd be paraded around in front of a tribe of strangers.

"Oh… um… thank you… but that's not necessary. I… they don't need to…"

"I insist. We have been waiting for our Eva for a very long time."

"I don't really do well at parties," I whispered to Jaka. "I've um, never been to one," I said shamefully embarrassed.

Jaka placed his hands on top of mine and I felt his confidence in me radiate through me. "Just be yourself my Eva, and that will be just fine."

With that he bowed, giving me the distinct signal that our meeting was over.

I left the tent feeling like a bundle of nervous energy, yet somehow, refreshed and ready at the same time. Although the chief had told me my journey would be difficult and he warned me of darkness and dangers along the way, he had also given me clarity and a goal to focus on. I knew now that I had to go back to the Troian Center and free the other orphans. According to Jaka, there were more of them that were like me in the Book of Secrets; Truiets with magical powers. He said there were four in particular that would need my help. He called them the four Pillars and said they were in danger because their power was instrumental in the Ravinori's goal of bringing their leader back.

Nova stood by my side, his eyes, questioning green pools. But,

I had no answers for him. My mind danced with Jaka's warnings echoing in my ears. Thoughts of dark forces whirled through my head. Jaka had said they'd been set in motion long before I was born. He cautioned me against the ancient cult of Ravinori that would stop at nothing to accomplish their goals. He said, they had formed to preserve Ravin's power hungry ways and to oppress the Truiets and steal their powers in order to bring Ravin back. I knew my tasks of freeing the orphans and protecting the Pillars would be far from simple, but I could feel Jaka's faith in my ability to succeed against all odds and it drove me onward. For the first time, I was starting to believe that I could actually fulfill the prophecy of the Eva; the chosen one who would bring our island to salvation.

Now, the hard part would be convincing everyone else. I knew I needed to start with my friends. I looked at Nova, standing loyally by my side outside the chief's tent. My heart ached at the thought of having to ask him to join me on this mission, but Jaka said I would need the help of all of my friends. Rallying them to head back to the Troian Center after we narrowly escaped would be no easy task.

Jaka told me Eja would be my appointed liaison from the Beto tribe, at my service to help me with any task. I knew what his first task would be, helping me come up with a plan to convince my friends that I wasn't crazy, before I asked them to return to the Troian Center with me. Eja seemed like as good a place to start as any, so I took a deep breath as I scanned what was left of the Beto camp for him.

"Eja," I called when I spotted him.

He gave me a wave and trotted over.

"I trust things went well with Jaka?" he asked me with a smile.

"It went much better than I had expected," I said as I took in his knowing smile.

Eja always knew more than he let on. I bet he had known that the chief would appoint him my Beto advisor and that I would enlist his help in convincing my friends that we needed to go back to the

Troian Center. He had, after all, read through the entire Book of Secrets with the chief and already knew that it was our only course of action.

Anticipating this, I simply said to him, "Shall we get started?"

He beamed, "The others are already back. I'll gather them for you."

As Eja went to work gathering my friends, Nova pulled me aside.

"So how are we going to do this?" he asked with a worried expression painted on his beautiful face.

I hated when he looked so worried. Especially when I knew I was the cause of it.

"Tippy?" he questioned, shaking me out of my all too frequent Nova trance.

"I don't know Nova, but I know however we do it, it'll work out."

"Tippy, stop," he said grabbing my wrist as I turned to walk in the direction Eja had gone. "You need to take this seriously."

"I am."

"No, I mean you need a plan. A real plan. You can't buy into the chief's 'whatever will be, will be' mumbo-jumbo."

"Nova, the chief is right. We need to stop worrying and start doing. I don't know how I got to be the Eva, or how I got to be here, in the forest with a magical Beto tribe that is supposed to be extinct, but look around you, here we are. Some things you can't plan for."

"Tippy! Do you not remember what we just went through escaping the Troian Center?" he shouted at me. "We had a plan and look how badly it went. We almost died! All of us! Greeley paralyzed us, then sent an army of Grifts after us and set half the rainforest on fire. The only reason we're still alive is because you had to kill her to stop her from killing us."

I wrenched my hand from his grasp furiously.

"Do you think I have forgotten that?" I whispered to him, fighting back the tears of shame that welled up at the mere mention of

Greeley's name. "I will NEVER forget what happened with Greeley. But that is precisely why we have to go back. We have no idea what the rest of the Johns and Janes are going through right now. What if they're all alone or worse, what if someone who's more evil than Greeley has taken over? You heard what Jaka said. There are more orphans like us, with powers they don't understand and we need to help them and keep them safe before they're discovered and their powers are manipulated."

"Tippy, I know, I know," Nova said, pulling me into an embrace. "I wasn't trying to upset you…"

"Stop!" I shouted at him.

I didn't want to be coddled or comforted. I couldn't believe he was throwing what had happened with Greeley back in my face. I'd only done what I had to do to protect myself and my friends.

"If you're not with me, you're against me Nova. I'm going back to the Troian Center, with or without you!" I yelled as I jerked myself free of him and marched past the group of my shocked friends that Eja had assembled.

I knew I had probably let my emotions get the best of me, overreacting because Nova had brought up Greeley. It was still such a raw subject. But I didn't care, I didn't want to apologize for my feelings. I wanted him to take me seriously and stop always questioning me. I knew he was probably just trying to protect me, but it made me feel like he only saw me as the same little girl he had met at the Troian Center and I wanted him to see me as so much more.

"Eja, where is the Beto tribe camping next?"

"I can show you the way," he replied.

"Good, walk with me so I can go over my ideas with you. We can fill the others in when we set up camp for the night," I called over my shoulder.

"What the heck was that all about?" Sparrow whispered to Journey.

"Another lovers' quarrel," he joked.

Remi rolled his eyes. "It sounded like Geneva was saying she wanted to go back to the Troian Center," he said to Sparrow, ignoring Journey's comment.

"She can't really want to go back to the Troian Center can she?" Sparrow replied.

"If she does, then I'm sure she has a reason for it," Jemma piped up, surprising everyone by coming to Geneva's defense.

Remi and Sparrow shot each other questioning looks.

"I'm sure she'll fill us in on her plan when we get to camp tonight, just like she said she would. You're all just wasting your breath speculating," Jemma said with a huff and picked up her pace, walking past Journey, Sparrow and Remi to catch up with Nova, who was striding angrily ahead of the group, towards the next Bellamorf tree.

CHAPTER XVIII

"Master, the Eva has made a decision."

"And …" he demanded. "What is it Kobel?"

"I can't really believe it myself master, but it has been written," he said in wonder. "The Eva will be returning to the Troian Center."

"You're sure?"

"Absolutely, master."

"Call back the men," he said with satisfaction as a wicked smile spread across his sharp face.

CHAPTER XIX

"We can't go back to the Troian Center right now, especially without a plan!" Nova yelled picking right back up where he had left off.

I sighed deeply. I was hoping that traveling to the new Beto camp would have cooled him down a bit. I knew all the hiking and morfing had worn me out. I was still trying to get the hang of morfing, but was having a hard time staving off the dizzying side effects from being sucked through the mystical portals offered by the ancient Bellamorf trees. It was much harder than just morfing from branch to branch like we had in morf tag. Remi said it had taken him a few days to get used to it and Sparrow attributed the lingering dizzy spells to my head injury. I suspected they were just being nice and attempting to make me feel better about my lackluster morfing abilities.

It was dusk and Eja had gathered everyone inside a tent that had been set up for me. It glowed yellow from all the candles inside. I stood before all of my friends, surveying their expectant faces before speaking. I tried to channel the calmness that Jaka had when I'd spoken with him. After a few more deep breaths, I walked over to the Book of Secrets, which was propped open atop a decaying tree stump, lined with melting candles. Eja was kneeling next to it and I nodded to him to start reading.

"...they will pillage the land and stop at nothing to obtain the magical powers they seek. They're allegiance is solely to Ravin and they worship his savage ways and operate without moral compass, only guided by an insatiable quest for power. The Ravinori, these mercenaries of greed, operate in a society of secret. Numbered and numb, they have imprisoned their subjects under the guise of patronage, imposing their cruel rules on the unspoken for. They wait, biding their time for the perfect opportunity to strike when their targets will be at their weakest, unguarded, their secrets unveiled and powers revealed. Unchecked and forgotten, the only hope for these orphaned souls is for the Eva to return and lead them to embrace their true identities. The powers that unleashed their secrets, will also band them together. All must oblige to defeat the Ravinori..."

I held my hand up to stop Eja.

"It goes on, but I think you all get the point," I said softly.

The vibe in the tent was electric. I could sense the rush of feelings my friends were emoting; shock, fear, anxiety, anger. I wanted to soothe them, so I dove into my speech, which I hoped would inspire them to return to the Troian Center with me.

"When I met with Jaka, he helped me understand my path and it leads back to the Troian Center. From what Eja just read from the Book of Secrets, it's clear to me that the Troian Center isn't just an orphanage. It has been acting as a prison run by the Ravinori! It's where all the orphans that were suspected to have magical powers were sent. Then they brainwashed us to forget our families and we were never allowed any freedom to develop our powers on our own. Jaka said that the Ravinori are behind the whole thing. I think they probably appointed Greeley to be our headmistress and oppress us. They have been working to find the Book of Secrets this whole time, so they can find out who has powers that they can use to bring Ravin back."

"And we led them right to it…" said Sparrow shell-shocked.

"Yes," I said, "but we still may have the element of surprise on our side since they were oblivious to the fact that the Book of Secrets was hidden right under their nose. They may not know we have it, which means they may still be occupying themselves with searching for it and that buys us some time. Eja has been deciphering it and if we can find the rest of the Truiets it speaks of and get to them before the Ravinori, we can help them."

"And if we can't?" asked Journey.

"If we can't, then the Ravinori win and we'll probably all be dead," growled Nova. "This is a suicide mission!"

"It's not!" I yelled standing my ground. "I would not have been appointed as your Eva if I was going to come up with a plan that would get us all killed. This is what I have to do to free our island. I need you all to trust me. I know that I don't have a perfect plan yet, but together we can come up with one. I know we can. But, the catch is, that we all have to agree. We all have to work together to succeed. It says it right in the Book of Secrets. 'The powers that unleashed their secrets, will also band them together. All must oblige.' That means all of us." I said staring at each of my friends, letting my gaze linger longest on Nova.

His hard stare seemed to soften ever so slightly and the moment I saw the fire in his green eyes go out, I knew I had won and he was with me.

I emerged from the tent and stretched my stiff legs. After an exhausting evening of talking and planning, we were finally getting somewhere. Everyone was on board to return to the Troian Center with me, but I had conceded to take some time to prepare. Nova and the others felt there were a few things we needed to do before we would be ready and they were probably right.

Eja and I needed to scour the Book of Secrets to know exactly who we were looking for. Practicing our powers was also on the agenda. Remi and Jemma didn't have a very good handle on theirs yet and as I was finding out, controlling your powers was a skill that required constant training. Nova promised to head that endeavor since he had the most experience with his powers. Journey wanted some time to track with some of the Beto scouts to find the safest path back to the Troian Center for us. He was always on the offense and worried that maybe some Grifts were still hunting us. We all agreed this was a good idea. I also wanted to get another chance to speak with Jaka. He had promised there would be time for him to tell me more of the Book of Gods and its legends.

With all of this on our agenda, we figured we would need a few weeks in the forest to prepare. Plus we still had my party to contend with. Eja cut our planning session short so we could start preparations. It seemed it was going to be a bigger event than I had anticipated. I figured I'd just shake hands with the tribes people and introduce myself, trying not to say or do anything stupid. But, to my dismay, there was a whole ceremony planned, with a feast and festive dress and dancing. It was set for tomorrow evening and I was already dreading it. I tried to put on a smile since Jemma and Sparrow were over the moon about the whole thing. Perhaps this would be a good time for some sisterly bonding.

I let them drag me to Jovi's tent, where we were going to prepare. Her family had graciously volunteered to take us in. They had apparently been feeding and clothing my friends since we'd arrived at the Beto camp. I hadn't met any of them besides Jovi yet, but if they were all as warm and energetic as she was, I knew I'd be in for a treat. Jovi was waiting for us outside of her tent with Quin. When she saw us, they both ran over.

"Mom! They're here!" she called as she ran towards us.

I successfully dodged Quin's pounce and she collided with Remi instead.

"Hi Geneva! Hi everyone! I hope you're hungry! Mom and I have been cooking all day and we were just putting the finishing touches on your outfits for tomorrow! Come and see! You're going to love them!"

As we followed Jovi back to the tent, a tall chestnut haired woman emerged. She folded her arms across her chest and gave Jovi a glance that instantly took the wild bounce out of her step.

"Jovi's mom?" I asked Sparrow.

"Yes, that's Vida."

"Jovi's mom is Vida?"

I don't know why that surprised me. I guess I expected the tribe's medicine woman to be old, but then again I had expected the chief to be old as well and he was far from it. It just struck me as odd that Jovi, this wild, free spirit would have such a strict mother. I hadn't even met her yet, but I could already tell she was a no-nonsense kind of woman. I swallowed hard as we approached.

"And where exactly are your shoes young lady?" Vida asked Jovi.

"Oh mom, I don't need shoes," Jovi smiled giving her mother a kiss on the cheek.

"We have company Jovi and you're not a wild animal you know!" she called after her pint-sized daughter, who ducked into the tent behind her.

"I beg to differ," called a voice from behind us.

I was slightly shocked to see one of the scouts we'd met earlier with Jaka, walking up behind us. He gave us a nod and smiled as he passed. He too gave Vida a kiss on the cheek and ducked past her into the tent.

"You should come out here and formally introduce yourselves!" Vida fumed, pushing a stray strand of chestnut hair back into place in its tidy bun.

We all stood silently in front of Vida for a moment. It was clear from the giggling and ruckus going on inside the tent, that they were not coming back out. Vida finally sighed and uncrossed her arms.

"I'm sorry. Try as I might, my children have no penchants for manners. They're strictly wild!" she said throwing her hands up.

As if on cue, Jovi and the scout growled and then exploded into laughter and Quin came darting out of the tent.

"Jovi! What did I say about that wex being in our tent!?" Vida hollered disappearing inside.

"Are we supposed to follow her?" I asked feeling awkward.

Journey just shrugged, but before the others could answer, Vida reemerged with both of her children. She was smiling now.

"These are my children. Talon and Jovi. I believe you've already met, but I still adhere to the old ways and make introductions properly," Vida said.

Both Jovi and Talon bowed dramatically and smiled at us. Talon had washed his skeletal mask off and he looked much less menacing. He was tall and thin and had the same long, wild hair and brightness about him as his sister Jovi. He was probably a few years older than Nova and almost as muscular as Journey. When he smiled at us, his deep dimples lit up his tan face. He wrapped his arm around his mother's shoulders and gave her a squeeze.

"Oh mother, we're just having a bit of fun. And we've already met, haven't we Geneva?"

Vida smacked him on the shoulder. "Son, we kneel when addressing our Eva!"

"Oh no, ma'am… that's really not necessary. I don't want people to bow to me."

"See mom, I told you she was cool!" Jovi whispered making me smile.

"And I did meet your son early this morning when I was speaking with the chief. He was very respectful," I added trying to get him out of hot water with his mom.

Talon gave me a thankful smile.

"Well, that will be decided at the ceremony. Until then we'll abide by the rules."

She turned to address me, bowing slightly. "If it pleases you, I'd like to serve dinner and get started with fitting you for your attire for tomorrow's ceremony?"

"Of course," I nodded and she held open the tent flap, inviting us into her humble home.

CHAPTER XX

After an appetizing dinner and lively conversation, I was starting to learn Vida's ways. She was stern on the outside, but it was only to mask her warm heart. She couldn't help but smile proudly as her children spoke, laughing at their outrageous tales. She had so selflessly invited us all into her home, sharing everything she had with us; food, clothes, laughter, advice. I watched as Sparrow drooled over every word she uttered, hoping to learn more healing tips from her. I hadn't been so sure about her at first, but her genuineness won me over.

Vida's home was full of beauty and love. It was sparse in terms of belongings. There was no table for us to gather at, only a few blankets and hammocks. My favorite part of the tent, were the walls. The interior walls of her tent were painted by the hands of her children. They had traced tiny hand prints, quotes, memories, drawings and even charted their height as they grew, comparing each measurement to a type of plant. Jovi was now the height of a wild iris and Talon, milk weed. I couldn't help noticing that there was a third set of hand prints and I'd only met two of her children. The name Kyo was painted next to them.

"Who's Kyo?' I asked before I could stop myself.

Talon and Jovi stopped talking and looked sadly at their mother. She smiled and squeezed Talon's outstretched hand.

"I'm sorry. I shouldn't be so intrusive," I said feeling the mood in the tent change.

"It's alright," Vida said tensely. "Why don't we clean up and get started on the fittings?"

I felt awful that I had killed the cheerful atmosphere. I helped the girls clear the table, while Vida sent the boys off to fetch more firewood. Jovi came to my side and slid her tiny hand into mine.

"Don't feel bad Geneva. Mom just doesn't like to talk about Kyo."

"I shouldn't have asked. It was rude of me."

"No, it's really fine. Talon and I talk to each other about him all the time. He was our older brother. Talon says talking about him keeps him alive in our memory. And I like hearing about him. Kyo and my father both died in the Flood. My mom was pregnant with me, so I never got to meet them. Talon said that's why she's so uptight about obeying all the ancient traditions and following the rules. She's afraid to upset the gods and have another Flood that will take the rest of us away from her."

"I'm really sorry Jovi."

"You don't need to be sorry. They're all in a better place now. Besides, there are many that have it worse than we do. I think we're pretty lucky. We still have a family and we get to live in this beautiful rainforest. Not locked away in an orphanage like you and your friends were."

I looked at Jovi in awe. She was so young, yet wise beyond her years. Even though she and her family had been through so much, she was still so innocent and optimistic. She was refreshing and inspiring to me.

"Besides, you're here now," she said cheerfully. "And you're the Eva and you can fix everything!"

Jovi's words haunted me for the rest of the night. She reminded me how heavy the burden upon my shoulders was. So many Betos, just like her, were looking up to me to save them and restore peace and equality to the island so they could come out of hiding. They'd all been suffering since the Flood, just like I had. I'm sure each of them had a story like Jovi's or mine. Family and friends ripped away from them, forever changing their hopes and dreams. At dinner Vida and Talon explained to me how the tribe had split up into small groups, continually traveling, never staying in one place for more than a night to minimize their risk of being found by Luxors. Luxors, where the military arm of Lux, and they had slaughtered or enslaved what was left of the Beto's once flourishing tribe after the Flood. Many friends and family members were forced to split up in order to achieve these small mobile groups. I felt the mounting pressure to help reunite them in the tone of our conversation. I sighed deeply as the heaviness in my chest took hold again.

"Ouch!" I squealed, when one of Vida's pins poked through the thin red fabric she was draping around me.

"Darling, I need you to stand still. I hate to keep poking you," Vida said.

"Sorry," I apologized.

"It's alright darling."

"My mother calls me darling," I mused.

"Does she?" Vida asked sounding surprised.

I realized how crazy that probably sounded, since everyone knew I was an orphan and I hadn't told anyone, except Remi, about speaking to my mother in these strange reflections and visions I'd been having. I wasn't sure if I should share that information just yet.

"Well in my dreams," I stammered trying to recover.

Vida just smiled and kept pinning.

"Vida, I never got to thank you for healing me after I fell into the cave. Sparrow said you helped set my arm and treat my wounds. She said you've been so kind, teaching her what you know about healing and taking all of us in. I'm really thankful for you."

"It's my pleasure dear."

"And your children are wonderful. I've only just met Talon, but he's so diligent and I love spending time with Jovi. She's so energetic and smart."

Vida smiled ruefully. "They take after their father I suppose."

"I'm really sorry that you lost him and your son in the Flood. It was rude of me to –"

"Who told you I lost them in the Flood?" she questioned me harshly.

She had stopped pinning now and was staring at me with fury in her piercing dark eyes.

"Um, Jo-Jovi," I stuttered.

Vida was silent for a moment, collecting her breath and her thoughts. I was holding my own breath, waiting for her to yell at me for rudely prying into her private life. But, after a little while, she simply went back to pinning the fabric she had expertly draped around my waist. This left me flabbergasted. I would have preferred she yell at me and get it over with. The silent treatment was torturous. After a few minutes of drawn out silence, I couldn't take it any longer.

"Vida, I'm really sorry. I shouldn't have asked about your son or said anything about your husband. I didn't mean to pry or assume anything… I just… sometime I just speak before I think and I … I didn't mean to make you mad."

"Geneva, I'm not mad at you."

Vida looked like she wanted to say more, but she was hesitant. Finally she sighed deeply.

"I guess I might as well tell you since you're the Eva. Perhaps my secret can serve you somehow. But, I will ask that you let it remain a secret for the protection of my children. Especially Jovi."

I nodded.

"Kyo did die in the Flood, but not the way they think. He shouldn't have died. We had enough warning and we got our whole family to safety in a cave that we had designated as a meeting place for such situations. There were a lot of Betos from our camp there, but when Kyo realized his girlfriend Dayna wasn't among them, he left to go in search of her. I begged and pleaded with him not to go, but he was blinded by young love and beyond reason. It broke my heart when he pulled free of my grasp and left the safety of the cave in search of Dayna. I knew I'd never see him again. And I never did," Vida said mournfully.

"After the Flood we searched for them, but the island was so devastated, it was impossible to find anything. We retreated with the few Beto survivors there were and tried to figure out how to live in this unfamiliar land that we had once called home. My husband was a great motivator and provider. He found himself helping and caring for others in the tribe and soon he was elected as chief. He became the next Jaka and the responsibility to protect and provide for his people stole him from me. The land was barren and our people were divided. They were living like savages, only looking out for themselves. Our once harmonious tribe had broken off into many smaller factions, all having separate chiefs and their own set of rules and motives. My husband knew it was imperative for our people's survival that we all reunite as one tribe and help each other cultivate the rainforest. He was having success bringing all the small groups back together too, but there was an altercation with the last sub-clan. They thought my husband was power hungry, trying to rule all the Betos. They rallied a charge against him. He tried to fight them with words, laying down his weapons as a show of good faith. All the other clan leaders were there to back him up and it almost worked, but at the last minute the rouge clan turned on them and slit my husband's throat. The others were able to put down the rouge tribe, and in the end it's what solidified the unification of the Betos back into one tribe, but it cost him his life."

The tent was tensely silent after Vida finished telling me her dismal tale.

"So you see Geneva, the Flood didn't take my son or my husband, love and leadership did."

"They were heros," I whispered as tears streamed down my cheeks.

"Don't fool yourself. There's nothing noble about dying, no matter what the reason. All it does is hurt the people that love you when you leave them."

"But your husband; he saved the Betos by reuniting them as one tribe."

"Yes, he was a great and selfless leader, but to be those things, he had to stop being a great husband and a great father. Leaders shouldn't have families Geneva. I know you may think I sound selfish, but I've experienced it firsthand. We were liabilities for him. We were threatened and targeted by those wishing to manipulate him and cause him pain. We made him vulnerable ..." she whispered, trailing off; her mind obviously reliving some sad past memory.

"Vida, I'm sorry for your losses. I can't imagine what it's like to lose your husband and your son - "

"No, you can't. And I hope you should never have to."

There was a wild anger, burning in her dark eyes when she spoke and it singed my heart when she looked at me.

"I haven't even told you the worst part yet Geneva."

I swallowed hard, knowing I didn't want to know, but that I didn't have the nerve to stop her from telling me.

"Do you know how they got my husband, the great Jaka, to agree to meet with the rouge faction? They kidnapped me and held me hostage until my husband agreed to meet with them. The only way they got him to lay down his sword, was by holding one to my throat.

And then, I had the great privilege of watching them murder him, before my very eyes, all the while knowing it was my fault. He never would have been there if it hadn't been for me," she said bitterly. "A short while after we buried my husband, I learned I was pregnant with Jovi. She was a tiny miracle and perhaps the only reason I was able to collect myself enough to continue on living. She saved me from the dark depression I was facing after the death of my husband and my oldest son, yet I see them in her face every day. She is a bittersweet reminder of love's vicious lease."

The air in the tent was suffocatingly still. I wanted to flee, to get to fresh air and chase her horrible story from my mind, but I was frozen. I stood perfectly still, as her steady hands expertly continued to pin my dress for the Eva ceremony that would seal me into a loveless fate.

After a short while she spoke to me again.

"I don't tell you these things to be cruel Geneva. I just don't want to see anyone suffer the way I have suffered. I love my children and my people and believe it or not I love you and I believe you can become a great leader. But, I feel it is my duty to warn you. I see the way those boys look at you. They spoke of nothing but your welling being after you were injured in the cave; doting on you the entire time you were recovering. I had to order them away to give you the peace you needed to rest and heal. They worship the ground you walk on. A word of advice Geneva; tread lightly on their hearts. You can only be responsible for one or the other; your country or your family. No heart is big enough for both."

Her words resonated hard inside my head. They were an echo of my own hesitations about becoming the Eva and what I would have to sacrifice. Vida was living proof of my worst fears; love, being used against me. I was lost, deep in the terrors of my own mind, when she spoke again, pulling me from my contemplations.

"I hope what I've shared with you will remain private. Talon knows his father died after the Flood. He realized the numbers didn't add up with Jovi's age long ago, but he's agreed to go along with my story for her sake. He knows me well enough to know I have their best interests at heart and I hope he trusts that I have my reasons for keeping certain secrets."

"You shouldn't keep secrets from them Vida. They're your children. They'd understand. And they'd want to know about their father," I pleaded.

"No! It's better this way. I'm thankful every day that Talon was so young and didn't witness what happened to his father. And, that Jovi was spared from the tragedy of all the death the Flood brought. I don't want them to know. I've fought too hard to keep this sadness from their lives."

"Vida, you *have* kept sadness from them. I see so much happiness in them. You're their mom and they love you. They wouldn't want to see you suffering the burden of this secret."

"It's funny how love works, isn't it? It's because I love them, that I must keep this secret."

Her tone was final and even after only meeting her today, I knew better than to push Vida any further.

"You're finished. Slip this off and send Sparrow in so I can fit her, please."

After I sent Sparrow in to see Vida, I wanted to put as much distance between myself and that tent as possible. My mind was reeling and my stomach felt queasy. I breezed past my friends that were gathered around the cozy campfire, mumbling an excuse before any of them had a chance to stop me.

I headed off into the forest for some solitude and found it near a babbling stream where I heaved my guts up, unable to contain the sorrow that Vida's story filled my heart with. The trouble with being an empath, was that I could feel the full force of people's emotions and

Vida's were overwhelming. I pitched until I had nothing left and then washed my face with the cool water from the stream. I was slurping handfuls of sweet water when I heard someone come up behind me.

"Are you alright?" Nova asked softly.

I turned to face him and my heart plummeted to my feet. He looked so beautifully surreal in the moonlight. The way the shadows rippled over his shirtless body made him look like he was only an illusion, and in that fleeting moment, I realized that maybe he was. After my conversation with Vida, the notion that someday Nova and I could be together, was merely a dream. This realization forced the breath from my lungs and I started to shake.

"I … no …" I wailed collapsing into his arms as he moved towards me.

"Hey, shhh…. Tippy. What's wrong? What happened?"

I just sobbed uncontrollably into his warm chest as his arms encircled me. Being this close to Nova was so comforting, yet excruciatingly painful all at the same time. It was a cruel taste of what I wanted, yet knew I could never have.

"Do you want to talk to me?" he whispered into my hair as he squeezed me tighter.

I just shook my head in protest, as I continued to shutter and cry. There was no way I could form coherent thoughts right now and I was afraid I'd say something I wasn't ready to. Something I couldn't take back, like the fact that I was madly in love with him, but that it didn't matter, because we could never be together if I was going to be the Eva.

"Do you want to let me see?" he asked.

"No! Promise me you won't read my thoughts Nova!" I begged, trembling at the thought of him getting the wrong idea by all the emotions that were flooding my mind right now.

"I promise Geneva. I won't do anything you don't want me to do. You know that right?"

I nodded and relaxed back into his arms.

"Just hold me…" I managed to choke out between sobs.

"Forever," he whispered into my hair.

CHAPTER XXI

Last night had been rough. I'd tossed and turned, fighting off dark visions of a friendless future. After a particularly cruel nightmare involving Nova and Remi, I finally gave in to the sleeplessness and slipped on some clothes and gathered up Niv for a twilight walk.

I ended up in the boughs of a Bellamorf tree, wishing I could somehow morf my issues away. I brought my journal and poured my bleeding heart out onto its pages. It always made me feel better to write things down. It didn't solve my problems, yet seeing them on paper seemed to make them more manageable. I guess it was like identifying an enemy, offering me a way to figure out how to best achieve victory.

I watched the sunrise and felt a peacefulness wash over me as the forest came to life. The birds sang with joy as the flowers opened their blooms, aching to spend a new day warmed by the sun. Niv eagerly hunted the branches for insects and I smiled as I watched him delightfully pounce when he found one.

How can a world this beautiful be so painful? I thought to myself as I bounded out of the tree.

When I reached the ground I had resolved not to let Vida's fate, be my own. Both my mother and Jaka had told me that I could write my own destiny and what better day to start than today!

I called to Niv and marched back towards camp, determined to conquer the day that would officially make me the Eva.

The camp was alive with excitement. There was truly something special about today. I sensed it in the sunrise and everyone could feel it in the air at camp. My friends were all in spectacular moods when I joined them for breakfast.

Nova glanced at me with a hint of concern, but when I smiled at him and telepathed "*I'm okay*," he seemed to relax.

"So how are you this morning?" Eja asked me cheerfully when he joined us.

"Good," I said. "A little nervous I suppose, but good."

"Excellent!" he said clapping his hands. "We still have a lot to do to prepare. I assume Talon, Vida and Jovi were appropriate hosts and helped prepare you with a brief history of the ceremony and what to expect?"

Everyone nodded and mumbled agreement as they continued to eat the delicious meal Vida had provided for breakfast.

I glanced at Nova, realizing I might have missed some of the history lesson while I was crying in the forest with him last night.

"I got ya covered," he winked.

"Splendid, then we have little time to waste. My Eva, I'll need you to come with me. Talon is expecting the rest of you," Eja said.

"But, I haven't finished breakfast," Jemma whined.

"I'm pretty sure Journey finished it for you," Remi said laughing as he caught Journey stuffing the last crumb from Jemma's plate into his mouth.

"Hey!" she yelled, but he was already on his feet before she could swat him.

"No wonder you're so thin Sparrow. All this time with Journey, I'm surprised he managed to leave you any scraps to eat!" Jemma called after Journey as he sauntered away, with Remi and Nova following.

I watched my friends walk away, bickering playfully and sighed. I was pleased they had come so far. Hopefully they could all get along long enough to make it through the Eva ceremony today.

I turned to Eja, "I'm all yours."

Eja directed me on a hunt to find the four elements of the Pillars. Earth, Wind, Water and Fire. We traipsed through the forest together, all the while being shadowed by a familiar looking Beto scout.

"Who is he again?" I asked Eja.

"That's Mali. He's one of the shadow scouts. You met him when you were first introduced to the chief. I assumed that you met him at Vida's last night also. He's Talon's best friend and he lives with them. Vida took him in after his family was killed by the Flood."

"Oh… right," I mumbled, mentally kicking myself for not sticking around the campfire with the others last night. Perhaps I should've asked Nova to fill me in before he went off with Talon.

"Why is he following us?"

"For your safety my Eva. You will always have a scout with you now that you're officially the Eva."

"We'll see about that," I muttered to myself, making a mental note to change that rule as my first act as Eva.

"Why are we doing this again?" I asked while I dug up dirt to put in a small vile that Eja was holding.

"They are for the chief to bless at the ceremony, thus connecting you to all the elements of this world on a deeper level. It's the foundation of the Eva ceremony," Eja said sounding put off. "Are you sure you're feeling okay?"

"Right. Yes, sorry. I'm fine. My mind is just … I don't know…" I trailed off feeling ashamed that I had missed the history lesson from Vida's family last night.

"It's alright. I'm sure you have a lot on your mind. Being the Eva is no easy task. You've been given a great responsibility."

My conversation with Vida didn't help any either, I thought regretfully.

"I know, I know! Great responsibility means great sacrifice and consequence. I get it," I moaned.

"I wasn't going to remind you of that. I was simply going to thank you," Eja said, immediately humbling me.

"Oh, well you're welcome, Eja."

After we collected all of the elements, we had a long trek back to camp. I decided to use my time wisely, picking Eja's brain a little.

"Eja? Do you know much about Vida and her family?"

"I know they are very kind, good people. Vida is loyal to the ways of our people. She helps counsel and uphold the ancient traditions. She's a wealth of knowledge and a talented healer, despite not having any Truiet powers."

"So, you trust her then?"

"Why do you ask that? Has she done something to make you think otherwise?"

"No. It's just, I only met her yesterday and I didn't really get a chance to know her all that well yet," I lied.

It seemed I probably knew Vida better than anyone else since she'd spilled all of her dark family secrets to me. I stopped walking and turned to face Eja.

"Can I ask you another question?"

"Of course."

"Do you think history repeats itself? That we're destined to suffer the same fate until we get it right?"

"My Eva, why are you asking me this?"

"Please. I just want your honest opinion."

"No, I don't believe that we are doomed to repeat the past. I believe in you, therefore I believe in freedom and limitless possibilities for our future."

I hugged Eja, startling him.

"Me too," I said. "I just wanted to make sure we understood each other."

"We all feel that way my Eva. All of the Betos believe in you. That's what we're celebrating today," he said eyeing me suspiciously. "Are you sure you're alright?"

"Yes. Fine. More than fine. Just some last minute jitters I suppose."

Once Eja seemed convinced I wasn't insane or that I wasn't going to freak out and run away, he directed me to a stream where Jemma and Sparrow were already gathering. He left us to bathe, directing us to return to Vida's tent when we were finished, to dress and prepare for the ceremony.

CHAPTER XXII

"Jemma, do you know how to put one of these on?" I asked holding up a long bolt of red fabric.

"Of course silly," she said, coming to my rescue.

She and Sparrow had already expertly draped their elegant saris into curve hugging dresses. Mine was hopelessly wrinkled and looked like I'd just gotten tangled in my bed linens.

"What did you do to it?" Jemma asked, sounding horrified when I handed her my balled up mess of a dress.

"I thought that Vida was sewing it into a dress or something! What was all that pinning about anyway?"

"*This* is for the ceremony. The dress she was pinning is for the party afterward," she scolded rolling her eyes at me.

"You really did a good job wrinkling it," Jemma fussed. "A little help Sparrow?"

Sparrow gladly used her amazing healing powers to restore the delicate fabric back to its original glory.

"That really is the most handy talent," Jemma said, her voice laced with envy while she expertly wrapped me. "Arms up," she ordered. "Now spin."

"Maybe I can teach you to do it? I was able to share it with Geneva," Sparrow offered while they both helped me get ready.

"Yes, but I'm a parallel," I said matter-of-factly.

Jemma looked disgruntled.

"But we *are* sisters, maybe we're both parallels?" I added, trying to defuse her mood.

"Don't patronize me Geneva," she said, putting the brush down she had been using to comb through my tangled hair. "It's obvious you're the talented one in our family. The chosen one. All I can do is track people. What use is that unless we're playing hide and seek?"

"It's really useful. If any of us are ever in danger or lost, you're the only one who can find us. Or, what about when we get back to the Troian Center? You're going to be our best chance in locating the Pillars and the other Truiets."

"It's a stupid power. You can train an animal to do what I do," she said dismally.

We had been getting along so well. I was determined to turn this conversation around. I studied Jemma's face. She still had a tiny cut above her eye from when she fled the Troian Center. Without thinking I grabbed both her arms and closed my eyes, concentrating hard on the healing power that Sparrow had shared with me.

"What are you doing?" Jemma cried, trying to squirm away from my hold.

"Hold still, I want to try something."

"No! I'm not your test subject!"

I opened my eyes and smiled. My sister's miniscule scab, above her dark eyebrow, was now completely gone. I let go of her arms as she pulled away from me.

"What's your problem? You're smiling like a lunatic."

"She healed your cut," Sparrow said, admiring my work.

"What?" Jemma cried. Her hand instinctively went to her eyebrow as she rushed to the large pot lid we were using as a mirror.

When she turned back to me, her dark eyes were ablaze with anger.

"So what! Are you just showing off now?" Jemma asked lividly. "It's not enough that you're prettier and that everyone loves you and that you're the chosen one. You're an echo, and a parallel and I'm nothing. I get it Eva, you don't have to flaunt it!"

I was stunned! I couldn't believe what I was hearing! Jemma thought *I* was the pretty one? I'd been envious of her my whole life! Hearing her insecurities made her seem more human and sisterly than I'd ever imagined she could be. I wanted to hug her, but I knew better.

"No! No, Jemma. That's not what I'm doing at all. I think that I can share my powers with you because I am all of those things. It's strange for one person to possess so many powers. I've been thinking about it and there has to be a reason. I think maybe it's so I can transfer powers to people who will use them for good and to further our cause. And, if it's going to work on anyone, it'll be you Jemma. You're my sister, my blood. There's always been a connection between us, some magnetism. I think the universe was trying to tell me this all along. Our fight on the ruble pile is what started all of this."

She was staring at me, eyes wide, but with less hate in them.

"Think about it," I urged.

Sparrow was watching us with baited breath.

"So, what are you saying?" she asked.

"I just healed you with a power that I acquired from Sparrow because I'm a parallel. But, I'm also an echo, so what is done to me is done to others and vice versa!"

"I don't follow."

"I used a power to heal you, thus giving you that same power you can use to heal me through my echo ability."

Both girls were looking at me like I'd lost my mind. Jemma was shaking her head and Sparrow just looked confused.

"I don't feel any different and if what you're saying were true, wouldn't I have healed you?" Jemma asked, nodding to the large bruises that remained on my arm from my fall in the cave.

"You weren't trying to," I said.

Jemma still looked skeptical.

"Geneva, if this works… do you know what this could mean?" Sparrow asked.

I nodded my head. It could have infinite possibilities, which delighted and frightened me simultaneously.

"It might work," Sparrow said with a shrug. "Couldn't hurt to try it."

"Try it," I encouraged Jemma.

"I don't even know what to do," she argued.

"Just place your hands on my bruise and concentrate. Close your eyes and picture my skin healed and flawless."

Jemma obliged and slowly closed her eyes as she took a deep breath.

"There's an awful lot of shrieking and giggling going on in there," Remi said, motioning to the tent where the girls were getting ready. "Do you think we should check on them?"

"Nah," Journey shrugged.

"What's taking them so long?" Nova said, as he paced back and forth waiting for the girls to finish getting ready.

For once, he and Remi seemed to be on the same page. They had spent all day helping set up the ceremony site and now he, Journey and Remi had nothing to do but wait. They'd been dressed and ready for hours and he was getting impatient of parading around in the ceremonial waist cloth they'd been instructed to wear.

"They're girls," Journey yawned.

He looked entirely too comfortable in his skimpy cloth, sitting on a tree stump, chewing a long blade of green grass. He had his arms folded behind his head lackadaisically.

"Journey, I'm seeing more than I ever wanted of you right now," Remi scoffed.

"If you don't like the view, look the other way," Journey said unapologetically.

"Seriously Journey, why are you so comfortable with these ridiculous outfits?" Nova chimed in.

Before the argument could escalate, Eja trotted up.

"Where are the girls?" he asked, unable to hide the mild panic from his voice.

"Still getting ready," Nova and Remi said in unison, pointing to the tent that was muffling squeals and laughter.

"Do it again!" Sparrow giggled.

"Okay, what color now?" Jemma asked.

"Peach to match her sari!" I exclaimed.

"Okay, peach it is!" Jemma said, grabbing Sparrow's face and concentrating.

"Bravo!" I exclaimed when Sparrow's lips changed to a soft, dewy shade of peach that matched her dress expertly.

We all exploded into laughter and applause. After Jemma had been able to heal my bruises, she couldn't get enough of her newly acquired healing powers. Sparrow had shown her a trick or two about how she could use her power to manipulate her hair styles and complexion. After that, we'd spiraled into an indulgent soiree of making each other over. I'd never had so much fun or felt like such a girl! It was grand! And Jemma was in her element. She was being fun and silly, and for the first time, I felt what the girls in her group must have felt. When Jemma's graces were upon you, it felt like the sun itself was worshiping you.

"Eva, let me do yours! You need perfectly, pouty red lips to match your dress!"

"Can you do my hair like yours too!?" I begged, envying her

black silky straight braid.

"I could, but why would you want to give up these beautiful blonde curls? They suit you so well sister," she said, as she kindly stroked my hair.

She was so kind and tender, I had to fight to remember that she was the same girl who had tortured me at the Troian Center. Perhaps we really could put that behind us and be sisters again.

Just as she finished dialing my lip color to perfection, we heard Eja clear his throat outside our tent.

"Ladies. Time is of the essence."

"Sorry, Eja. We're almost ready," I called. "Just putting on the final touches."

"We really must be going. I'm sure you all look beautiful, as usual," he said.

We all blushed and exploded into another fit of laughter.

"Okay, we're ready," I said, after I'd collected myself.

Eja pulled open the tent flap and we emerged one by one, into the fading sunlight of the afternoon.

Nova stopped pacing, and Journey and Remi stood, when their eyes settled upon us. They'd never seen us so dressed up before, and truth be told, I'd never felt so beautiful. The sheen of my delicate red sari bounced the filtered sunlight back in the most flattering way. With each movement, different shades were illuminated, making the fabric come to life. The beautiful, hand forged jewelry that Vida had lent us shimmered, reflecting rays of gold as brilliant as if they were stolen from the sun itself.

The boys were speechless. The stunned expressions on their faces were what we'd been hoping for, but it still made us all blush and giggle all over again. Jemma loved the attention. She marched forward and linked arms with Nova.

"Shall we?" she crooned.

Nova hesitated against her pull, with his gaze still locked on me.

I felt my cheeks flush and had to avert my eyes. When I glanced back up through my bashful, pale lashes, I saw he had given in to Jemma's persistence. I watched his tan, toned back moving away from me, as a pang of jealousy awoke inside my heart.

CHAPTER XXIII

We made our way to the Eva ceremony. Jemma with Nova, Sparrow with Journey, and me hanging back with Remi and Eja. I balked when we emerged from the brush, into the clearing where everyone was waiting. The beautiful scene momentarily took my breath away. The lush landscape was elegantly decorated with red flowers that matched my dress in every size and shape imaginable. They hung overhead, draped in luscious strands. They lined the aisle, separating the sea of strangers and they were gathered in elaborately arranged bunches around the large stone altar.

"Why is everything red?" I whispered to Eja. Then I cringed, realizing it was probably explained in the history lesson I'd skipped.

"Isn't it your favorite color?" Eja asked sounding slightly terrified. "The chief noticed the flower you had in your hair the day he met you and thought it must be something you loved if you were wearing it to make your introduction, so he modeled everything in that hue for tonight's affairs."

"Oh yes, it's perfect. I love red," I smiled, remembering that it was Jovi who gave me that flower.

How appropriate that my spirited little Jovi had influenced

the entire Eva ceremony. It made me smile and relax for a moment, knowing she'd had such a big part in planning tonight's festivities. I tried to hang onto that thought, but when I saw the endless sea of Betos before me, I could feel the panic setting in.

"Why are there so many people?" I whispered nervously.

"Geneva, you are our Eva. We have been praying for the prophecy of our savior to return since it's inception. Betos from all over the island have come to witness you.

"How many Betos are here?"

"Many. Our Island is vast and it has been safer for us to exist in smaller groups, where we could travel more easily and live simply. Now that you are here, that may all change," Eja said, beaming.

I struggled against the crushing expectations. I knew this day was coming and meeting the Betos was a simple task compared to what lay ahead of me, but already I could feel the tiny beads of sweat forming on my brow and the heaviness pressing back against my rapid heartbeat.

Remi noticed my nerves and came over to comfort me.

"I can walk in with you if you'd like?"

"Thanks Remi," I said trying to collect my breathing.

"No, actually you all need to proceed ahead of Geneva to the right side of the Altar," Eja said, pointing to the massive moss covered boulders in front of the large group of tribes people.

Jaka was seated comfortably upon one of them, with his eyes closed in meditation. He was wearing a beautifully stitched robe of reds and yellows, along with an elaborate headdress to match. I studied the calmness of his face and tried to channel his energy. Once I focused on it, I could feel him sending me soothing vibrations. I slowed my breathing and let his strength wash over me, encouraging my own. The moment I knew I was ready to proceed, Jaka opened his eyes and nodded.

The music boomed forth, startling me as Eja urged my friends forward. Jemma perked right up, straightening tall and pulling her shoulders back as she glided down the aisle away from me. Nova gave me a wink over his shoulder and followed shortly behind her. Next was Sparrow. She gave my hand a gentle squeeze of encouragement before flitting away from me, into the sea of foreign faces. Eja had to hold Journey back when he tried to instantly follow behind her. His protectiveness over Sparrow was second nature by now and Eja ended up letting him go sooner than he wished after Journey gave him a menacing glare.

I watched, as all of my friends climbed atop the stone altar and sat next to Jaka. Remi was the last one to join them. Once he was settled, the music changed to a more grand rapture. It must have been my cue, because Eja genuflected and then let his arm gracefully point to the path before me. Everyone was on their feet now and I could hear my heart pounding in my ears, as I took my first unsure steps forward.

The crowd burst into applause as I moved towards them. I took deep breaths and tried to fight my nerves, but I felt dizzy with fear. I stopped abruptly after only managing five feeble steps towards the altar.

I looked back to Eja and mouthed, "I can't do this."

"*Yes you can,*" I heard in my head.

I turned back to the stage at the sound of Nova's voice inside my mind.

"*Come to me Tippy. Just walk up here, to me.*"

"*Nova, I can't. I'm not ready for this. I don't want to let all these people down.*"

"You could never let them down Tippy. You have already saved us, all of us. You're more than we ever could have hoped for. But for now, you don't need to think about any of that. Just pretend they're not here. Just focus on me. Pretend tonight is just for us. Come on, just come to me."

I took a deep breath and focused on Nova's beautiful face. It was easy to get lost in his dazzling green eyes and devastating dimples. Everything faded away as I lost myself in him, letting his voice guide me, drawing me closer with each step. I let my mind wander into the most terrific daydream, where the aisle was transformed into a flower lined path, which was leading me to Nova, on our wedding day. He was smiling warmly at me, waiting patiently, as I made my way towards him.

I didn't even flinch as the hundreds of guests I passed knelt and praised me. I smiled as the petals of bright red blossoms showered down magically from above me, kissing my skin lightly as they fell, like the soft flutter of butterfly wings. I was no longer nervous or shaking. I felt like I was floating and my heart was lighter than air, filled with love and gratefulness. I couldn't contain my smile. Joy radiated through me as I grinned from ear to ear. I even felt tears of joy streaming down my pale cheeks. I noticed them on Nova's face as well, as they glistened in the fading sunlight.

I finally made it to the altar and Nova was there, extending his hand to me. I felt it close warmly around my fingers and the fantasy evaporated into the setting sun, taking my peace with it.

I sat quietly through the ceremony, barely listening to the words Jaka was saying. I was mesmerized by the daydream I'd been lost in. It was so real! Was it more than my imagination? A vision maybe? I'd been having more of them lately. Could I be so lucky to have a future where I could marry Nova? I chanced a glance at him and he was already staring at me. My cheeks instantly blushed and he winked, spurring an even more crimson shade to my cheeks. I prayed that my mind had been closed off to Nova during that vision or daydream or whatever that was. He had an unfair advantage being able to read people's minds and even implant thoughts of his own.

My breath caught in my throat! Had Nova implanted that vision in my mind?! Did he feel that way about me? Was that a glimpse of the future he wanted too? I could barely contain my excitement.

No, Geneva, do not overreact, I scolded myself. *It was probably just your imagination running away with you again. You always do this. You get your hopes up about Nova and then it all comes crashing down when you realize you've blown your relationship way out of proportion in your mind. Not to mention the stressful conversation you had with Vida last night that pretty much made you give up on the idea of Nova all together!*

I looked at Nova again, trying to hide my confliction as my mind spiraled out of control. He smiled at me and my heart melted again.

He has to like me the way I like him! It can't be possible to feel this way about someone without them feeling the same way, right? It's just too cruel, I whined internally.

Get it together, my pessimistic voice of reason chimed in. *That vision could have been nothing more than a trick he used to get you down the aisle because he knew it would work. Besides, you're going to focus on being the Eva, not boys!*

No, that would be too cruel to use my feelings against me like that. Nova may not be wildly, head over heels about me, but I know he cares about me too much to play with my emotions like that.

Jaka may not have given him a choice, chided my self-doubt.

It probably looked like I was hyperventilating or having some sort of panic attack to the Betos watching me. My breathing was erratic and my eyes were darting from my lap to Nova and back rapidly as I scoured over the multitude of scenarios that could have caused my vision, arguing with myself about what had truly happened.

Suddenly, I felt Nova's warm hand upon mine. He gently squeezed it as I looked at him, letting my protective walls slip away the instant he touched me. I wanted to crawl into his arms and have him tell me he loved me too and that I shouldn't be embarrassed of that vision, because it's what he wanted as well. And, that it didn't matter what Vida said, we'd find a way to be together and have it all. Maybe he knew that and that's why he was reaching out for me. He couldn't bear to see me so conflicted.

"Nova..." I whispered.

He let go of my hand and slid gracefully from the stone he was sitting on to his knees. I instinctively rose to my feet and felt my blood pressure spike!

Was this happening? Was Nova proposing to me? In front of everyone?

I looked around, feeling self-conscious that everyone was watching and was astonished to see that they weren't. Everyone was kneeling; all bowing to me. My cheeks flushed scarlet, and for once I found myself grateful that everyone was bowing to me. It spared me the humiliation that they'd seen my horrible misperception, thinking I was being proposed to.

Hopeless romantic fool, I chastised myself.

Jaka must have been introducing me and I missed the entire thing because I was so wrapped up in my own mental melodrama with Nova. Nova was simply trying to clue me in that Jaka was telling me something.

Jaka rose from his genuflect and spoke to me telepathically.

"These are your people Eva. They are your responsibility now. Speak to them."

"I don't know what to say."

"Listen to them. They are speaking to you now."

As I looked out at the sea of kneeling people, I saw he was right. When I focused, I could hear them praying and rejoicing. They were all so thankful and open. They all felt such loyalty and trust in me. It was beyond humbling. I wanted more than anything, for them to be right. I wanted to be their savior, their Eva.

While I studied them, the beauty of the forest in the fading daylight caught me off guard. Reminiscent of my nuptial daydream, the landscape spoke to me as well, making me feel connected to it, like I was seeing my home for the first time. The waning sun cast a golden glow that made everything come to life. The lush green forest, was the most electric shade of chartreus that seemed to absorb the lowering sunlight, saving it for its own vanity. The red tropical blossoms, suspended magically from the canopy of vines, swayed in the gentle breeze that filled the forest with their fragrant aroma. I watched as a clan of lava pixies danced among their boughs mischievously. Their light illuminating their delicate features as they hid among the flowers, sporadically shedding petals that cascaded silently over the Betos.

When I returned my gaze to the Betos, every one of their faces seemed brighter, warmer, more alive. Something was different about them. I couldn't tell if it was the golden sunlight that had softened their features or if it was that they were so joyful in their belief that the prophecy was now fulfilled. Either way, the Betos no longer looked so wild and foreign to me. They instead, strangely felt like family. Rather than fearing I'd let them down, I now felt protective of them. Their bold tribal tattoos ceased to frighten me, instead they spoke to me of the struggles they had endured, battles they'd won, demons they'd conquered. When I looked out over them, it was hard for me to be so consumed with myself, and my own desires and fears. For the first time since reading the truth about my destiny in the Book of Secrets, I stopped thinking about how being the Eva was going to change me. I suddenly realized how selfish and single-minded I'd been and it allowed me to truly see the Betos and that changed what I saw.

This beautiful society, suddenly looked fragile among the wildness of the rainforest, balanced precariously between me and the Ravinori. They looked small and naked, exposed to an impending darkness, which I knew I must shield them from. I was overcome with emotions and I took a few steps toward them and I started speaking before I knew what I was going to say.

"Stand…"

Instantly, everyone was on their feet. That had come out like more of a command than the request I intended it to be.

"Please stand," I corrected. "You don't need to bow to me. Ever. I want to stand with you, live among you, and fight for you. I am one of you. At least I want to be, if you'll let me. I am the one who is privileged to lead you, honored that you call me your Eva. And I vow to you, that I will do everything in my power to fulfill the prophecy. No one should have to live in secret and in fear, because that is not living. We all deserve more. Much, much more."

Applause erupted in the forest and the Betos were joyously chanting.

"Eva! Eva! Eva!"

Their chant burst into song as music suddenly began. I turned to Jaka and he smiled warmly at me and gave a subtle nod. I knew I had done well without him having to say anything, telepathically or otherwise and that filled me with warmth and positivity. He stepped to my side and clasped my hand in his, pausing for a moment before raising it to an even wilder response from the crowd.

"Tonight we celebrate our EVA!"

CHAPTER XXIV

"Master, her power grows. I can feel the Eva's connection to the elements. The Beto's must be conducting the induction ceremony."

"Good. Let those ancient fools have their ceremony. If there is any truth to their ways, it will strengthen her connection to the Pillars and give her more power, which will only serve us better. Keep me informed Kobel."

"Yes master."

CHAPTER XXV

The forest whirled around me as I danced with my friends, new and old. I couldn't ever remember such a beautiful or happy event, as the party in my honor after the ceremony. The music was nonstop and we couldn't help ourselves from bouncing to the primal beats. Sparrow, Jemma and I whirled and twirled, giggling and squealing with delight in our party dresses that Vida hand helped us change into. We swirled our skirts and changed the colors of the fabric to suit our mood, while we frolicked with our friends. Journey was smiling and I even heard him laugh! It was a real, truly joyful, belly laugh. It shocked me, but made me smile all the more. He kept scooping Sparrow up and spinning her around, until they collapsed in laughter.

Jemma was in her glory. She bounced from one dance partner, to the next, on the torched lined dance floor. They all bowed to her and she curtsied, smiling from ear to ear. Her long black mane came unplaited and fell like a dark, cascading waterfall down her back, dancing to a rhythm all its own, as she spun her way across the petal trodden ground.

I had started the night dancing with Remi, but that was short lived. Once Mali boldly cut in, everyone got the same idea. It seemed I too, would be making the rounds on the dance floor tonight. Everyone wanted to shake my hand or dance with me. The Betos all had such kind things to say and offered me words of encouragement. I was having a wonderful time meeting everyone and was astonished how much fun it was to come out of my shell and embrace this life. But, when Nova finally cut in and the music slowed to a more romantic melody, I was relieved for the break, realizing how exhausted I was from spinning and pirouetting all night long. Plus, I couldn't deny how nice it felt to be in his warm arms. He gave me a rare, full smile. These days he usually looked worried and I got little more than a quick smirk or a wink out of him. But, this was a full on, dazzling, mega-watt Nova smile and my inner goddess and pessimistic subconscious both melted into a useless puddle of drool, leaving me speechless and Nova-dazed.

"Where do you go Tippy?"

"Hmm…?" I mused.

"When I talk to you, you seem to zone out a lot lately. I'm just wondering where you go or what you're thinking about. Or, who? It has to be something pretty good, because sometimes I'm using all my tricks to try to get your attention and you give me nothing."

I stared into his liquid green eyes in astonishment. He had my attention now!

"You really don't know?"

"No, but I would love to."

"You could just look inside my mind and you'd know everything."

"You asked me not to do that. And believe me, it's hard not to, but I try to respect all your wishes Tippy."

"So, you weren't in my mind earlier, when I froze at the beginning of the ceremony?"

"No. I was just telepathing to you. I thought if you could just talk to me, I could help you get over your fear. We're good when we're together, just you and me, without any interruptions. Like in the forest last night."

I stared at him, warily weighing his words.

"I promise I wasn't in your mind! Last night or tonight," he stressed, when he saw I looked skeptical.

I decided I believed him and pulled him into a tighter embrace.

"Sometimes I wish you would see inside my mind," I murmured shyly into his neck, standing on my toes so I could rest my head on his shoulder and drink in his intoxicating smell. "Then you'd be able to see all the things I'm too afraid to say."

"All you have to do is say the words Tippy. Let me in," Nova said pulling me closer still.

"I'm too embarrassed," I whispered.

"What could you possibly have to be embarrassed about?"

"My feelings… for you."

He stopped swaying with me and pulled away from me ever so slightly so he could look down into my clear blue eyes. I'd never seen him look so honest and nervous before; like the boy he was, rather than the man he'd been forced to become. I could feel his hands shaking as they moved from my waist to intertwine with mine.

"And how do you feel for me?" he whispered cautiously, while squeezing my tingling hands.

"Nova… I – "

"Did you tell him!? Did you tell him what we can do?!" Jemma interrupted.

How was it possible for her to have such impeccably inconvenient timing?!

"Jemma, we're in the middle of something!" Nova hissed harshly at her.

The hostility in his voice caught me off guard, but I found myself smirking subconsciously. Jemma completely ignored his tone or the fact that she was interrupting us. Perhaps she was immune or oblivious to the idea that her presence wasn't always welcomed.

But, it was fine. The instant she had shown up, the spell was broken and I knew the moment had passed. She'd probably saved me some embarrassment from declaring my love for Nova in such a public place. This conversation was far from over, but it was suited for somewhere more private, where we weren't under the watchful eyes of an entire civilization and open to so much interruption.

"You didn't tell him Eva?" Jemma questioned me, looking surprised. "Well, what where you two talking about this whole time that you didn't get to the most exciting news!?"

I shrugged and Jemma rolled her eyes.

"Watch," she said, as she put her hand on my head.

I felt my hair fall flat and heavy on my shoulders. It felt silky and straight as it brushed my skin. Then, I saw Nova's eye bulge.

"What did you do? Put it back right now Jemma!"

"What? You don't like it? We look more like sisters now!" she squealed clapping in delight.

I ran my fingers though my silky, straight hair and jumped when I saw the black strands sliding through my fingers. Its contrast with my stark white skin was so vivid; it reminded me of the night sky against the moon.

"Stop it Jemma. I don't know how you did that or what you think you're doing, but you need to put her back the way she's meant to be right now." Nova scolded, as he glanced warily around at the Betos, who had stopped dancing and were now staring at us.

"Geez, fine. I will! You don't have to be such a party pooper about it."

"I see why you didn't mention it to him," Jemma grumbled quietly to me, as I felt my hair spring lightly back to its normal texture.

The relief on Nova's face showed that Jemma had restored my appearance. By now, Remi had come over to see what was going on. He was gawking at me, still in shock from seeing me look like Jemma no doubt. Sparrow and Journey came bounding up as I reflexively raked my fingers though my flaxen curls, settling them into their natural style.

"Pretty neat, huh?" Sparrow giggled breathlessly.

"You knew about this?" Remi asked sounding betrayed.

"Yeah, Geneva shared healing powers with Jemma and we were having a little fun with it earlier, while we were getting ready."

"Why are you all being so weird about this? We were just having fun! I don't see what the big deal is?" Jemma stewed.

"The *big deal,* is that our powers aren't just for *having a little fun,*" Nova scolded. "And, before you start sharing powers, don't you think we should talk to the chief about it?" he directed at me.

"Oh, I see what's going on here, it's just not okay for *me* to have fun with my powers! I don't even have any good powers! I'm good at following people! Big deal! You all can do amazing things! Eva and Sparrow were just being nice to me and sharing what they can do. We thought you'd be excited. This is a good thing. If we can share all our powers, it means we'll be stronger and able to protect each other better," Jemma argued.

I could see she was winning Journey's approval as he nodded at what she was saying.

"Well, I don't think you should be making decisions that affect the group without talking to all of us first," Nova growled at Jemma.

"Why don't we go find Eja and see what he thinks? Maybe he can ask Jaka his opinion," I interjected before this argument got any more heated.

Everyone agreed and we set off to find Eja in the crowd of celebrating Betos.

As I started to follow my sister and the others, Nova caught my hand, holding me back from the group momentarily.

"Hey, can we continue our conversation later?" Nova asked, his pleasantness returning.

"Yes. Let's just find somewhere more private, where we can talk."

"Promise?"

"Promise."

CHAPTER XXVI

We found Eja in a crowd surrounding the altar, where Beto artists were marking people with tribal tattoos. Many of them were lined up waiting their turn. They were cheering and high fiving each other as they came down off the altar. They all had so many tattoos already, I couldn't tell what was new and what they'd already been adorned with. The air was heavy with the smell of herbs, blended together to make a natural ink used to paint the tribe members. As I watched a group of women mashing the ingredients in stone bowls, I had a thought and turned to Eja, examining his flawless cocoa skin.

"Eja? Why don't you have any tattoos?"

"Well, you have to earn them," he said simply.

"And you have to have your family give you your first one, right Talon?" Jovi piped up.

She had appeared with Talon and Mali.

"That's right, light weight," Talon said, as he picked his sister up and let her perch on his shoulders so she could get a better view over the crowd.

"Talon gave me my first tattoo, look!" Jovi boasted pointing to the thin band that followed the curve of her delicate collar bone.

I looked at her brother and he had the same one. So did Mali, and everyone else for that matter.

"What does it mean?" I asked.

"Beto!" Jovi said proudly. "We all have them."

"So I've noticed," I said softly, looking at Eja. He let his eyes fall, ever so slightly, with a hint of shame.

"Check out my newest one," Mali said grabbing my attention.

When I saw a familiar symbol painted on his shoulder, my mouth fell open in shock.

"Mali!" I almost screamed. "Why did you do that?"

"LVX! It's your symbol. We're all getting it," he said, motioning to the line of Beto's waiting for tattoos.

"Oh my god," I whispered, grabbing Nova's arm to steady myself.

"I got it too," Jovi said from atop Talon's shoulders, pulling up her shirt sleeve to reveal the freshly painted symbol; LVX.

"Lux. It means enlightening, unity and rebirth!" she rattled off proudly.

"That's not - "

Eja pulled me away before I could finish my sentence.

"Eja, who's idea was this? That's not what my tattoo means? It doesn't spell Lux, it's just a number, a brand the Troian Center gave me because I wasn't even worthy of a name in their eyes."

"I know that. And maybe that's what it means to you, but that's not what it means to them."

I searched his eyes, but still felt uneasy about the idea of my number tattooed on all of these people.

"What if someone is mistaken for me because they have my tattoo?" I worried.

Eja smiled warmly at me. "No offense meant my Eva, but that would never happen," he said lightly touching a strand of my blonde curls.

"Okay. True," I agreed. "But, I don't know about this … I don't want them to get the wrong idea about what it means. I don't want to mislead anyone."

"Meaning is in the eye of the beholder. Look how proud they are. You have arrived and they are celebrating you the only way they know how. Tattoos are what we do in our culture. Every Beto has the tribe credo painted on them at birth by a family member. Then each family has their own crest. The rest are earned; hero, hunter, provider, protector, healer, seer... They're a badge of honor."

I heard the pride and longing in Eja's voice as he spoke, and as I watched the Betos proudly showing off their new LVX tattoos, I realized he was right. It made them feel like they were a part of the resurgence of our island, the rebirth of their civilization. There was such a pure magic and happiness in their hope, that I knew it couldn't be wrong. I let my heart embrace the emotions that the Betos where sharing in this unique experience.

I could feel the brightness of their faith, shining even more happiness on the festivities in the forest. But, I also couldn't help notice how Eja seemed to be fighting his own despair as we watched groups of Betos our own age, comparing their new ink. There was a sadness and longing in his eyes that he was trying to disguise. I recognized it, because it's how I often looked during my entire existence at the Troian Center. It was really hard when you felt like you didn't fit in. I hated to see a friend suffer.

"Eja, you've never really told me anything about your family," I said softly, hoping he'd open up to me.

"There's not much to tell my Eva. Like many others, my family died in the Flood."

"I'm sorry," I whispered, feeling his pain. "You must have been very young?"

"About your age I suppose."

"Can I ask you why you didn't get the Beto tattoo that everyone else has?"

"I am told I was very ill when I was born and no one thought I would survive so I wasn't given the tattoo. Then the Flood struck and my entire family perished."

"Jovi said your family has to give you your first tattoo?"

"Yes, it is a sacred tradition. Our tattoos hold immense importance and a little bit of magic. They link us and they define us. They aren't given lightly. It is said that your family must be the one to give you your first tattoo; passing with it the continuation of your bloodline. If someone other than your family tries to apply this first tattoo it won't remain. It will vanish with one full rotation of the sun. And without that first all-important tattoo, no others will stick. So this is why my skin is destined to stay forever desolate."

Suddenly, I had an idea. I pulled Eja with me and went to gather the rest of my friends.

"What's going on?" Remi asked.

I turned to Eja, and took his hand.

"I just need you to trust me," I urged.

He looked mildly skeptical.

"Jovi, can you come with me too?"

"Sure!" she squealed, scrambling down from her brother's shoulders.

"Okay, now I need all of you to come with me. There's something I have to do."

My friends followed as I pulled Eja up to the altar with me and asked one of the women if I could borrow her bowl of magic herbal ink and a brush. She looked quite shocked, but obliged nonetheless.

"My Eva, what are you doing?" Eja questioned.

"Do you trust me Eja?"

"Devotedly," he replied without hesitation.

"Sit here and close your eyes."

Eja obeyed while the others huddled around me, watching to see what I was up to. I dipped the brush in the inky blackness and was surprised by the thickness of the liquid. I motioned for Jovi to come stand next to Eja and I studied her Beto tattoo, preparing to recreate it on Eja's narrow collar bone.

The ink was cold and Eja gave an involuntary shiver the first time I touched the brush to his bare skin.

"I need you to be as still as possible," I urged.

He complied and I worked quickly, mimicking the intricate thatched pattern that wove through bold geometric shapes. When I was finished, I stepped back to admire my work. It looked perfect.

"There," I said, smiling confidently. "Now you are a proper Beto!"

"My Eva, I appreciate the kind gesture, but this tattoo won't stick. It has to be performed by family. Only family - "

"We'll just have to wait and see won't we Eja? Besides, I'm not finished just yet," I said dipping my brush back in the sticky liquid as I eyed a spot that I needed to touch up.

Eja, looked uncomfortable now, with so many eyes watching him.

"My Eva, please. You don't need to waste any more time on me."

"Eja, you *are* my family. All of you are my family!" I said turning to look at my friends. "We're all orphans, but we found each other and made our own family. We take care of each other and look out for each other. We've found refuge, shelter, comfort, loyalty and trust in each other. We've shared loss, joy, love, battles, hardships, and triumphs together. If that's not the definition of family I don't know what is. What good is being the Eva if I can't have a family? In my destiny, you are all my family."

Wild applause broke out when I finished speaking, startling all of us. Apparently, everyone had been listening to my speech to Eja and they approved. Cheers and hollers rose above the clapping and I blushed for a moment, but I stood proudly behind my words. I meant what I said to Eja. He and my friends were the closest thing to family that I'd ever had and I was meant to protect them by being their Eva so I was choosing to start now. Tattooing Eja was a small gesture in the grand scheme of things, but I knew, better than most, how powerful the need to belong could be.

I looked back at Eja who had tears of appreciation in his eyes. I had one more tattoo in mind for him. I whispered to Jovi and she took the paint brush from my hand and quickly stroked a design on a nearby rock. She handed back the brush and smiled at me admiring her art. I mimicked its design on Eja's back.

"Brother," I said.

"Thank you," he telepathed to me.

"You're very welcome."

CHAPTER XXVII

"Master, you have to see this!"

"What? Have you located the book? The girl?"

"No master, but look," the old man said, pointing to a symbol that blazed boldly on the fragile pages of the Book of Gods that lay open before him.

The tall man, ran his hand slowly along his shining, black hair, which was neatly pulled back, as he stared at the pages. His reaction, bubbling beneath the surface, was delayed and Kobel pushed to make sure he understood the meaning.

"Master, it's the symbol from the prophecy. A nation united, under one flag, one true ruler; the Eva."

"I know what it is Kobel!" he thundered as he upended the table, sending the Book of Gods skittering across the floor. "It changes nothing!"

After a brief silence, in which he composed himself, smoothing his hair back into place, the menacing man said, "I don't want to hear from you until you've located them."

CHAPTER XXVIII

I had Jovi help me tattoo LVX on my friends, along with what I'd come up with as our family crest. It was a mixture of the golden laurel wreath from Lux's flag and the thick tribal bands of the Betos. The first time I finished painting the design, it struck me with an eerie sense of déjà vu. I felt certain I had seen the symbol somewhere before, but couldn't place my finger on where. It danced before me, taunting my failing memory. I shook off the notion and focused on the symmetry of the design. Lux and Betos, Citizens and Locals; my friends and I were the perfect blend of the two, so I thought it was a fitting representation. Journey loved it and was the first to volunteer for his tattoo after I painted it on Eja. I marked it in a crescent shape around his number that the Troian Center had tattooed us with, thus turning their symbol of oppression, into one of hope. The rest of my friends all followed suit, volunteering their numbered shoulders for restoration.

Soon, we were all admiring our tacky ink. Even Jemma was excitedly talking about her new tattoos. Eja was elated to be a part of the discussion, even if he was still a tad bit skeptical that it would remain. I decided to let him ride the high of getting his first tattoo for the rest of the night. I figured my question about sharing powers with Jemma could wait until morning.

The festivities continued well into the heart of the night. There was singing, dancing, feasting and more dancing. I could barely keep the sleep from pulling at my eyelids when I finally decided to call it a night. I had promised Nova we'd have our talk, but when I went to find him, he was having a great time playing a gourd guitar with a group of Betos and I didn't have the heart to interrupt him. I started making my way back to my tent, when Remi caught up to me.

"I've been looking for you," he said. "Well actually, someone else has been looking for you. I just decided to help him."

Remi pulled a twitchy Niv from behind his back.

"Oh Niv! What are you doing out here buddy?" I crooned, scratching him under his chin and cradling him in my arms, while I showered him with kisses.

"I think he was lonely," Remi shrugged.

"Or cold," I said giving a shiver.

I hadn't realized how cold it was until we left the torch lit area of the ceremony site. Out in the open, the heavy, night air of the forest, had a habit of settling its cold cloak upon you.

"Are you cold?" Remi asked, looking to offer me his shirt by habit. "Oh…" he said, sounding puzzled when he realized he wasn't wearing one.

We both burst into laughter.

"I'll never get used to how little clothes they wear!" Remi laughed.

"Me either," I giggled.

We continued laughing and talking about the fun events of the night as we walked towards our tents.

"Well, this is me," I said pausing beside a particularly sun-bleached tent, in a row of dozens of other identical ones.

"Okay," Remi said. "I'm in that one if you need me for anything," he pointed a short distance away.

It was sweet the way Remi worried about me. I doubted he even knew he was doing it. I guess he'd always been that way when I think about it. When we were younger, at the Troian Center, he always made sure we knew each other's schedule on the rare occasions that we weren't together. Back then, I'd just thought it was a necessary means of survival, since all we had to rely on was each other. But, I think he was looking after me in his own way. And, when I was sneaking off into the forest to practice my powers, he risked everything to follow me, because he could tell something was off and he wanted to make sure I knew he was there to help me. Then, when I tethered my soul to Niv's, he'd even known me well enough to know he'd have to protect Niv too.

Remi had always been there to save me in many different ways and it seemed that I was taking notice of it more lately. Maybe it was that kiss in the cave that really opened my eyes to truly see him recently. Whatever it was, I was finding my heart swelling gratefully to have Remi in my life and to have the privilege of calling him my best friend.

He was about to turn away and head to his tent, when I quickly hugged him.

"What was that for?" he asked with a big smile, when I finally let him go.

"Just for being such a great friend."

"It's nothing," he shrugged.

"Well it's something to me Remi. We've been through a lot. Even before all of this," I said, gesturing to the sleepy forest surrounding us. "I'm just really lucky to have someone that knows me so well in my life. You've been by my side since the very beginning."

"Thick as thieves," he said with a sly smile.

"Thick as thieves!" I laughed and hugged Remi again.

We hadn't used that phrase in ages! One of our favorite professors said it to us once and it stuck. We used to call ourselves the 'little thieves' and sometimes Jemma and her friends would refer to us as such, thinking they were being rude and funny, but we just grinned at each other, secretly loving our nickname.

I let go of Remi's embrace, but he caught my hands as they slid off of his bare chest and my breath caught in my throat for a moment. I wasn't used to Remi making me feel nervous. I was so comfortable with our friendship, that sometimes I forgot he wanted more.

"Remi..."

"I was just going to say that I'm really proud of you Geneva. I know you're nervous about this whole Eva thing, but you did an incredible job on your first official day."

"Thanks Remi," I said positively grinning.

"And, it doesn't hurt that you look beautiful tonight," he added bashfully, making my cheeks burn and blush.

"Thanks."

"Goodnight little thief," he smiled, kissing my cheek and giving my hands a squeeze before letting go.

They felt suddenly cold without his warm hands surrounding them and it made me shiver, as I watched him disappear into his tent.

I turned to duck into my own, when I saw Nova standing a short distance away, staring at me. My heart plummeted. I knew he'd probably just seen Remi and I, and would read more into it than he should. He had a bad habit of that. I guess we both did. We'd had such a great night that I didn't want it to end on a bad note.

"Nova!" I called and started towards him, but he turned away from me and retreated back towards the party.

I sighed deeply, trying to calm the panic in my heart. For once I decided not to go after Nova. I wanted to take a more mature approach. I was hoping by giving Nova the night to cool off, we could avoid an argument. It was a gamble, but I shook off my fears and returned to my tent. I was beginning to learn that Nova and I had the same stubborn streak, and the best thing to do was to give us our space when we were in the middle of a jealous row. When I didn't, it always ended in a fight and I was much too exhausted for that tonight. Not to mention, I didn't want getting in a fight with my jealous boyfriend, to be my first act as the official Eva. Instead, I settled into my hammock and grabbed my journal, hoping that writing would calm my nerves.

Dear Diary,

Today was one for the history books. I made a lot of sisterly progress with Jemma. I shared powers with her and I was officially inducted as the Eva to all the Betos, at the most beautiful ceremony I ever could have imagined. It was so beautiful that for a moment, I found myself daydreaming that I was at my own wedding, marrying Nova of course. I know, no surprise there, right?

Nova and I actually had a really great time and the start of a pretty serious moment on the dance floor, but with her effortless flare, Jemma, the queen of bad timing, interrupted us before I could actually get the nerve up to say how I feel about him. On one hand, I'm relieved, because it wasn't really the time or place for that kind of discussion; surrounded by hundreds of Betos and all of our friends. Her intrusion also saved me from admitting that I'm madly in love with him, because once I do that, there's no going back. He'll either laugh at me and I'll feel ashamed and awkward forever, or we'll actually give us a try... I know, I know.... I've been scribbling about how much I love him in your pages since I got this diary, but tonight, I came so close to telling him how I feel and that frightens me because it makes it so real. Maybe, preserving the fantasy of Nova and what we could be, is better than taking a chance.

What if we try and it doesn't work out? What if we break up and he breaks my heart? Would I never recover from that? What if it does work out? Am I ready for what a serious relationship means? Nova is older than me. He's probably so much more experienced than I am. I'm blushing just thinking about the prospect of it. He'd probably be better off with someone like Jemma or the dozens of other Beto girls who have been throwing themselves at his feet since we got here. I just feel like I can't compete with them. He's Nova! He's the most amazing, beautiful, talented, bravest, kindest person I've ever met. Why would he want to be with me? I'm not just a normal girl. I'm the Eva. I come with a whole slew of problems. I have a country to unite and rule, and crazy unheard of powers that I don't even really know how to control that well. I'm sure there's probably some that I don't even know I have yet. What if I accidentally hurt him with one of them? Or what if someone hurts him to get at me? And, how could I forget that I have an army of crazy Ravin supporters hunting me? Yeah, I think it's safe to say that I'm no ordinary girl.

And then there's Remi. I have to tell Nova that I kissed him. I hate keeping it a secret, but I know it won't go over well no matter what I say. Remi has always been my best friend and I've never looked at him any other way, but now, after that kiss and him telling me he has feelings for me, I feel so confused. My heart and head are a jumbled mess... I probably should just save all of us the heartache and stay single...

CHAPTER XXIX

Once her last dance partner graciously excused himself, Jemma was surprised to find herself alone at the party.

"Where did everyone go?" she muttered to herself scanning the dance floor. "I can't believe they never even said goodnight!"

Then she had a thought. "Oh, if they think they're going to all go off and have an after-party without me…" she said, half running towards the tents, panicking at the thought of being left out of the fun.

The first tent she came to, was Geneva's. It was still and quiet, but it looked like there was candlelight flickering inside.

"Eva?" she whispered poking her head in.

Her sister lay asleep in her hammock, with Niv nestled beside her. Jemma noticed that the candle next to her was still burning and crept inside to blow it out. She paused for a moment, gazing at her long-lost sister's pale features, glowing in the moonlight. She still found it hard to believe that her baby sister had come back to her. Never in a million life times, would she have imagined she could be so lucky to be reunited with her. She had given up hope of ever seeing her again after the Flood. It was cruel to think they had grown up together, but never really knew each other. Losing her family in the Flood had hardened Jemma's heart and ironically, she took her anger out, most severely, on Jane #65 at the Troian Center.

Jemma shook her head and swiped away a tear as she pondered the irony of their situation. Their circumstances were unique in the fact that Jemma remembered more of Geneva since she was the older sibling. Like how she used to sing to her and gave her the nickname of Eva, long before it meant she was the savoir of Hullabee Island. To Jemma, they'd forged an inseparable bond as sisters, and it hurt that Geneva couldn't remember it.

Jemma moved closer, instinctively humming a soft lullaby that she used to sing to help Geneva sleep when she was a baby. When she realized what she was doing, she quickly stopped herself for fear that Geneva would wake and catch her in such a vulnerable moment.

She regained her composure and leaned over to blow out the candle. That's when she saw it. The worn and tattered journal, that lay open next to the glowing flame. Its pages were exposed, beckoning her to sneak a peek. Jemma knew it was wrong, but the temptation was too much!

She told herself it was to get to know her little sister better, but once she read the alluring musings about Nova, she couldn't put it down.

"How typical that we share the same taste in men," Jemma whispered to herself bitterly as she flipped the page. "I guess that's just another thing I want, that Eva will get!"

Her eyes widened as they focused on the passage outlining Remi's kiss and her mouth dropped open! She gasped, then quickly covered her mouth to stifle her tiny yelp, but not before she dropped the journal. Jemma noticed Geneva starting to stir and quickly blew out the candle and fled from the tent.

Once outside the tent flap, she breathed in the safety of the surrounding stillness. Everyone must be asleep and she was confident no one had seen her go in or out of Geneva's tent.

"That little harlot!" Jemma whispered to herself as she slipped through the night, towards her own tent.

After slinking inside, she still found herself bewildered by her discoveries. It was obvious to the entire world that Geneva loved Nova, but no one ever would have suspected she had Remi on the side!

"And I was all ready to give her Nova! Huh! Maybe she's more devious than I give her credit for. After all, she *is* my sister," Jemma smirked, as she gave voice to her thoughts. "Well, two can play at this game. Bring it on sister."

Jemma blew out her candles and lay down for the night, storing away her newly acquired revelation. She smiled as she closed her eyes, knowing she'd spend the night dreaming of how best to use it to her advantage.

CHAPTER XXX

Kobel knocked on the heavy door that had been propped open, peeking inside to find his master seated at his ornate desk. He was eating a peach, skinning it effortlessly with a razor sharp blade. The black ivory hilt of the dagger, glinted as it caught the afternoon light filtering in from the high, narrow windows.

Kobel didn't wait to be waved in. He'd seen his boss like this before, obsessively pouring over maps and manuscripts. He didn't even look up, but he seemed to know who had entered the room regardless.

"What is it Kobel? I'm busy."

"Master, I really wish you wouldn't use that for eating," the old man said as he approached the desk. "It's a sacred relic, you know?"

"Did you come here to badger me about my table manners or did you have a valid reason for interrupting me?"

"I've located the Eva. She's moving west along the interior ridgeline of the forest."

"West! I thought you said she would be returning to the Troian Center?"

"That's still the plan, but they're stalling, preparing."

"So, she knows about us then?"

"Yes master, I believe so. She has the ear of the Beto leader. He has his shadow scouts with him at all times, cloaking his thoughts, so I have no way of knowing what he's shared about us, but we have to expect the worst."

"If Jaka is helping her, then we're running out of time Kobel."

"I gather more information each time the Eva uses her powers. And, I've discovered she keeps an enchanted journal. When she uses it, I can connect to her; learn her thoughts, her secrets. Last night she left it open and I've found their location."

"Well, what are we waiting for? Send the mercenaries!"

"The Betos are protecting her and they're very wise. They move to a new location every day. They travel through the Bellamorf trees. It's impossible to pinpoint their next move."

"Nothing is impossible Kobel! I'll flood the forest with my men if that's what it takes! Burn the whole place down if you need to!"

"There may be another way master," Kobel said, timidly.

"What is it?"

"I may be able to connect to her mind. If she's weak enough, I may be able to influence her thoughts, get her to come to us. I just need some time master."

"I'm not wasting any more time. I'm sending the mercenaries."

CHAPTER XXXI

The next morning, when the sunlight started seeping in through the seams in the tent, I awoke well rested. I rousted Niv from his sleep. He was always grumpy when he woke up and his rumpled fur made me giggle. I tussled his silky hair and scooped him off my chest as I swung my legs off my hammock. I noticed my journal was laying open on the floor. I must have fallen asleep writing again.

"Restore," I mumbled as I rubbed the sleep from my eyes and watched the words vanish.

I stretched and quickly changed, eager to meet up with everyone this morning and continue our plans for returning to the Troian Center.

Niv ran off to forage for food and I headed back toward the center of camp. The Betos were all finishing the last of their packing, preparing to move on to their next destinations. It was obvious that the majority of the visiting Betos were already gone. Those that remained, waved and smiled at me. I returned their greetings, grinning when they caught themselves about to bow to me.

I passed over the trodden earth, strewn with flattened petals. They were the only remaining evidence of the ceremony. I smiled fondly at the memories we'd made here. I stopped to pick up a velvet soft red petal, feeling the nostalgic need for a souvenir. I drank in its delicate, sweet scent and laughed to myself. Because of Jovi, I had a feeling the rest of my reign as Eva would be synonymous with the color red and that idea warmed my heart. I cherished the time I spent with Jovi and I loved the fact that every time I saw a red blossom, I'd think of her.

Suddenly Jovi was at my side, as if she knew I was thinking of her. She was breathless and excited as always and cut me off before I could even rib her about the red flowers.

"Good morning Geneva! I made you something!" she said, shoving a large folded palm frond into my hand. "Well two things really. My mom made you breakfast," she said holding up a basket, "and I made you this," she said, pointing to the package in my hands. "Open it! Open it!" she squealed.

"Alright, alright!" I laughed at her exuberance.

I unfolded the large leaf and it revealed a small fold of leather, lined with deep blue patterned satin. It reminded me of the shining night sky, speckled with stars. The leather pouch was expertly woven together with a single, long piece of twine. I marveled at the beautiful tool marks that adorned the leather with geometric shapes, matching the crest I had painted onto all of my friends at the ceremony last night.

"Jovi.... It's beautiful," I said, tearing up, while slowly turning her gift over in my hands.

"It's for Niv! It's a marmouse pouch! I noticed last night that you didn't have anywhere to put him when you were all dressed up, so I stayed up all night making it! Now you have a pretty bag for him to ride in so he doesn't have to miss any parties! And, I put your crest on it too!"

"Jovi! That's the most thoughtful gift I've ever heard of. Niv will love this. Thank you so much," I said hugging her and meaning every word.

"It's the least I could do with all the trouble Quin causes him," she said sheepishly.

"It's perfect," I said squeezing her again. "Absolutely perfect."

Jovi never ceased to amaze me. I was already admiring how she'd impacted my life and then she goes and does something like this? No one had ever given me a gift before. Being orphans, we didn't own anything or celebrate our birthdays. We just barely survived. We were more concerned with food and shelter. It's not to say I didn't envy the finer things I saw when I visited Lux, but gifts were lavish things that just weren't part of our lives. I looked at Jovi, this tiny girl lived simply as well. She didn't have many things of her own, nothing more than she needed, yet I knew she wanted nothing more. Perhaps the most lavish thing she owned was her hopeful innocence. It allowed her to be eternally kind and have a full and giving heart. She had found it in herself to make me something more extravagant than she even had for herself, simply because she wanted to. I was starting to see why Vida wanted to keep her secrets from Jovi. I hugged her tightly and swiped away the unexpected tears of joy that overwhelmed me.

"Are you okay?" Jovi asked, noticing my tear streaked cheeks when I released her. "You like it, don't you?"

"Yes! Yes, Jovi! I love it more than you know," I said, smiling at her and taking her hand. "Come on, join us at our meeting."

We all met at the center of camp to continue where we had left off with our planning. Everyone seemed to be in great spirits, still riding the high from the post ceremony festivities the night before. They were all examining their newly painted tattoos as I walked up. Everyone except Nova. He was glumly standing away from the group, working on sharpening the head of a spear. His mood didn't strike me as odd after the way he took off last night. He was no doubt, still stewing over what he thought he saw between Remi and I. I shrugged it off and figured we'd address our issues later. Right now, we had real matters, which effected us all and possibly the fate of our whole civilization, to deal with.

"Your marks are holding strong Eja," I said with a smile, pointing to the tattoos I'd painted on him.

"Ah, yes for now they are, but it takes a full celestial rotation. We will have to wait and see if it pleases the sun tomorrow morning my Eva," he said. But I could tell he was having trouble keeping the hope out of his normally steady voice.

"So, where did we leave off?" Remi asked.

"Based on our findings in the Book of Secrets that 'all must oblige,' we decided that we will all return to the Troian Center at the earliest time, after the proper preparations have been made. Which include acceptable training on how to use our powers and procuring the safest route of travel," Eja rattled off as though he was reading from a book.

I smiled at him, grateful for his impeccable memory.

"As you requested my Eva, I've come up with a schedule for scouting, training and studying the Book of Secrets. We can start today as soon as we address a few more things on the agenda," he smiled.

"Great, let's get started," I said.

The few more things on the agenda, turned into a lengthy discussion. During which, we ate all of the sweet bread Jovi had brought us. But, the good news was, we came to some solid decisions and a plan was taking shape. We decided Eja would come with us. Even though he wasn't bound to help us by the Book of Secrets, he had happily volunteered to accompany us. I was grateful to him and happy to have him along, since he was the best one of us to read and translate the Book of Secrets. With his flawless memory, he was practically a walking history book.

Sparrow suggested it would be a good idea to bring Quin with us. The wex was so fast and stealthy, she would be an excellent way to deliver messages to the Beto tribe, should we run into any trouble or need their help. I didn't like the idea at all, because Quin was useless without Jovi and I was already too attached to the young Beto girl as it was. Involving her in our mission would put her at risk and that was out of the question. There were so many unknowns awaiting us at the Troian Center, but of course that didn't scare Jovi. She was eager to be part of the team and I was furious when I was out voted. And to make matters worse, I was also nominated to ask Jovi's mom for her permission to include Jovi in our expedition. That seemed like the scariest part of the mission so far.

Since I wasn't eager to start my day with another discussion with Vida, I asked Eja if he thought I'd be able to get a meeting with Jaka.

"Yes, he always has time for you my Eva. May I ask what it's in regard to?"

"Well, a few things really. I shared a power with Jemma yesterday and it sort of spawned an argument among the group."

"Oh?" Eja asked, raising his faint eyebrows. "And why is this the first I'm hearing of it?"

"I thought it best to table any decision making until after the ceremony. We all deserve a night off to have some fun once in a while, right?"

He nodded. "What else did you want to ask the chief?"

"Let's just start with that," I said, not wanting to get into my visions with Eja.

"I will find him and arrange a meeting. In the meantime, why don't you study my most recent translations in the Book of Secrets with Remi and Sparrow, while the others practice powers with Nova?"

"Works for me," I smiled.

CHAPTER XXXII

I was working hard to concentrate on what Sparrow and Remi were reading from the Book of Secrets, but I kept getting distracted by the shouts and applause coming from behind me. Journey and Nova were aggressively sparring each other, while Jovi and Jemma cheered. Nova was sending blasts of flames Journey's way, as he used his hunter skills to dodge them, even turning a few to stone right before they hit him. It was terrifying and amazing to watch.

"That seems a bit excessive for practicing powers," I mumbled under my breath.

"Geneva, are you listening to anything Remi just read?" Sparrow asked disapprovingly as she caught me glancing over my shoulder.

"I'm sorry. I'm trying, but they're making quite a racket!"

"Just ignore them. They're showing off for some reason," she said.

"I'll try. Sorry Remi, continue," I apologized.

"It's okay. You're not missing much. It's just a bunch of names we don't recognize and vague descriptions," Remi grumbled.

"Remi, it's important that we read through all of this. It might seem inconsequential now, but I'm sure it'll help us identify the

Pillars," Sparrow chided.

"How? Rhys, Hazel, Mase, Finn, Jax, Kalen ... we've been over this. We don't know any of them. Names don't help us when we only know each other as numbers at the Troian Center. And all it says about the Pillars is that each possesses qualities similar to their element. What kind of help is that? The water sign is going to be wet and the earth sign is going to be what... dirty?"

"Remi, it's not a literal translation," Sparrow sighed.

"You can say that again. I'm not even sure why Eja's wasting his time translating it. None of it makes any sense."

"I think it's describing different uses of the elements. For instance, the earth Pillar might be able to cause earthquakes, or volcanic eruptions, or crevices. That kind of thing," I offered.

"Well if that's the case, then maybe Journey's the earth Pillar. He's manipulating the earth right now. Look, he just turned that branch to stone," Remi pointed, sounding impressed.

We all turned to watch Journey and Nova skillfully battle.

"That's a terrible thing to say Remi. He's not a Pillar," Sparrow hissed. "The stone thing is the only power he has regarding the earth. If he was the earth Pillar he'd be turning the ground into quicksand or opening up big crevices under Nova or something."

"Okay, Sparrow. You're right. I'm sorry, I shouldn't have said that," Remi apologized, seeing he'd upset her.

Journey may not be the earth Pillar, but it was much harder to deny that Nova was the fire Pillar, I thought dismally, as I watched him ignite a ring of flames around Journey.

I can't say the thought hadn't crossed my mind the moment I'd learned about the Pillars, but I'd protectively pushed it from my mind each time it crept back. Everything in me hoped that it couldn't be true. I didn't want any of my friends to be Pillars; targeted weapons coveted by the Ravinor. I knew Sparrow was right. The answers were hidden somewhere within the pages of the Book of Secrets. I sighed and resigned myself to return to its pages.

I gave it my all, but I couldn't stop listening to Nova and Journey battling each other. It sounded like they were going to take down half the forest! I had a feeling Nova was still blowing off some steam from what he thought he saw last night. He was hot headed but it wasn't like him to stay mad for so long.

"Ahh!" Journey grimaced. "Take it easy Nova. We're just practicing!"

We all turned around to see what happened and the blood drained from Sparrow's face when she saw the crimson gash on Journey's arm.

"Journey!" she cried, running to his side.

We were all on our feet now, rushing to see what was going on.

"Nova!" I scolded.

"What the heck are you doing? We're all on the same team!" Remi yelled

"Are we?" Nova challenged, getting in Remi's face.

Remi put his hands up and backed away as I darted between them.

"Nova. Nova!" I called, trying to get him to look at me.

When he finally did, I could see the pain in his eyes.

"What's going on?" I asked, pulling him away from the others while Sparrow worked on healing Journey.

"Nothing, I just got carried away. I should go apologize to Journey."

I glanced over and saw that Journey was fine. He had a big grin on his face, while Sparrow and Jemma fussed over him.

"He's fine. He knows you didn't mean it. I'd actually really like you to come with me. I need to speak with the chief about something and I was hoping you'd come with me?"

He looked at me like he wasn't sure he wanted to come.

"Please Nova? Maybe it'll give us some time to finally talk after…"

"Yeah, I think that'd be good for us," he said forcing a grin. "Come on."

As we walked back towards camp, Eja was running to greet us.

"Good! I was just coming to get you. It seems you and the chief are on the same wavelength this morning. When I went to request a meeting on your behalf, he told me he was hoping he'd have time to speak to you about a pressing matter."

"Is everything alright?" I asked.

"I'd rather let the chief explain," Eja replied.

His response did little to ease my nerves, as Nova and I followed Eja back to the chief's tent.

We ducked through the soft hides of the tent flaps to find the chief sitting cross-legged, in the center, on his mat. He nodded to acknowledge our arrival, but his eyes remained closed in thought. This time I noticed the scouts. Mali and Talon were stoically standing in the shadows, still as statues, except for a fleeting smile in our direction.

"Eva, thank you for coming," the chief said, pulling my attention back to him. "I have a pressing matter I'd like to speak to you about, but I understand you have something you'd like to discuss with me as well?"

"Yes, Jaka. I wanted to ask your opinion about sharing powers," I said jumping right into it.

I wanted to get to what the chief needed to tell me as quickly as possible.

"I shared a power with Jemma yesterday and –"

"Deus!" Jaka gasped. "You were able to share a power with your sister?"

I nodded slowly, unsure of whether that was a good thing or a bad thing, from Jaka's tone.

"I told you sharing powers was a big deal," Nova telapathed.

I cut my eyes at him briefly, before returning my gaze to the chief's bewildered expression.

"It all makes sense now. Pardon my outburst Eva, but I have been wondering about your sister. From what we were able to translate from the Book of Secrets, we know that your sister is your opposite, your shadow self. If you are light, she is dark, where you are timid, she is fierce. Nature has created her as your balance. It has always seemed odd to me though, that while you are all powerful, she is an empty vessel, void of any real powers!" Jaka said with rapid enthusiasm.

Yeah, Jemma's not too fond of that role, I thought to myself.

"Eva, I believe you were able to share your powers with your sister, because she was created specifically to help you manage them."

"Manage them?" I asked.

"Yes! No one person was meant to possess so much power Eva. And, it's only going to get worse when you encounter the Pillars. Their powers will be much stronger than any others you've gathered. It will take its toll on you. You may start to have headaches, hallucinations, nose bleeds, ringing in your ears. Eventually, you may even lose control of your powers if you aren't careful. And if that happens when you come across the Pillars, you risk being overpowered by the elements; earth, wind, water, fire. The results of which, would be catastrophic."

My hands were shaking now. It was as if I could see my future in his words.

"It's been happening already, hasn't it?" Nova accused.

I tried to deny it, by my trembling body gave me away.

"Are visions part of it?" I asked shamefully. "I've been having more of them and sometimes I have trouble telling my visions and reality apart."

"Yes, and I'm not surprised you're having them more often. You've been around my shadow scouts. They have powers that allow them to 'see.' You're parallel ability has probably picked up on that, absorbing their power and heightening your susceptibility to visions. I believe your visions will eventually become compromised because your mind is overcome with powers. It will become increasingly difficult for you to trust yourself. The shadow scouts have had a lifetime of training to control their sight, but I'm afraid time is not a luxury you have," Jaka replied. "I'm sorry to have to tell you these things Eva, but I wouldn't be doing my duty if I didn't warn you."

I stifled a sob, thinking back to the beautiful vision I'd had of marrying Nova and the conflicting visions my mother had shown me.

"Eva, it's nothing to be ashamed of. Now that you know you can share powers with Jemma, you have a solution," Eja encouraged.

"She doesn't trust her," Nova interjected, knowing my thoughts before I even formed them. *"She doesn't trust anyone,"* he added, for only me to hear.

I could see the hurt in his eyes. The fact that I had been hiding my visions from him, on top of making decisions to share powers without consulting him made Nova feel incredibly betrayed. Not to mention that he thought he saw something going on between Remi and I. I could see that it had all been piling up and I understood his foul mood earlier.

"Is this true?" Jaka asked, interrupting my thoughts.

I nodded shamefully.

"It is very important that you trust her, before you share your powers with her. It is a huge responsibility for you both and you need to be able to support each other. Sharing powers is similar to tethering. It's a sacred and serious act, which will uniquely connect you for life."

I swallowed hard. It had been so easy to share a power with Jemma. I guess I hadn't thought of the consequences.

"It's just that this is still so new to us. I only just found out that I had a sister. Jemma and I are still figuring each other out," I argued.

"I understand and I encourage you to continue to build your relationship with your sister, but I caution you not to take too long.

You need to share your powers with Jemma while you still can. If you wait too long, it may not be an option."

After a brief pause to let the weight of his words sink in, Jaka said, "This brings me to our next matter on the subject of your powers."

My mind was so busy trying to figure out if I could trust Jemma, that I had forgotten Jaka had wanted to talk to me about something as well.

"I'm going to have to respectfully ask all of you not to use your powers unless a situation deems them detrimentally essential."

"What?!" Nova and I both squawked at the same time.

"I know this is terribly inconvenient, but after Mali's most recent vision, I've come to the conclusion that each time you use your powers, I can feel the pull of the Ravinori, much stronger and closer. It's almost as if they are tapped into them somehow, channeling them."

"Do they know where we are? Do they know we're here?" I whispered, barely able to contain my fear.

"No, I don't believe so. If they did, they'd already be here. But, I do believe they know you are a source of great power and they will be coming for you. By choice or by force, they plan to use you to help resurrect Ravin."

CHAPTER XXXIII

My head was spinning. Based on Mali's vision, we'd agreed not to use our powers, unless it was a life or death situation. The chief suspected this would stop the Ravinori from somehow channeling our powers to pinpoint us. Nova had argued that not being able to train was going to hurt our preparations for returning to the Troian Center. We all agreed, but there didn't seem to be a solution around it as far as using our powers were concerned. It was just too dangerous.

Mali and Talon volunteered to help train us in fighting tactics as an alternative. It was a kind offer, which we'd politely accepted, but I felt as Nova did; without our powers, we didn't stand a chance.

The chief had also suggested that I speak to Jemma about sharing powers with her. He said he'd be happy to speak to her of the responsibility of possessing powers if it would help. I had politely accepted his offer, but said I would try to speak to her on my own first.

"How are we supposed to prepare? This is complete rubbish!" Nova cursed after we left the chief's tent.

"I think the bigger issue is that I have to give half of my powers to Jemma," I argued. "That's going to make her just as powerful as me! And, you know she's going to let that go to her head," I grumbled.

"You know if you gave her a chance, you'd see she's really not that bad. She actually wants to help you. She wants to be your sister, but you just won't let her in. You're too busy keeping your secrets," Nova said, his voice raising.

"What's that supposed to mean!" I answered, halting in his path.

"I'm going to give you two a moment," Eja said, silently excusing himself.

"You know what it means!" Nova hollered at me.

"I know you think I'm full of secrets Nova, but you're wrong! What you saw last night with Remi was nothing! You're the one who blew it way out of context!"

"I know what I saw Geneva! We were supposed to finally *talk* last night and when I came to find you, you were with him! And he was kissing you!"

"He kissed me goodnight! On my cheek!"

"Well… that's not what it looked like, so how was I supposed to know that? You knew I'd seen you and you weren't going to clear it up were you!? You were going to keep it to yourself, like everything else."

"Like what else Nova!"

"I don't know, but I know you're hiding something from me. You've been so – closed off lately. I don't know what to think. You won't let me in," he said throwing his hands up in the air. "And now I find out you're having visions?! You can't control them can you? What else are you keeping a secret? Are you having headaches and nose bleeds?"

"No! Just ringing in my ears from time to time," I admitted, "but it doesn't matter. I know what to expect now and I'm fine. I'll deal with it."

"I just want to help you Tippy … why won't you let me?" he pleaded, his face softening.

My heart panged, longing to just run into his arms, where I always felt better; like everything was somehow going to be okay.

"Because Nova, I don't think anyone can help me. You've all done so much for me already. Sacrificed so much. I don't need to burden you with anything more."

"You're not a burden. You know that, right? You have to know that."

I bit my lower lip to fight the pain I felt in my heart. Tears were stinging my eyes as I fought them back. I knew if I let them slip, cascading down my face, that Nova would catch them. He'd catch me and my splintering heart in his wonderful embrace and never let me go. How I wanted that, more than anything else in this world, but Vida's words haunted me, making me second guess my ability to be the Eva and be with Nova. And now, the chief was cautioning me that I might lose control of my powers.

I was essentially a ticking time bomb and more than wanting to let myself love Nova, I wanted to protect him. I couldn't lose myself in him, if I couldn't trust myself not to hurt him, even if it wasn't on purpose. It was a risk I wasn't willing to take, but I knew if I told him how I felt, he'd never let me pull away. I'd never forgive myself if I hurt the boy I loved, but I knew my heart would never forgive me for denying it.

So once again I had to keep my love for Nova to myself. I let my love's secret fire, silently stoke my determination to fulfill my destiny, in the hopes that someday, I might have a chance to finally tell Nova the words I longed to say. For now, I painted them on the inside of my closed eyelids as I pushed him further away, where I knew he'd be safe.

"I know that I am the Eva and if I say I don't need your help, then I don't need it."

I strode away from Nova, turning my back on his hurt expression before I lost my resolve. I caught up with Eja and asked him to gather the others so I could fill them in on the news. I knew they wouldn't be happy about not using their powers, but I had promised Jaka I'd relay his orders. I wanted to do it as soon as possible, so I could explain that it also meant we'd be hiking to our next campsite, rather than morfing.

Another unfortunate set back, I thought to myself as I waited for Eja to gather my friends. I suddenly felt a suspicious notion creep up my spine, setting my hair on end. *What if all of this is part of the Ravinori's plan?* It felt an awful lot like they were setting things in our way to change our direction or slow us down.

"Just try and stop us," I said out loud, challenging the universe and whoever else might be listening.

Then, I set off to find my friends with a renewed determination.

CHAPTER XXXIV

As I stretched in the moonlight, I breathed in the cool night air outside the tent where my friends and I had been gathered for the past few hours. I hadn't realized how stuffy it had been inside, but with all the candles burning through the night and some of us being full of hot air, I guess we'd let off a lot of steam, going round and round with our crazy schemes and ideas now that we had to regroup since learning we couldn't use our powers.

A sudden breeze picked up and I shuttered involuntarily as a shiver ripped through me. I tried rubbing down the goose flesh that was forming on my damp skin when I felt something warm brush against my leg. I looked down to see two brown saucer eyes, sleepily blinking up at me.

"Niv," I crooned, bending down to sweep him up in my arms.

I cradled him to my chest and buried my face in his thick, wispy fur, breathing in his comforting scent. He smelled like sweet hay and safety. Somewhere along the way, this sweet little marmouse had become my security blanket. I scratched him behind the ears and he cuddled deeper into my arms, nosing his snout into my armpit, as I giggled. It was his favorite spot. I was glad some things never changed. It seemed Niv didn't care that I was the Eva now. I was still just the girl who saved him from a tarcat and he simply loved me for it. I was hoping he still would, after I told him that his less than favorite new friend, Quin, would be following us back to the Troian Center.

Before I could break the news to Niv, Remi emerged from the tent. The soft, yellow glow from the tent illuminated his cherub-like features, and he cast me a shy smile. Remi had been behind me all the way about sticking with our plans to return to the Troian Center even though we couldn't practice our powers. He'd even supported my reservations about sharing my powers with Jemma. I was really surprised at his unabashed support for me and was reminded how grateful I was to have him as my friend.

"Hey," Remi said, shivering, "it's cold out here!"

"Yeah, I was surprised by that too," I admitted.

"Kind of reminds me of the cave," Remi observed. Then his cheeks flushed and that familiar foot in mouth expression crossed his face. "....uh, sorry. I didn't mean to bring that up."

I flushed too. The mere mention of the cave brought our awkward kiss back to the surface, but then I laughed.

"It really does remind me of the cave!" I said while giggling. "Don't worry about it Remi, we're best friends. We're bound to have some awkward moments over all these years, right?"

He paused momentarily, looking at me fondly.

"Right," he shrugged. "Hey, let's go find a fire and get warmed up," he suggested.

We walked arm in arm, huddled together for warmth, chatting and petting a cooing Niv as we went.

"Thanks for backing me up in there Remi."

"You know you can always count on me," he said. "Besides, you made some valid points."

"Thanks."

"Apparently Jemma thought you did too."

"Yeah that was really surprising. I didn't expect her to be so agreeable, but I have a feeling it's just her way of trying to win me over so I'll share some powers with her."

"Earlier today she was actually sticking up for you too and that was before she knew about the chief wanting you to share powers."

"Really?" I asked unable to keep the surprise out of my voice.

"Yep."

"I can never figure her out," I sighed, wondering if Nova was right and I wasn't giving Jemma enough credit.

It was hard not to think of her as Jane #31, who'd spent her days torturing Remi and I at the Troian Center. I shivered at the memories. I could see a small fire crackling a few yards away and picked up my pace, aching to thaw my chilly limbs. We were nearing a Beto family's campsite, when a bright sliver of dancing moonlight caught my attention.

"Did you see that?" I asked Remi, pointing in the direction of the shimmering reflection.

"What? The pond?" Remi asked.

Without answering, I handed Niv off to Remi and changed my course. I was drawn towards the pond before I even knew why. Something about the dancing silver reflection was calling me. Its effortless movement seemed too light, too graceful. I stood still, quietly watching the shadow ballet, before she appeared to me again.

"Mom!" I cried and ran to the water's edge, forgetting my chill and dropping to my knees.

"My darling," Nesia replied lovingly as she shimmered into focus.

"Mom! You're here!" I sobbed. "I knew it was you! I knew you'd come back to me."

"Of course I'm here my darling. I'm always with you, whenever you need me. You only have to look within yourself to see me."

"But, you left me when we were in the cave! I have so many more questions for you. I want you to stay with me," I wailed, letting my fingers sink into the cold, soft earth that met the water.

"Geneva, it's not safe for me to be present always, but when you truly need me, I will be there. You are stronger than you know dear one. I saved you in the cave because you needed me then. I can't touch you, because I don't live in the same world as you do, but as you get stronger, I do too. Now that you've unlocked your identity, you've truly opened your eyes and you can see me. I'm right here, watching over you, like I've always been."

"Oh mom," I sobbed.

I was shaking like a leaf, crying with abandon. The tears flowed out of me, a bitter mix of joy and sorrow. My mother was here, yet she wasn't. I could talk to her, but I couldn't hug her or touch her. She still didn't belong to the realm of the living and she never would. It was strange how she was here with me, floating on the water's surface, just out of reach. Something about that, made it hurt even worse than before. It was as if I was losing my mother all over again.

I felt Remi's hand on my shoulder. I didn't have to turn around to see him. His reflection next to my mother's, gave him away.

"Geneva?" he called softly.

I wondered if he could see her too or if he just thought I was losing my mind. But the next sentence he said, gave me my answer.

"Your sister needs to see this."

I ran as fast as my legs could carry me. Cutting through the cold night air, I headed back in the direction of the tent, where I had left the others. It was still glowing orange with warmth from the candlelight within. I burst through the tent flaps and stopped breathing.

I didn't have a chance to catch my breath from my sprint back to find Jemma and tell her about our mother, because what I saw inside the tent punched what wind I had left out of my lungs. I stood, flabbergasted, as I gawked unable to process the scene before me. No matter how many times I blinked or rubbed the hot tears from blurring my vision, the view was the same. Two figures, swaying in sleep, limbs lazily intertwined in a hammock. His golden hair was just visible over her onyx mane. I had no intention of waking them, but my voice, fueled by the pain in my heart, jealously betrayed me with a gasp of horror and Jemma woke, turning to stare at me.

Rage blossomed like a flower inside my chest, choking the breath from my lungs. I stumbled backwards out of the tent and teetered aimlessly about before crashing into Remi. With his arms around me, I burst into tears.

"Geneva! What's wrong? What happened?" Remi asked, concern coating his voice.

"Jemma! She's what's wrong!" I screeched. "She's evil! I'm never sharing my powers with her. She just wants to take everything that's mine!"

My wailing must have woken the Betos in the nearby tents, because I could see candlelight flicker to life and a few tent flaps open. I was angrier now, than I was sad. I pounded my fists against my legs in fury and mentally cursed Jemma for making me display this tantrum for the others to see.

Eja emerged from the shadows and rushed to my side.

"Geneva?" he spoke timidly.

When I didn't answer, Remi spoke up.

"She was just coming up here to find Jemma and tell her that we'd seen their mother in the pond..."

"Deus!" Eja exclaimed, cutting Remi off.

We all looked at him with confused expressions, waiting for him to elaborate or at least translate whatever he'd just said.

"I should have known," he muttered to himself. Then he looked up at me and said, "Come with me. We have work to do!"

Eja had me lead him back to the water's edge, where I'd last seen my mother and as I had expected she wasn't there when we returned.

The moon had risen higher in the sky by the time we returned and it rippled just out of reach in the water's reflection.

"She was right here, I swear!" I said to Eja. "You saw her this time too, right Remi?" I asked with a hint of panic in my voice.

"You've seen you're mother before?" Eja asked, in astonishment.

"Yes, I saw her when I fell into the cave. She saved me from drowning. And, I also saw her when we were at the New Year Gala in Lux."

Eja was staring at me now. I realized that I probably hadn't told anyone, besides Remi, about seeing my mother in the mirror when we were at the Gala. I'd tried to tell Nova, but I'd gotten distracted by Jemma's antics and I wasn't exactly sure what I had seen anyway. Plus, there hadn't really been time to try to figure it out. Everything had spiraled out of control that night. And since then, we'd been on a chaotic quest for the Book of Secrets and it never seemed like the right time to bring it up.

"Okay, let me start from the beginning," I said.

I filled them in on my encounter with my mother's reflection in the mirror backstage at the New Year Gala. I told them how that was the first time that I had seen Nesia and really started to believe the Legend of Lux could be real. Of course, at that time, I still had no idea who I was or that Nesia was my mother. I did remember how strange it felt seeing her for the first time though. Some unspoken magnetism had drawn me towards her and when my palm had connected with the glass it was like an electric shock. I had the same feeling when my mother saved me from drowning in the cavernous lake. It was painful, yet powerful all at once. I didn't want the feeling to stop, but I knew I couldn't physically tolerate it for very long. It was like staring at the sun.

"That's because her touch can kill you Geneva," Eja piped up. "It goes against everything in nature to converse with those on the other side. Your mother is dead, she's not of this world, she shouldn't be able to connect to anyone here, but she was a deity, a goddess of legend. If you're able to see her, it's only because she is channeling sacrificial magic. I've heard of gods and goddesses using the powers they obtain from offerings to increase their divine power. It's dark magic Geneva. What you're experiencing now, being able to see and touch your mother, it shouldn't be able to happen. There are tales of it of course, but I never knew of anyone who was able to find Ponte Deorum."

Remi and I stared blankly back at Eja, again waiting for him to translate. He kept forgetting that we didn't speak Truietian.

"Right, sorry. I keep forgetting," he said, reading my thoughts. "Ponte Deorum is something that people from every civilization have searched for or even fought wars over, it means Bridge of the Gods."

The phrase sent chills rolling down my spine, the same way the water was rhythmically rippling the moon's reflection away from me.

"Eja, I didn't find any bridge. It's like I said, I just see her reflection sometimes in different places and we can speak to each other."

"Geneva?" Remi spoke slowly, "I think what Eja is trying to tell you, is that you *are* the Bridge of the Gods."

"What?" I asked, looking at Eja, who was hesitantly nodding at me. "I'm what? I'm the bridge?" I gasped, letting the words hang in the cool night air as they slowly sunk in.

My mind started whirling. Why was it that whenever I finally had a grasp on my life, something else was thrown at me? This was possibly the biggest and craziest thing yet. Finding out you're part of a Legend that turns out to be true? Check. Accepting that you're the chosen one to save your island and lead your people to a better life? Hard to swallow, but yep, check. Getting stuck with your arch nemesis as your long lost sister? Pretty awful, but we can build on that, right? But this? The fact that I was the bridge between the living and the dead? This was too much.

I felt like I was floating, like I'd left my body. I hovered above myself and watched my slight frame slowly melt into a crouch. I was holding my head, my white blonde hair glowing in the moonlight as it cascaded around my shoulders, hiding the frustration of my furrowed brow. Remi and Eja's faces were painted with expressions of sadness and worry. I suddenly understood why they looked so gloomy and uneasy as they watched me try to come to grips with the responsibility of being the gate keeper between worlds. This was more than I could handle. I was taking deep breaths and trying to remain calm, but I could feel the weight of this news pulling me under.

I watched as my shoulders heaved up and down, raking in ragged breaths. Remi and Eja moved closer to me. Remi knelt down. He was saying something to me, but I couldn't hear him. I felt myself drifting away. I was losing focus; too many thoughts and visions were whirling through my mind. I watched Eja put a comforting hand on my shoulder, but I couldn't feel it. As I drifted away from myself, I saw four figures come into view. They rounded the bend in the path and came upon the three of us, huddled near the pond. The tallest figure came faster now. He was shouting something and then he grabbed my body, shaking my shoulders. I felt it! I felt him; hot and fierce in my heart, when I heard my name upon his lips.

"Tippy!" Nova shouted, shaking me back into my body. "Tippy!"

I didn't want to come back, back to my complicated life, but I couldn't resist him. He was the sun and I was Icarus. I could already feel myself melting back into my body, in the heat of Nova's presence.

I opened my eyes and foolishly looked up at his brilliantly appointed face.

"Damn you," was all I managed to get out, before I drown in my own darkness.

Blackness.

CHAPTER XXXV

"Geneva?"

I opened my eyes to Sparrow hovering over me. She looked concerned. Her delicate features were pinched, her lips in a thin, tight line. Her fine brown hair was pulled back from her face, but a few uncooperative pieces strayed and she constantly kept tucking them behind her ear as she watched me.

I sighed deeply as I sat up, swinging my legs over the hammock so I could sit upright. Niv was none too happy that I'd disturbed him from his slumber and he grumpily chattered as he leapt down off my lap and under the blankets I'd strewn off, apparently not ready to start his day yet.

"How long was I out this time?" I asked sleepily.

"Not long. Just since last night," Sparrow replied.

"Oh. Good," I said. But as the events of the previous night filled my head, it instantly began to ache.

"Geneva, you were only down for a little while, but a lot is going on."

"Like what?" I asked, standing to look around the tent for something to wear.

"Here," Sparrow said, handing me a sack of fresh clothes.

I was grateful she was always so prepared.

"And for once I'd like to be the one getting some answers," she said, surprising me, while I stuffed my head through the pale linen shirt. When I poked my head through the other side, I stared at her.

"Sparrow? What's wrong?"

"What's wrong? Everything is wrong! How can you even ask that Geneva?"

"Whoa, Sparrow. I remember what's going on, I know the situation we're in, but the last time I checked you and I were friends. Why are you yelling at me?"

Sparrow took a deep breath and looked crestfallen when she responded.

"I'm sorry Geneva. We *are* friends. It's just, so much is changing. I can't keep up with everything. Like what the heck happened last night? You blacked out or something and your nose was bleeding. I had a hard time getting it to stop. Remi said, from what he could tell, you didn't hit your head or anything, it just started bleeding."

I put my hand to my nose as a reflex. Everything felt fine, but the chief's words echoed in my mind.... *'you'll get headaches, nose bleeds, ringing in your ears....'* Everything he'd predicted was happening. I shook that realization away.

"I'm fine," I whispered.

Sparrow didn't look satisfied.

"Everyone's talking around camp. They're saying you're losing control of your powers."

"I said, I'm fine. I just need to focus a bit more and if people would stop dropping bombshells on me, it wouldn't be so hard."

"What bombshell?"

"Never mind," I muttered not wanting to get into the Ponte Deorum with Sparrow just yet.

"Okay, well then maybe you'd like to tell me why you're so angry with Nova? I thought you two were, were.... dating?"

"We are definitely *not* dating!" I huffed as I finished dressing. "Why don't you ask Jemma if she's dating him?"

"Jemma?!" Sparrow questioned. "I thought you two were getting along better. She was being so considerate to you during our planning meeting yesterday, asking your opinion on things and supporting your ideas. She seemed like she was really trying to be sisterly."

"Well, she wasn't being very *sisterly* when she was shacking up with Nova last night, was she?" I barked.

"WHAT?" squealed Sparrow!

"Yeah, I ran all the way back to the tent to tell Jemma that I'd seen our mother in the pond, only to look like a complete fool walking in on the two of them cuddling in the same hammock!"

My voice cracked as the painful memory choked me. I quickly brushed away the tears that were welling in my eyes.

"No wonder you were so mad," Sparrow said in a hushed voice. "Well, this probably won't make you very happy then."

"What won't make me happy?"

"Eja and Remi filled us in on what happened last night and Jemma lost it. She was hysterical that your mother had been there and she'd missed it. Nova was the only one who could console her. And..."

I was fuming. "And what else?!" I demanded.

"I think he stayed with her all night," Sparrow shyly admitted.

"Oh! I *hate* her! How is it possible that she's my sister!?" I screamed. I was pacing and suddenly felt the tent was too small a space. "I can't think in here," I said brushing past Sparrow as I grabbed my shoulder bag. "Can you feed Niv his breakfast? I need to get some air," I called back to her.

I set off aimlessly walking. I always did my best thinking when I was alone. I needed space to clear my head and gather my thoughts.

Vida's words were echoing in my head. She'd been right to tell me that love would only hurt me. We had things to do today to prepare for our expedition back to the Troian Center. I should be focusing on that, not distracting myself with Jemma and Nova! If he was falling for Jemma's antics then fine, he could keep her. I was nothing like my sister. I wasn't needy or fragile, so if that's what Nova liked, then I'd been wrong to think he and I would ever work.

Even just thinking these thoughts, that Nova and I didn't belong together, cut me to the core. I had to stop and catch my breath. My ears were ringing again. I focused on slowing my pulse and relaxing my breathing until it subsided. I cursed my foolish heart and scolded it to toughen up. I refused to let Jemma hurt me anymore. I had expected it from her, but feeling betrayed by Nova was what hurt the worst. I trusted him and felt so open and comfortable with him. And even though I'd seen Nova and Jemma together, my heart still refused to believe it, foolishly making me cling to every kiss and kindness Nova had shown me.

I screamed and shook my head, pushing those feelings away. I was done with Nova. I couldn't afford to let him be anything more than a friend. I already knew that and this was the final sign. I was the Eva. I had so many more important things to focus on. An entire civilization was counting on me for salvation. With responsibilities like that, I needed to heed Vida and Jaka's warnings; I couldn't afford to fall in love and I needed to get a grip on my powers fast!

"There you are."

As if on cue, Nova appeared. My heart flip flopped and I grimaced.

Time to face the day I told myself. I turned to address him, steeling myself not to give him or Jemma the satisfaction that their secret romance was getting to me. *I could keep a secret too*, I thought to myself.

"Morning Nova," I said sweetly, as I ducked the hug he tried to give me.

He looked confused, but recovered, shrugging it off.

"I was hoping to catch up with you earlier, but I wanted to let you get your rest. I stopped by your tent this morning to see how you were doing and Sparrow said I'd just missed you."

"Yep, I'm fine. Ready to get today started. We have a lot to do. Have you seen Journey this morning? I think I'm going to go scouting with him to check out the route back since we can't practice our powers."

Nova looked at me skeptically. "He left at dawn with Mali and some of the other Beto trackers."

"Hmm. Oh well," I shrugged. "I guess I'll just go find Jovi and see how Quin's training is going then."

I started back towards camp, but Nova caught my wrist as I marched past him.

"Hold up," he said. "Tippy, what's wrong?"

"Nothing's wrong, and I'm getting tired of everyone asking me that," I said. "I'd just like to get on with my day."

"Tippy," he said, lowering his face closer to mine.

He was looking at me like he was searching for something, but I refused to meet his eyes. I knew I wasn't strong enough yet. I needed time to build up my defenses. I would break if I stared into those emerald pools that could reach my soul and I didn't want him to see that he'd hurt me. My pain was my secret to keep. I needed to be stronger than that.

"Tippy, it's me. I know you. I know when something's wrong and I'm worried about you. I'm worried about last night. What was that? What happened last night?" Nova pressed. "You were screaming and then you were having a massive nose bleed."

"Well, I guess you don't know me that well Nova, because you're wrong, I'm fine," I said, pulling my arm from his grasp. "I need to talk to the chief about last night before discussing it with anyone else, so if you'll excuse me, I'm going to find Jovi now."

"Tippy, wait! I think there's someone you need to talk to first."

I paused, waiting for him to continue.

"I came out here to find you because I want you to go see Jemma," he said.

I rolled my eyes and turned on my heels. "That's not going to happen."

"Tippy!" he called, striding after me.

I cursed my short legs as his lanky ones easily closed the gap between us, until he was blocking my path.

"What's wrong with you today? Your sister needs you."

"Why? She has you doesn't she?"

"Why are you being so childish?" he scolded. "She's really upset that you got to see her mother last night and she didn't."

"I got to see a lot of things I wasn't expecting to see last night, Nova!"

"What the heck is that supposed to mean?" he asked, looking completely perplexed.

My heart faltered at the look of genuine hurt on his face and I knew I had to get out of there before I crumbled, giving into the pain of my pitiful, broken heart.

"I'm going to find Jovi," I called as I turned, squaring my shoulders.

I left Nova standing alone, dumbfounded, while I dragged my battered heart away, willing my stinging eyes to hold back the tears that were threatening.

CHAPTER XXXVI

"Kobel! My men haven't found them. Are you sure the location you gave is correct?"

"Yes master, but this Eva … she's unusually powerful. And as I told you, the Betos are smart, they keep her moving to keep her hidden."

"Well, where is she now?"

"That's just it. There's something strange about her. Last night there was an overwhelming surge of power and now, nothing. It's like she went dark; just shut the powers off."

"Are you telling me you lost her!?"

"No master. It's just I've never encountered so much power coming from one individual before. Perhaps she has already made contact with some of the Pillars? We must be careful master. She won't be easily controlled."

"Nonsense Kobel. She's a child, raised under my watchful eye. She never had time to learn how to control her powers. She has no idea what she's truly capable of. Even with the Betos helping her, she's not prepared to face us. Tell the men to keep searching. Find her!"

CHAPTER XXXVII

I busied myself searching the bustling Beto camp for Jovi. I didn't see the tiny girl or her playful sidekick, Quin, anywhere. Once again, everyone was tearing down their tents and packing up their belongings to move to the next location. Their nomadic way of life seemed so strange to me. It was so different from the familiar walls of the Troian Center. I had lived inside the same coquina shelled walls for all of my life. All that I remembered anyway. I realized, I envied the Beto way of life and the sense of adventure it offered.

I watched the Beto children skillfully roll up their hammocks and possessions. They seemed so carefree as they chatted with each other, completing tasks to help their family bundle up their lives into neatly folded sacks that they could carry with them, before morfing to a new location, courtesy of the amazing Bellamorf trees all over the forest. Or at least that's what they used to do, until I came along and ruined everything. Traveling wasn't as fun now that we couldn't use powers. That meant traveling by morfing was out and I was just starting to get the hang of it. It was old fashioned hiking from here on out.

I sulked as I watched the last of the damp cool air quickly burn off with the morning sun. The forest was hot and humid once more. I took shelter from the heat under the canopy of moss covered trees, leaning up against a trunk, so I was out of the way of Beto traffic.

I felt my stomach begin to growl as I realized I hadn't eaten breakfast. I rummaged around in my bag for any crumbs Niv might have left me, but I came up empty. My only reprieve was that my journal was still inside my shoulder bag. I pulled it out, running my hands across it's worn cover. I opened it slowly and mumbled "reveal" when I saw no one was watching me. I knew we weren't supposed to be using powers, but I wasn't sure an enchanted journal really counted and I was desperate for an escape from my aching heart.

Dear Journal,

I feel so lost. My heart has led me into a battlefield and now it feels like it's been shredded by a thousand tiny paper cuts. I saw Nova and Jemma together last night and I haven't been able to catch my breath since. Nova, who's always been my North star, seems to have led me astray. I feel like all of this is Jemma's fault. I've seen the way she looks at Nova and she knows how I feel about him. She has to right? I thought everyone did. Now she even has me doubting myself. But there's no doubting that I saw the two of them snuggled in a hammock together. I only saw them for a moment but it was long enough that I will never forget the stabbing pain it drove into my heart. I can't believe Nova hasn't even come to me to try to explain or apologize. He's always been so decent to me and always seems to know when I need an explanation to see that however mad his methods, he has my best interests at heart. But not this time. He had his chance just now to come clean and he just looked at me like I was the crazy one. He even had the gall to tell me to go console Jemma. That's NOT going to happen. But, none of that matters, it's not like he could explain this away. How was flirting with Jemma to help me? It's devastated me.

How could he betray me like that? He knows how I feel about Jemma. He knows she's never been kind to me and that it's so hard for me to accept that she's my sister. Why did he keep trying to push us together? He was always telling me to forgive her and give her another chance. Maybe I had resisted too much and had forced him to spend so much time with Jemma, trying to mend our relationship that I had driven them together. It's true that I have been acting childishly where Jemma was concerned, but I can't help it. She brings out the worst in me. Could this be my fault? Oh it would be too much to take if that were true, that I had done this! But I thought Nova loved me. I know now that I love him. I haven't been brave enough to tell him that, but I thought he truly knew my soul and would never betray what we had, whatever that is… or was. We've never actually classified it. He had never asked me to be his girlfriend. I had wanted him to ask me, but so many things got in the way. Remi, being one of those things. He's my best friend and he kissed me! I may have kissed him back before I knew what was happening. I don't know, it all happened so fast!

Oh none of this matters anyway. I'm being so emotional and thinking about who I love and who loves me, but it's all a lost cause because I'm doomed to be the Ponte Deorum. Why worry about fighting for Nova or anything else when I'll probably be dead?

My torturous thoughts were interrupted when I overheard familiar voices.

"She's not coming?"

"No. Jemma, I tried talking to her but… Please don't cry," Nova pleaded.

"She hates me!"

"She doesn't hate you," Nova consoled. "She's just… she's just overwhelmed right now."

"Of course she does! She won't share her powers with me, even though I'm the only one who can help her and she didn't even let me have a chance to talk to my own mother," Jemma sniveled. "She is such a spoiled brat!"

"She is being kind of childish," Nova replied and my heart tore a little more.

"She is, isn't she?" Jemma said, perking up with a girly giggle.

I couldn't take anymore. I hardened my battered heart and commanded my legs to carry me away from the sounds of her laughter.

I walked with my head down and arms wrapped tightly around me. I was desperately trying to keep my emotions in check. I was lost in thought when I heard a familiar howl.

"Jovi! There you are!" I exclaimed, when I finally came upon her and Quin deep in the woods. She was covered in scratch marks and had leaves stuck in her brown hair. She looked like she must have just wrestled Quin out of the nearby tree that was still dropping leaves.

"I've been looking for you all morning," I said.

"You have?" questioned the petite girl, her brown eyes, bright and wide. "Am I in trouble?"

"No. No, just the opposite. I need your help."

"Oh! Anything," she said, smiling until her dimples showed.

"I was wondering how Quin's training was going? Do you think she'll be ready for our return to the Troian Center soon?"

She resembled a bird, pondering a new discovery. Jovi's head bobbed from side to side. She looked inquisitively at Quin and then me and then back at Quin. "How long until we return?" she asked.

"Well I'm not sure yet. A few weeks maybe?" I said.

This peaked her interest, so I continued; filling her in on what we still had to accomplish before we were ready to return to the Troian Center.

"I'm still going to get to go with you, right?" she asked awe struck.

Even though I knew Jovi was a Truiet and I had been outvoted by my friends, I still felt it was too dangerous to bring someone so young and untrained to the Troian Center. But, I had a feeling that letting us borrow Quin, would hinge on Jovi coming with us.

"Well, you'll definitely be part of our team," I said, hoping it would entice her. "But we'll have to convince your mom and that's not going to be a simple task."

"Oh mom is easy! Yay! I finally get to do something!" she squealed with delight, hugging the wiggling wex tightly. "What should we work on with Quin today?"

I sighed and dove into what I knew would be a harrowing training session with Quin.

After a less than impressive demonstration of Quin's listening skills, I sent Jovi off with a list of cues to work on with the wex. Then, I spent the rest of the day avoiding Nova and Jemma as much as possible. Every time I saw either of them, the image of them entwined in the hammock singed my memory, flushing my cheeks scarlet with heartache.

Whenever I tried to think of anything but the two of them together, my mind wondered back to what Eja had told me about the Bridge of the Gods. It was unthinkable that I could be the link to the other side, yet I felt that heavy, uneasy feeling sink back into my chest. It was settling in, making itself comfortable, as if it were planning on staying awhile. I hated that feeling of foreboding doom. I didn't need it weighing me down right now, not when I was about to lead my friends on an uncertain voyage back to the Troian Center. Even the humid midday climate couldn't prevent me from shivering, when my mind flashed back to the harsh memories of our narrow escape from the Troian Center.

As I ducked into my tent, I continued to wonder if it were really true, that I was the one person that could connect the living and the dead. Perhaps it was just some Eva thing or just something that my mother was able to do. I decided however, if it were true, this Ponte Deorum, it was definitely something I wanted to keep to myself. If it got out, who knows what could happen. Eja said every civilization would covet such a power and I could see why, everyone loses someone they love at some point; it's the nature of life, yet so is the longing after such loss. That kind of longing can make you desperate. And it's a desperate heart that can devour a soul.

I had to find Eja. I wanted to talk to him more about his Bridge of the Gods theory and see if it was possible for him to keep it to himself or at least within our group. I knew Remi wouldn't be gossiping about it, that just wasn't his way and Sparrow hadn't mentioned anything about Ponte Deorum this morning. Maybe she just assumed it was normal for the Eva to be able to converse with her dead mother? So, maybe there was hope that Eja hadn't shared this with the others yet.

CHAPTER XXXVIII

I found Eja sitting in his tent, the Book of Secrets propped open in his lap, papers with scribbled notes strewn about haphazardly.

"Geneva! I'm so glad you're awake. We have much to discuss today!" he said enthusiastically.

"Um, yeah there's some things I'd like to discuss with you as well," I said, clearing a spot on the ground to sit down next to him, among his mess of papers.

"About this whole Ponte Deorum thing…" I started, "is there any way you're wrong about that?"

"I'm afraid not Geneva. It's remarkable! You shouldn't be able to do it, yet you can."

"Story of my life," I mumbled.

I sighed deeply as the heaviness in my chest stretched out, making itself comfortable.

"I've been researching it since last night. I can't really find any solid information about it. It's definitely not in the Book of Secrets. But I know I remember it being referenced vaguely in an old legend. I was hoping that maybe the chief would remember it and share it with you, since I was unable to locate the legend I'm thinking of."

"You're really sure it's not just part of my Eva powers or something special just between me and my mom? She's the only one I've ever seen. I don't go around seeing ghosts or anything like that," I added hopefully.

"No, I've read every prophecy about the Eva, the coming of the chosen one, etc. Ponte Deorum isn't mentioned anywhere. It's a dark power of legend. Perhaps the biggest legend of them all. There's no one on this earth that doesn't long to reconnect with a loved one they've lost. But nothing comes without a price. This is an evil kind of magic Geneva. The Eva is all about enlightenment and rebirth for our people. You are supposed to light our way into the future, not connect us to the darkness of the past."

I heard the finality in Eja's tone, but I argued with him anyway.

"But Eja, isn't it true I can do so much more than you thought I should be able to do? Like the fissures and visions and being an Echo. And if the Bridge of the Gods power was part of my destiny, maybe it was smart not to write it all down, because if it's as coveted as you say, then people would be coming after me to try to…"

My voice cracked as visions of my torture and death swam rapidly through my mind and I couldn't finish my sentence. I doubled over, overwhelmed by the throbbing pain searing my mind. I could tell Eja had glimpsed my visions from his grim expression, but he kindly put a hand on my knee and said, "We won't let that happen Geneva."

"I don't want to tell the others. I don't want to add any more for them to worry about."

"Geneva, knowledge is power. Sharing this is your decision, but I think keeping things from them will not help protect them. We're all in this together. You can trust us. We'll keep your secret."

I nodded, knowing he was right. Keeping this from my friends probably wouldn't help anything, but telling them would make it feel real and I wasn't ready for that. I swallowed back my tears, grateful that Eja hadn't told anyone else about the Bridge of the Gods yet. It was my secret to share and I needed to be the one to tell my friends about it, since I was going to have to ask them to guard it for me. I had once again, endangered my friends by dragging them into my messy life. I hadn't meant to, but once I let them all know about my ability to talk to the deceased, I would be making them accomplices to my doomed fate. But, I knew Eja was right, not telling them wouldn't make them any safer. They at least deserved the truth. I owed them that.

"I think you need to see the chief about last night. He's already expecting you. I'm going to gather the others so we can adjust our agenda and make preparations. There is much to be done Geneva," Eja said as he rose and walked soundlessly from the tent.

"I understand that you had a powerful vision last night?" Jaka asked me.

I was sitting in his tent, where he had summoned me. I decided if I was going to get this all out in the open, that everyone else might as well be here, so I didn't have to repeat myself.

As my eyes adjusted to the dim light inside the warm shelter, I looked around at the faces of my friends. Nova, Remi and Journey all looked tense, while Sparrow looked terrified and Jemma looked aloof as ever. Eja gave me a nod of encouragement as I hesitated answering the chief.

"Sort of," I replied finally. "It was more than a vision though … it was an encounter."

"An encounter? With whom?" Jaka asked, arching his eyebrows.

"My mother."

Jaka, who was almost always in control of his emotions, stifled a gasp.

"Deus! It cannot be true," he muttered mostly to himself as he stared at me with new intrigue. "Ponte Deorum."

Once he uttered the words, they felt true. I had dreaded that Eja was right the whole time, yet somehow still held a glimmer of hope that he'd been mistaken in naming me the Bridge of the Gods; used to connect the living world with the dead. But, when the chief said the words aloud, it made them feel real, squashing all delusions of hope.

I rushed through the events of last night, filling Jaka and my friends in on where I'd seen my mother, and how I'd tried to tell Jemma. I skipped over the part about finding my backstabbing sister hitting on the love of my life! I jumped ahead to where Eja intercepted me and we went back to find my mother, but she'd vanished. I gave them a brief recap of the other times I'd seen my mother, just like I'd told Eja and Remi last night. Finally, rounding it all out, with how Eja had deduced that I was the Ponte Deorum and now we needed to figure out how to protect me from becoming the most sought after tool in the universe.

"Did I miss anything?" I asked, looking at Eja and Remi.

They both shook their heads. I looked from them, to the pale, shocked faces of my friends. All of them were completely silent. I could feel their worry for my safety, along with a hopefulness and shame that I soon recognized with dread. Each of my friends had lost their families; parents, siblings, friends. Each of them realized that I could connect them to their lost loved ones, yet they knew they couldn't and shouldn't ask me too, because of how dangerous using that kind of dark magic was.

I was crestfallen and felt like I was suffocating from the sorrow that filled the tent. I looked to Jaka for some sign as to whether we were meant to continue sitting in the stuffy shelter or if he would excuse us so he could think on the matter. Hoping for the latter, I was disappointed to see him motion to his scouts to fetch something for him.

"So you're convinced that I am this Ponte Deorum then?" I asked, while impatiently waiting for Jaka to say something.

He slowly nodded.

"Is there any way to stop it? Or get rid of it?" I asked.

He looked lost in thought and didn't respond.

"I don't want this power. It's too much! And why didn't we already know about it? I don't remember reading anything about it in the Book of Secrets."

"That's because it's not in the Book of Secrets my Eva. I'm afraid it is somewhere much worse, The Book of Gods. All the pieces are fitting together now. I believe this is why the Ravinori are hunting for you and perhaps how they are connecting to you." He paused, looking deeply saddened. "You should have shared the encounters you had with your mother with us earlier."

"I didn't know they were important," I whispered.

"Sharing information with those who are fighting to help you, is always important. You mustn't keep secrets from your allies Geneva. I know you might think some things aren't important or that by keeping information from us you are sparing us, but it is just the opposite. Secrets are scars we wear on our souls. They hold us back from progress and can even damage us beyond repair. After hearing this new information, it is even more imperative that you share your powers with Jemma. The sooner the better. It's a miracle you are still standing with that amount of power coursing through you."

I swallowed hard. Even though Jaka's voice was soft, his words fell sharply upon me. I felt ashamed and foolish. I had told myself all of those things. That I didn't need to share my thoughts or feelings, that I could keep my time with my mother to myself, that I could carry some burdens on my own to spare my friends, that I didn't need to share my powers with Jemma, I could handle it. But, deep down, I'd known all along, that keeping such secrets was selfish and wrong. Perhaps becoming the Bridge of the Gods was my punishment for my deceitful ways.

"If I told you earlier, could you have stopped it? The Ponte Deorum, I mean?" I asked the chief.

"No, do not dwell on the past my Eva. What's done is done, perhaps it was meant to be. You are who you are and nothing can change that. But I believe that in war, it is good to know as much as we can about ourselves and our enemies, so that we can be better prepared for what we are up against."

War? I gulped, repeating the ominous word to myself. Just then, one of Jaka's scouts returned carrying a large dusty book. I recognized him under his face paint. It was Talon, and when I caught his eye, he looked saddened. The usual, mischievous lightness in his eyes was missing. Instead his jaw was set and his shoulders rigid and square. His whole demeanor put me on edge even more than I already was.

"Ah, thank you," Jaka said, taking the leather bound manuscript.

Eja let out a tiny gasp of awe.

"What is that?" I whispered to Eja, while we all intently watched the chief flip slowly through its delicate pages.

"Striga Carta," he replied. "Sorry, the witches book," he corrected, when he saw that I didn't comprehend.

"Is it a book of spells?"

"No, it's more like a history book. It's full of legends and lore from other lands. It was recovered off a vessel that we found wrecked upon our beaches. No one knows where it came from, but it tells of many mystical plants and creatures that are found on our island. It even has rudimentary maps that look to be of Hullabee Island."

"Why is it called the Witches Book?" I asked, mildly annoyed that a history book had been given such a menacing name.

"Because," Jaka interrupted, "it was written by a very wise woman who we believe, was trying to find our island. She conceived that Hullabee Island was the key to unlocking the origin of the four realms. And she was a witch."

I sucked in my breath, vacuuming out the remaining stale air in the tent and replacing it with terror.

Of course it had been too much to hope that the ancient book propped open on Jaka's lap was merely a history book; full of boring stories of settlers and explorers like the ones we'd learned about in our History and Trade lessons at the Troian Center. I had a sinking feeling that the history in the Striga Carta would be a lot more terrifying and reveal more than I wanted to know.

"Here, it is!" Jaka said to himself with satisfaction.

He looked up from the pages, as thin and brittle as onion skin, to see our anxious faces and cleared his throat before continuing.

"Have you heard that history repeats itself? That we are destined to suffer the same fate until we correct our past mistakes? That is what Striga believed. She believed it so much that she set sail on a perilous sea voyage to try to right the wrongs of her ancestors, who were described in this very legend. It all started with two immortals, Kull and Aris. They were fighting for the affection of a beautiful girl, named Zophia. Both were obsessed with her beauty and were boasting their powers in order to impress her. Each of them immortal, they possessed the same powers and prowess. They were handsome, strong, athletic, and equal in every way. Zophia liked them both and didn't know which of her suitors to choose. Kull grew worried that she was not impressed enough with him and that she might choose Aris instead. He was determined to set himself apart from Aris, so he set out to find a way to make himself more desirable."

My eyes darted between Nova and Remi, haunting my mind with the memories of their relentless quarreling over my affection. I didn't like the direction this story was going.

"It is said, that during his quest, Kull came across a mysterious elder who knew of his plight and promised he could help. He told Kull of a magical weapon that could take the life of an immortal. The elder told Kull, that if he killed a fellow immortal, he would gain all that they possessed, including their power. Thus, making him more powerful than any other immortal in existence. This enticed Kull.

It was exactly what he needed to set him apart from Aris. His greed overruled his suspicion of the strange elder. He hadn't thought of eliminating Aris as an option, but now that it was, he was desperate to make it happen. Kull would have done anything to win the hand of the fair Zophia," Jaka said pausing to stare ominously at Nova.

"What happened?!" Jemma impatiently questioned.

"Kull greedily used the fabled weapon to kill Aris. Thus starting the first war."

Sparrow gasped while everyone else but Journey remained speechless.

"What was the weapon?" he asked.

"It isn't known, but it is believed to be many different things. A bow, a sword, a knife, but I think it is something much worse. Something that lies within each of us, waiting to strike. The heart is a wild thing, that's why it lives in a cage made of bone, buried deep within us. It is so easily poisoned by simple things like hate, greed, jealousy. In my experience, these are the most destructive of weapons, if left to grow untended."

"What happened to Zophia?" I asked.

"Ah, yes. Zophia. She is an imperative part of this story."

"She had fallen madly in love with Aris while Kull was off trying to find ways to gain power to impress her. They were set to be married under the first pink moon, but it so happened that Kull killed Aris on the eve of their nuptials. When Zophia heard what had happened, she was sick with grief. She ran to find Aris, not wanting to believe he could be dead. When she found his slain and bloodied body she was devastated and a deep madness began to set within Zophia. She threw herself over him and wept while staring up at the heavy, pink moon and from that day forward, it became known as the blood moon, bringing death and devastation in its wake.

The other immortals found out what was done to Aris and went after Kull for retribution. Kull fought them off, killing many of them easily with a simple blade. The blade has become a bit of a legend itself, since it had a hand in slaying immortals. It seemed that the death of one immortal had broken the magic that kept them all immortal. This caused a war to break out. It has been called many names; the first war, the holy war, the immortal war. But, whatever it's called, one thing remains true; it has shaped our very existence," Jaka said somberly.

He paused, lost in his own thoughts for a moment.

"Where was I?" he asked after a short break.

"Zophia?" Jemma prodded. "You were telling us what happened to her."

"Ah yes. Zophia. Dressed in her wedding gown, she lay over Aris's body during the entire war, shielding him and praying he would somehow come back to her. It is believed that this act, is what spared her life. The warring immortals likely thought her body was already slain as she lay over Aris, covered in his blood.

When she finally raised her head from her beloved's, all she saw was red. Red blood, spilled from those she loved. Red rage, towards Kull, who had senselessly started this war and a red moon, reflecting the violence it had seen. Zophia rose to her feet and vowed to find a way to punish Kull for what he'd done and most importantly, to reunite herself with her soul mate Aris.

She went in search of the mysterious elder who had given Kull the immortal weapon. When she found him, she was poised to kill him for instigating the horrible events, but he pleaded for his life, saying he could help Zophia as well. She paused long enough to hear him say he could give her what she wanted most, her heart's true desire; Aris. She listened to his bargain and they struck a deal that both felt was fair. Zophia set off to put actions into motion that have shaped this world and many others.

Zophia found Kull on the battlefield and threw herself at his feet, declaring him triumphant. She told him she loved him and that she wanted him to stop the war and spend eternity with her. Kull was intrigued, but he was also enjoying the fear and respect he was gaining by slaying immortals in the war. He'd become accustom to stealing powers from those he killed and wasn't eager to give that up. So Zophia enticed him with a proposition that the elder said he was sure Kull couldn't pass up. She told Kull she knew of a secret ritual that would change the world. It would transform Kull and herself into the supreme immortal rulers of all beings. They would be all powerful and live eternally together.

The elder had been right. Kull immediately agreed that they must participate in this secret ritual. So Zophia took his knife and led him to the top of the highest mountain peak and they waited for the elder to prepare the ritual. The fragile old man, limped about, chanting in a foreign tongue for hours, drawing marks all over their bodies. The sky grew dark and the wind picked up. Soon the sky ignited with cracks of fire and a sound that rumbled deep within their bones. Kull was growing impatient with him, but Zophia reassured him that the elder knew what he was doing and this was all part of the ritual.

The sky opened up, lashing them with stinging rain and hail. Zophia's white dress suddenly turned red as the rain washed the blood from her hair. Kull was frightened for her. He thought his lovely bride-to-be was bleeding, injured by the hail from the storm. When he said so, Zophia laughed cruelly, her eyes wild. She told him it was the blood of her true love, Aris, and that she'd never washed it from her hair, intending to keep him with her always.

She pulled out his blade, turning it on him and cursed him for taking her true love from her, saying that if she could not be with Aris and be happy, then Kull didn't deserve happiness either. She grabbed hold of Kull's trembling arms and started screaming the same chanting words as the elder, while holding the blade to his throat.

In that moment Kull knew that Zophia had tricked him. She

laughed madly as the ground beneath their feet began to split into a deep crevice. The earth opened up, groaning and shuttering into an endless abyss, running straight to the core of the universe. Kull tried to get away, but it was too late. Zophia pulled them both into the mouth of the hungry mountain. When she was satisfied by the look of pure terror and despair on Kull's face, she laughed and closed her eyes, praying for the falling to stop and the darkness to take her and lead her back to her true love Aris."

"Did it work?" Sparrow asked anxiously, when Jaka left us hanging.

"Their sacrifice did end the war," he said. "When their souls had finally been devoured, the mountain erupted with their blood, cleansing the earth with molten lava from the volcano their sacrifice had created. This is how the four realms were created; Heaven, Hell, Earth and Limbo. The elder had had a plan all along, to create four new and powerful realms that he planned to rule. He created the heavens where the virtuous immortals were sent. He deemed them gods and goddesses and they could peacefully live out their days in a new realm, safe from the dangers of earth. Those who had fought with Kull and killed were vanquished. Cast out, they were doomed to live all of eternity as demons in a treacherous realm named hell. He created earth, a fragile realm full of life, creatures and mortals to entertain him. Lastly, he created Limbo at the request of Zophia. She wanted the worst punishment possible for Kull. A space between spaces where he couldn't be part of any realm; where there was no peace, no life, no death, just an endless abyss of pain and suffering that would stretch on for all of time."

"So she got to be with Aris in heaven then, right?" Jemma interrupted.

"Not exactly," Jaka said. "You see, Zophia had been so blinded by her hatred for Kull that she hadn't asked enough questions of the elder and he had tricked her too. He trapped her in the in-between, cursed to usher souls between the four realms. She became a portal that the elder could use to travel to any realm, making him the most powerful being of all. This had been the plan he was orchestrating the whole time. He had used Kull's greed and selfishness to his advantage to start the war. Then he preyed upon Zophia's grief and emotions, getting her to give up her soul in order to punish Kull. She had actually supplied the elder with the idea of Limbo, giving him what he needed to finalize his plan; her soul and a way to roam between all the realms and rule them all."

"What happened to Aris and Kull?" Sparrow asked.

"Aris did go to heaven like the elder had promised, but those in heaven are ethereal spirits, invisible to us and even to poor Zophia. It's believed that Zophia could hear Aris speaking to her, but she couldn't see him and it was slowly driving her mad. In our culture, Aris means heaven and is often described as a calm cloud or mist. Now Kull is the opposite. Kull means hell and is always represented by fire."

"But he wasn't supposed to go to hell," Nova said, speaking for the first time in a while. "You said Kull was supposed to go to Limbo."

"Ah, you didn't let me finish telling you how the story ends," Jaka replied.

I heard the chief speaking, picking up the story where he'd left off, but I couldn't peel my eyes off of Nova. His beautiful face had paled three shades whiter than I'd ever seen. He looked sickly and haunted and I felt his nerves tingle from across the room as I watched him clench his fists and set his jaw to stop him from shaking.

"... Zophia called out to the elder in fury. He came to her to thank her for her part in his plan. She recoiled in shock and fear when she first saw him, because she didn't recognize him. He had given up his old, tired mortal body that she was used to seeing shrouded in dirty robes and was now possessing a new one. But not just any body, it was a perfect human specimen of stunning physique and it used to belong to Kull. Zophia was angry and hurt that he had tricked her.

She begged him to do as he had promised, but the silver tongued man scolded her, saying he had kept his word. Aris was in heaven as she had asked and she would have been there too, but she had asked him to create an even worse place for Kull. So, when the elder created Limbo, per her request, he had to make her the bridge connecting all the realms, where she would be able to watch over Kull's suffering, while still being connected to Aris. Since Limbo was a place that no longer required a body, he felt that Kull wouldn't mind if he borrowed his. After all, it would be a shame to waste such a fine body, when his own was so old and frail. He assured her that Kull's spirit was rotting in Limbo, engulfed in eternal anguish, as she had asked.

Zophia cried that this hadn't been what she'd meant and he simply shook his head and told her to be more careful what she wished for in the future.

As the elder, now in Kull's body, walked away from her, she asked him for one thing before he left. She at least wanted to know the true name of the one who had condemned her to an eternity in the in-between. He laughed and agreed that he at least owed her that. He revealed to her, his true name before he left."

We all stared at Jaka, waiting anxiously for him to say it, but deep down I already knew. I could feel it in my bones.

"His name was Ravin."

"Ravin?" I asked, after everyone calmed down. "How could he be Ravin? I thought Ravin was the man in the Legend of Lux, that caused the Flood and murdered my aunt Mora. The man my mother and father hunted to the ends of the earth?"

"Ravin is just a name. In our culture, it means devil. Perhaps it is two different men with the same name, or perhaps he is the same man in both legends," Jaka said. "Or maybe Ravin is just a name used to represent evil. Devil, is just the word evil without the 'D' after all."

I was shivering, as a slow chill crept up my spine. Was it possible that I was going up against the devil himself? I couldn't wrap my mind around something so vast, so I returned my focus to the problem at hand.

"But, you said you were starting to see how we are all connected. I still don't get it. Other than the fact that this Ravin could be the same man… how does it all fit together? What's my role in it?"

"Don't you see the theme?" Jaka asked. "Four realms, four Pillars?"

I felt like I did, yet it was somehow just outside my grasp. Each time I tried to focus and pull a single idea from my whirling mind, I would get sharp pains in my head. Heaven, hell, earth, limbo, water, fire, earth, wind. I kept repeating the four Pillars and the four realms over and over in my mind until they were all muddled together. Suddenly it clicked.

Jaka must have figured it out from the look on my face, and he smiled.

"How?" was all I said.

"That is the part that Striga figured out. You see, Zophia was the portal to all the realms for a very long time. She was the original Ponte Deorum and she met many different beings as they all passed through her to where they were going. One day, she met a very special witch named Divina and when she heard Zophia's story she wanted to help her. She taught Zophia a spell that would end her purgatory and get her out of being the Bridge of the Gods. But Divina warned that there was no coming back from this spell. It wouldn't give her back her life, it would end it, along with her suffering. Zophia was desperate after years of serving Ravin as the Ponte Deorum so she begged for Divina to teach her the spell and she did.

In it, Zophia had to tear what was left of her soul into four equal pieces, one for each realm that Ravin had connected her to. She gave her tears to heaven, so that they could become water to cleanse and sustain the humans that she'd grown fond of watching over. She gave her breath to limbo, so that her words would live upon the cold wind that dwelled there and continue to haunt those who had been condemned to suffer for eternity. She gave her heart to hell, because it had been the fire of love and flames of hate that had ignited her passion to the brink of destruction, landing her in this predicament. And lastly, she gave her bones to the earth, where she asked that they be buried so that she could find peace and rest at last."

My skin dimpled with goose bumps as Jaka read the chilling words from the Striga Carta.

"Zophia created the four Pillars," I whispered.

"Yes. That is what Striga believed and I believe it too. Divina happened to be an ancestor of Striga's and that's how I've come to remember this story. Striga wrote about it in this book," he said pointing to the crusty leather bound book on his lap. "The legend about the first war is from a different manuscript believed to be possessed by the Ravinori. It's called the Book of Gods, but Striga recounts the legend here and she was privy to it because the story was passed down to her through generations by her family. A family of witches, who at one time, must have been a part of the Ravinori's inner circle to have knowledge of the legend. She tracked the origin of the legend here, to Hullabee Island. She was on her way to our island by ship when she met her demise."

"Do the Ravinori know about the last part? The four Pillars part?" Nova asked.

"I believe so, and that is why they are searching for the four Pillars and why the Book of Secrets tells you that you have to protect them. All of the legends point to the Eva as the one that can save all of us by saving the four Pillars. Striga wrote that she believed the Eva would be the reincarnation of Zophia."

"So the Ravinori think that if they can find the four Pillars, and put them back together again, that they can re-create the Ponte Deorum and bring Ravin back from wherever he's been all this time!"

Journey said putting the pieces together proudly.

"They just haven't figured out that I am the Ponte Deorum yet," I said. "They know that the Eva is supposed to be a Pillar tracker because she'll be the reincarnation of Zophia?"

The chief nodded. "Yes and I think they are using that knowledge to track you by tapping into the elements, since you must possess a small part of each original element. They should call to you when you come in contact with a Pillar."

My stomach dropped as I thought of the uncanny pull I had towards Nova. My head was spinning. This was the biggest revelation yet. Jaka's words whirled through my hazy mind like a revolving door.

Ravin… four realms … four Pillars… volcanos… sacrifice… the Flood. It was overwhelming how similar parts of the legends were. Like puzzle pieces that you couldn't quite make fit, yet you knew somehow they did. I just couldn't quite see the big picture yet, though I urged my brain to stretch past its limits.

"Jaka? When you said history repeats itself, what did you mean?" I asked seeing visions of Kull and Aris fighting over Zophia in the first war and then Ravin trying to make Mora love him and now… me and -

I couldn't finish my thought because blood had started seeping from my nose, perhaps overwhelmed by the horrible connection my mind was trying to get my heart to make.

Remi and Nova rushed to my side, both offering to help me stop the bleeding at the same time. Nova pulling off his shirt to mop up the blood, while Remi tilted my head back, gently pinching the bridge of my nose. I pushed them both away as I swiped the blood from my horror struck face with the back of my trembling hand. I could taste its' bitter metallic flavor in my mouth as my heart sank. Everyone in the tent had now come to the same conclusion I'd been dancing with moments ago. I had my own Kull and Aris, I just called them by two different names; Nova and Remi.

CHAPTER XXXIX

I refused to believe it.

"No!" I said getting to my feet. "If history is just going to keep repeating itself then why are we even here? Why am I killing myself to defeat the Ravinori and restore peace to Hullabee Island?"

"Nature craves balance Geneva," Eja said softly, trying to diffuse my outburst. "Striga believed that what Ravin did in both legends upset the balance and ever since, it has been trying to right a wrong. That's why similar situations continue to present themselves to our ancestors, in hopes that one of us will get it right. We need to choose love over hate, humbleness over pride, selflessness over greed. That's why you have finally come to us, to right the wrongs, to deliver us."

"So what? Free-will means nothing? I have no choice? How am I supposed to even know if I'm making the same mistakes as my ancestors! If I'm a reincarnation of Zophia or whomever, won't I just make the same mistakes as she did?"

"Like choose me?" Remi whispered.

His face was so crestfallen that it was painful for me to look at him. I wanted to hug him and tell him it wasn't true and that everything was going to be alright. But how could I? He'd been in the tent the entire time and heard the whole vicious tale. His likeness to Aris was undeniable. He even possessed the power to render himself invisible, just as Aris had been invisible to Zophia in heaven. Remi wrapped his arms around his folded knees and hung his head. I hated seeing my best friend so upset, but I was at a loss. I was searching for something to say, when Nova's voice interrupted me.

"Ah come on, don't look so glum. You're a better choice than me," he said. "You get to be heaven and I'm hell. This must be music to your ears."

"Nova," I scolded. "You know that's not true!"

"Isn't it though? You were just thinking it, weren't you? I'm fire, he's invisible and you're the bridge between us. Sounds like a story I've heard before and it's not going to have a very happy ending."

"It's a legend," I argued. "This is all just speculation. I'm sure if we read more about it –"

"What? You can re-write a better ending?" he demanded, green flames dancing with anger in his deep emerald eyes.

"I think not," he said as he stood to storm out of the tent in a hurry.

I turned to the chief as I scrambled to my feet.

"Jaka, I think you've given us more than we can handle for right now. We could all use some fresh air and a little time to process this new information if that's okay with you."

He nodded, but I was already halfway out the door chasing after Nova. So much for my mature approach of giving Nova space when he was mad, I thought as I dashed after him. But I'd seen the pure torturous pain in his eyes, I felt the sting of it, mirrored in my own heart and I didn't want him to have to deal with this burden alone.

I was surprised to find that night had fallen when I stumbled out of the tent. It took a moment for my eyes to adjust to the lack of light. The air was heavy and cool. It clung to the nervous sweat that had gathered on my skin, making me shiver.

"Nova!" I called, taking off in the direction I'd last seen him run. "Nova! Stop running away from me. You know I'll find you. I can just use my hunter powers –"

"Don't! We're not supposed to use powers!" his voice scolded me telepathically.

"Okay, so when did telepathy become a normal skill?"

No reply.

"I'm just going to keep doing it until you come out here and talk to me!"

"Fine," came his voice as he emerged from the thick forest underbrush, not too far in the distance.

He was walking towards me, still shirtless, his blond hair a disheveled mop of gold. I shook the thought from my mind that his locks resembled golden flames lightly caressing his head. He stopped a few inches away from me, close enough for me to feel the heat radiating from his toned body. I could see a fury still burning within his wild green eyes. When he looked deep into my eyes like this, I lost my voice.

"You wanted to talk Tippy, so talk."

"Are you even going to listen to me?" I asked referring to the harshness in his tone.

"I just don't see what the use for talking is? It's not going to change the facts."

"Facts!? They're not facts Nova. It's just a bunch of stupid legends. Old stories written by crazy witches and fanatic Ravin worshipers. They don't mean anything."

"You don't believe that and you know it. If you didn't believe in that stuff you wouldn't believe you're the Eva, but you are and you do believe it. I felt it in the tent. You pulled away from me, you're scared."

"Of course I'm scared! Every time I think I have my head wrapped around my fate, someone drops another huge legend or power in my lap and everything changes! It's not easy having your destiny mapped out for you and only being fed bits and pieces along the way. I'm terrified that I'm going to screw this up and make the wrong choice."

"I'll make it for you. Chose Remi."

"Nova –"

"No, I'm no good for you. You heard what Jaka said in there. I'm Kull!"

"No you're not!"

"I am. I'm all of those things. I'm dangerous, hot tempered, I possess fire, I'm impulsive and when it comes to you I don't think straight. There's no limit to what I'd do to protect you; even if it meant killing, and you know it. I'd do anything I could, if I thought it would keep me from losing you, but it's no use."

Nova's eyes were dancing wildly now and his breath was heavy and fast. He'd moved closer to me and grabbed my arms just above my boney elbows. His hands were trembling and hot. He slid them slowly up my arms until they reached my shoulders. He leaned in closer still and bent down, resting his forehead on mine, closing his eyes tightly, like he was trying to fight something painful. My breath had quickened too, but it caught in my throat when his thumbs slid over my collarbones, lightly caressing them.

"Nova…" I whispered fighting to make my brain continue to think through his close proximity. It felt as if his body threatened to swallow mine whole; and I wanted to let it. "It's not true," I whispered.

"It is," he murmured. "You know it is. I'm no good for you. I think you've known it all along. This whole time, you could feel it, couldn't you? That there was something different about us. When we're together our connection is so…"

"Intoxicating?" I offered.

He nodded and moved his hands up my neck, so they were now cupping my delicate jaw bones. He tilted my head back, forcing me to look up at him.

"You need to stay away from me Geneva. We can't be together. No matter how bad we want to be."

His voice was heady and urgent. I didn't know who he was trying harder to convince, me or himself.

"But I … Nova, I –"

"No! Don't say it. Please, just don't say it. This is hard enough as it is. I know how you feel because I feel it too. But maybe it's not real. It's just some stupid connection forced upon us by nature or our ancestors. I know it's not fair, but you need to be with Remi. You have to break the cycle of history repeating itself and always ending in tragedy."

"No! I won't. I won't chose either of you. That way I won't make the wrong choice. And I will not allow some legend to take away my free-will! If I can't be with the person I want to be with more than anything, than I'd rather be alone. It's better for all of us. I'll keep my head clear of all of this destiny nonsense and concentrate on finding the Pillars and saving the island."

Nova's whole body was trembling now. His eyes glistened and I saw a single tear threatening to break free. To me, that single teardrop held the weight of a waterfall and I couldn't bear to watch it. I squeezed my eyes shut and he pulled me into a fierce embrace. I could feel his heart hammering against me. *A caged animal* I thought, the chief's words still fresh in my mind. How was it that the beast that beat within us, could get it so wrong when it came to love? My own heart felt like I'd driven stakes into it with every word that threatened to defy its cravings for Nova. But, I was determined to beat it into submission, no matter how much it killed me, so that I could be the Eva that my people deserved.

CHAPTER XL

"I've done it master. In a weak moment, she let me in. I'm in her mind right now. I can try to manipulate her thoughts. I can get her to come to us and lead us to the Pillars."

"I thought I told you not to waste your time on this nonsense," he bellowed, dramatically clearing his massive desk of the papers he'd been studying before Kobel interrupted him.

For a brief moment, they were the only sound in the room as they fluttered like dead leaves to the floor. The tall man behind the desk stood, looming before Kobel, who now looked frightened.

"Master, I would never defy you. I was following your orders, trying to pinpoint the Eva's location. It's been very difficult lately. I think she knows that we're using powers to track her because she hasn't been using them. No one around her has been using them. The Bellamorfs aren't even being used to travel anymore. I'd all but given up hope, when suddenly, like a beacon, her voice rang out in my mind. She can telepath and when I picked up on her conversation, she must have pulled me into her mind."

"What was she saying?"

"She was speaking to a Pillar."

"She's found a Pillar?" he asked tentatively.

"Yes master."

"Which one?"

"Fire."

"If you manipulate her mind, can you bring them both to me? The Eva and the fire Pillar?"

Kobel smiled, showing what remained of his grey, decaying teeth.

"That should be easy master. They're in love."

Both men laughed wickedly. Kobel's wheezing mirth, mixed with his master's deep booming laughter, as he sat back down, stretching out behind his dark desk, weaving his hands behind his head in a satisfying way.

"Do it Kobel. Bend her mind and bring them to me."

CHAPTER XLI

After not nearly enough time, I heard the others calling for me. I peeled myself from Nova reluctantly and he let go of me, except for my hand. His warm fingers had caught mine when I tried to pull away from him. Not a word was spoken between us, yet somehow he was telling me this was it. He was letting me go. I felt my heart contract with panic. It scrambled to hammer against my ribs in protest, but just like that, Nova let go of my hand and the wind rushed from my lungs. It felt like I'd been kicked in the chest. I tried to catch my breath, but I couldn't. My vision tunneled and I swayed, falling to my knees without Nova to steady me.

I called out to him from the ground, but as he anxiously spoke to me, I couldn't hear his words. Soon I saw more faces. Remi, Journey, my sister. My ears were ringing so loudly that it forced my eyes closed. I felt like I was swaying and when I opened my eyes I saw the stars moving above me. I was being carried through the forest. Carried by someone or something strong. I tried to speak but it was as if I was choking on something thick and warm, filling my throat and lungs. My stomach lurched and my body convulsed fighting against the choking liquid. I screamed out in pain and fear and then everything faded away.

Blackness.

When I opened my eyes, Nova's face was inches from mine. Relief instantly washed over him, changing his expression back to the handsome, charming one he'd worn when I'd first met him. He kissed my face all over. My forehead, my cheeks, my fluttering eye lids and finally my lips. I drank in the sweetness of his affection, craving it when he pulled away.

"Tippy, oh thank god you're okay."

"What happened?" I mumbled, feeling sluggish with sleep.

"It doesn't matter. I was wrong. I was wrong about all of it. We need to be together. I can see that now. Being apart will do us no good, but we have to leave here. We have to leave right now!"

"Leave? Where will we go? What about the legend and history repeating itself?"

"Do you trust me?"

"Yes."

"Then I need you to come with me right now."

I followed Nova out of the tent and into the night. We ran through the forest until we reached a spot where he'd hidden a horse. He lifted me up onto its back and then mounted behind me.

"Wait. Nova, where are we going? Are we really leaving? What about our friends?"

"They can't come with us Tippy. It can only be us. This is our time and it's about time we put ourselves first for once."

"But – "

Sensing my doubt, he wrapped his arms around me and whispered into my ear, "Your life will always be filled with uncertainty Tippy. At some point you have to take a risk. You have to trust in love and fate and each other. I want someone to face this crazy life with. I want to face it with you. Together."

I was spell bound and I nodded, knowing I'd follow him anywhere. He kissed me as my heart did cartwheels inside my chest.

With that he heeled the horse and we galloped away into the darkness. After putting a good distance between us and the Beto camp, Nova pulled up our steed. He was spent and we were all in need of some rest, so we found a quiet opening in the forest canopy to bed down for the night. We left the horse to graze on the dew damp grass, while Nova spread a blanket out in the sodden meadow, to protect us from the chill of night. The air was cool, but sweet and alive with dancing lava pixies and the song of the night creatures.

My heart was pounding as I sat down on the blanket. I'd never done something so bold. We had no plan, we'd abandoned our friends and family, and my destiny, but I'd never felt so alive.

"Nova, what changed your mind? I thought you said you were no good for me?"

"Well, we proved we're no good apart either and I will not sit by and watch you suffer. I was a fool to think we could be apart," he said gazing down at me, the stars of the night sky surrounding his beautiful silhouette. "I can't be without you, any more than I can be without air."

"But the legend," I whispered as he closed the space between us, touching his lips to mine.

"What about it?" he said between kisses.

"There'll be consequences."

"Let the heavens fall for all I care. As long as I'm with you, I'm happy," he grinned.

My heart shuttered with glee. Nova was saying every word I'd ever wished to hear upon his breath. I couldn't stop smiling as he kissed and embraced me on the soft meadow floor.

"But if this ever isn't what you want… if you get tired of being on the run with me, just say the words and we can go back," he said as I breathlessly stared into his vivid green eyes.

"Never," was all I said as I pulled him closer, until he blocked out the light of the moon and stars and all I saw was him as I drifted into the happiest moment of my life thus far.

CHAPTER XLII

I awoke well rested. I stretched my stiff limbs and yawned in the warm sunlight that cradled my aching body. When my sleepy eyes finally focused on my new surroundings I balked, sitting bolt upright.

"Good, you're awake," Remi said smiling down at me.

"Remi?" I asked in utter confusion. "But… I thought… Where's Nova?"

"Hold on, I've gotta get Eja. Don't move."

Remi ran from the tent, leaving me alone to contemplate how I'd gotten here. The last thing I remembered was … my cheeks flushed as my mind was flooded with the memories of Nova and I escaping together to spend the night in the forest, on the run from our lives and problems. But, how did I end up back here at the Beto camp.

I stood up, ignoring Remi's orders and peeked my head out of the tent. We were in the same place I remembered fleeing last night. My head felt so hazy and my balance faltered. I was stumbling back to the hammock I'd awoken in, when Eja and Remi came back into the tent. They both helped steady me so I could sit down.

"I told you not to move," Remi scolded.

"What happened last night?" I asked looking at both of them.

"My mind is so foggy and I thought..." I trailed off. "I don't remember how I got here?"

"You passed out again last night. I think you were having visions. It was sort of like you were possessed. You got up and were sleep walking or something. You kept trying to get to Nova and when we tried to stop you, you started screaming and thrashing around, and your nose was bleeding badly. Vida had to give you something to sedate you," Remi said, looking apologetic.

"What?" I asked feeling crushed.

Was any of what happened last night real? Did I dream it? Was it a vision or a cruel hallucination? I should have known it was all too good to be true, but it had felt so real. My heart felt like it was in my throat and my head was pounding.

"Where's Nova?" I asked again, trying to catch my breath. "I need to talk to him."

Remi looked uncomfortable and didn't reply.

"Where is he!?" I demanded.

"Geneva, we need you to remain calm," Eja said.

"What aren't you telling me!? Is he hurt?!" I cried getting to my feet unsteadily. I took a step and nearly collapsed, but Remi moved quickly and caught me.

"No, Eva, he's fine. The chief just doesn't want him to see you right now."

"What!?" I screeched in outrage.

"You two were talking last night right before you passed out. We're not sure if he did something to upset you, so the chief is just being cautious. He's trying to keep you calm until we can help you."

"Nova didn't do anything!" I yelled. "He's not dangerous. He's not Kull!"

"My Eva, please calm down. You are probably still feeling the effects of the sleeping potion we gave you. We need you to remain calm. It should wear off shortly," Eja assured me.

"You drugged me?" I whispered, astonished as I looked from Eja to Remi.

"It wasn't like that," Remi said, unable to mask his devastation. "We were trying to help you."

"In the meantime, the chief is on his way to see you. He says it's imperative that you share your powers with Jemma right now. We can't wait any longer," Eja interjected.

"No! I'm not ready. I don't trust her," I argued feeling defensive.

"I'm afraid you don't have the luxury of time," Jaka said as he entered the tent with my sister by his side.

"Hello my Eva, I'm glad you are awake and I'm sorry that we had to drug you last night, but I'm sure Eja explained it was for your own good. You're powers are overwhelming you. We cannot wait any longer. You are in danger of being consumed by all the power you possess."

"But – ," I started.

"Trying to contain all of them is making you a beacon for the Ravinori. If you share your powers with Jemma, it'll hopefully throw them off your trail, protecting all of us. That's what you want isn't it?" Jaka asked.

He was right, but I felt backed into a corner. I didn't trust my back stabbing sister one bit, but that didn't seem to matter to anyone. So I tried a different tactic.

"What if my powers are too much for Jemma? Isn't anyone concerned for her safety?"

Her eyes got big and she turned to the chief. "They won't hurt me will they?"

"When she shared her healing power with you, it didn't hurt did it?"

"No…"

"Well then there's no reason to believe this will be any different."

I could see the chief wasn't going to let up.

"Fine! Let's just get this over with," I muttered. "What do you want me to do?"

"I'd like you to share each one of your powers with your sister. One at a time please and slowly, to make sure she can handle them."

I walked over to Jemma and looked into her dark, conniving eyes. Her lips twitched up as she tried to suppress a triumphant smirk. It killed me that she was getting everything she wanted. My powers, my boyfriend… and she didn't have to suffer any of the consequences. I raised my hands and clamped them down hard on her shoulders. She did the same.

"Are you ready?" I asked begrudgingly.

"Of course," she smiled sweetly.

"It may hurt. Are you sure you can handle it?"

"If *you* can handle it, I can handle it."

"Fine. Just remember you asked for this."

"Bring it on sis," she smirked coyly. "Oh and since I heard the notion of you and Nova being an item is off the table, I'd prefer you share that nifty little empath power of yours first. I'd *love* to know what he's feeling inside that pretty head of his."

I gawked at her.

"Don't worry. I'll take good care of him."

In that moment, as the rage coursed through my veins, I decided I was going to make sharing my powers with Jemma as difficult and painful as possible.

I dug my nails into her skin and closed my eyes, channeling all my energy, anger and power towards my sister and I didn't stop. Not even when she buckled and screamed out in pain. Not when my nose started bleeding again and Remi looked like he was going to jump out of his skin. I kept going, until finally the tightness in my chest and the buzzing in my ears had diminished.

I released Jemma's trembling arms and she fully collapsed to the ground. Small droplets of blood were oozing from where I had dug my nails in. I felt sick, as bile quickly and unexpectedly rose up from my gut and I rushed from the tent to heave the contents of my stomach.

I sat outside the tent for a long time, listening to Jemma groan and cry. Niv crawled into my lap and I scooped him up, burying my face into his soft fur. I felt awful. I couldn't believe that I'd let such hatred take hold of me. I was frightened of myself. Maybe the chief was right, maybe I was beginning to be consumed by my own powers. At least I prayed that was the case. I would have never thought I could hurt someone. But as I formed the thought, Greeley's face filled my mind and I found myself vomiting again.

I felt a cool hand on my shoulder and looked up to see Eja standing over me.

"It is done," he said.

"What does that mean? Is she going to be okay?"

"Yes, your sister is very strong. Vida has given her something to help her sleep, but she should be fine by morning."

"I didn't mean to hurt her like that. I – ," I stopped short and let my head drop in shame.

"What's wrong?"

"That's a lie. I think I did mean to hurt her. I was thinking about how angry she makes me and how unfair this all is and I wanted her to suffer, just like I suffer. But I lost control… I'm no good at this. I should never have been chosen to be the Eva."

"That's not true Geneva. You've done more good than you know," Eja said.

"Like what?"

"Like this."

I looked up to see what he was talking about. He was pointing to his chest. His marks were still there. The tattoos had stuck!

"Oh Eja! It worked!"

"It seems you were right, we are a family after all," he smiled.

"You've made me a legitimate member of the Beto society Geneva and that means the world to me. I will always owe you my deepest gratitude."

This perked me up a bit. I returned his smile and hugged him.

"So you owe me huh? Enough to let me talk to Nova?"

"My Eva…"

"Please Eja. I need to talk to him. I'm so confused about what I remember from last night. I need to know what was real and what wasn't. Besides, I shared my powers with Jemma. I should be able to control myself now, right?"

He nodded slowly.

"What better way to test it, than seeing if Nova and I can have a normal conversation?"

"You make a good point," he said. He looked over his shoulder. Camp was pretty deserted. Everyone was occupied in the tent with Jemma. "Come on," Eja said.

CHAPTER XLIII

Kobel's eyes flew open wide and he gasped for air.

"What is it Kobel? Did it work?"

Kobel ran to the table, where the Book of Gods lay open. He stared at it, panic washing the remaining color from his age-creased face. After a moment of watching the empty page before him, he slowly pulled his brimless white cap from his head, mashing it against his chest, defeated.

"I've lost her master."

"What do you mean? Did she stop using her powers? Is she blocking you somehow?"

"No, master. I mean she may have been gravely injured."

"What!?" he growled. "What did you do?"

"I don't know. I may have pushed too hard. But, it was working, she was responding to me, but then suddenly, nothing. It's like she just vanished. Everything went dark and now, the little bit of power that was still pulsing, pulling me towards her, … it's almost nonexistent. And not like before, when she'd just stopped using her powers. This time it feels different, more permanent. Like her powers are at half life, or expiring."

"You fool! You ruined everything!" he thundered, grabbing Kobel by the throat and lifting him off of the floor with one hand. "We needed the Eva alive and with her powers!" he hissed into the old man's face as he pushed him against the stone wall with crushing force. Kobel's legs twitched as he struggled. One of his sandals came off, skittering to the floor while Kobel sputtered for air.

"Master … we can still complete the ritual without her," he managed to squeak out.

"How?" he asked, letting Kobel fall to the floor in a heap of white robes.

"We only need the Pillars. We can draw enough power from sacrificing them to do what we need."

"And just how do you suppose we find them without her? She was a descendant of the goddess Zophia. We needed her help to track them down and her blood to bind the spell!"

"She has a sister. They share the same blood. The Eva has already located the fire Pillar. We only have to find the other three. I'm thinking we can use the sister for that as well."

"I don't care whose blood we have to spill, but we will complete the ritual! Dispatch the rest of the mercenaries. Surround the forest and flush them out."

CHAPTER XLIV

"Hey," I whispered, causing Nova to jump.

I thought he'd heard me come up behind him, but he must've been lost in thought. I watched as a mix of emotions rapidly washed over his perfect features. He looked surprised and happy to see me, like he was going to reach out and hug me, but then a dark, sadness stopped him and the familiar light in his eyes clouded over.

"You shouldn't be here," was all he said as he leaned back against the tree he was near, hunching his shoulders.

"No, it's okay. I'm okay now."

"What do you mean?"

"I shared my powers with Jemma," I said, mustering up as much excitement as I could, given how against it I'd been.

He shook his head and laughed. "I didn't think you'd do it. What do I know though?"

"You know a lot. You know I didn't want to do it. But, what choice did I have?"

"I do feel a bit better," I added when he didn't reply.

Nova just kept looking down.

"Nova," I said, reaching out to touch his arm.

He recoiled away from me like I was poison.

"Don't! Don't touch me Geneva, it's not safe. I'm not safe."

"What are you talking about?"

"Last night. I let you go and... and..." his eyes grew darker. There were deep shadows under them like he hadn't slept. "The chief doesn't think it's a good idea for us to be alone together after what happened last night."

"What about what I want?"

He still wouldn't look at me.

"Will you at least tell me what happened last night?"

Still nothing.

"Look, I at least would like to know what I imagined and what was real."

"What do you mean?"

"Well, I remember talking to you and deciding ... " It was too hard to get into it again. My heart wasn't strong enough after all the wounds I'd inflicted lately. "We decided I should just focus on finding the Pillars. I remembering being sad and hugging you, and then... " I trailed off again.

"Then what?"

"I think I imagined the rest. I think I had a vision or hallucination or my mind just made up its own reality since the truth was too much to take. I dreamt that we ran away together and we never looked back. We said to hell with all of these legends and prophecies and we just took off."

Nova was looking at me now. It was as if I was watching his heart break all over again. It seemed worse now in the daylight, without the cloak of night to soften his despair. He looked like he wanted to reach out to me so badly, but he didn't. I could see the wall go back up, closing me off from his vulnerability and true feelings.

"That's not what happened Tippy. You collapsed. You were convulsing, having some sort of seizure I think. You were screaming and I couldn't get you to calm down. Your nose was gushing and you were choking on it. I was trying to help you, but you kept screaming at me like you didn't even know me. Talon came and got you. He carried you back to camp and Vida treated you. She gave you something to calm you down. I don't know what happened after that. They wouldn't let me in the tent. They had Mali and Journey standing outside my tent all night like they thought I was going to do something to hurt you," he said sounding hurt.

"Later that night Sparrow said you got up and were looking for me. She said you were in a trance and trying to find me. Vida didn't want to wake you, she said it could be dangerous, but you started to wander away from camp so they had to, but you were deranged beyond reason and they had to drug you again. That's all I know. They don't want me near you and they're probably right."

We stood silently apart for a moment, each gazing into the forest lost in our own thoughts. I was quietly grieving the life I'd dreamt of for Nova and I as runaways. I didn't know what he was thinking, but I knew it couldn't be good because when I looked at his face, he was grinding his jaw muscles. Something he only did when he was wrestling his own inner demons.

"Thank you for telling me what happened Nova. I really do feel better now. I don't know what happened last night, but one thing I do know, is that you didn't cause it. I know you'd never hurt me and I don't accept that we need to stay apart. We're doing just fine right now. Besides, I'll need your help if we're going to find the other Pillars."

He looked at me without any emotion and nodded. "If you need my help, you'll have it."

❖ ❖ ❖

Everyone was in a somber mood after the events of the past week, but today was a new day and I was determined to do something productive with it. Jemma had recovered from our power sharing.

She was in surprisingly good spirits, even around me. I guess since she'd gotten what she wanted, she wasn't holding my brutal methods against me.

I was just happy that I wasn't having anymore crazy fainting spells or visions or nose bleeds. We'd all had time to process what the chief had told us about the Ponte Deorum, Striga Carta, and the legend about the four realms. It was still a lot to take in, but like all things, time made it easier to digest somehow.

I asked Eja to get everyone together for the first time since we'd all learned I was the Ponte Deorum. We gathered inside his tent. The floor was littered with papers and journals, all strewn about in a wide radius encircling the Book of Secrets.

"So, I know a lot has happened and it's a lot more complicated than we first thought now that we know I'm the Ponte Deorum. But, I think if we all work together, we can still accomplish our goals," I said hopefully.

I looked around at the faces of my friends, but none of them shared my optimism. Remi looked pained and I could tell he was trying to keep it together for my sake. Sparrow was sitting alone, her ever present shadow, Journey hadn't returned from scouting yet. She was fragilely folded next to Remi, with her worry written clearly across her delicate face. She unwound an arm that she had wrapped tightly around her long fawnlike legs to swipe at her loose strands of hair. A single tear escaped her glassy amber eyes. She was rocking back and forth, her fears and anxieties mirroring my own manifestations. I could feel the worry in the room, even after sharing my powers with Jemma. I was thankful that they were dulled to half power in moments like these. I hated having to feel everyone else's pain and fears on top of my own.

I was grateful to Remi when he put his arm around Sparrow's slender shoulders. It instantly dimmed her pain, allowing me a comforting reprieve from her emotions. Without Sparrow's fears overpowering my mind, I was able to feel the mood of the rest of the room and I was surprised to find joy mixed in among the worry and sympathy my friends were emoting on my behalf.

Of course, once I traced it back to its source, I should have known Jemma would have been reacting that way. I was amazed she was actually able to contain her delight. She was making a great show of acting sad so that she could cry on Nova's shoulder, but I could read her like an open book. Maybe it was sisterly intuition? Maybe it was because we were even more connected after sharing powers? I could see the slight curve of her heart shaped lips, lift into a grin every so often, while she pretended to weep for me. It was obvious to me that she was rejoicing inside about how I probably wouldn't be around long enough to compete for Nova's affection, now that I had the added danger of being the Ponte Deorum to shoulder.

She is not my competition, I scolded myself. *I can't be with Nova. Not right now anyway.*

I shook my head and cleared my mind, refocusing before addressing the group again.

"I've spoken to the chief and he's agreed to allow us to stay behind. I know packing up and moving each day has made it really hard to get much accomplished. Not to mention that it's exhausting now that we're not able to use our powers to travel by morfing. I think it just makes more sense for us to stay in one spot, especially with the tribe moving further and further away from the Troian Center, which would only make our inevitable trek back even harder."

"We're going to be alone?" Sparrow asked sounding frightened.

"No, we'll have protection," I replied. "And it's only for a day. I want to return to the Troian Center the day after next."

"Two days?" Remi asked, sounding leery.

"Yes, I know it's soon, and we have a lot of work to do, but we can't use powers and we're just wasting time here if we can't train. Journey said he and the scouts have mapped out a safe route back.

They're doing the final check now," I said, trying to reassure everyone.

"The chief has agreed to let us stay as long as Mali and Talon stay with us. He said they volunteered to offer us protection and guidance should we need it. Vida and her family will stay behind as well, to cook and care for us," Eja informed the group.

As if on cue, Jovi came in with our dinner. It was a welcomed interruption, I thought, suddenly realizing how hungry I was. My stomach growled as the air filled with the wonderful aroma of the meal; corn cakes with figs and tree frog stew.

Even though I'd had a few rocky moments with Vida, I was very grateful that she had offered to stay with us. She was an incredible healer, even without using powers and she was an even better cook, I thought as I dug into the stew Jovi brought me. I let Niv gobble up the remaining crumbs from my meal, while Eja recapped our strategy for finding the Pillars. I knew I should be paying attention, but my mind wandered. We'd been over the Book of Secrets a million times. We knew who was looking for who. Going over it again was taxing. Besides, Jaka said I'd feel it when the Pillars were near. I was basically a one woman Pillar-tracker.

All I could think about as Eja reiterated the characteristics of each Pillar's element, was how miserable it made me to watch my elated sister flirting with Nova. It reignited the flame for him that I'd barely snuffed out and I couldn't stop thinking that there had to be some way to get Nova back. Perhaps if I saved the Pillars and defeated the Ravinori, that would be it? I would have fulfilled my destiny as the Eva and would be free to live the rest of my days as I saw fit. I knew I was grasping at straws, but it was the only glimmer of hope I had right now and I was clinging to it with all of my might.

CHAPTER XLV

I stroked Niv's silky fur while I lay in my hammock. I'd retreated to my tent immediately after our group meeting. Taking in everyone's emotions had exhausted me. Plus, I couldn't bear to be in the same room with Jemma and Nova. I needed some time to gather my thoughts, so I pulled my journal from my tattered shoulder bag. It had been my solace in times like these, I repeated the charm that would only reveal its contents to me and I opened my journal, finding comfort in its pages once more.

I reread some of my previous entries from the last year. Looking back now, my worries back then seemed so simple and trivial. I would give anything to have my biggest worries be, *Will I ever learn my real name?* Or *Will I learn to sing?* Or *Will I make more friends?* It was crazy how much my life had changed in a year. I'd accomplished a lot. At the time all the new things I was dealing with, like learning I had powers and trying to control them, to finding the Book of Secrets, all seemed like insurmountable tasks, yet I'd done them. This gave me hope for the future. If I could just get past this next step, maybe I could figure the rest out along the way.

I opened the journal to a blank page and started writing. It was the first time I'd written since learning I was the Ponte Deorum. It felt like it was the first entry to the rest of my life.

Dear Journal

I don't even know where to begin. So much has happened since I've last written. My life continues to change beyond my wildest dreams. Sadly, I don't know if this change is for the better. I guess the saying is true, "be careful what you wish for." I wished I knew my name and that I had a family and friends and maybe even a boyfriend. Well I got all of those things, but just like a devious genie in a lamp might grant your wishes, there was no guarantee they'd be executed the way you had hoped. This realization makes me feel even more of a kinship to Zophia, whom I'm supposedly a reincarnation of. I bet she had never imagined that her true love would be murdered by a jealous suitor and she would be tricked into becoming the portal to the four realms of the universe.

I don't know who had it worse, me or her? I'm sadly hopeful it's her. After all, I'm the Eva, the chosen one, meant to restore peace and equality to all on Hullabee Island. I can't be doomed to fail with a destiny like that, can I? There is so much responsibility in this role, so much I'm unprepared for. I feel grateful to know who I am, but I also feel like I've given up the carefree childhood I'd hoped to have. Learning my true identity seemed to let the veil of naivety slip from my life and now I can see things for how they truly are; dark and depressing.

Like the fact that I can't even enjoy that I do have a family. My mother is a ghost, a dead goddess to be exact, but I can see her and talk to her, which apparently means I'm the Bridge of the Gods or Ponte Deorum as the Betos call it.

Things between Jemma and I don't seem to be going too well either. It feels so strange to have a sister; here in the flesh and blood. But she's not what I expected. It seems she doesn't believe in "blood being thicker than water." Before finding out Jemma was my sister, she had been my nemesis, making my life at the Troian Center a living hell. Then, after she had found out the truth from the Book of Secrets, there had been a time when

I really believed that maybe she wanted to start over and really be my sister and I had almost been gullible enough to buy it. But with everything she's put me through since, I should have trusted my gut. She's done nothing but hurt me.

Jemma is the same rotten Jane #31 I knew from the Troian Center. She only looks out for herself and it seems that she truly does get everything she wants. I had to share my powers with her since they were becoming too much for me, so now Jemma is as powerful as I am, yet without the bounty of the Eva and Ponte Deorum looming over her head. And now, she's set her sights on Nova. I'm not even sure if she actually has feelings for him or if she just wants to hurt me. The one thing I do know, is that Jemma always gets what she wants.

I still don't know what actually happened between the two of them in the hammock. Nova seems unwilling to admit he and Jemma are anything but friends. Sparrow tells me I've got it all wrong, and maybe she's right. I know the tendency of a jealous heart to see its deepest fears. It's what Nova thinks every time Remi and I are near each other. Whatever I thought I saw, it's nothing compared to the excruciating pain I feel now, as I sit by and watch Jemma take over the life I want; my friends, my powers, my Nova.

But since I've found out that I'm the Ponte Deorum, I have to remind myself that perhaps this is all happening the way it's meant to. Maybe it's better to let Jemma have it all. That way I can distance myself from everyone, because these days I feel like I can sense the end. The dangers I feel and see in my visions are so real that I have almost accepted that I'm marching to my death. And that terrifies me. I don't want to die, but I think I've always known that being the Eva would call for the ultimate sacrifice and cost me my life. But, if in the end, it protects the people I love, then I will have served a purpose. And what more can you ask for in life?

However, I do know, that no matter how it all goes down, I'm not going without a fight.

CHAPTER XLVI

The sunlight streamed in through the seams in the tent, casting beautiful displays of floating dust, suspended in a slow motion waltz, as if under some spell cast by the sun. My pale eyelashes fluttered lazily awake as I rubbed the sleep from them. I swung out of my hammock and stretched, inhaling the sweet scents of the forest's early morning dew. For a split second I felt normal, hopeful even, but then the heavy sinking feeling in my chest slammed me back to my harsh reality.

Today was our last day in the forest. We were planning to head back to the Troian Center tomorrow at dawn. Journey had reported that he and the scouts had mapped out a secure path for us to take. They had spent a lot of time finding the safest route, where there didn't seem to be any activity from hunters, predators or Grifts. Even Mali and Talon were convinced we were finally ready.

I was a bundle of tingling nerves as I got dressed and prepared to meet my friends one last time to go over our plan.

"Morning," yawned Remi, slinging an arm over my shoulder as soon as I emerged from my tent. "Have you had breakfast yet? I heard Vida made fresh sugar cane cakes!"

"Oh really?"

"Come on, let's go get 'em while they're hot!" he said prodding me along.

Remi had always been much more of a morning person than me. I yawned and protested half-heartedly as he pushed me towards the sweet smell of freshly baked bread while he chattered on and on. As we passed by the other tents, I saw Nova push open his tent flap and gawk at Remi and I as we walked past him arm in arm. I don't think Remi noticed him staring at us, but I was secretly smiling inside when I saw the look of shock and possibly jealousy on his face. In a shameful place, I tried to keep buried deep inside, it was good to know Nova still cared about me enough to look envious.

Remi had been right, the sugar cane cakes were delicious. Jovi's mom was a genius when it came to cooking. I think we had all put on some much needed weight since she'd been cooking for us and we were grateful for every meal. I would sure miss her cooking when we were back at the Troian Center, but luckily she made extra cakes for us to take on our trek back.

I sat cross-legged on the floor next to Remi as he chatted with Eja and Sparrow while watching Niv forage for our crumbs. Journey and Jovi were still eating, deep in conversation about the best ways to train a wex. She obviously wasn't revolted by his horrible tendency to talk with his mouth full. Nova, was being standoffish and Jemma hadn't emerged from her tent yet, which was fine by me.

When she finally did, I heard her and Nova arguing with each other.

"You said you were going to wait for me," Jemma pouted.

"Yeah, well you were taking forever," Nova grumbled.

"I'm still getting used to these powers. They make me feel strange. You said you were going to help me with them Nova," she whined.

"And I will," he said softening his tone.

"Well, you could have started by walking me to breakfast ..." Jemma huffed, testing Nova's patience.

"Jemma! That has nothing to do with your powers. You can make it 20 feet from your own tent to breakfast," he scolded. And then he added under his breath, "Besides, something came up."

My ego soared. Maybe I was that something. Maybe seeing me with Remi made him realize he didn't want to give up on us. Besides, he and Jemma didn't seem very cozy this morning. I tried to suppress my smile and focus on the task at hand as Eja called us all over to the Book of Secrets.

We poured over the Book of Secrets for hours. Since we'd already thoroughly researched the Pillars and we knew we'd be relying on my built in Pillar tracking skills, for the most part anyway, we decided to go back to exploring some of the names we'd come across in the Book of Secrets.

We were going over the names it listed for others with powers and trying to match them up with who we thought they might be describing from the Troian Center. It was a daunting task. It's not like the book came with photos of who they were describing. They only came with a name and that was really no use to us because each orphan at the Center had been stripped of their names and identities. Instead, they were known only as John or Jane and the number they were tattooed with.

Also making the task more difficult, was the fact that there were so many orphans at the Center and we really didn't know any of the Johns or Janes outside of our own year. At least Nova knew some of the older orphans since he was a year older than the rest of us. Jemma made herself useful by reminding us that she was so popular and that she knew some of the older orphans too. Even Sparrow and Journey had some insight on others in our year that they knew, but Remi and I seemed to be utterly useless. I guess years of being shy, unpopular outcasts was really hurting our chances of finding these other Truiets.

"What about Jane #16? Do you think she could be Kaylen?" Journey offered.

"No way. I think she sounds more like Jane #53," Nova argued.

"I was thinking #53 sounded like Staley," Journey said pointing to a translated passage in the book.

"Oh, I was thinking Staley was a guy's name."

"What do you think Eva?" Eja asked as the arguing continued.

He still didn't seem to catch onto my feeling of helplessness after I shrugged for what felt like the hundredth time someone asked for my opinion on who so-and-so could be.

Remi gave me an encouraging nudge with his shoulder. I was relieved that at least one person here totally understood me. It made me smile and gave me enough confidence to interrupt the lively debate between Nova and Journey about who they each insisted probably had magical powers.

"This is going nowhere you guys. We're supposed to be looking for Pillars, not arguing over who you all know at the Troian Center. I wish the Book of Secrets listed names for the Pillars. Even just family names would be useful. Can we go back to the section about the Pillars again Eja? There has to be something we can use there."

"We can definitely revisit it my Eva, but it's clear that the names of the Pillars aren't listed for their protection and because their powers change hands so often; being passed down through the generations."

I sighed in frustration. The Book of Secrets was nothing but a riddle. It gave us names for people who didn't use them and element characteristics for people who had names.

"How do we even know the Pillars are here on Hullabee Island?" Remi asked.

"That part we know, because the Ravinori are here searching for them as well. Their sole purpose is to find them and use them to bring Ravin back. They wouldn't be here on our island if the Pillars weren't here. Let me just find that passage … " Eja trailed off, flipping through the pages.

"Ah here it is."

" '… it is power they seek, so those that possess the most will risk the most. There are four individuals the Ravinori covet the most to create and control the four Pillars of this world, Earth, Wind, Water and Fire. It is said that those who control these elements can control the world.' "

The humid forest air hung heavy above us. It was laced with silence and somberness after Eja finished reading. I looked around at my friends. Each of their faces set with a stern expression. My eyes finally rested on Nova. It was clear to me that he was fire. Everything about him screamed fire to me, even before I had seen him produce his flame in the forest that fateful night. Even without the chief comparing him to Kull. Nova's bright emerald eyes always had a glow about them, as if lit from within by some mysterious internal inferno. His combustible personality, the way I could so quickly ignite his temper, the way he made my skin flush with heat when he was near, the spark I felt whenever he touched me, the way his blond hair curled in sections, like flames, licking his forehead. There was no doubt in my mind that Nova was the fire Pillar. And I could tell when his gaze met mine that he knew it too. The reality of the situation made our feuding seem trivial. All I wanted to do now, was protect him.

CHAPTER XLVII

We ended our meeting without any new direction. We would focus our search on the Pillars as planned. Once they were safe, I knew I would focus on rescuing the rest of the Johns and Janes at the Troian Center. I wouldn't rest until every last one of them was freed of that evil institution that had imprisoned us.

Everyone seemed ready to divide and conquer. Sparrow and Jemma would seek water, Remi and I would search for wind and Journey and Nova would look for earth. In an unspoken agreement, we all seemed to know that searching for fire was futile since Nova seemed to fit the bill. While we were wrapping up the last of the details, I saw Nova slip away and I couldn't help worrying about him, so I excused myself and went after him.

"Nova, wait up," I called to him, jogging to catch up.

When I got to his side I could see that he was wiping away the remains of tears from his glimmering green eyes. I was so taken aback I didn't know what to say. Nova was always so strong, so brave. To see him cry stunned me, so I did the only thing that felt right. I closed the space between us and hugged him tight. It felt so good to feel his warm chest against me again. He hugged me back and I felt a new conviction to fight the Ravinori. It would be over my dead body that I'd let anyone hurt this boy.

"Nova, it's going to be alright. We're going to find the others and we're going to get you all away from here and hide you from the Ravinori. I won't let anything happen to you."

"Tippy, it's not that."

I looked up at him, "It's not?" I said confused.

He smiled down at me. "Well okay, it's a little of that. But something else too."

I continued looking at him, waiting for him to elaborate. He let our embrace end and sat down on a mossy trunk, patting it for me to join him.

"After hearing all those names in there, it made me think of my sister."

"Ivy," I said solemnly, remembering Eja rattling that name off of the list of dozens of others in the Book of Secrets.

"Yes. It made me think that maybe she's still alive and I'm paralyzed by the hope that she is. I mean what if she's somewhere out there Tippy? What if she needs my help?"

I looked at the sadness in his eyes and could feel his pain.

"I've been talking to Jemma about this. I mean Jemma thought you were dead and you had no recollection of her at all because you were so young. My sister was your age when the Flood hit. You survived. Maybe she did too!" he said sounding hopeful.

"Is that why you've been spending so much time with Jemma?"

"Yeah. That and trying to help her manage all your powers, which is kind of impossible since we can't actually use them," he groaned. "Why else?"

My heart soared. Could all of my jealousy be completely misconstrued?

"I thought ..." I paused when the image of them in the hammock popped back into my mind.

"Tippy, if there's a chance that my sister could be out there, I have to try ..."

"Nova…" I started, softly placing my hand on his.

"Don't Tippy. Don't say that it's not possible."

"I wasn't going too. It's just that I don't think you should focus on that right now. Right now we need to focus on getting back to the Troian Center safely and finding the other Pillars before the Ravinori do. Then, we have to try to get you all somewhere safe."

"I know," he sighed, sounding resigned.

It made my heart ache to see him this way.

"After we do all of that, I promise I'll help you find out about Ivy."

He smiled at me and finally squeezed my hand back.

We returned back to camp to find everyone starting to prepare for our long trek home. Eja went to meet with Jaka one last time, while Journey and Nova caught up with Mali and Talon and the rest of the scouts for their final reconnaissance mission. The rest of us stayed behind with the daunting job of packing.

I tried to focus on packing, but it was useless. My mind kept wandering; swirling with images of Nova and Jemma, terrifying visions where Nova was consumed by fire and I could do nothing to save him. It went on and on, each vision worse than the last, until I shook myself from my last trepidation and gave up on packing all together.

The day was still young and I was determined to enjoy what might be my last day of happiness in the forest I'd come to love. I walked over to where Jovi and Vida were bundling our rations.

"Is there anything I can do to help?" I offered.

"I was just getting ready to go gather some ingredients for mom," Jovi replied. "Do you want to come with me?"

"Jovi, our Eva has more important things to do than scour the forest for fruit and berries with you, darling."

"Nonsense. I'd love to help," I said with a wink at Jovi. "I bet I could get Sparrow and Jemma to help us too and then we'd probably be back in time to have some fun. How does that sound?"

"Uh, you're supposed to stay here Geneva," Remi called over his shoulder as he rolled up a blanket.

"Says who?"

"Nova and the scouts."

"Well, I say I'm more useful helping Jovi gather food for our trip. The Eva can't let her people starve now can she?" I said, turning stubbornly away from him and grabbing a basket.

Jovi, followed suit and we marched into the forest, stopping briefly to convince Sparrow and Jemma to join us.

CHAPTER XLVIII

Jovi and I were having the best time gathering fruit in the forest. Her enthusiasm was contagious and she turned the task into a game. We were running and laughing as we competed to see who could find the most fruit. We took turns hiding and springing on each other too. I got Jovi so good on one occasion that she shrieked and threw her entire basket of berries into the air. We spent the next twenty minutes or so collecting them off the forest floor.

I loved that it was impossible to be in a sour mood when I was with Jovi. I found myself drawn to her for that very reason. The stress of my role as Eva, my feelings for Remi and Nova, my distrust of Jemma; it all seemed to take a back seat when Jovi and I spent time together.

She had so many questions for me. It felt strange to seem worldly to someone. After all, I had only ever known the Troian Center as my home. I got to go to Lux, once a year for the New Year Gala, but besides that, I really hadn't been anywhere. But to Jovi, who'd never left the forest, I guess my stories of the Locker and Lux sounded like fairytales.

"Do you think someday I'll get to go to Lux?" Jovi asked.

"Yes. I know you will."

"How?!" she asked wide-eyed.

"Well, I'm the Eva. I'm here to make sure that we all have the right to go to Lux or anywhere we want."

"So I won't have to hide in the forest forever?"

"Exactly."

"Promise?"

"I promise."

"Eeek!!!" Jovi squeezed her arms around me. "Thank you, thank you, thank you!"

"Do you think Quin can come to Lux?"

"Well, if you can get her to mind her manners, I don't see why not."

"Quin! Quin!" Jovi called in her sing-songy voice as she darted away from me in search of her wex.

"Did you hear that Quin?! We're going to get to go to Lux someday!"

I shook my head and laughed as I watched Jovi's head bouncing by, barely visible above the thick undergrowth.

"Not too far, alright Jovi?" I called after her.

"I know the way," she called back.

"I don't!" I hollered.

The forest always got me turned around. We moved so often that I never had a chance to get my bearings. If I used my powers I knew I could find my way back, but the chief had forbidden it since that's how he thought the Ravinori were tracking us.

"Sorry. I'm back," Jovi said, instantly back at my side. "I can't find Quin though."

"She knows the way back."

We pressed on, loading our baskets with mangos, avocados and berries.

"So, what shall I wear when I go to Lux?" Jovi asked.

"Anything you want."

"I heard everyone dresses in white and they wear flowers in their hair. Is that true?

"Yes, Lux is very beautiful. Did you know some of the women even dye their hair elegant pastel shades? And they all wear stunning jewelry!"

She stopped walking and bit her lip.

"What's wrong?"

"I don't have anything beautiful to wear," Jovi pouted.

I smiled and knelt down to her level.

"Jovi, you are beautiful no matter what you wear. You're a beautiful person on the inside and that's where it matters most. Besides, with all the goodies you have collected, I'm sure we can make you look wonderful you little pack-rat!"

At that she giggled.

"You're right."

"Good, now come on. I think we've collected enough. Let's go find Sparrow and Jemma and head back."

She sighed, but resigned to head back to camp.

"What did you wear when you went to Lux?" she asked after we walked a short while.

"Well, I was with the other orphans from the Troian Center. We all wore the same thing. Our white uniforms."

"And your hair?"

"Sparrow helped me braid my hair. She has a way of mending things and making them pretty," I smiled, remembering how I had been astonished when I saw my refection for the first time on the way to the last Gala.

Jovi was staring at my hair, as if trying to figure out what it would look like when it wasn't a tangled blonde mess of curls.

"What's got you so interested in Lux?"

"Well, I was saying that I'd never seen anyone look more beautiful than you did at the Eva ceremony but then Remi said you looked even more beautiful when you were at Lux for the New Year Gala last year," she blushed. "I want someone to say that about me."

"Remi said that?"

"Yes," she giggled. "He has a crush on you."

"I wouldn't say that. Remi is my best friend. We just say nice things about each other."

"No, he definitely has a crush. He talks about you all the time and I overheard him talking about you to Sparrow just yesterday. Do you have a crush on him too?!" she asked excitedly.

"Jovi, it's not kind to eavesdrop on people or to ask them such personal questions," I scolded.

"Sorry," she said, dipping her head in shame. "I didn't mean to."

"It's alright. Let's just find the girls and get back. It'll be dark soon."

We walked in silence the rest of the way. I was lost in thought about Remi after what Jovi said. Did he really still have feelings for me? I thought we had agreed to just be friends? It's true that after what happened in the cave, I'd opened my eyes to Remi more. I had never thought of him as anything other than my best friend and I think I was scared of taking a chance that he could be anything more. If I messed it up, and with my track record, I'm sure I would, I didn't want to risk losing his friendship. But, it appears that not making a decision might cause me to lose his friendship, along with a few others.

I wished he would stop talking about how much he liked me to Sparrow! I suspected she had a crush on him and that had to make her miserable to listen to him drone on about me. It's how I felt anytime Nova uttered my sister's name. Not to mention, I'm pretty sure that Journey is madly in love with Sparrow, and he'd probably be uncontrollable if he lost her to Remi. And, then there's the way Remi and Nova have been fighting. The two of them can't agree that the sky is blue. They'd been at each other's throats lately and I've been doing my best to ignore it, but I could feel it making everyone uncomfortable.

The whole thing was a royal mess, but I didn't know what to do about it. Should I just confront them all and hash it out already? I'm sure we'd all walk away a bit wounded, but maybe that'd be better than the tension we were all feeling. At least it would give us all a chance to heal and move on before we started our quest to the Troian Center together.

I was so deep in thought that a branch Jovi pushed out of her path came back at me harshly across the face, causing me to jump back to reality. And not a moment too soon. I heard the snap of the twig echo through the entirely too quiet forest. There should be birds chirping, monkeys calling, but there was nothing. The forest was still. My hunter powers burst into high alert as I swiftly grabbed Jovi's shoulders and pulled her to the forest floor.

"Geneva," she protested, but when her eyes locked with mine, they grew large with fear as she saw the urgency of my expression.

I lifted a single shaking finger to my lips. Jovi swallowed hard and nodded back at me.

CHAPTER XLIX

"Where's Geneva?" Nova asked as soon as he found Remi back at camp.

"I don't know, I'm not her keeper."

"That's exactly what you are!" Nova growled. "I told you to stay behind and look after her while Journey and I went with the scouts."

"Well Nova, if you knew anything about Geneva at all, you'd know she doesn't like to be told what to do. It pretty much makes her do the opposite of what you want her to do."

"So what'd you tell her to do?"

"Stay here with me and pack, while the girls went out to gather fruit."

Nova exchanged a nervous glance with Journey and took off towards the bustling center of camp where dinner was being prepared.

"What's going on?" Remi asked, matching stride with Journey as he headed in the same direction as Nova.

"We found evidence we're being followed and whoever it is, is nearby."

By the time Remi and Journey caught up with Nova again, he'd been joined by Talon and Mali. They all looked rattled.

"The women returned hours ago with their gatherings but Jemma, Sparrow, my sister and Geneva were not with them. They should have been back by now," Talon said.

"Come on Journey, we have to go find them. They might be in trouble," Nova barked as he laced a leather vest over his chest and collected spears for himself and Journey.

"We'll come with you," Talon said, motioning to Mali. "I know where Jovi likes to go."

Nova nodded gladly.

"I'm coming too," Remi said.

"No, you're not. You'll just slow us down. We don't have time to babysit you in the forest. Their lives might be at stake," Nova snarled

But Remi didn't back down.

"You're not the only one who cares about her, you know?"

Nova had already been walking away, but he turned abruptly to face Remi, who hadn't expected him to turn back. The sudden face off caught him off guard and he stumbled backwards. He would've fallen if Nova didn't catch him by his shirt collar.

"Do you ever notice, that when I leave her with you, these kinds of things happen? The cave, the pond and now this? I am always cleaning up after you and I'm glad to, because I love her. I would go into hell to save her. Would you?" he challenged.

Remi was stunned by the venom in Nova's tone, and hurt by the truth in his accusations. He was coming right out and saying it, drawing lines in the sand; Nova loved her and thought he was better for Geneva. Remi's voice was caught in his throat. He'd never heard Nova say anything so plainly, not laced with sarcasm and insults. His honesty stung, because deep down, Remi thought he was right.

"That's what I thought," Nova said, shaking his head in disgust. He let go of Remi. "You can barely stay on your own two feet, let alone rescue anyone."

Nova turned and stormed away into the forest to catch up with

Journey and the others.

I held Jovi's hand tightly and closed my eyes, willing my hunter's mind to stretch to encompass my surroundings. I could hear faint voices of men in the distance. From the sound of their footfall, I could tell there were six of them and from the weight of their steps they seemed to be heavily armed. That meant they weren't Betos and probably not even Grifts. They didn't normally carry weapons. I could hear the clanking of steel and mesh armor and smell the putrid scent of gun powder.

Soldiers? In the forest? Could it be? Maybe they were hunters? Maybe they'd been sent for me? Whoever it was, I didn't have much time to think about it, because what was certain was that they were moving towards us. We needed to get to an area where we could take cover. Crouching in the sparse undergrowth wasn't going to cut it. There was a large bank of thistle palms about a hundred yards away. If we moved now and kept low, we could make it there and stay downwind and out of sight.

"Jovi, I need you to follow me. You need to stay silent and stay as low as you can to the ground."

She nodded, her eyes wide with fear, but eager to obey.

We covered the ground quickly, side by side. Once we got to the thorny bushes I coaxed Jovi inside among the razor sharp branches. It was slow going, but we made it. With the protective cover of the wide fan leaves, I chanced a peek to see if I could spot the men I'd heard. What I saw stole my breath. Jemma and Sparrow were traipsing along without a care in the world, headed right in the path of the hunting party.

I knew I wasn't supposed to use my powers, but if I didn't warn Jemma and Sparrow, they'd surely be caught.

"Jemma! Sparrow! Drop down to the ground right now!"

I knew they heard me because they both paused and then

suddenly I saw Sparrow reach out and grab Jemma's arm before they both swiftly dropped out of view. They were hidden in the tall grass, but as soon as I breathed a sigh of relief, I saw the underbrush swaying and parting to my left. The voices of the men grew louder. They would be upon Sparrow and Jemma any minute. There was no time to call them to join us in the protection of the thistles. I was racking my brain for what powers I could use to help them. There wasn't time for anything!

I grabbed a few small stones and threw them as hard as I could in the opposite direction of the girls. I was hoping the noise would draw the men off our path. It had the desired effect when the stones struck a tree, causing a flock of birds into a frenzied flight.

"Something's spooked the birds. Let's go check it out," one of the men called.

Once they changed course, I contacted Sparrow and Jemma again.

"There's hunters in the forest. Jovi and I are in the thistle palms. Stay low and get over here now!"

I waited impatiently for a response.

Nothing.

"Jovi. I need you to stay here and stay silent. I'm going to go get them."

"No! Don't leave. Please don't leave me!"

"Jovi. It's going to be alright. Just stay here. Don't move okay?"

Before she could argue any further, I kissed her on top of her head and vanished. I could tell my invisibility was working from the look of sheer terror on Jovi's face. When I was sure she wasn't going to bolt, I left the safety of the thick line of thistle palms. I ran in the direction I'd last seen the girls and stumbled upon them laying in the same spot.

I fell on top of them, clamping my hands over both their mouths so they wouldn't scream and give us away.

"Come with me now!"

Neither of them argued. They were shaking and petrified when I grabbed each of their hands to share my power of invisibility. Once it was working in full force, we took off running towards the dense cluster of thistle palms. We were in the short clearing about 30 feet from the protection of the palms when the men came into clear view. I felt Sparrow balk in fear when her eyes locked on the heavily armed men. I pulled her forward, propelling her and Jemma ahead of me into the unforgiving thorns.

My entrance wasn't as graceful this time and my skin tore as it snagged on the razor sharp thorns. We rejoined Jovi and she breathed a sigh of relief, hugging me tightly when I let myself come back into sight. I held my finger back up to my lips and surveyed my friends. Their eyes bulging, and skin dripping ribbons of blood from where the thorns had caught them. Something warm and wet dripped into my eye. I swiped at it and pulled my hand away, bloody. I must have cut my forehead on the thorns. Jovi pulled a rag from her basket and offered it to me. I smiled at her and held it to my head as I tried to fight the waves of queasiness that flipped through my stomach.

I hated the sight and smell of blood. But we were safe, hidden from the men for now and that was the most important thing. We sat silently, watching the group of men stalking their way through the forest. They were definitely not Grifts and they seemed more than local hunters. They moved with lethal precision, like they'd been trained to do so. They wore all black and were adorned with strange, dark masks, barely visible beneath the hoods they wore. They carried weapons; staffs, bows, spears, swords and heavy shields. I was trying to make out the crest on them when I heard a twig snap loudly next to me.

The men stopped. The one in front lifted his hand in a fist, signaling to the others to turn around and head back. I panicked as I watched them flank out. They'd almost been through our area. We were just about free and clear. Who'd snapped a twig?! I was furious and scared as I turned to my friends to see what had made the noise. The looks on their faces matched mine when my eyes finally landed on the culprit.

A large tarcat flattened his ears and narrowed the slits of his bright yellow eyes at me, while he licked his vicious lips with hunger.

Remi charged through the forest, already out of breath and cut up from the unforgiving vegetation when he caught up to Nova and the others.

"Ah, so we go into hell together then?" Nova said, not taking his eyes off the horizon.

"Together," Remi said, as Journey shook his head with a smile and handed him a staff.

Nova nodded, gaining a small bit of respect for Remi in that moment.

It's about time, he thought to himself.

The boys moved through the forest quickly and silently. They fanned out, spaced a few yards away from each other so they could cover more ground. The sun was setting and once it got below the canopy of trees, the forest would fall into darkness. Time was of the essence. Even without the threat of hunters, the forest was not a safe place to be alone at night.

"Over here," Talon called.

The boys all changed course to meet him. He was holding a panting wex under his arm.

"Quin?" Remi whispered.

This wasn't a good sign and they all knew it.

"She never leaves my sister," Talon said, unable to hide the worry in his voice.

"Maybe that means she's not too far from here?" Remi offered trying to give hope to the grim situation.

"Luckily I know someone who can ask her," Nova said.

Everyone looked to him as he patted his shoulder and Niv scurried out of his pack and perched by his neck. The little marmouse sniffed the air rapidly, while twitching his nose and combing his long whiskers.

Quin, whined when she saw him. Niv's ears perked and he snapped to attention, locking eyes with the wex. He started chattering angrily, but Nova stroked his bristled coat.

"Niv, it's okay. We need your help. Tippy needs your help. She's lost in the forest with Jovi, Sparrow and Jemma. Quin was with them and she came to find us. Can you talk to Quin and find out where they are?"

"Um, what's going on here?" Journey asked skeptically as he watched Nova talking to Niv.

Remi shook his head, "Just trust him, it works."

Talon and Mali looked doubtful as well, but Talon held Quin up to Niv and they chattered and squeaked back and forth, until Niv scurried back up Nova's arm and perched on his shoulder again.

"Okay buddy, we need you to take us to her."

With that, Niv leapt from Nova's shoulders and took off into the forest.

"Come on," Nova called as he chased after the little marmouse, motioning for the others to follow.

CHAPTER L

The smell of blood must have drawn the tarcat to us. His rucked, white snout was drooling as he bared his needle sharp teeth at us. His breath was hot and putrid as he chuffed and hissed. He was crouched low, coiling his haunches, as he twitched his black tail with agitation. I watched as his spotted ribs fanned out and in, out and in, with each terrifying breath he took, inching his way towards us on his belly. His white fur, was tinged yellow where it met the earth, like he'd spent a great deal of time hiding in wait for prey, as he was now.

I pulled Jovi behind me to shield her from him and grabbed Sparrow and my sister's hands to pull them behind me as well.

"Move slowly," I cautioned them. *"He smells the blood, cover up your wounds."*

I felt them moving behind me, doing their best to carefully cover up their cuts, but I knew it was too late. The tarcat was already upon us. No doubt, drawn to the smell of our bleeding gashes thanks to the thorns. There was no way he'd leave us in one piece. We were a tantalizing meal, just begging to be devoured. At least I had given them something to do, something to keep their minds busy on anything other than the fact that we were cornered. If we ran, we'd be caught by the hunting party that was closing in on us. If we stayed, we'd surely be ripped to shreds by this ferocious tarcat. My mind shuttered at the memory of the last tarcat attack I'd witnessed.

I had been the one to sick Khan and Ria on their master, headmistress Greeley. Bile rose from the pit of my stomach as the violent images of her death tore through my mind. I closed my eyes trying to stop them.

"No, Greeley … please stop," I murmured through gritted teeth, begging the vision to leave my mind.

Now was not the time for my mind to slip into haunting memories. I needed to focus and think clearly if we were going to find a way out of this mess.

"You set me free" came a familiar, unsettling voice.

My eye lids flew open and met the luminescent yellow eyes of the tarcat before me. He no longer had his ears pinned back. They were pricked towards me in surprise.

"Khan?" I telepathed back to the tarcat in bewilderment.

He nodded his head in confirmation.

"I owe you a great deal for the freedom you've given me," he purred as he genuflected. *"How can I repay you?"*

I didn't know what to say or think. How could it be that the same tarcat I freed was now sitting before me offering my freedom?

Just then the hunters snapped another twig, catching all of our attention. They were creeping dangerously close to us now. They had our bluff of thistle palms surrounded. Khan looked back at me with his wise, bright eyes. He purred for a moment and I laid my hand on his broad soft brow. At my touch, he closed his iridescent yellow-green cat eyes and for a fleeting instant, I felt his love and loyalty and compassion. He was a misunderstood creature, who'd been imprisoned at the Troian Center just as I had. I opened my mouth to apologize to him, but before I had the chance, he sprang into action, leaping from the safety of the palms out toward the startled hunters.

Khan thrashed and roared, scattering the hunters. I saw one go down and lay still. Khan lifted his face to look back at me, his once white coat was now stained red, from muzzle to chest.

"Run!" was the last word he ever uttered to me.

I didn't wait to see what happened next. I quickly cloaked us with my invisibility power and pulled the girls from the tearing thorns. We ran as fast as we could, holding hands and never looking back. The screams from the men were terrifying. I heard Khan's roar booming through the forest. It was getting further from us, as he drew them away. Jovi stumbled and I lost hold of her hand. We all became visible when I lost contact. I scooped her up as I heard a blood curdling scream from Khan that made my skin turn cold.

Jemma and Sparrow both turned to me with looks of shock and fear. I shook my head and offered both of them my hands.

"Cover your ears Jovi," was all I said as we pressed on, away from the sad, wounded calls of the tarcat who had saved our lives.

After running until my muscles ached, I heard a familiar chattering and then a streak of fur launched itself at me.

I knelt down and collected my excited marmouse.

"Niv!?" I exclaimed in confusion. "Why are you in the middle of the forest?"

"Over there! I see them!" came Nova's voice.

I nearly burst into tears at the sound of his voice! If Nova was here, we were saved! I scratched Niv between his ears and held him tight, knowing that once again, my amazing marmouse had saved my life. I let him kiss my face and tickle me with his feathery whiskers.

"You led Nova to us, didn't you my sweet boy?" I crooned to him.

My adrenaline had worn off by the time Nova and the others reached us. I couldn't stop shaking. Jovi ran straight into her brother's arms, while Quin raced circles around them. Jovi had been so brave the entire time, but now, in the safety of Talon's arms, she exploded into tears. I felt like I could have done the same thing the moment Nova engulfed me in his embrace.

All of our petty arguments instantly evaporated in moments like this. Our squabbles seemed so insignificant now, because when it came down to it, Nova was always there for me and I knew as long as there was an ounce of breath left in his body, he'd go to the ends of the earth for me. I let him examine me at arm's length, reassuring him that all of my cuts were superficial. Remi came over to make sure I was alright too. I hugged him tight to help relieve the worry in his eyes. I asked him to take Niv for me because his claws kept catching my skin where the thorns had torn into me. Remi reluctantly let me out of his embrace and called Niv to him. Niv had always loved Remi and he jumped merrily from my arms, to his shoulder. I reached out for Nova and collapsed into his arms once more. He scooped me up, cradling me as he carried me the rest of the way back to camp.

Journey and Mali helped Sparrow and Jemma back as well, while Talon carried Jovi. When we could see the glowing firelight of camp, I heard Vida shouting to us and then felt hands all over me. She gently helped us to her tent. Jaka was there to receive us as well. He helped Vida tend to our wounds. The boys were shooed from our tent so we could be bathed and treated with a healing salve.

I drank a warm tea that I was offered and it made me feel drowsy. I fought my heavy eyelids, wanting to stay awake to make sure that Jovi, Sparrow and my sister were okay. I blinked and tried to stop my head from nodding, but it was no use.

The chief came over to me and laid his hand gently on my forehead. "Sleep my child. Tomorrow is another day."

CHAPTER LI

"What do you mean you failed!?" seethed the man with the shiny, black hair.

"Master, I'm sorry I failed you," the wounded mercenary replied through his disheveled armor as he knelt at his master's feet in front of his peers. "The Eva is fast and cunning. She heard our unit approaching somehow and she had time to prepare. She had a tarcat on her side. She made him attack us and he took out the other five men in my unit, while she and her friends escaped. But don't worry, I killed the vile beast, though I'm lucky to have escaped with my life."

"Oh? I wouldn't say you're lucky," he growled.

In one swift, fluid motion, the tall man pulled a black handled knife from his belt and brought it down upon the injured warrior in front of him. The only thing that the other men saw, was the shining, gleam of silver, before they watched their comrade's head fall from his shoulders.

The room full of mercenaries was deathly still as they watched their master slowly wipe the blade of his scythe on his black robes before sheathing it.

"Now, listen closely men. You will not return here until you have the Book of Secrets and the Eva and her friends. I need them alive, but be prepared to kill anyone or anything else that gets in your way. I hope I've been clear; failure is *not* an option!"

CHAPTER LII

Nova's face, silhouetted by sunlight, was the first thing I saw when I opened my eyes. He looked so beautiful that I thought I might still be asleep, having another dream about Nova and I, where we weren't orphans or chosen ones. Just two normal people, free to be together and live happily ever after. He blinked his vivid green eyes and leaned in closer to kiss me on the cheek. I could smell his sweet scent and feel his warmth as he came near. I didn't want this dream to end.

"Good morning sunshine," he whispered. "We were wondering when you were going to wake up."

"We?" I murmured rubbing the sleep out of my eyes.

Nova took a step back and I saw that my tiny tent was filled with about a dozen Betos! My cheeks flushed, feeling suddenly self-conscious. I popped up and surveyed my visitors. Jaka, Vida, Talon, Mali, Remi, Eja and a few other Beto scouts where all looking at me expectantly.

"What's going on?!" I asked, my heart in my throat as I scrambled to my feet.

"Nothing, happened. Everyone's alright," Remi offered reading the concern on my face.

"We didn't mean to alarm you my Eva," Jaka spoke. "We just need to speak to you about the attack."

"Where's Jemma and the others?" I asked as I looked around the tent where they had been last night.

"We sent them on to a new site earlier this morning. They morfed for safety reasons. I think that's the safest way to travel given yesterday's events. We were reluctant to wake you until you were finished healing. You suffered the most wounds."

"Figures," Nova whispered for only me to hear.

I glared at him and he gave me a wink.

"But, as you can imagine," Jaka continued. "Time is of crucial importance. Talon and the scouts said they saw evidence of hunters in the forest, but they didn't actually see who it was. I was hoping you would share what you saw with us so we can be better prepared for what we might encounter."

"I can do better than that," I said staring at Eja.

He seemed to understand instantly what I wanted to do and he stepped forward, reaching out his hand.

Everyone was silent after what I'd showed them through Eja's amazing power to share memories. I looked around the room and all of their faces were horrorstruck, both by the gruesome attack between Khan and the soldiers, and of the wrath of the men now hunting us.

I let go of Eja's hand and everyone followed suit. He stared at me tragically and I could feel his pity and fear for me. His emotions were echoed by everyone else in the room and it was making my head spin. It was too hard to be near all that emotion, I needed air. I excused myself from the tent and sat down outside, next to Niv who was napping in a patch of sunlight. I stroked his warm fur and he gave a content groan, as he rolled onto his back so I could scratch his belly.

"Why does everything have to be so difficult buddy?" I whined.

From the devastated looks on everyone's faces, they knew who the men in the forest last night were and it wasn't good. I could tell they weren't just hunters. I'd known deep down as soon as I saw their masks and weaponry that they were part of the Ravinori. The looks on everyone's faces just now confirmed it.

Jaka came outside and I immediately moved to stand, but he motioned for me to stay seated and he joined me.

"They were Ravinori weren't they?" I asked.

"Yes, mercenaries," Jaka replied. "The Ravinori's most elite and lethal soldiers. They call themselves the phantoms and it's lucky that you possess such intuitive powers that you were able to detect they were near. They pride themselves on their swift and soundless attacks."

"They're looking for me?"

"Yes."

"I can't stay here Jaka. I'm putting everyone in danger as long as you're harboring me."

"It is an honor to our people to help serve our Eva. Your will shall save us all and that will not be without sacrifice."

"I used my powers last night. They surely know I'm here and they won't give up now. It's not safe for me to stay here. I'm just going to drag innocent people into my mess if I stay here."

"We will make preparations for you to leave soon, but not before you are ready. This attack has taught us that it is clearly not safe for you in the forest. I'll make arrangements for you to travel through the Bellamorf network. Their channels are not marked. We've always been afraid to map their locations in case they should fall into the wrong hands. With Eja's help, I can show you the way in my mind, but it will take time to prepare."

I shook my head and let it hang, fighting off tears. Jaka took my hand.

"We are not afraid my Eva. Do not despair. We have stayed hidden in this forest for many years. We are not defeated yet. Now thanks to you, we know our enemy. There is hope in knowing your enemy."

CHAPTER LIII

Shortly after my talk with Jaka, we left camp. We mounted some wild ponies that Talon and Mali had procured and rode them silently through the tangled forest, towards the nearest Bellamorf tree so we could catch up to the rest of the tribe that had left earlier to make a new camp.

There weren't enough horses for all of us, so I rode with Remi since his riding skills weren't that great. He seemed to enjoy the look of disgust on Nova's face when I offered to ride with him after he got bucked off in the first two seconds he was on his mount.

"You can wipe that smirk off your face now," I commented when we were out of earshot.

"What?" Remi replied coyly.

I gave him a frustrated elbow.

"Okay, okay. I'm sorry. I won't antagonize him."

"Promise?"

"Well, how long are you talking about? Just today or - "

"Remi!" I scolded. "What's gotten into you? You know we almost died last night right? I'm in no mood to joke."

"Precisely! Last night proves life is short. We need to take joy in every moment while we can."

I sighed deeply, but didn't respond.

"Alright, I promise! No more fun," Remi conceded.

"Thank you. Besides, Nova doesn't need to be encouraged to dislike you anymore than he already does. And you're lucky he doesn't know about our kiss, so stop gloating! You're just causing trouble for me. We all need to work together if we're going to get through this."

"And why haven't you just told Nova about our kiss if it didn't mean anything?" Remi challenged. "Do you want to know what I think?"

"Not really, but I'm sure you're going to tell me anyway,"

"It's because you know you liked kissing me."

I was glad Remi was riding behind me so he couldn't see my cheeks burn red. For some reason, I hadn't been able to stop thinking about that kiss, but I had to. And, I had to make him stop thinking about it too.

"Remi, you have to stop. We've been through this. It's not like that between us okay? You're my best friend and I'm not ready to lose that."

"I know, I know. I mean the world to you, blah blah, blah. You can say that all you want, but it's not going to change the way I feel about you. I felt it when we kissed. Maybe you don't know it yet, but you love me and I'm going to be here waiting when you figure that out Geneva."

"Remi, that's just it. I don't want you to waste your time waiting for me to figure out what I want! I have enough to worry about right now without you and Nova putting pressure on me."

"Well, I'm not putting any pressure on you. Don't worry, I'm not going to make you chose between us or anything dramatic like that. But as far as waiting, that's not your decision to make for me. It's my heart, I'll waste it how I want," he said defiantly.

I sighed deeply and shook my head. These boys were incorrigible.

I was relieved to reach camp and see that everyone was alright. Jovi, Sparrow and Jemma were completely healed from their scratches thanks to Vida's expert care and Sparrow's healing powers. They were all a little shook up, understandably.

"Where is everyone else?" I asked, noticing that the camp looked pretty sparse.

"Jaka put everyone on alert after he learned of the attack," Sparrow told me. "A lot of them left last night. He said it's safer for us to spread out and try to throw the hunters off our trail."

"We're only allowed to travel by Bellamorf now," Jovi added.

"So, I've heard," I said, my concern growing.

I hated the idea of endangering the Betos. I wanted to start our trek to the Troian Center as soon as possible and put a safe distance between us and the Betos. I knew every moment more I spent with them was putting them at risk. I was the reason the mercenaries were invading the forest. The Ravinori only wanted me. If I hadn't come into the forest, the Betos wouldn't be in danger.

"Can I talk to you for a minute?" Nova said interrupting my thoughts.

"Sure," I shrugged, letting him pull me away from the others.

"Not too far," Talon called when we reached the edge of the soft orange light cast by the nearby campfire.

"Tippy, don't even think about it," Nova whispered to me.

"Think about what?" I asked.

"I know what you're thinking. You're not going to sneak off in the middle of the night. That does none of us any good."

"Nova! That's not what I was thinking and you've got to stay out of my head!"

"Don't lie to me. I know you well enough to know that's what you were thinking without having to read your mind. It's written all over your face."

"Then you should know I'm right! If I stay here, I'm just putting innocent people in danger. The Ravinori only want me."

"That's not true. They're looking for the Pillars too and that means me. And, what good does it do any of us if the Ravinori get you? You're the only one who can defeat them and we have to do it together! You're the one who convinced us of that, remember?"

I sighed in defeat knowing he was right.

"Besides, you know if you sneak off that I'm just going to have to come rescue you."

I rolled my eyes at him, but knew he was only speaking the truth. And I knew from experience if Nova came, then Remi was going to come and then everyone would get dragged into my mess as usual. Staying to figure out a plan would be better than running blindly into the abyss.

I shook my head and tried to fight off my eagerness to flee. I felt guilty even thinking it, but I knew Nova was probably reading my mind anyway so I said it.

"Nova, do you ever wish we could both just run away?" I whispered.

He looked at me in shock.

"Together, I mean. Sometimes I wonder if maybe we went far enough away from here... Maybe our problems wouldn't follow us and we could be..." I paused, staring into his intense eyes as my own welled with emotion, thinking back to my dream. I wanted to say *"together"* but, the words froze in my throat. I swallowed hard and was only able to say, "... normal?"

"Every day," he smiled painfully. "I think about that every day."

CHAPTER LIV

The next morning, after morfing to a new campsite at daybreak, Jaka gathered us together in his tent. He had Eja show us a path he and the scouts had mapped out for our return to the Troian Center. Eja shared their vision with us, using his unique powers that let us see into his mind. This way, we could view a map that would never have to be written down, ensuring our path would remain secret and there wouldn't be the risk of it falling into the hands of the Ravinori.

Jaka's plan consisted of traveling by morfing the majority of the way along the secret chain of Bellamorf trees that existed strategically throughout the rainforest.

"There are a few instances where you may have to travel short distances by foot, but for the most part, I think it's your swiftest way back to the Troian Center."

"What about using powers? Won't morfing only alert the Ravinori to our whereabouts?" I asked.

"Not if we all morf in different directions," Mali smiled.

"Split up?" Sparrow asked apprehensively.

"No way! That's not a good idea!" Nova interjected.

"Let him finish," Eja urged.

"Jaka has sent word to the other Betos in the forest. If we all morf, in different directions at the same time, there will be too many of us traveling for the Ravinori to track at once. It'll be like a lottery and they'd have to get really lucky to find our group," Mali finished.

"Who's in our group?" I asked.

"Mali and I will escort you, and your friends, while Jaka goes with my family and the rest of the tribe," Talon said. "As long as that's okay with you, my Eva," he added for good measure.

I pondered their plan for a moment and felt tentatively optimistic.

"I think it could work," I admitted surveying the map Eja was projecting with his mind. "When do we leave?"

"Tomorrow, at dawn."

We had a lot to do before we were ready to leave and no time to waste. The Ravinori encounter had made us all leave in a hurry and we were scrambling to find our belongings. I quickly went to work delegating tasks to get us on track. We only had three tents to share between all of us at camp, so I sent the boys to work setting them up, designating one for the girls, one for them and one for Vida and the chief.

Eja was pouring over the Book of Secrets while Jovi was helping Jemma and Sparrow weave shoes for the trek. I spent my time helping Remi gather supplies and food for our expedition. Everyone was busying themselves with a useful task. It was good to see us all come together to accomplish a goal in a civil manner. There was no bickering or volleying for attention. Everyone just put their heads down and worked. It was a little victory, but I took pride in it.

As I watched everyone finishing the last of the packing, I thought now would be a good time to speak to Vida. I needed to apologize to her about putting Jovi in danger last night. I should have listened to Remi and just stayed at camp. If I had, we would have avoided the run in with the mercenaries and left for the Troian Center already, instead of scrambling to come up with this new plan.

I found her inside her tent preparing healing ointments for us to take with us.

"Vida? May I come in?" I asked.

"Of course," she said without looking up.

I admired the cheerful walls of her tent fleetingly as I sat down next to her, briefly stalling. Vida was such an intimidating woman. She had been through so much in her life and I knew it had hardened her, but I admired her perseverance and her ability to endure. To me, she seemed like a born leader. I hoped that in the short time I'd spent with her, I might have picked up some of her traits. I know I aspired to.

"Was there something you needed my Eva?" she asked.

"Oh, um, yes. I mean, I didn't need anything, I just wanted to apologize for the other night and thank you for healing me and my friends."

"You're welcome, but it was mostly your friend Sparrow that did the healing. She's quite talented."

I swelled with pride, hearing Vida praise Sparrow. I too had noticed that Sparrow was coming into her own. Working with Vida had been good for her. I could see her confidence soaring since we'd been here.

"I'll be sure to pass along the compliment and my thanks to her," I smiled. "But I also wanted to apologize for dragging your family into all of this as well. I'm very sorry that I put Jovi in danger last night."

"You have nothing to apologize for my Eva. We've been in danger for years. If anything, you have brought us closer to the brink of peace then we've been in ages. We don't expect that luxury to come without sacrifice."

"But I don't want you to have to sacrifice anymore," I whispered.

She stopped what she was doing and finally looked at me. Her eyes bore into my soul. I could tell she was angry that I was referring to her secret past.

"I know you feel responsible for us as a people and as our Eva, I admire that genuine quality, but it needn't go further than that."

"But Jovi –"

"Jovi is not any safer here in the forest with me. The tarcat and the Ravinori attack last night is proof of that. She has a destiny to fulfill as well and that is why I'm sending her with you to the Troian Center."

All the breath rushed from my lungs.

"You're what?"

But Vida had returned to tending her potion.

"You can't do that. I came here to tell you that I wanted to keep her safe and that means keeping her here with you. I know she wants to go with us. The others think she'll be useful helping us communicate through Quin, but I don't want to risk it. We weren't even out of the forest last night and I already put her in danger. I can't bear the thought of anything happening to her because of me!"

Vida threw down her ladle and turned rapidly towards me. Her face was inches from mine when she spoke.

"This is what I've been trying to tell you all along. You can't be attached like this. You can't have these deep relationships! I love my daughter; that is my job, not yours. You need to lead her! You need to lead all of us and you can't do that with a clear head if your heart is pulling you in so many directions! Don't you get that yet?!"

I could feel her breath on my face as she yelled at me. Her eyes were wild and her auburn hair was coming loose from its bun, giving her a savage look. I could see the fear and heartache that she normally kept buried deep down, locked away somewhere with her dark secrets. Now, it was plain in her eyes. She terrified me and I nodded as I scrambled a few paces away from her. She must have caught the fear in my expression and it shocked her into composing herself. Vida immediately retreated pawing at her hair and smoothing out her dress.

"I'm sorry, my Eva. Please forgive my outburst," she apologized, lowering her eyes to the ground in shame.

"It's okay," I whispered, still backing away.

"It's my daughter's wish to accompany you to the Troian Center because she believes she can help you. I believe she can be an asset to you and I will not prohibit her from going. Of course you are our Eva and if you wish her to stay here, than I shall do my best to honor your wishes.

I nodded as I retreated from the tent. Once outside, my legs felt shaky. Nova took one look at me and jogged to my side.

"You alright?" he asked.

I couldn't respond. I was too busy scanning the camp for Jovi. I found her by our tent and ran over to her, intent on convincing her and the others that she needed to stay here, despite what her mother said. I knew Vida was right, that I needed to stop letting my heart rule me, but it was too late when it came to Jovi. I'd already formed a rare bond with this girl and no amount of logic or reason would stop me from doing everything in my power to save her if she was in danger. And that's exactly what this trip was; dangerous.

I ignored Nova's calls as I ran past Sparrow and Eja organizing our packs and Remi inspecting the food that Vida had rationed us. I stopped breathlessly in front of Jemma and Journey. They were talking with Jovi and it looked like they were helping her pack a bag of her own.

"What's going on?" I asked as I watched Jovi haphazardly jamming her belongings into a burlap sack.

"I'm coming with you!" she beamed. "Isn't that great!?"

"What?" I said shooting Journey an annoyed look. "No! No, this isn't a good idea. We need to talk about this. After last night I'm not okay with this. It's too dangerous," I said, pleading with Journey and Jemma.

"You don't want me to come?" Jovi asked sounding hurt.

"No, that's not it. I just want you to be safe! I love spending time with you Jovi, you know that, right?"

She nodded timidly.

"I don't want what happened last night to happen again. I'll never forgive myself if something happens to you," I said.

"But I want to help," she pleaded.

"She wants to help Eva," Jemma chimed in, being as unhelpful as ever. I glared at her.

"You were out voted remember? Jovi is coming with us," Journey added without stopping what he was doing.

He wasn't taking me seriously, so I pushed myself in between him and his pack.

"I don't care about the stupid vote! I'm the Eva and I don't think it's a good idea Journey," I challenged.

"Well, it's a little late now Eva. Bottom line is if we're taking Quin, we're taking Jovi. No one else can control that wex like she can and she's our only way of communicating with the Betos."

As if on cue, Quin came barreling at us. Journey, tried to get out of her way, but she changed course, narrowly darting through his muscular legs, tripping him up. He grumbled as he picked himself off the ground and brushed the moss angrily off his knees. He narrowed his eyes at me and said, "The kid's coming with us!" Then he turned to Jovi and said, "Don't make me regret this kid, get that wex under control."

"Yes sir!" Jovi said and she sprang into action, running after Quin.

I was out of sorts for the rest of the day. It seemed that the sun was refusing to set, as time dragged on inside our hot little tent. We'd already had dinner and gone over the plan too many times. No matter what I said or who I pleaded with, the verdict remained the same; it seemed that Jovi was coming with us. It turned out that there really was nowhere else for her to go. The Betos had decided to remain disbanded until we made it to the Troian Center. That meant that the only people left would be Vida and Jaka, and everyone's argument was that she was safer with us since there were more us to protect her.

I sat, legs folded, brow furrowed, on the edge of our cramped tent. Eja was reading the Book of Secrets aloud again, describing the characteristics of the four Pillars that we would be looking for. We'd been over this dozens of times since we found the book and I knew it would reveal nothing new.

"I've gotta get some air," I said suddenly standing and exiting the tent.

I instantly felt better once I got outside. It was cooler and quieter. I felt like I was suffocating in there with all the thoughts and emotions of my friends running through my head. I welcomed Niv when he crawled into my lap.

"You like it better out here too, huh little buddy?" I said scratching him between the ears.

He chattered gratefully as I continued to pet him and soak up the silent serenity of the rainforest.

I groaned when I heard someone push though the tent flaps to join me, thinking it was either Remi or Nova checking on me. To my relief it was Sparrow, who sat down next to me. She quietly watched the sun sinking below the canopy of lush trees without speaking a word. I always appreciated her company. She had a knack for reading my moods and was happy to sit quietly with me.

When the sunlight was merely a faint afterglow, she reached over and squeezed my hand.

"It's going to be okay. I know we're one big dysfunctional family and all, but we've got each other's backs," she smiled.

"Thanks Sparrow," I replied. "And thanks for cleaning up my mess from yesterday."

"What do you mean?"

"Vida said you healed all our wounds from the thistle palm thorns. She was giving you a lot of well-deserved praise."

"She was?" Sparrow asked perking up.

"Yeah. And she's right. You've really come into your own out here. You're a great healer and a really great friend. I'm sorry that I probably don't tell you that enough. I hope you know how much I appreciate you. I should probably tell everyone how much they each mean to me before tomorrow," I sulked glumly.

"Geneva, it's going to be okay. Don't worry about tomorrow, we all know what's at stake and you have to know you didn't force us into this. We want to fight alongside of you. And that's because we all know how much you care about us," she smiled putting a gentle hand on my shoulder.

"Thanks Sparrow. When did you become so grown up? I'm really proud of you."

"Thanks Geneva. I'm proud of all of us. I think we've all come a long way."

I forced myself to return her smile, but couldn't help thinking how we still had such a long way to go.

CHAPTER LV

"Why are you wasting my time showing me all of these random thoughts that are running around her head? What do I care about the mundane musings of a teenage girl?"

"Because master, look. She's frightened and if we pay attention, we can see her biggest fears and use them against her."

"Can you implant fears into her head that we can use against her later?" the dark haired man asked deviously.

"Yes, of course master, but I don't think we need to. She's already terrified of her destiny and of us."

"Kobel, I don't employ you to think, I employ you to execute my wishes."

"Yes master," Kobel cowered.

"Besides, the mercenaries are closing in. Why should they have all the fun? What's a few more nightmares for good measure?" he laughed.

"As you wish master."

CHAPTER LVI

After a long and sleepless night, full of terrifying visions or nightmares, it was finally time to make our way back to the Troian Center. The air seemed to hum with the electric anticipation of this long awaited moment. I found myself shaking out the pins and needles of anxiety that pulsed through me as I dressed. The feeling was both ominous and exciting. Either way, I felt relieved to finally be doing something productive. I was ready to face my destiny. No matter what the voyage back would bring us, at least it was better to confront it head on, instead of waiting for evil to come and find us.

We departed camp before daybreak, following Mali to the Bellamorf tree, with Talon bringing up the rear. Our mood was tense and no one spoke as we crept single file through the forest. The dew still lay heavy in the air, adding a chill to the already eerie pre-dawn trek. The forest was still asleep as we moved through it with stealth. The twilight hours were when the night creatures were returning to their roosts, while the diurnal species had yet to wake. The quiet glow of dawn was growing as we caught our first glimpse of a Bellamorf tree looming majestically ahead of us.

After inspecting the tree, Mali waved us forward and helped

us climb into its tangled limbs where we took shelter from the cool morning air, awaiting the signal that it was time to morf.

"Alright, it's almost time," Talon said looking towards the brightening horizon. "As soon as the sun breaks we're going to morf. Everyone link hands and follow Mali. I'll be right behind you."

We nodded and reached for each other's hands. A tense tingle buzzed through me as we linked hands. I found myself wondering how this group of tragic teens had been selected to save an entire civilization. It was quite a tall order for a ragtag group of orphans.

The horizon was ablaze with a bright orange glow as the sun got ready to crest above the trees. The Bellamorf tree sprung to life, beginning to shake and groan as leaves swirled in the powerful wind that Talon had summoned.

"Get ready!" he called over the sound of rustling leaves.

"Now!" he yelled as the fiery yellow ball of sunlight burst over the canopy, bathing the forest in light.

Success! We all landed in the next Bellamorf tree as we had intended; some more gracefully than others. I of course, was one of the clumsy ones, narrowly managing to regain my balance and stay on my feet with the help of Remi steadying me. I smiled my gratitude at him and he just shrugged and smiled back. Just another day in his life as my best friend.

Talon landed above us moments later. He and Mali exchanged some sort of hand signals that only they understood and then they directed us to climb out of the tree. It was hard work since we couldn't use any of our powers to assist us. That would have been a dead giveaway, sure to draw the Ravinori. I was really missing being able to bound down the massive trees effortlessly. By the time we reached the ground, I was covered in splinters and sweat.

I surveyed my friends and everyone looked a little worse for wear. I was starting to worry about this plan. Traveling by morfing was no easy task and this was only our first jump.

"Great job everyone. A dozen or so more jumps just like that and we'll be at the edge of the forest in no time," I encouraged.

"We have a lot of morfing ahead of us," Talon said. "Let's keep moving."

Everything went according to plan for the next few hours. We hiked and climbed our way through the forest. Morfing where we could and hiking between expanses that were too large to jump. Talon and Mali were keeping watch, always scouting the area before letting us move on. They were so vigilant that I actually tried to relax for a while and enjoy the simple beauty of the forest and the company of my friends. Although we were moving with care, I had a strange foreboding feeling in the pit of my stomach that this may be the last time I could relish such happiness.

I tried to fight my ominous thoughts as I watched the sunlight filtering in from high above the rainforest canopy, casting dust moats for us to pass through. I found myself wishing we could somehow remain encapsulated in their stillness. I envied their world of slow motion. I wished I could somehow live in its suspended safety, instead of the rapidly changing reality I lived in. I shook myself from my own trance and found myself watching Jovi. The decision to let her join us still haunted me. She was so young and so innocent. I would never forgive myself if I let anything happen to her. I stared after her as she added a skip to every few steps to keep up with the others in our group. She was still barefoot, despite having made herself shoes upon her mother's insistence. Her long brown hair was already escaping the neat braid Vida had put it in. The good news was, Quin was actually obediently jogging at her side for a change.

"She'll be alright," Remi said from behind me, reading my thoughts as only a best friend can.

I paused for a beat to let him come along side me.

"She's so young Remi. I don't want to drag her into the mess that we left at the Troian Center."

"She's tough, she can handle it. Besides, I'm pretty sure if we hadn't let her come, she would have followed Quin back to us after we sent word to the Betos that we'd arrived at the Center. It's probably safer for her this way."

I looked at the tan, energetic girl bouncing in front of me and smiled, realizing Remi was probably right. She was staying in line with the group and urging Quin to do the same so none of us would have anything to say about bringing her along with us. I smiled as I watched the tiny girl marching, fearlessly, into our unknown future. I hated that this was her reality, but I knew that having her so nearby would continually inspire me to fulfill my destiny. I sighed and linked my arm with Remi's, squeezing it to thank him for making me feel better.

"You doing alright with your pack?" he asked.

"Yes, thanks. It's fine."

"Okay, well let me know if it gets too heavy? I'm going to catch up to Journey and find out how far we are from the next tree."

I nodded to him and watched as he picked his way past the others to the front of our group. Chivalrous Remi. Hmm … this was new. There was a lot of new things I was starting to notice about him. Maybe being out in the forest agreed with him, like it did Sparrow. His skin wasn't so pale anymore and lean muscles now rippled just below his healthy, tanned skin. He seemed more confident too. It looked good on him I thought with a smile.

Sparrow interrupted my thoughts.

"What are you smirking about?" she asked.

"Oh nothing," I lied when she broke my concentration.

She was carrying Niv, who was defiantly living on our shoulders to show his protest for Quin joining our group. He chattered and leapt to my shoulder when Sparrow was close enough.

"Oh Niv, come on, Quin's not that bad," I laughed as I scratched him under the chin. "Look, she's following Jovi very obediently."

Niv squeaked his disagreement and disappeared into my pack. Sparrow and I both giggled.

"So do you think we'll be able to find them all?" Sparrow asked. "The others Pillars?"

"I do. We all found each other somehow and I truly believe we were meant to. Together, with all of our individual skills and powers, we'll have everything we need to find the others and help them."

"How do you do it? How do you stay so confident and positive?" she asked shyly.

"Truthfully?" I asked. "I learned that from you Sparrow."

She beamed back at me and gave me a quick hug. When she released me, I could see her old sparkle had returned to her amber eyes. I couldn't put my finger on it before, but I knew there was something off, but now that it was back, it was obvious. The gravity of our situation was weighing on her too.

"Thanks, Eva. I think I needed that."

"You're welcome Sparrow. I meant it. You've always been there for me and you've helped boost me up when I thought we were a lost cause so many times in the last year. You're a great friend, so I'm happy to return the favor."

"I *am* a pretty great friend," she joked, the joy evident in her larky voice.

"We're more than friends, we're sisters, remember?" I said laughing with her.

"That's right!" Sparrow chirped.

"Too bad you're not my real sister," I sighed as I fixed my gaze on the back of Jemma's perfect raven mane swaying down her tan flawless back. Nova was already carrying her pack.

"What's going on with you two?" Sparrow asked.

"Which two?" I sighed, thinking how Sparrow could have been referring to either Jemma or Nova.

It seemed I couldn't make up my mind about either of them these days.

Sparrow laughed, "Well I was referring to Jemma."

"I don't know. Honestly I haven't talked to her much since I gave her half my powers. It's too painful to see her and Nova together. She knows I like him and she obviously doesn't care. I don't even want to bother with her. I have too many other important things to worry about, besides my backstabbing sister."

"So you're not even going to fight for Nova?!" replied Sparrow sounding shocked.

"Why bother? It's Jemma. I mean look at her. What boy would choose me, over her?"

"Seriously!?" Sparrow squealed. "You don't give yourself enough credit and you're not trying to get *any* boy to like you, we're talking about Nova! He's crazy about you! You two are destined to be together. Like star-crossed lovers….." she exaggerated, quoting a play we had read once.

"Oh stop," I said, playfully shoving her. "You really think he likes me though?"

"Please! He *loves* you. You really don't have any idea how the boys look at you do you?"

"Boys?" I asked.

"Yes, boys. Nova and Remi in particular."

"Oh, right. Remi," I said suddenly embarrassed, thinking back to our kiss.

"So what are you going to do Eva?"

"I don't know Sparrow. It really doesn't matter does it? I'm the Eva, and not to mention the Ponte Deorum, so it's not like I'll really have time to have a love life anyway. I'm sure I'm going to be spending all my time trying to dodge Ravinori hunters and just stay alive."

"Maybe that's true, but isn't that even more reason to live in the now? You need to enjoy every second. Take it all in and spend your time with the people you care about most."

She was starting to sound like Remi, but I nodded, knowing she was right. It awoke an ache in my heart as I stared at Nova's tan muscular back.

"So who is it you want to be with Eva?"

It was Nova. It had always been Nova. But, my heart protested itself, remembering the searing pain of seeing Nova and Jemma together, along with all the warnings from Vida and the legends.

"It's Nova, but…."

"But nothing. Just talk to him! For once, just tell him how you feel. If any two people need to talk it's you two!"

"It's not that simple. You heard the legend … "

"Geneva, even a legend can't keep you two apart if you're both honest with each other."

"You're right," I sighed. "But not right now. I'll talk to him tonight when we camp. I don't want Jemma around or anyone else overhearing us."

"That's probably a good plan. I can try to distract her to give you two some time to talk if you want?" Sparrow offered.

"That would be great!" I said, but I still felt uneasy. "You really think he likes me over Jemma?" I asked.

"Absolutely."

"It just seems like he spends a lot of time with her."

"Whatever his reasons, I'm sure that you're the one he loves."

I smiled at Sparrow as my spirits lifted with her confidence in Nova's feelings for me.

Sparrow and I walked side by side in silence for a while, but I kept getting the feeling that our conversation wasn't over in her mind. Like she wanted to ask me something more and finally she did.

"So you really don't have any feelings for Remi?" she asked.

"I mean it's complicated. I love him, but in more of a brotherly way, I guess. I've known him forever, he's my best friend. It's a different kind of love."

"So you wouldn't be mad if he wanted to date someone else?" she asked timidly.

"Like who?" I asked caught off guard. But I never got the answer to that question.

CHAPTER LVII

Talon signaled to Mali and we all halted.

My stomach plummeted and my heart started pounding. I could hear a dim roar in the distance. Was something wrong? Had the Ravinori found us? We all instinctively crouched while Talon scoped out the threat. He was only gone a moment, but time seemed to stretch into an endless abyss. I protectively watched over Jovi and my friends, all of their eyes, wide with alert and fear.

"All clear," rang Talon's voice, shattering the tense silence.

I released my breath that I hadn't realized I'd been holding and stood.

"We're at the vine bridge. The last Bellamorf tree before we make camp is just on the other side of the ravine. We'll need to cross one at a time because I don't know how well the old vines will hold. We haven't crossed this boundary since the Flood."

I glanced nervously at the rickety old vine bridge that hung over the rushing waterfall. Its wooden rungs looked slick with moss and rot. A few pieces were missing, probably claimed by humid weather and old age. It left huge gaps in our path that did little to ease my mind about crossing. As I leaned over the edge to inspect it closer, I noticed the knotted vines holding the hazardous heap together were frayed in parts, with clumps of vegetation reaching from either bank, clinging to the knotted vines, threatening to reclaim them for the rainforest.

"Is this really the only way across?" Sparrow asked.

"Yeah, can't we use powers or just have morfed from that last tree?" Jemma chimed in.

"You know we can't use our powers," Remi said "and I'm pretty sure if we could have just morfed over we would have."

"It's too far to morf," Mali confirmed.

"We'll be fine to cross on foot. Betos have traveled this path for centuries."

"Yeah, that's what worries me," Remi gulped, looking at the bridge. "I don't think the centuries have been kind."

"I'll go first," Talon offered. "If it'll hold me, it'll hold all of you."

"And if it doesn't?"

"We'll cross that bridge when we come to it I guess," he joked, giving me a big grin.

Journey laughed, but the rest of us looked on tensely. This was no time to joke, but my worry was wasted on Talon. He lived for adventures like these and nothing scared him. He was a trained Beto scout and if anyone could lead us across this bridge, it would be him. He motioned to Mali, again exchanging signals I didn't understand before tightening his pack and heading into the mist of the hanging bridge.

10…11…12…13… The seconds ticked by in agonizing silence since Talon had disappeared from view. The sheer force of the powerful waterfall nearby created a thick mist that rose from the river below us. It hung in the middle of the vine bridge like an eerie grey curtain, blocking our view of the other side. Occasionally the wind would push a small clearing in the mist, giving us a hazy glimpse of Talon as he slowly made his way across the bridge. But now, after he was through the halfway point, we'd lost all sight of him.

I continued to count the seconds in my head as I held my breath. Jovi, slipped her hand in mine and I squeezed it.

"He's going to be alright," I said trying to comfort her over the thundering sound of the waterfall.

"I know," she smiled. "I came over to tell you not to worry. My brother is the best and bravest Beto scout there is. You don't have to worry about him."

My admiration for Jovi grew even more. While her brother was in the face of danger, she was calm and collected, worrying about comforting me.

"All clear!" rang Talon's voice finally.

It sounded far away, muffled by the sound of the raging water, but he was safely to the other side and we all let out a little cheer!

"Who's next?" I asked.

We each painstakingly waited our turn to cross the hanging vine bridge. When it was finally my turn, only Mali and Nova remained on the bank with me. I took a deep breath and stared at the gently swaying bridge. My hands were shaking as I reached out to grab hold of the first brittle posts on each side. I looked back at Nova one last time. He smiled at me and gave me his token wink. My heart suddenly surged with overwhelming fear that I might lose him. I turned on my heels and ran to Nova. I threw my arms around his neck and hugged him tightly as he stumbled back a few steps, caught by surprise.

"Tippy – " he started.

But I cut him off by holding my finger to his warm lips.

"I love you," I whispered breathlessly into his ear.

He was so shocked and speechless that he didn't respond. I let my hands slip from around his neck and I kissed his cheek as I slid to the ground and retreated back to the bridge with renewed determination.

After finally being brave enough to tell Nova how I truly felt, crossing the bridge seemed easy. I felt especially light on my feet, like I was walking on air after my confession. I purposely hadn't given him a chance to respond, but at least I had left my heart on my sleeve, or rather on the bank with Nova. I didn't want to risk crossing the bridge without the boy I loved knowing how I felt. It was liberating and I found myself conquering many fears as I quickly traversed the bridge. I wasn't thinking or worrying, I was simply doing. I was aware of the present moment and somehow felt more alive. Each step brought me closer to the other side, metaphorically and literally. I ignored the groaning of the vines and rotten wood and charged forward with my heart open.

I was only twenty yards from the bank now and I was starting to be able to make out my friends waiting for me on the other side. At first they just looked like looming dark shadows, but as I moved closer I could see their faces. I smiled back at Remi, who was waiting as close to the bridge as he could get. I waved to him and had just picked up my pace, when I felt the bridge give a jerk and groan loudly. I stopped and instinctively put both hands on the vine railings, gripping tightly. Remi mirrored my concerned expression as Talon came to his side to see what was going on.

Suddenly, Talon's eyes narrowed and as he opened his mouth to say something, I felt the bridge give a violent jerk! I flew to the side and my feet slipped off the slick wooden planks. My grip was steady though and I pulled myself back up. As soon as I was back on my feet, the bridge erupted wildly. It was bucking left and right and I heard shouts coming from all around me.

I held on tighter and zeroed in on Remi's voice.

"Run! Run!" he was screaming.

When his words finally connected with my mind, my feet came to life and I sprinted the last few yards of the bridge until I collided with Remi and Talon.

"What's going on?" I cried.

"Ravinori," was all Talon said as he breezed past me back onto the bridge, disappearing into the mist.

All hell was breaking loose. Talon had disappeared onto the bridge and Jemma, Jovi and Sparrow were screaming. I looked at their frightened faces and told the boys to stay with them and get them to the next Bellamorf tree as I turned to reenter the bridge, my heart prodding me to find Nova and rescue my friends. After all, it was my fault they were in this mess.

"Geneva! Wait. Don't go back!" Remi called, but I was already on the bridge. It was lurching and swaying as I descended to the center. Once in the mist I saw dark figures battling each other, but I couldn't tell who was who! Everything just looked like swirling shadows. I searched frantically for Nova but couldn't find him!

I screamed when I was grabbed hard from behind.

Hands were suddenly on me, pulling me up and I fought back screaming and thrashing wildly.

"It's me!" boomed Journey's low voice in my ear.

"Journey, let me go!" I said climbing to my feet with his help on the bucking bridge. "You were supposed to get everyone out of here! I need to find Nova."

"We're not going to abandon you. We'll all help you find him," he said motioning to a group of shadows behind him.

"Are you mad!?" I screamed as my heart sunk when I realized that he'd brought everyone back onto the bridge.

"Jovi has an idea," he said. "And I think it's just crazy enough to work."

"Journey, this bridge can't hold us all!"

"That's what we're counting on," he said.

Journey didn't fill me in on the plan, instead he shoved something into my hand.

"Don't lose them!" was all he said, when I snuck a peek at what he'd given me.

I didn't have time to argue, because suddenly a large dark figure was on top of us. I ducked and pocketed Journey's items while he pummeled our attackers. When I opened my eyes again I had engaged my hunter powers and could see clearly through the fog. The assailant looked just like the ones I'd seen a few days ago in the forest. Dark mask, black hood and weaponry; he was a member of the Ravinori phantom mercenary.

"Hunter powers," I called to Journey.

He nodded and fought off the masked figure as he tried to get back up. A few more blows from Journey and the man went down. The masked heap in front of Journey was sliding off the bridge and it was pulling us all towards the side with his weight. The bridge groaned and splintered further. I heard the girls scream and saw Jovi slipping.

"Journey, grab him!" I yelled.

He tried but was too late. The masked man fell off the bridge and plummeted out of sight, flailing and screaming as he went. I didn't have time to stop and think about what I'd just witnessed. My veins had gone cold when I saw Jovi slipping. I bounded over Journey and grabbed her. Wrapping my hands around her slender wrist and helping Sparrow and Jemma pull her back onto the bridge.

The four of us huddled on the bridge for a brief second of relief before I heard Journey call for me.

"Whatever you're planning to do, do it now and get them out of here!" I yelled to Remi and Eja as I scrambled to my feet and bounded back to Journey.

"Two more coming at us!" he called.

We both crouched low, waiting for them to get close enough to identify. Once their dark masks came into view I lobbed an orb up, temporarily blinding them. Journey pulled up a section of rotten wood and turned it to stone. He slammed it into the men with a sickening, bone crushing sound and they both went down. We looked at each other for a moment and then back at the men that ceased to move. I felt sick and dizzy but I knew I didn't have time to waste. I jumped to my feet and started screaming for Nova, Mali and Talon, but all I was met with was more Ravinori warriors.

Journey and I continued to take them out as we made our way further into the fog of the churning bridge.

"Nova! Nova!!!!" I called; more frantically each time I was met with silence. "*Nova, we're all on the bridge. You need to get to us! We have a plan,*" I telepathed, hoping somehow I'd be able to get through to him.

Finally he answered, but it wasn't what I was hoping for.

"Tippy, we're not going to make it. Whatever you're planning, do it now. We're surrounded. Get out now! Journey, take care of her! Get them all out of here now!"

"NO!!!" I cried, desperately looking at Journey who was now blocking my way. "I'm not leaving him Journey! I can't!"

"I know," he replied looking sad. He squeezed my shoulder sympathetically and then stood up, grabbing me under my armpits and hauling me over the railing of the bridge.

"Morf," was all he said.

I didn't have time to react before he let me go. I felt myself falling, flailing and screaming. I was consumed by shock and terror. I tried to control my frantic mind, but the wind rushing past my head made it hard to think. When I could finally form a thought it was an angry one, directed at Journey.

Had Journey really just thrown me from the bridge? Was he really so dull that he thought this was saving me!? Morf? How was I supposed to Morf from mid air? That maniac! It's not like he threw a Bellamorf tree off the bridge with me!

Suddenly my mind was screaming at me over the jack hammering of my heart! My pocket! I reached in and felt my slender fingers close around what I had been praying was still there. I pulled out the thin, veiny leaves of the Bellamorf tree that Journey had planted in my hand moments earlier and instantly took back all the horrible thoughts I'd just had about my brilliant friend.

CHAPTER LVIII

I landed in the Bellamorf tree we had previously been in before crossing the hanging vine bridge and to my pleasant surprise, Jovi, Jemma and Sparrow were there!

"Jovi!" I cried scrambling to her through the tree limbs. "You're a genius!" I said, hugging her tight. "How did you know to carry the Bellamorf leaves with you?"

"I always do," she shrugged. "Journey came up with the idea of taking the bridge down with the Ravinori on it, I just figured morfing would be the best way to get us all off of it," she said beaming.

"Where are the others?" I asked nervously.

At that moment, Remi and Eja morfed onto a branch next to me.

"Remi! Eja!" I cried, hugging them both with relief.

"Journey's making a run to get leaves to the others and then he's going to cut the bridge," Remi said. "They should be here any minute," he added when he saw the pale look on my face.

We sat silently, waiting for our friends and family to appear in the Bellamorf tree. But all was still for much too long. I had a sinking feeling in the pit of my stomach.

"Something must be wrong," I whispered to Remi, but as the words escaped my lips, the wind picked up and shapes started to materialize in the tree limbs.

Relief washed over me as I got to my feet, but something wasn't right. They didn't land gracefully like they'd been doing all day. Instead, the boys spiraled through the limbs, smashing and crashing as they went, until the ground broke their fall.

The commotion didn't stop there. I heard them screaming, calling for help. I recognized Nova's voice right away and bounded breathlessly to his side. My stomach lurched when I landed next to him on the leaf littered ground. He was covered in blood and gripping Journey tightly.

"Oh my god! Nova? There's so much blood! What happened?"

"It's not mine, its Journey's! I think they got an artery," he said, releasing his grip on Journey's arm slightly to reveal the wound.

Warm blood spurted angrily onto my neck when I tried to get a look. I fought the bile that burned angrily in my throat.

"Sparrow!" I screamed, but she was already by my side. "I'm going to need your help," I whispered.

Her cheeks were flushed and streaming with tears, but her hands were steady as she laid them on Journey. She looked determined as she nodded to Nova, who restrained Journey as we prepared to heal him. We both clamped our hands on either side of the gushing wound on his arm and I closed my eyes to block out the blood and concentrate on healing Journey.

I felt Sparrow's warm, healing power take hold, rushing from my heart down my limbs, to my hands on either side of Journey's pulsing forearm. Sparrow's hands were overlapping mine and I could feel her powers pouring through me to Journey, but only for a moment. My powers continued to surge, rushing forth, overpowering Sparrow's. My hand grew hot! Too hot!

"No, stop!" I cried, my eyes flying open as I realized I was losing control.

But it was too late. Flames burst from my hands, attacking Journey's wound and flinging Sparrow and I backwards. My ears were ringing with the shrieks of my friends. When I found my feet, I sprinted to Sparrow whose hand was being savagely licked by bright orange flames. I tackled her and stamped them out. By the time I got to Journey, Nova had managed to stifle his flames. Luckily Nova had enough practice with fire to remain level headed.

"What the hell was that?" he asked.

"I don't know! My powers… I'm losing control of them! I was only trying to use the healing power the way you taught me," I said looking from Nova to Sparrow.

Her face was twisted in pain and fear.

"I'm sorry," I whispered to her, tears welling in my eyes.

I fell to my knees next to Nova and Journey.

"I'm so sorry," I sobbed.

"It's okay. Look," Journey said through gritted teeth.

He held up his arm with painstaking effort.

"Well the good news is, the flames cauterized the wound and stopped the bleeding," Nova said. "The bad news; it's not the neatest job of healing I've ever seen."

We all looked at the bright white scar that had bubbled to the surface of his skin, marring his otherwise spectacular forearm.

"It's alright," Journey said with a trace of a smile. "I've actually been trying to get a gnarly scar there for ages," he joked.

"I think I can still fix it," Sparrow squeaked, trying to stifle a sob.

"I don't want you to fix it Sparrow. It's a badge of honor," he grinned. "Oh, come here," he called to her when he saw the tears flowing from her eyes. He pulled her close, embracing her tightly with his good arm.

"What about you?" he asked, peeling her folded fingers away from the palm of her burnt hand as gently as he could.

She winced a little and Journey immediately released her hand. My stomach flip flopped with guilt.

"It's alright, just a little tender," Sparrow said, trying to smile to spare my feelings.

"We match," Journey said with too big a smile, as he looked down at the white blistering skin on her palm.

"Journey, unlike you, I haven't been striving for scars!" Sparrow said pulling her hand away from him.

"Oh come on. You've healed every cut or scrape I've ever had so expertly that I don't have any scars. Scars are cool! Guys like scars, and we earned these. Besides, it makes you look tough!"

"I *am* tough," Sparrow said with mild annoyance.

I backed away from my bickering friends. They might be okay with their new scars but I wasn't. I couldn't believe I had lost control of my powers like that. Sure, this time it had actually worked out that I shot flames from my hands to sear Journey's wound, but that hadn't been my intention. Scars were a mild side effect, but it could have been worse. Much worse. I thought the whole point of sharing my powers with Jemma was supposed to prevent this. Apparently it wasn't helping enough. I needed to find a way to get my powers under control or I was going to become a liability.

Journey was still ribbing Sparrow, while I was wallowing in my own despair and guilt.

"It's not funny Journey. This isn't something to joke about. You could have been killed!"

"Oh come on Sparrow, we just defeated the big, bad Ravinori phantom mercenaries! We're allowed to celebrate a little. Right mates?" he said glancing behind me to where Mali and Talon had appeared.

They'd morfed onto a thick lower branch of the Bellamorf tree. I was relieved to see them and started towards them when the look on Mali's face stopped me dead in my tracks. A frigid chill stemming from my heart, ran through my body like a bolt of lightning, leaving goose flesh all the way to my scalp.

"No," I whispered even though I knew that nothing I could do or say was going to change what I saw.

Mali sat on the steady branch cradling his best friend, whose limp limbs dangled lifelessly from his lap. Everything around me seemed to go still; silent. Everything except the slow drip of blood from Talon's open hand. The Bellamorf tree looked deadly, as it rained slow droplets of blood from Talon's extended index finger, which pointed directly at me.

This haunting, ominous vision was all I could focus on as my friends rushed around me. Shell-shocked, I could do nothing but fall to my knees. It seemed like everything was moving in slow motion. My mind couldn't grasp what my eyes were seeing. I found myself hoping and praying that this was some sort of vision or nightmare, but something finally broke through the gloomy, quicksand of my mind. Jovi's hysterical screams shattered my thoughts and slammed me back to the tragic reality we were face with. This was no vision. Talon was dead.

CHAPTER LIX

"Kobel, what's taking them so long? The mercenaries should have reported back by now. They haven't lost them have they?"

"No master. The Betos thought they were being clever by having multiple groups morf at once, but the Eva is easy to track now that I've tapped into her mind."

"Well tap into her mind now! I want to see what's taking the men so long."

Kobel stood over the large map that had been splayed out over the massive desk in his master's office. He held his left hand steadily above it and waited for the man with the dark hair to unsheathe the blade he carried with him. When he stabbed the shining blade of the dagger into Kobel's open palm, the old man winced with pain. Kobel grimaced as he squeezed his hand closed, allowing his blood to drip onto the map.

The droplets of blood pooled like possessed beads of mercury, into one location; a waterfall. Kobel dipped his index finger into his blood and then touched it to his master's forehead. Both men closed their eyes, tapping into the Eva's mind.

They saw what she saw; panic, battle, death and destruction.

They watched as the Eva and her brave comrades skillfully battled the Ravinori soldiers, fending them off with an astonishing display of power and fighting ability. Kobel and his master were bewildered by their seamless communication, anticipating the mercenaries every move. They weren't all lucky though, the phantom mercenaries injured a few of the Eva's defenders. At least one suffered a mortal wound as he defiantly held his position, blocking the exit from the crumbling bridge.

Kobel gasped in horror as they watched the vine bridge plummeting to the ravenous waters of the gorge below. The water bubbled to a frothy pink, as the mercenaries met their demise in the churning current beneath the destroyed bridge.

The man with the long black hair slowly opened his eyes. He rocked his head back and roared furiously.

"I WILL HAVE HER HEAD!"

CHAPTER LX

"I don't know what happened next," I said to the chief. "I already told you, we ran back onto the bridge to fight the Ravinori. We took as many out as we could and then morfed to safety. The boys stayed behind so we could get away… I can't tell you anything that happened after that because I wasn't there! We've already been over this. Why are we wasting time?"

"Geneva, it's okay," Remi soothed from my side.

"No! It's not okay. None of this is okay! Talon is dead! He's dead! And it's my fault!"

My voice cracked. I was reaching hysteria but I didn't care!

"We have to leave now! I'm not staying here a moment longer. No one else is going to die because of me!"

I turned to rush from the chief's tent, but Vida was blocking my path. I stopped short of running into her and sucked in my breath. I hadn't spoken to her since we returned to camp. We had sent Quin with word of the attack and the chief had sent scouts to retrieve us. They took us all to a cave to hide while they assessed the threat of danger, and waited for Jaka and Vida to arrive.

She had rushed to Jovi's side and then spent the rest of the day sobbing over her son, while we'd been going over and over the attack with Jaka.

"May I ask one thing of you before you go my Eva," she said bowing her head.

"Yes, anything Vida," I whispered.

"Please stay for the funeral to honor my son."

I couldn't form any words. Hot tears streamed from my blood shot eyes as I nodded. Then, the most unexpected thing happened. Vida wrapped her arms around me and pulled me in close. She held me tight while we both sobbed, shaking and exhausted with grief.

That night I couldn't sleep. I'd never felt so tired or drained, but every time I shut my eyes I saw Talon's face. I gave up sleeping and grabbed my journal. I thought writing might help me get my emotions out, but it was too dark in the cave. Jaka had told us he preferred we all stay inside the cave even though Mali had assured him that all of the Ravinori that attacked us had perished. He said Talon's final task, which had cost him his life, had been cutting the vine bridge down with all of the Ravinori phantom mercenaries on it. That's when one of them had managed to plunge a sword into his chest, while Mali could do nothing but watch. He said he'd barely been able to get to Talon and morf them from the plummeting bridge, before it collided with the raging river below. But, he was sure it had swept away whatever Ravinori warriors it met, saying no one could have survived that fall. And, when he described the way the water had churned into a red mass grave of ravaging liquid, I believed him.

I'd fought alongside of Mali and I trusted him inexplicably. I decided if Mali said the threat was gone, then it was good enough for me. Besides, I needed some air. I poked my head out of the small opening of the cave and was greeted by the songs of the night birds. I crept out into the lively night atmosphere of the forest and looked up at the beautiful starry sky, drinking in the cool night air.

"Beautiful night isn't it?"

"Mali!" I shrieked. "You scared me!"

"Sorry. Couldn't sleep."

"Me either."

"I was just out here checking out Talon's view," he said as he leaned back against the cave wall and gazed upwards to the spectacular shimmering sky.

"What do you mean?"

"Ah, I forget you know so little about Beto culture," he said patting the wall next to him.

"Yeah, sorry," I said sheepishly.

"It's okay. Don't be embarrassed. I know you haven't really had a chance to learn everything yet. Don't worry, you'll get there. I'll give you a crash course for now and it'll be helpful in preparing you for tomorrow."

"Tomorrow?"

"The funeral."

"Oh," I said, feeling my heart instantly plummet.

It's not like I'd forgotten about it, or could even if I wanted to. Talon seemed to be haunting my every moment since I'd seen him laying lifelessly in Mali's lap. I felt that I was the reason he had been killed and that was an enormous guilt to carry around. *Why should I get to live and he should not? I'm alive and he's dead.* These thoughts and many more like them, were whirling around in my brain so much that I guess I hadn't had room to think much about the funeral, but suddenly I felt even more overwhelmed.

"I've never been to a funeral," I said once I settled in next to Mali, leaning into the coolness of the mossy cave wall behind me.

"Well, Beto funerals are beautiful," Mali said. "When a Beto passes away, we believe that they pass on to another realm," he said nodding up to the sky. "Everyone gathers at twilight and we bow remembering the person who has passed as we await the sunrise."

"What happens at sunrise?"

"Betos believe that the sun rises each day to help usher all the souls that have passed on. The light and warmth of the sun guides the souls so that they don't get lost on their journey to their final resting place among the stars. It's said that a tiny bit of their soul remains with the sun, to help power it and guide others. It's also how we can stay connected to the ones we've lost. They watch over us every day, guiding us with their light, warming us with their love. Then when night falls, they shine bright from the heavens, filling the sky with their beauty. So you see, the ones we lose are never very far. They always remain with us, you just have to know where to look."

I looked over at Mali. He's eyes where shining brightly as he gazed straight up to the vast night sky. I had a feeling he was studying it closely so that tomorrow night, he might find Talon's star and be comforted knowing where his best friend lay resting, watching over him.

There was such beauty in his words that I found myself longing for them to be true. I too wanted to believe that all those I'd loved and lost were always with me. I wiped the tears that were streaming from my cheeks and once the dry tightness in my throat dissipated, I reached over to grab Mali's hand.

"Thank you," was all I could manage.

He seemed to know what I meant anyway and he returned my heartfelt hand gesture as we studied the night sky together.

CHAPTER LXI

Just as Mali said, our day began at twilight. We all moved silently through the forest until we came to a clearing. There were dozens upon dozens of other Betos already there. Just as many as had attended my Eva ceremony had turned out for Talon's funeral. They were already kneeling in orderly rows, each of them with their arms stretched forward and foreheads touching the ground. It was an eerie sight, watching their backs slightly rise and fall in the last fading bit of moonlight.

My friends and I joined them. We each fell in line, kneeling quietly among the worshiping Betos. I thought about what Mali had told me last night. I found myself clinging to his words, for I found hope and peace in them and I needed that. I also wished for hope and peace for Talon and his mother Vida and his little sister Jovi. I couldn't wrap my mind around someone being here one moment and then so completely gone the next. It made everything so fleeting and fragile and I found myself having trouble breathing every time I let these thoughts take over.

I felt my chest constricting as I pictured Talon running past me, so full of life, into the face of danger on the vine bridge. He had been selflessly willing to fight for me, taking my place in front of the sword so that I might continue to fight and save our people. The guilt was pounding my soul, weighing me down and just when I thought I couldn't take it, I felt the sun suddenly warming my skin.

I opened my eyes without moving my head from the ground and I saw light. It was noticeably brighter than it had been when I had closed my eyes moments ago. The sun was rising. I felt my skin grow warmer now. The crown of my head and my shoulders felt as if they were being kissed by the sun. I kept my eyes open and let the sun burst in through the tendrils of blonde hair that cascaded down around me. I felt the light encircling me, engulfing my heart and filling the broken pieces of my soul. I was sobbing, but these tears were filled with joy.

I felt the air around me moving and I lifted my head to see the most glorious sunrise I'd ever witnessed. The huge orange ball of light floated before us, just over the ridge of the clearing. It looked as if it were so close that you could touch it if you dared. My mouth was open in awe and I squinted my eyes against its overpowering brightness. I smiled, thinking how the sun was much like my friend Talon; bright, bold, and fearless.

I felt Nova reach over and take my hand. I never took my eyes off the sunrise, but I was so grateful that he was beside me to share in this moment of beauty and tranquility as we watched the light spreading across the horizon. It was gradual, yet fast all at once.

When the sun had reached a place just above her head, Vida stood up to address us. Jovi was by her side, holding her mother's hand and biting her lower lip, trying to remain strong.

"I want to thank you all for coming today to celebrate my son, Talon. For those of you who knew him, today is bittersweet, but I know Talon would have wanted us to focus on the sweet. I am comforted to know he is surrounded now by so many who care for him, just as he was surrounded by his friends when he passed and will now be surrounded by all of our loved ones who have passed on. As his mother, I am eternally proud of my son and so grateful for every moment I spent with him. I did my best to nurture and teach him, yet I feel like I am the lucky one, because he taught me so much about life, courage, bravery, and kindness. I will do my very best to honor him each and every day, and to live my life with the zest he always showed and I will take comfort in knowing he will be shining down on all of us, bathing us with the warmth of his love in the new light of every day and guiding us each night in the brightness of his star alongside our ancestors."

Vida closed her eyes and put her palms together, bringing them slowly to her lips. She kissed her steepled fingers and then raised them up to the sky, slowly shaping them into a heart that was instantly filled with bursting sunlight. Everyone around me followed suit, mimicking her gesture. I released my hand from Nova's and raised them up to the sun as I said farewell to my noble friend Talon.

We said our tearful goodbyes to Mali, who'd decided to stay behind to protect Jaka and Vida. Then we waved farewell to the remaining Beto tribe members as we prepared to set off for our trek back to the Troian Center. They were already a group of few words and since the funeral, everyone was especially somber. They mostly just nodded to us, but Jovi's mom had given us all tearful hugs and wished us a safe voyage. She wanted us to send word with Quin as soon as we arrived. After promising her that we would and assuring her that we had enough to eat, she let us go.

As the distance between us and the Betos grew, I turned to look over my shoulder. The last image of my days in the forest with the Beto tribe was of Vida watching us go, griping an empty basket to her chest while stoically resisting wiping the tears that streaked her cheeks as she watched her only remaining child march with us into the unknown.

We hadn't wanted to bring Jovi with us after losing Talon, but Vida had insisted that she was safer with us and that it was Jovi's duty to serve us and none of us were in the position to argue with a grieving mother. Plus, what I knew of Vida and Jovi, was that they were both very determined and headstrong and fighting them on this would only delay the inevitable. I had resigned to let Jovi come along, but at the same time I'd made a vow to myself to protect her above all else. I would rather die, than let her fate be the same as her brother's.

It concerned me that we still weren't sure how the Ravinori had found us. But, I refused to stay at camp with the Betos a moment longer and continue to endanger others while we tried to figure it out. I hoped our swift departure might help us reach the Troian Center before the Ravinori had time to regroup and mount another attack.

We were traveling quickly; morfing when we could and hiking at a determined pace. There was little talking. Everyone was alert and on edge after what we'd encountered on our last attempt to reach the Troian Center.

With the vine bridge out we had to take a different way. The route was more direct, but more exposed. Journey had been against it, but we hadn't any other alternatives. He led the group, using his hunter skills to ensure our safety. We now knew the Ravinori were on to us and not using our powers before hadn't prevented them from finding us. We knew it was still risky to use them, but at least this way we'd sense them coming.

We'd been on foot for half the day. The hours passed uneventfully until suddenly, Quin's howl sliced through the air, bringing our group to a halt in an overly dense area of the forest. I'd been using my hunter skills and her howl felt like it pierced my eardrums. I crouched grabbing both my ears in response.

The undergrowth was thick and had slowed our pace already. It was dim here, yet still bright enough to see where we were going with the sunlight that filtered down in sporadic beams, bathing us with warmth as we passed through them. But, I had trouble extending my view beyond our group in the thick jungle to see what had startled Quin.

"Jovi, get control of Quin," Jemma whined looking aggravated.

"Sorry," Jovi said, starting to follow Quin in the direction she had darted, "I'll get her."

"No, wait," Journey commanded looking serious. "Eva, do you hear that?"

I closed my eyes and concentrated. There was a faint humming sound growing overhead.

"Yes," I said as I walked up closer to him, motioning for Jovi and the others to come closer until we were huddled together.

"I hear it too," Jemma added sounding frightened. "What is that sound?" she asked looking to Journey.

The others were starting to look a bit spooked now. Not being privy to our hunter power, they were unable to hear what we could.

"I think it's civer ants," he said. "Everyone huddle low, get under the brush. Quickly. We can't let them see us."

"But I have to get Quin!" cried Jovi, resisting as I pulled her towards a large thistle palm. She wiggled free of my grasp and started to run towards the sound of Quin's howling that was starting to be drowned out by the hum of whatever was approaching.

I stood to go after her but Journey's large arm held me back.

"Don't be stupid," he said.

He was right, but I was starting to panic. I could no longer see the top of Jovi's head over the wild underbrush of the forest. I could barely make out her shrill cries for her beloved wex. Suddenly the sky went dark, as if a blanket had been thrown over the forest canopy, cutting off our vital beams of sunlight.

We all looked to where the sky had been moments before. Journey and I saw them first; civer ants. Thousands of them. Their wings were beating so fast it was stirring up a wicked wind in the forest. I shielded my eyes as I used my hunter vision to rapidly scan the forest for Jovi. I'd promised her mother I would take care of her and I intended to keep that promise. I couldn't even be angry with Jovi. She had just lost her brother and was now even more attached to her wex. I understood her love for her pet. I knew I would have done the same for Niv, who I felt safely nestled in my pack. I slipped it off and handed it to Remi giving him a pleading look before I ran into the churning forest before anyone could stop me.

CHAPTER LXII

I barely heard my friends screaming my name behind me as I charged into the thick brush. I headed in the last direction I'd seen a glimpse of Jovi. I tried calling her name but it was useless. My voice was drowned out by the deafening hum of the civer ants. I kept low, trying to stay out of sight.

Although they were small and looked deceptively harmless, civer ants were notoriously vicious. They were the buzzards of our island, and a swarm of them could strip a carcass to the bone faster than you could blink. As long as you didn't aggravate them, they were quite useful, scavenging the island and riding it of sick or deceased creatures. I didn't know what drew them to our area, but I was pretty sure that Quin's incessant howling might qualify as a source of aggravation.

I noticed they were no longer traveling, but rather hovering above us. Their wings were beating so furiously they created a biting wind. The swarm had stopped just ahead of me, their dense mass blotting out the sun. I was terrified they'd found Quin or worse, Jovi. The only thing we had going for us was that they had horrible eyesight. They used their sense of smell to locate their prey, which was usually something already dead, but they'd make exceptions if they were particularly hungry and by the way they were swarming, it seemed like they were targeting something.

Suddenly, the wind parted the ferns just right and I spotted Jovi, she was huddled under a palm frond, clutching Quin in her arms. Her brown eyes were wild with fear. I was afraid that the civer ants were onto them now. Perhaps they had locked onto Quin's heady smell, because they were continuing to hover above them. If they didn't suspect us, they should have moved on by now. I couldn't chance waiting any longer. If I didn't get to Jovi before the civer ants did, there would be nothing left of her and Quin, but a pile of clean, white bones. I shook the acrid taste this image created out of my mouth and darted straight for them.

When I reached Jovi she wrapped her thin limbs around me instantly and buried her face into my neck, sobbing uncontrollably. I wanted nothing more than to comfort her, but there wasn't any time. The flying ants had spotted us and all at once they changed course, moving into position with deadly precision.

I didn't have a plan and it was too late to formulate one. My instincts kicked in and before I knew it I was running, bobbing and weaving through the thick forest, carrying Jovi, with Quin on my heels. Palmetto's slashed at our skin, ripping bloody ribbons into us with their serrated leaves. I knew I was no match for the speed of the civer ants, even without carrying a little girl. This fight was useless and would soon be over. I heard Jovi gasp with fear and call my name.

"Geneva! They're going to catch us!" she cried looking over my shoulder.

"Don't watch Jovi. Close your eyes!" I called to her. "Think of your favorite memory."

I didn't want her last image to be of a swarm of killer ants descending upon us. I had to do something but I didn't know what to do and I was out of time. I closed my eyes and took my own advice. The image of Nova and I atop the Bellamorf tree popped into my mind. That was it! The wind! Jovi had controlled the wind in the Bellamorf tree so we could play that magical game of morf tag. If she could do it here, if she could make the wind strong enough, maybe she could blow the civer ants away from us long enough for us to get away.

"Jovi! I need you to call the wind, just like you do for morf tag."

"But …" she started.

"Do it now Jovi!"

I felt her hands untwist from around my neck and suddenly the wind picked up. The trees and leaves swirled around us. I chanced a glance over my shoulder and saw that the civer ants were fighting a head wind that was slowing them down. I stopped running, long enough to put Jovi down and grab her free hand, sharing in her power to control the wind. It felt like lightning surging between us and it was hard to hold onto to her tiny hand, but it was working. I held my other hand up like she was and could feel the air responding to me. It swirled in powerful gusts, howling with fury and pushing the civer ants away from us in a cyclone of chaos.

"It's working Jovi!" I called to her over the roar of the wind, but she didn't respond. I looked at her, expecting to see her giving me one of her dazzling smiles, but instead was shocked to see her nose was bleeding and her eyes were rolled back in her head!

"Oh my god! Jovi!" I called, releasing my grasp on her hand. The wind died down instantly and the forest fell silent, as Jovi's tiny body collapsed into my arms.

I shook her and called her name over and over to no avail. Suddenly Quin growled. I followed her gaze to the black cloud that was reforming, and swarming back towards us. The civer ants weren't giving up so easily. They were back for revenge! Our momentary reprieve came to an abrupt halt as the angry, dark mass was upon us before I had time to do anything but throw my body over Jovi's.

A blinding light blazed behind my closed eyelids and there was a buzzing that was growing incessantly louder. Was this heaven? Or were the civer ants striping away my senses with their overpowering swarm? When I opened my eyes I found it was a little of both.

In the final seconds before the civer ants had closed in on us, I must have created some sort of fissure-like orb. I remember looking up to see the terrifying black mass about to engulf us and the only thing I could think of was "light!" I knew I had cast an orb, hoping it would have thrown them off course as a last ditch effort, but I knew deep down it would only momentarily delay the inevitable. But, I was bewildered to see that I'd done much more than that! I must have created a fissure as well. I shouldn't be that surprised, really. It always seemed to happen when I was scared or my emotions were extremely heightened. Getting eating by a swarm of vicious civer ants certainly seemed to do the trick.

Quin, Jovi and I were in the protected bubble of one of my fissures, but what was strange was that it was glowing with the light of one of my orbs. Outside the bright shielding membrane, I could see and hear the civer ants angrily testing the boundaries of the barrier, which was keeping them from their prey. I turned to comfort Jovi and tell her not to worry, that my fissures were very strong and I could hold it until the civer ants lost interest in us, but she still didn't respond. I swept her tangled brown hair from her unconscious face and called her name.

"Jovi! Jovi! Wake up! Please wake up."

Quin cowered and let out a sullen wimper.

"I know Quin. It's okay. She'll be okay."

I tried to wake Jovi, but she didn't respond. I could see her eyelids flickering, her nose bloodied and her face pinched, as if she were in pain. It seemed like she was stuck inside a nightmare that I couldn't wake her from. I wanted to use my healing power to fix whatever was causing this, but I was frightened after my last attempt on Journey had gone so wrong. Jovi was just a little girl. I doubted she'd recover from a mistake as easily as Journey had. Plus, I would need all my strength and concentration for that and that meant I couldn't keep the barrier of the fissure up. I looked out at the swarm of civer ants surrounding us. Giving up the fissure didn't seem to be an option.

"Persistent buggers aren't you!" I called angrily at them.

Quin howled and whimpered again.

"Quin, shhh. I'm trying to think."

She crawled over to me and laid her head on my crossed legs where Jovi's head was resting. She put her paws over her ears and I stopped to listen to the wex. Really listen to her. She was trying to tell me something. I could speak to animals after all. Maybe Quin could help me.

"What is it girl? What are you trying to tell me?"

Quin whined again, but I heard her this time. "*It's too much. It hurts. She's not strong enough.*"

"Oh no!" Eja's words instantly popped into my mind, haunting me as I remember him telling me the dangers of being an echo and sharing powers. Perhaps I had transferred some of my power through her and it was too much for her. Jovi was just a little girl. And now to make matters worse, I had trapped her inside a fissure with me. Time slowed inside of them and it could become too powerful for some, even trapping them forever. Plus, this fissure was different than anything I'd ever done before. I could feel it pulsing with power and heat from the bright glow of blue orb light that surged around us. I had to get Jovi out of here. But how?

"*I want to help! I can help!*"

I looked into the eager black eyes of the wex. She really did love Jovi. I could feel how much she wanted to help her. She was on her feet now, muscles coiled under her curly coat of russet fur, as she bounced from side to side with excitement.

"You're right Quin. You can help us. But you're going to have to be really fast. Are you sure you're ready for this?"

She answered me with an enthusiastic howl.

Quin burrowed out of the protective bubble of the fissure in seconds. She emerged on the other side and took off without hesitation. Within three strides she was up to full speed. She howled as she ran to get the civer ants' attention. A streak of screaming chestnut fur was all I saw as she disappeared into the forest, drawing the civer ants with her.

I dropped the fissure as soon as it was safe. The orb light dissipated instantly and it took a moment for my eyes to adjust to the dim forest. I scooped Jovi up. She gasped for breath, but didn't open her eyes. I had to get her somewhere flat where I could lay her down and try to heal her. I frantically scanned the horizon, nothing but trees and thick underbrush. But then I saw I large boulder. It was smooth and had a sloped top, spotted here and there with moss. It looked like the perfect spot to lay Jovi's tiny body.

I cradled her as I jogged to the huge rock and awkwardly placed her atop it as gently as I could.

"You're going to be okay Jovi. It's okay. You just need to wake up. Quin is leading the civer ants away from us and I'm going to fix you. Everything's going to be okay."

I kept murmuring soothing words of assurance to Jovi as I prepared to heal her. I wiped the blood from her nose with the sleeve of my shirt and then laid my trembling hands on her forehead and chest and closed my eyes. I took a deep breath and said a silent prayer that my powers would obey me. I did my best to push the thought of my past healing mishap from my memory. I cleared my mind and concentrated on sending my healing essence to her. I felt a warm energy surge from within me and suddenly she shuttered and swayed under my touch. That wasn't right! My eyes flew open, but what I saw was so unexpected I screamed and jumped back!

The huge boulder was moving! And it wasn't a boulder at all!

Four thick and scaly legs had sprouted from the rock, lifting it from the forest floor where it had been sitting moments ago. It trembled, dislodging bits of dirt and moss as it moved. I leapt up and grabbed Jovi from atop the moving boulder just as a head uncoiled itself from somewhere within the massive rock.

"What is the meaning of this?" growled its voice.

The rock was talking to me! I couldn't believe my eyes or ears. Its neck continued to uncoil, stretching longer and closer to me. The creature blinked its hooded yellow eyes as if it was waking from a long slumber. When they focused on me, they narrowed to angry slits as its neck stretched impossibly longer. I'd backed away as far as I could, but now I was cornered against a hammock of tree trunks and vines. I pressed my back into the sharp bark and tried to turn Jovi away from the beast, sheltering her with my arms.

I gasped as it unleashed a blue forked tongue! It was tasting the air with it over and over as it took a thunderous step closer.

"I asked you a question child!" it bellowed.

"How do you know I can hear you?" I asked in shock.

"I know a great many things," it replied.

"What are you?"

"I'm a rover tortoise. Now answer my question child. Why did you wake me?"

"I'm sorry, uh sir. I didn't mean to wake you. I didn't know you were . . . , well, I thought you were a rock! My friend is hurt and I'm trying to help her. I needed somewhere safe to lay her while I tried to heal her."

"Ah, so you're a Truiet healer? Why didn't you say so? We rovers are friends of the Truiets. We're just as ancient too, you know. We natives need to stick together. Come inside, I'll help you heal the child."

His head retreated back into his massive shell and I was left with my mouth gaping, Jovi listless in my arms.

Had a giant turtle just invited me into his shell? Was he crazy or was I? I felt like one of us was a bit mad and my money was on the old tortoise as I heard a racket of chaos coming from within his shell. It sounded like dishes smashing. I was starting to back away from him when he called to me again.

"Are you coming child?"

"Um, thank you, sir, but I don't think there's room in there for all of us," I said cautiously peering into the hole at the front of his shell.

"Nonsense!" he said popping his head out so rapidly, that I squeaked, unable to completely stifle my shock.

"Follow me this instant. From the looks of that girl there isn't time to spare." Then he retreated inside again.

I looked down at Jovi and swallowed hard. He was right, she was getting paler and her nose was still bleeding, soaking through the front of her shirt and mine as well.

"Well, here goes nothing," I thought as I edged us closer to the opening in the tortoise's shell.

It was dark inside. The opening looked large enough for my head, but I still didn't see how or where we were supposed to go?

"Jovi, I hope this works," I whispered as I laid her at the edge of the opening.

I felt a magical force take hold of us and whisk me off of my feet.

CHAPTER LXIII

I looked around the interior of the shell in complete wonder. It was amazing! Its vastness was incredible and completely impossible. I was sitting where I'd landed on a beautiful Persian rug, woven in hues of reds and golds, in a large room littered haphazardly with too much furniture and glowing lamps. I knew I was inside of the strange rover tortoise, but I didn't understand how it was possible that his interior was so expansive. It resembled a cozy home! There was obviously magic at work here.

Despite the dozens of lamps in what appeared to be a sitting room, it was dark inside. I was waiting for my eyes to dilate, while I clutched Jovi when the tortoise's voice bellowed around me.

"Bring her in here,"

"In where?"

"The kitchen. The table should be cleared off. You can lay her there."

"Where are you," I called to the tortoise's echoing voice as I stood in the vast belly of the beast. "How did we get in here?"

"You really don't know anything about rover's do you? There's no time for a history lesson now dearie. Put the child on the table and heal her! Once you're done I'll give you some special tea that will help her sleep so she can recover faster."

"Okay," I said, sprung to action by Jovi's ragged breathing.

I made my way through the maze of furniture and found the small cluttered kitchen. The table was cleared off as promised and I laid Jovi upon it and picked up where I'd left off, sending my healing powers to her. I was relieved that my powers responded flawlessly. It seemed I had enough strength to control them after all. When I'd finished, I found her color had been restored and her breathing returned to normal. If it weren't for the dried blood on her face, she looked like she might just be sleeping.

"Alright… sir, I'm finished. Where's that tea?"

The room shook as the tortoise bellowed. "Isby! Tea!"

"And stop calling me sir. The name's Hollis."

Before I could ask who Isby was, I saw a blur of black and white feathers wiz by me, squawking with discontent. The large bird slammed to a halt on the cluttered kitchen counter, sending a shower of dishes cascading onto the floor. It flitted around the kitchen, occasionally stopping to drop different ingredients into a battered tea cup. He ruffled his feathers grumpily while he worked, knocking things out of his way and making an even bigger mess of the already disastrous kitchen. Finally, he flew over to me with the tea cup clutched in his large, clawed feet and dropped it unceremoniously, without warning. Luckily, I'd been watching him like a hawk and was fast enough to catch it without spilling most of its contents.

"What is this?" I asked.

Isby just kept on flying out of the room without an answer. I peered at the sluggish grey liquid and shuttered when I caught a whiff.

"Make sure your friend drinks it all," thundered Hollis's voice, startling me.

"What is it again?" I asked him, while cautiously sniffing its familiar sulfuric scent.

"You sure do ask a lot of questions don't you? I told you, it'll help her rest and heal faster. It's an old Truiet recipe. Make sure she drinks it slowly, it should be rather thick."

The strange, giant tortoise had been helpful so far and he seemed to be a friend of the Truiets, so I took a deep breath and lifted Jovi's head, tilting the tea cup slowly to meet her lips.

"Please work," I whispered.

After I'd finished getting Jovi to drink the healing potion that Isby had made I felt relieved. Her cheeks had pinked up and her lips were the color of over ripe grapefruit flesh. Jovi smiled when I brushed her hair from her face and washed the dried blood from her nose. Her eyes still didn't open but Hollis assured me that it was the desired effect of the potion and it would wear off when she was fully rejuvenated.

"So, how did you know how to make this potion?"

"I told you, the Truiets are friends of the rovers. We look out for each other."

"How did you know I was a Truiet?"

"I could feel your power when you were trying to heal your friend. You have extraordinary strength for a child."

"Thanks," I said warily.

I was glad that he didn't seem to know I was the Eva but I had a feeling he might soon find out. My friends were still out there and would be looking for Jovi and I once they felt the threat of civer ants was gone. Hopefully Hollis would be willing to help me with one more thing.

"Hollis, I really appreciate you helping me. I wonder if I could ask you for one more favor?"

"What is it child?"

"Well, my friends, they're Truiets too, and they're still in the forest. We got separated when a swarm of civer ants attacked us.

Anyway, I need to find them, and since Jovi is sleeping, I can't really leave her to go do that. Would you be able to help me find them and bring us too them?"

"Civer ants? Why would they attack children?"

"I don't know, but I really need to find my friends. Will you help me?"

"Certainly. Where did you last see them? I'll send Isby out to scout for them. ISBY!"

The room thundered as Hollis's voice boomed through it, seeking out Isby. The ornery bird flew at me from a darkened corner and I barely had time to duck as it soared over my head. Hollis filled Isby in on my request and sent him out on the task of finding my friends. He squawked disapprovingly, spreading his shiny, black wings and making quite a racket.

"That's enough Isby," said Hollis and with that, the grumpy bird took a few hops while staring at me before lifting off and flying from sight.

"I don't think Isby likes me very much," I said.

"Oh don't mind him. He's always that way. Ill-tempered since the day I met him."

"Does he live… in you?"

The room shook as Hollis gave a rumbling belly laugh. "Of course child. He's my obliguile."

"What's an obliguile?"

"You really don't know anything about rovers, do you? How is it that a Truiet child, like yourself, is so uneducated about its kin?"

"Well, I was orphaned by the Flood and grew up at an orphanage called the Troian Center. Have you heard of it?"

By his gasp, I assumed he had.

"That is an atrocity! You should have been raised among your people, learning our way! No wonder you have so many questions."

Hollis spent what felt like an eternity filling me in on rovers, while we waited for the grouchy bird to return. As it turns out, Hollis told me he found Isby when he was just a fledgling. He was just hatching when a black jungle mamba had come upon his nest. The massive snake greedily gobbled up all the eggs and was about to make Isby his last meal, when Hollis rescued him. Saving his life had made Isby an obliguile, indebted to serve Hollis to repay him for saving his life. Apparently, every rover needs one to tend to their magical interior. As I looked around at the shabby state of things, I wondered if Hollis knew how poor a job Isby was doing?

I drummed my fingers on the overstuffed chesterfield I sat in, watching the patterns they created in the dust. I was growing impatient waiting for Isby, but Hollis didn't seem to notice. He happily continued to tell me all about rovers. I tried to pay attention to the sing song rhythm of his voice, as he relived the history of his kind.

He told me how rovers are the oldest living descendants of the Truiets. That they had existed on this island well before any other god or man. They roamed the island peacefully, keeping to themselves until one day a child who was fleeing a tarcat stumbled upon one. The story goes that the rover was so huge that the child was able to crawl inside his shell for shelter to hide from the vicious tarcat. It turned out that the child's parents were immortals and to thank the tortoise for saving their child, they granted him immortality and gave him magical powers, turning the interior of his shell into a spacious shelter for others and the ability to converse with all living things. It is said that much later on, the same rover tortoise came upon another child in the forest in need of shelter during a horrible storm. He let the child climb inside and after the storm had passed, he lent his magic to the boy named Jaka, who shared it with the Beto people, creating the Truiets to connect man and nature harmoniously.

"...but it all went horribly wrong."

"I'm familiar with the rest of the legend," I said.

"They taught you the Legend of Lux at the Troian Center, did they?" Hollis asked, sounding surprised.

"Well not exactly..."

Now it was my turn to tell Hollis about myself. I told him about my life at the Troian Center and how I had recently discovered my sorted past in the Book of Secrets, and how it had spawned our quest to return to the Center, where we hoped to find and free the other Truiets that were being held there. I didn't get into too much detail about who we were particularly searching for. I figured the less anyone knew about our search for the four Pillars the better, and besides that, I had a pretty good suspicion that another one of them had been right under our noses this whole time. After I finished talking with Hollis, I decided I needed to check on Jovi and explore my hunch.

"Hollis, thank you for everything. I'm going to go check on Jovi while we wait for Isby to return."

"You are most welcome my Eva. I am but your humble servant. I will do everything in my power to help you."

I found her laying where I had left her on the worn wooden kitchen table. She looked peaceful, covered with a tattered blanket, her head resting on a soft floor cushion. I stroked her hair and her eyelids fluttered open.

"Geneva?" she whispered as she tried to sit.

"Let me help you up Jovi," I replied, cautiously helping her rise.

"Where are we?" she asked with wonder.

"It's a bit of a long story. What's the last thing you remember?"

She looked blankly up at me and when I saw tears begin to well on the rims of her brown saucer eyes, I knew she remembered it all.

"Quin?" was all she managed to squeak out before she burst into tears.

"It's okay Jovi." I said, pulling the tiny girl to my chest. I stroked her soft brown hair as she sobbed against me. "Quin's okay. She is so brave! I told her how proud you would be of her! She saved us."

Jovi stopped crying and raised her head to look up at me. "She did?"

"Yes! She dug a tunnel out of the fissure and led the civer ants away from all of us."

"But what if they catch her?" she asked, her lower lip quivering.

"She's too fast. They'll never catch her."

There was a brief pause while Jovi was pondering something.

"Quin *is* really fast," she said, smiling now.

"The fastest," I said hugging her again, relieved to see her bright spirit returning, while secretly praying Quin really had been able to outrun the civer ants. It would devastate Jovi if Quin didn't survive. I shook the depressing thought from my mind and refocused on another pressing issue.

I figured now was as good a time as any to talk to Jovi about what I suspected. If I was right, I didn't want anyone else to be around for this discussion.

"Jovi, there's something I have to ask you."

"I know," the little girl said looking down, legs swinging back and forth nervously as they dangled from the table.

"You do?"

"Yes, and I'm sorry."

"What are you sorry about?"

"I'm sorry I didn't tell you and I'm sorry I'm not better at it. My mom made me promise not to ever use my power when she found out what I could do."

I shook my head. So, Vida did know what Jovi could do. No wonder she wanted her to come with us. She must have expected that we'd figure it out. I knew she just wanted to keep her daughter safe, but that doesn't excuse her for keeping this secret from me. Hadn't Jaka just told us how important it was that we were honest with each other? And this wasn't just some little, insignificant attribute she'd forgotten to mention. Her daughter was a Pillar! One of the very people we were risking our lives to save!

Jovi's head was in her hands now as she sobbed quietly. "I'm so sorry Geneva. I should have told you, but she made me promise not to. She didn't know if she could trust you, but I did. She said this power is too dangerous and that you'd figure it out when you were meant to. That's why she wanted me to come with you. She said you'd need me. But, I'm sorry I'm no good. I never get to practice. Except for when we play morf tag, but she doesn't know about that."

I collected my thoughts, as I let the unsettling fact, that Jovi was a Pillar, wash over me. I had suspected the possibility of her having some sort of power relating to the wind when I saw her controlling the squalls during morf tag. I had dismissed the thought almost instantly though, attributing morf tag to the unique magic of the Bellamorf tree that all Betos had access to. Not to mention, my friends had all seen her morf tag display as well and none of them offered her up as an option during our Pillar discussions. Plus, she was just a child. None of this made sense.

I sat next to Jovi in silence. I was trying to figure out what this all meant. What it meant for us, for her. How was it possible that this little girl was one of the four Pillars that controlled the elements? She was so young and didn't even fully understand how to control her power. I doubted she even knew how powerful a gift controlling the wind was. Or, that it might be a curse, coveted by an evil force.

When I looked at her thin frame and delicate features, I wanted to cry. Why? Why was this happening to all the people I cared about? First Nova and now Jovi? Why did she have to be one of the four? She wasn't ready for the consequences of such power.

Jovi was fidgeting with the hole-riddled blanket draped over her lap while I lost myself in thought.

"Geneva?" Jovi said, interrupting my sullen musings.

"Yeah?"

"I'm scared."

I pulled her close and hugged her tight.

"Me too," I whispered into her hair. "Me too."

I made a decision right then and there. I wasn't going to lose any more people that I loved. I pulled Jovi out of my embrace and looked deep into her honest brown eyes.

"Listen to me Jovi. I need you to do something for me. Can you keep a secret?"

CHAPTER LXIV

Just as I finished swearing Jovi to secrecy, Isby came squawking back into the room. He circled my head and then flew back out of the rover tortoise, beckoning me to follow.

"Jovi, I think he found the others. Can you stay here while I go out and get them?"

"But, I want to come too….."

Before I could argue with her, Hollis interrupted us.

"I think you should both stay inside where it's safe. I will follow Isby and bring you to your friends."

"Hollis, thank you. That is very kind, but I really don't mind going out to follow Isby. Besides, my friends might be a little frightened of you."

"Nonsense! It is my duty to help you my Eva. Please let me fulfill it. I insist."

Then without warning the room swayed into motion and it was obvious that Hollis wasn't waiting for my response. He was already on the move, hopefully heading in the direction of my friends.

It took me a while to get used to Hollis's undulating motion. It's what I imagined being on a boat might be like; swaying in the sea.

After quite a dizzying trek, Isby flew back into the room and circled around us noisily before disappearing into the darkness of Hollis's impossibly large interior. Shortly after, I heard voices. I ran to the edge of the sitting room and was confused when I didn't see a door. It was where Isby had been coming and going and it was where we'd landed when we first arrived in the cozy interior of the rover tortoise. But, right now, I was faced with a solid wall.

"Hollis! How do I get out?"

"I'm not certain it's safe for you outside my Eva. We're surrounded by six others and two of them have spears!"

I smiled, the two with spears had to be Nova and Journey. "Can you tell me what they look like?"

"Two females, four males. One has gold hair almost as light as yours."

Nova! My heart sang his name as my mind thought it.

"They're with me. They're the ones I'm looking for. If you let me out I can tell them you're a friend and they'll put away their spears."

"I'm still not sure it's safe..." Hollis hesitated.

It was sweet the way the rover tortoise was protecting Jovi and I, but also kind of frustrating. I needed to find a way to reason with him.

"Hollis, just as it is your duty to protect me, it is my duty as the Eva to protect my friends. Please let me out so I may speak to them."

"As you wish," he conceded and suddenly the wall in front of me vanished and I could see the bright daylight streaming in and hear the voices of my friends clearly. It was definitely them; Nova, Journey, Remi, Eja, Sparrow and Jemma. But the loudest voice I heard was Quin's and I was flooded with relief that she had survived!

"Quin!" Jovi squealed with delight, leaping to her feet. She bolted past me and was already hugging the excited wex by the time I landed on the ground next to her.

"I don't believe it! You found a real live rover," Journey was saying as he circled around and around the giant tortoise.

I turned to look at the rover tortoise as I dusted myself off. The top of Hollis's shell rose slightly above Journey's head, blocking him from my view until he bent down to examine the tortoise's scaly brown legs. They resembled coarsely barked tree trunks, until you noticed the thick yellow nails at their base.

I was still amazed that Jovi and I had been inside of his spacious interior. Even though I'd experienced it first hand, I was still full of questions and disbelief. Hollis was large for a tortoise, but there was no way you'd ever suspect he was large enough to house a house!

The others all looked dumbfounded, their mouths agape and eyes wide. All except Jovi, who was tangled in the curly fur coat of her beloved wex, being showered with kisses. She was all smiles and giggles as she crooned her thanks to Quin for saving us from the civer ants.

"His name is Hollis" I said, "and he helped save us."

"This … *thing* saved you?" Remi asked in disbelief.

He was only half looking at Hollis. He'd been distracted by the stain on my shirt, pawing at it with worry written across his deep brown eyes.

"Oh, I'm fine, it's not mine." I said, having momentarily forgotten about the blood on my shirt. "It's Jovi's. She had a little nose bleed."

I grabbed Remi's hand and squeezed it reassuringly, smiling when I saw Niv peek out of his pack. I let him scramble up to my shoulders and received my own shower of kisses from him. Once Niv was satisfied with his affection and settled down, I realized the others were still looking at me expectantly.

"Oh, yeah, sorry. I deterred the civer ants long enough to send Quin off as a decoy. When they followed her, I knew I needed to find a place to heal Jovi and I put her on top of Hollis, thinking he was a large boulder. Once I figured out what he really was, he let us hide inside and helped us find our way back to you all."

Eja laughed light heartedly, shaking his head at my mistake, most likely thinking that any normal Beto would have known Hollis's shell was no boulder. I blushed a bit at my inexperience, but smiled anyway. No one seemed to be judging me for my mistake now that they had found Jovi and I in one piece. Everyone was actually in great spirits after narrowly escaping our brush with the civer ants and certain death.

"Jovi, are you alright? There's blood all over your shirt?" Sparrow asked, circling around the little girl, picking twigs and leaves out of her tangled hair like a protective mother hen.

"She fell while we were fleeing and bumped her nose pretty hard," I interjected before Jovi could answer. Jovi looked up at Sparrow and nodded her confirmation, flashing her infectious smile.

"It was just a little nose bleed. I'm fine. See?" she said, rolling up her shirt sleeves to reveal she was intact and spinning in a dramatic circle while Quin tried to jump into her arms. She collapsed into a pile of swirling fur and laughter.

"Good enough for me," Sparrow said stifling a laugh and looking more relaxed.

Sparrow, Eja and I were all chatting rapidly, filling each other in on what happened after I'd left the group to go after Jovi and Quin. Everyone else continued circling Hollis, still in awe.

"How did you stop the civers?" interrupted a shrill voice.

Ah, leave it to Jemma to spoil the mood.

"Yeah, how'd you get rid of them?" Journey asked, his interest peaked.

I guess I knew I'd have to tell them what happened at some point, but I'd secretly been hoping they'd be so happy to see us that maybe they wouldn't ask too many questions. I hated lying to my friends, my palms had already begun to sweat just thinking about it. But, I needed to protect Jovi. Everyone was staring at me expectantly now. Especially Nova, with his beautiful piercing stare and I was starting to second guess our cover story.

"She was awesome!" Jovi piped up. The focus of the group shifted to her, catching me by surprise.

"You should have seen her! She blew them away! Literally! She made this big gust of wind and that blew the civer ants away from us, but they came back! So then she made this big bright protective bubble and they couldn't get to us! That's when Quin saved the day! She tunneled out and led them away from us so we could escape. Then, we found Hollis and he let us inside so we would be protected in case they came back again! Geneva and Quin are my heroes!" she said while hugging Quin tight to her chest and smiling at me. "Oh and you too Hollis! Thank you for helping us."

"Huh? What!" mumbled the startled rover tortoise.

We couldn't help but laugh at Hollis's confused expression. He must have fallen asleep during Jovi's tall tale and I was thankful for that because I wasn't sure how much of our battle with the civer ants he had seen and I didn't want him contradicting our story.

"Jovi was just thanking you for taking us in."

"Oh! Honored to do it. I am a friend to all Truiets. Anything you shall need, I am privileged to help you with my Eva," he said while lowering his head into a bow.

Nova spoke up, "There is something you can help us with."

He had been strangely quiet up until this point. I looked at him quizzically, not sure what he was about to say to Hollis.

"We're traveling to the Troian Center. We've already encountered some dangerous obstacles along the way. Do you think you could help us get there?"

"Oh, Nova that's not necessary. Hollis has been kind enough to help us so much already…"

"Nonsense. I too think you have encountered some peculiar dangers with the civer ants. They don't normally behave that way, you know? I'd be delighted to grant you safe passage to your destination."

"Really, Hollis, it's too much to ask of you," I glared at Nova.

I didn't want to be stuck inside Hollis's cluttered, swaying shell for the long journey back to the Troian Center. Especially with that ornery bird, Isby and the even more intolerable, Jemma. Not that I wasn't grateful for Hollis's help and his interior was large, but the eight of us in such a confined space was surly a recipe for disaster. I'd rather take my chances in the forest and move quickly like we had planned, before the Ravinori could regroup. Plus, Jovi had expertly lied to the group about what really happened when the civer ants attacked and I was still worried that the truth might come out if we stayed here and dwelled on it, but I could see it was too late. My friends were too excited to pass up the rare opportunity to travel by Rover. Everyone was already nodding and thanking Hollis for his generous offer. I was apparently the only one who didn't think this was a good idea.

"It is decided, I will take on this noble duty my Eva. I exist to serve you," he said with another bow.

I sighed deeply as I watched my friends gather up there things and one by one disappear into the giant tortoise's shell. Nova breezed past me and stopped for a moment to glare at me.

"It's good to know you listen to someone," he said with a hostility that surprised me.

"What's that supposed to mean?" I asked.

"It is decided," he said mimicking Hollis, sarcastically; disappearing into the magic shell before I could offer a witty retort.

I'd returned to Hollis's now bustling interior as I stewed over Nova's standoffish behavior.

"What's his problem?" I mumbled to myself.

The others were all walking around Hollis's spacious interior in awe. They were conversing with each other and inspecting their new surroundings. They seemed elated with Hollis's invitation to transport us to the Troian Center, but I was miffed. I stood where we had entered, arms crossed in protest, mirroring Nova's cold stance, across the room.

"What's whose problem?"

I turned to see Jemma standing next to me. I must have been so deep in thought that I didn't notice her come up. She really had a knack for bad timing.

"Now's not a good time Jemma," I replied.

"It's never a good time with you is it?"

"What did you say?" I asked, my voice and blood pressure rising.

"What's your problem with me anyway? I'm your sister and I've done nothing but try to be a good sister to you."

"Are you kidding me?" I was shaking with anger. "If this is you *trying* to be a good sister.... Well you can STOP TRYING!" I screamed at her.

"You're such a spoiled brat Geneva! You think just because you're the *EVA* everyone just has to do whatever you say? Well I don't care who you are!" Jemma taunted and poked my collarbone with her slender, pointed finger!

My mind was exploding. I was seeing angry, white spots of rage, dancing in my vision. Jemma's pretty face was pinched and mean, just as I remembered her from our days at the Troian Center, when she made it her mission to make my life miserable. It was like déjà vu of the rubble pile. I was trying desperately not to launch myself at her, but everything in my being was fighting against me. I was shaking as I raised my hands and tried to form my next sentence carefully while controlling my livid temper.

"Jemma," I hissed through gritted teeth.

"What Geneva? What are you gonna do?"

"Nothing, she's not going to do anything," said Sparrow, cautiously stepping between us, putting her hand on mine, calming the shaking.

"Sparrow, I can handle this," I whispered to her.

"Oh, really? Can you?" Jemma jeered.

By now everyone was watching us, but I didn't care. At least I didn't until I saw Nova. He was shaking his head with disapproval shining in his eyes. My heart dropped and I felt a lump forming in my throat. I had to get out of here before I started crying. I wouldn't give Jemma that satisfaction. I turned my attention back to her wickedly beautiful face.

"Yes. I can Jemma. And that's why *I'm* the Eva and you are not!" and with that, I turned on my heels and stalked away from her, pulling Sparrow by the hand behind me.

I didn't have a plan. I just wanted to put some distance between Jemma and myself, so I headed into the dark patch I'd seen the last time I was inside the giant rover tortoise. Luckily I'd been right, and the shadows parted ways, leading to a dark hallway. I was relieved it hadn't been a dead end and I wouldn't have to face the embarrassment of walking back into the living room to face the others. I could feel their eyes staring after me as we left the room. I pushed the thoughts of the rest of my friends from my mind and trudged forward down the dimly lit hallways. It twisted like a narrow maze lined with a collection of different doors along the way. They were different colors and sizes and shapes. The first two I tried were locked, but finally I came upon a short royal blue door with an antique gold nob. I twisted it and it creaked open.

It took a moment for my eyes to adjust to the dim light inside the room. It was painted a deep hue of purple and the floor was littered with dozens of large gold silk pillows. There were giant triangular shaped paintings, made to look like ornately framed windows. They were glowing with some sort of magical light, which gave the illusion of natural outdoor light. The room seemed safe enough and I could feel my emotions threatening to spill over, so I pulled Sparrow in behind me and shut the door, before collapsing in a heap on the pillows.

"What was that?" Sparrow asked.

I couldn't answer her. I was already sobbing. I was so

overwhelmed. Overwhelmed by the fact that my sister hated me and probably always would, overwhelmed by Nova's new disapproving attitude towards me, overwhelmed by the web of lies I was spinning to protect Jovi, overwhelmed by the fact that's she was a Pillar and she'd almost died today, overwhelmed that her brother had died. It was all too much. I just needed a release. I screamed into a silken gold pillow and pounded it with my fists, sending little clouds of dust floating into the air. Sparrow was by my side, rubbing my back and pushing my tangled hair out of my eyes.

"Breathe," she said. "Take deep breaths Geneva. It's going to be okay."

"It's not going to be okay! None of this is okay!" I sobbed.

Sparrow sat silently with me as I wailed, sputtering and coughing until I had nothing left. I was exhausted, but I pulled myself together, embarrassed by my outburst.

"I'm sorry Sparrow," I whispered.

"You don't need to apologize. You've been through a lot. We all have. I get it. But can I just say, you were brilliant back there! You didn't fall for Jemma's taunts. I can't believe you stood up to her like that! She looked like such a fool standing there with her mouth gaping after you spun on your heels," Sparrow mused excitedly.

"I'm pretty sure I made a fool of myself too," I said, still sullen.

"What do you mean?"

"Did you see the way Nova was looking at me? I've never seen him look so, so....disappointed in me."

"Oh Geneva, you really just need to talk to him and it'll all work out."

"Sparrow, I know you're always looking on the bright side, but I really don't think you're right this time. We're so hot and cold and we fight all the time. Plus, he's always spending so much time with my horrible sister ... although..."

"Although what?"

"He told me he's spending time with her because he's trying to see if Jemma can give him any indicators that will prove his siter might still be alive."

"Well that's a perfectly good explanation."

"I don't know Sparrow. It's just too complicated. And then there's the whole Kull and Aris prophecy that he can't get past."

"Oh please! If you'd seen him after you took off after Jovi you wouldn't have any doubt," Sparrow said rolling her eyes and waving off my gloomy state.

"What do you mean?"

"Geneva, he was out of his mind with worry. Journey had to tackle him and practically strangle him to keep him from going after you. The two of them almost got into it, but luckily Remi stayed level headed enough to break it up. He convinced everyone that with the civer ants nearby the best plan of action was to stay put and that he knew you would come back to look for us the first chance you got."

I smiled proudly hearing about Remi's brave actions. He really did know me best. But then I was back to shaking my head thinking about Nova. It confused me to hear his reaction.

"If he cares about me, he really has a stupid way of showing it," I huffed crossing my arms.

"Oh, you're both fools! Beautiful little fools," she said quoting from our lessons again. Then she sighed and dramatically collapsed onto her back in the pile of pillows.

I sighed and laid back onto the soft pillows as well, letting a smile spread slowly across my face, thinking of Nova actually caring about me.

"He is beautiful," I said with a sigh.

"Will you please talk to him already?"

"I sort of did. I started to anyway.

"What do you mean?"

"I told him I loved him right before we crossed the vine bridge."

"You did!? What did he say?"

"Nothing. But, there really wasn't time."

We were both silent, momentarily lost in the painful memories of that day.

"Well, you should try again," Sparrow said breaking the silence.

I was about to reply when I heard the door creak open and lifted my head to see Jovi peeking into our little room of pillows.

"There you are! Everyone is looking for you two," she called, playfully kicking a pillow in our direction.

I snatched it out the air as it sailed over my head. Sparrow and I both looked at each other and then simultaneously threw pillows at her.

"Hey!" she squealed ducking just in time. Without skipping a beat, she was tossing pillows back at us.

This started a full-fledged pillow war! Blurs of luxurious gold fabric were sailing overhead as the room filled with laughter. Leave it to Jovi to bring her gleefulness everywhere. Even into my dark pit of despair and exhaustion.

After a good ten minutes of brilliant battle, we were all breathless and giggling among the mounds of stuffed silk. I gazed up at the white feathers floating weightlessly above us, seemingly frozen in the false sunlight. I flicked my wrists making them spin in tiny cyclones on the light gusts of wind I now effortlessly controlled with my latest power. Sparrow oohed and awed, while I winked at Jovi.

"So, why is everyone looking for us?" I asked Jovi, knowing it was time to get down to business.

"Nova was talking to Hollis about the civer ants and they think that the Ravinori sent them to attack us! He said they would never act that way on their own. Nova wants to have a meeting to go over our plan for when we get to the Troian Center because he's afraid they might be expecting us!"

I looked nervously at Sparrow. The light-heartedness that we'd had moments before, had been sucked out of the room. It was time to get back to reality. Nova was probably right about the Ravinori. The civer ant attack had been bothering me too, but I didn't know that much about them to be completely sure. I wished we could have just talked about it one on one. I hated feeling foolish in front of the group.

I sighed as I stood, dusting the feathers off of myself.

"Okay, let's go have a meeting."

CHAPTER LXV

"What do you mean they got away? No one gets away from the civer ants!"

"Master, I'm sorry, but I told you the Eva is very gifted. Even with her diminishing powers, she's very cunning and seems to have many unknown weapons at her disposal."

"Of course she does, Kobel. She's the Eva! But we are the Ravinori, and I will not be made to look like a fool! This has gone on long enough. Where is she right now? I'm going to go after her myself and end this once and for all!"

"Master, I'm terribly afraid to tell you that they've disappeared. All of them. They've completely vanished."

"What do you mean, Kobel? She's powerful, but she can't defy the laws of nature. If she exists you should be able to see her. Is that not what your purpose is?" the tall man asked venomously. "Unless … you're wrong, and the civer attack was successful? They've been known to devour a whole body in seconds, but I specifically instructed them not to harm them. They were just supposed to bring them to me."

"No master. I watched the civer ants be defeated by the Eva and her friends. I'm sure they survived. But, they split up and I lost track of them, trying to trace too many at once. I'm sure they're still alive. They must just be using some sort of new power to conceal their whereabouts. I will find them master. I live to serve you."

"Be sure that you do Kobel or I will have no use for you. And, it is as you said, 'you live to serve' and if you no longer serve a purpose, you shall no longer live!"

CHAPTER LXVI

We followed Jovi back through the winding hallway. She seemed strangely at home in the rover tortoise. She skipped and chattered nonstop as we trailed behind her. She finally led us to an open doorway, which she promptly disappeared through.

Warm light spilled out into the hallway and something made me pause mid step. It was Nova's silhouette, leaning casually against the door jam. The light peppered his golden hair and highlighted his perfect jaw line. His face was mostly hidden in the shadows and I couldn't gage his mood. I didn't know which Nova to expect, the one who worried about me or the one who was disappointed in me. Sparrow brushed my shoulder as she pushed past me and whispered, "Talk to him."

"I'll be inside in a minute," I called after her as I paused outside the doorway in front of Nova.

"There you are," he said with a hint of annoyance.

I took a deep breath and said, "Nova, I need to talk to you."

"About what?"

I paused before answering. I could see my friends gathering around a large antique looking table just inside the room we were standing in front of.

"I'd rather not say here."

Nova pushed himself off of the door jam and was standing close to me now, completely bathed in light. I could see worry wash across his face.

"Is everything alright? Are you okay?" he asked, his hand instinctively going to mine.

It was such a simple and genuine gesture, but it sent an electric jolt through my being. How could I ever deny I had feelings for him? It would be impossible. Just holding his hand was pure joy.

"Tippy?" he prodded.

"Yeah... Yes," I stammered when I realized I was stuck in my Nova daze and hadn't answered him. "Everything's fine. I just wanted to talk to you about something I've been thinking about."

"Come on you two," called Journey from inside the room.

"Coming!" called Nova. "Tippy, can we talk after this meeting? We've been waiting for quite a while and I think everyone's getting a bit restless," Nova said.

"Sure, it can wait," I said giving him a reassuring smile, while mentally wishing I could kick Journey for interrupting us!

"Are you sure?"

"I'm sure," I said returning the squeeze he gave my hand.

As we entered the room, I was once again astonished by Hollis's never ending interior. The room was round and as large as one of our lesson rooms at the Troian Center. It had high, arched ceilings with dark wooden beams sporadically placed above us. The walls were the color of scorched wheat and adorned with beautifully painted frescos. I was pulled away from examining them further when Hollis's voice boomed, echoing through the room.

"Are we ready to start?"

"Yes, we're all here. We're ready Hollis," replied Nova.

Hollis cleared his throat theatrically before proudly welcoming us.

"Welcome to the rotunda. It has been quite some time since I hosted Truiets here and I am beyond proud to serve you on such a noble cause. I want to put your minds at ease and let you know that those who are after you, won't be able to find you here. Rovers are a safe haven, immune to the Truiet techniques of tracing. After speaking with most of you and gathering information from what Isby and I have recently observed in the forest, I've come to the conclusion that there are dark forces working against you. As we discussed, your quest back to the Troian Center will be safest if I usher you there myself. A task I'm honored to take on."

The room swayed slightly under our feet and I imagined Hollis was bowing.

"Hollis, what makes you think that there are dark forces after us?" I asked.

"Many things my Eva. The civer ants are a fine example. They never behave irrationally as you all have described. They don't attack. They are scavengers. They clean the island of carcasses. They don't go out of their way to take down perfectly healthy prey."

With the little I did know about civer ants, their behavior did seem peculiar. The others all seemed to be nodding in agreement, but I wasn't so easily convinced.

"What could have made them behave that way Hollis?"

"The Ravinori of course. No other dark forces would possess enough power to control animals like that."

I shuttered, instantly thinking of the way Greeley had controlled her tarcats, Ria and Khan.

"Are you sure it's the Ravinori?"

"Positive. The civer ants are one of their master's favorite weapons."

We all stared blankly around the rotunda waiting for Hollis to explain.

"You do know who I'm speaking of, don't you?" he asked after our silence.

"I'm afraid we don't," I said.

"Malakai Venir, of couse."

Again, no one responded. We met each other's wandering stares simultaneously, waiting for Hollis to elaborate.

"Ah, well then I have much to tell you! Allow me to introduce you to the leader of the Ravinori."

As Hollis spoke, the walls inside the rotunda burst to life. The frescos came alive, their scenes fading away to show moving images. It was like the visions my mother had shown me in the cave, but these were sharper and all focused on the same, tall, dark haired man. They seemed to be a chronicle of his development from adolescence to what I was assuming was his current state. Past to present, the images were haunting. The walls displayed the things of nightmares; evil, torture, malice, murder.

"His name is Malakai Vanir. He's the most powerful man on Hullabee Island. He's head counselor of Lux, in charge of the Luxor militia, the prisons and now, the Troian Center. He's the suspected leader of the Ravinori, probably heading the hunt for you and your friends. Rumor has it, that he has found a way to extract power from the souls of the lost Truiets. If it's true, it would make him as powerful as you, my Eva. It's assumed that's how he has risen so quickly up the ranks of society. But alas, money and power are not enough for him. He wants total domination and for that, he needs you."

"How does he get his Truiet powers?" I asked.

"From the Flood debris of course. You didn't think they spent years cleaning up all that rubble for nothing did you?"

"Flood work," I whispered, thinking back to the years I spent sorting stones at the Troian Center.

"Yes," Hollis encouraged. "Now you're getting it. You see, when the Flood happened, it was because nature was unbalanced. There must always be balance. When everyone died, their souls split, being divided equally among the four realms. You do know that story, don't you?"

"Yes," we answered in unison.

"So, a part of the soul went to each realm, bone to earth, tears to heaven, breath to limbo, heart to hell. You know, ashes to ashes and such … Anyway, something unique happened to all the magic that was left behind. The magic powers didn't belong to any realm, so each Truiet left the power they'd possessed behind, where it was encapsulated by the lava, turning it into the stones, or rubble as you call it. That's why the Ravinori had the city of Lux commission all the rubble to be recovered, under the guise of cleaning up the island during Flood work. The order was truly given by Malakai, so he could claim every last drop of lost power for the Ravinori, with the hope of bringing Ravin back. That's been the sole goal of their secret society and Malakai believes that if he's the one to bring Ravin back, he'll be allowed to serve eternally by his master's side; right hand man to the devil."

"Is that true?" I asked, looking to Eja. "I've never heard that part about the powers being trapped in the stones."

As if reading from a book that we couldn't see, Eja recited a quote from some ancient legend he knew, "The struggle for powers had started the strife and upset the balance of nature. Through self-sacrifice, balance was restored and the powers were sealed away; all that remained after the cleansing Flood, would be trapped for all eternity, so that they would never ignite another war."

I instantly thought back to how I used to swear the gems and stones in the rubble pile where speaking to me. That was back when I was younger, before I knew there was truth in legends and fairytales.

"Can he do that?" Journey asked, breaking me from my memories. "Can he bring Ravin back?"

"It's all rumors; whispers we forest folk hear. But, I hope we never find out," Hollis answered.

We all looked nervously at each other, shocked by this news.

"Hollis, how do you know all of this?" Remi asked.

"Isby and I have our ways. We are not easily noticed and lips are loosest when you think no one is listening."

"Why is this the first we're hearing of it?" I asked.

"Perhaps the Ravinori wanted it that way."

I looked around at the shell-shocked faces of my friends. Another bombshell had been dropped in our laps. I took some comfort from Jaka's words that echoed through my mind. 'There is power in knowing your enemy,' he'd said.

"I feel I should warn you, if Malakai sent the civer ants after you, you can bet that they already know your course and he will be waiting for you."

"Hollis, even if Malakai is this all powerful leader of the Ravinori, how could he have known where to find us unless *someone* tipped him off? How could he possibly have known where to send the civer ants?" I asked.

Just then, Isby squawked from his perch by the door, picking at his glossy feathers. Even though Hollis had vouched for him, I didn't trust him one bit. For all I knew, he could be one of Malakai's spies.

"Malakai is very powerful. He has his ways. I've heard he has a powerful alchemist in his service and he employs him to use dark magic to serve his needs."

"Even so, we've been careful. We knew the Ravinori were out there. We've encountered them already. We even had the Beto's best scouts checking the area to make sure it was safe before we started our voyage. Nothing indicated they knew we were heading back to the Troian Center," I challenged.

"Ah yes, you are skeptical. I might add that I could be skeptical of you my Eva. You have not been completely honest with me."

My palms began to sweat as I nervously scanned the room, searching each of my friends' faces to see if they would give something away, eluding to what dishonesty Hollis could be referring too. In that moment, it became overwhelmingly obvious that I had way too many secrets. I truly didn't know which one Hollis was referring to.

The room was so silent I was sure the others would hear my thundering heart. I took a deep breath and was about to deny lying to Hollis when Remi saved me.

"Hollis, if I may interrupt? Our Eva has many to protect and she has to be cautious when sharing information. She tends to err on the side of vagueness for our safety and surely means no offense to you by it."

I looked at Remi with astonishment. I'd never heard him speak so confidently or eloquently. Apparently I wasn't the only one shocked by his diplomatic speech. Sparrow's mouth was hanging open and everyone was staring at him with looks of wonder.

Remi seemed to notice my stare and gave me a smile. I returned it, regaining my composure.

"Yes, Hollis. I apologize for any offense. Remi's right though. I'm only trying to protect my friends."

"A noble quality of our Eva indeed," Hollis said. "I apologize for my harsh tone."

"I apologize as well."

"Well, I hope by now you know you can trust me and that you will take my warning to heart."

I waited for him to continue, still confused as to what secret he had figured out. Then, I realized he must be waiting for me to reply.

"Yes, Hollis. We do trust you and are very grateful for your help and advice."

"Good, because the matter of Ponte Deorum is a very serious one."

My face went pale and I instantly felt a chill run up my spine.

Hollis mentioning Ponte Deorum had knocked the wind out of me. How had he figured it out? Surely, no one in our group would have told him this tremendously vital secret. Besides Jaka, Vida, and my friends, no one else knew. Eja had sworn us all to secrecy. I thought Hollis may have figured out that Jovi and I lied about the way we escaped the civer ants or that she was a Pillar, or maybe that I had been in one of his rooms without permisson, or that I was in love with Nova or that I had kissed Remi; anything but this! My world was whirling and I was having trouble focusing on what Hollis was saying.

"... the Ravinori mustn't find out that you are the Bridge of the Gods. Malakai will come after you with all his force, for it is this eternal power that he seeks most, in order to bring back their one true leader."

Hollis paused theatrically, but I knew what he was going to say next and it made me break out in a cold sweat.

"Ravin."

The sound of his name made my stomach lurch and I had to put both hands on the table and grip tightly to keep myself upright. How could this be happening?

Suddenly, all eyes in the room were on me and I could immediately feel desperate, longing and hopefulness emoting from my friends. This was a room filled with orphans. We had all lost parents, siblings, and family in the Flood. Of course we could all see why this was such a coveted power.

But Hollis wasn't telling us anything new. Maybe *he* hadn't known I was the Ponte Deorum, but I did, and so did all of my friends. I was more upset that one of them had betrayed my trust and told a rover tortoise, we'd only just met, the biggest secret of my existence, putting all of us at risk.

"I want to know how you know this, Hollis," I said through gritted teeth.

"I told you. I'm ancient. The oldest living descendants of - "

"NO!" I cut him off. "Not how do you know about the Ponte Deorum. I want to know *who* told you that *I* am the Ponte Deorum."

"Well …" he stuttered, but he didn't have to tell me.

As I searched the faces of my friends, I settled instantly on particular face; Jemma's. It was pinched and she refused to meet my gaze. Guilty!

"I knew it! I knew it was you Jemma!" I shouted, lunging from my seat.

"Hey, whoa," Journey called, reacting fast enough to catch me before I could reach my traitorous sister.

"You don't know it was her," Eja said calmly, trying to diffuse the situation.

"It was her," I hissed. "You're not denying it are you?" I called, narrowing my eyes and focusing my seething hatred at Jemma.

"Oh come off it Eva. You're not the only one this effects! You shared your powers with me. Maybe that makes me part of the Bridge of the Gods too! I have a right to know how this works."

"This wasn't your secret to share Jemma! You swore you wouldn't tell anyone about the Ponte Deorum. I'll never trust you again Jemma! You only care about yourself!" I yelled.

"That's not true! I was thinking of all of us and who we could bring back. Like our mother! Why can't we use the Ponte Deorum to bring back our mother?" shouted Jemma, already in tears and moving towards me from the head of the table. "Maybe we could bring them all back! Why should we have to suffer any longer?"

Nova blocked her way and she wailed, struggling against him.

"Do you think I don't wish I could bring her back? I wish I could bring all of them back! Mom, Dad, Talon, Ivy, Dehani …," I whispered.

My heart shattered as I mentioned the names of our deceased family and friends. It was too painful to continue a list that long.

"That's not how it works Jemma," I said sadly.

"You don't even know how it works! But that's fine, I'm not going to let you stop me from doing what you're too afraid to. You gave me half of *all* your powers. I bet that includes the Ponte Deorum too."

"Is that true? Is she the Ponte Deorum too?" Sparrow asked sounding worried.

"I don't believe that's possible," Eja said.

"Why not?!" Jemma yelled. "I can be powerful too! I can have a purpose. I'm not afraid of greatness. You just need to give me a chance," she scolded. "What if I can bring them back? All of them. Everyone we've ever lost. Don't you even want to explore our options just a little bit?" she pleaded to the room.

"SILENCE!" bellowed Hollis, putting an end to the chaos and shouting in the rotunda. "It is not that simple. There can only be one Ponte Deorum. And if you say you've witnessed Geneva exhibit this privilege, then she is the one and only, true Ponte Deorum. Another important thing you should know, is that the Ponte Deorum can only bring one from the other side back to this world, and it will most likely cost you your life."

Now this *was* new. Jaka hadn't told me that bringing someone back would kill me. Again every eye in the room was on me.

"How?" I asked. "How do I do it Hollis?"

"My Eva, this is not something I can recommend in good conscience. It is wrong to fool with nature by connecting to the other side and there are consequences. Steep consequences."

"I need to know how it's done Hollis. How am I to protect myself and others if I know nothing about this!?"

"Very well my Eva. I shall not deny you, I am but your humble servant. Whomever is the Ponte Deorum possesses the power to see through the veil between worlds."

"Veil?" asked Jovi startling me. I hadn't noticed that she'd moved to my side.

"Yes, think of it like an invisible wall that separates the living from the dead."

Jovi swallowed hard and curled her slender fingers around mine, griping my hand hard. I forced a smile for her sake and pulled her close, stroking her hair while Hollis continued to tell us about the Bridge of the Gods.

"Every time you summon someone from the other side, the veil thins and can allow those from the other side to reach through to this world. This is a very dangerous act even in itself. Alas, an even more perilous act is required to start the transition to bring someone back from the other side. It requires an exchange of matter."

I hated the sound of that; exchange of matter. Unfortunately, I had to ask Hollis to explain further so that I could avoid doing it.

"How do you exchange matter Hollis?"

"Ah that part is really quite simple. You just have to touch someone from the other side. Although I hear it's quite painful. Even painful enough to kill you."

My heart plunged and I tasted bile. I had touched my mother when I was drowning in the cavern lake and when I first saw her in the mirror at the New Year Gala. It felt like grabbing onto a lightning rod. I had tried to touch her when I last saw her in the pond in the Beto camp, but she pulled away from me and said it was dangerous. My mind was reeling.

"You just have to touch someone to bring them back?" asked Jemma hopefully, ignoring Hollis's warning of danger.

"Well, yes. But it doesn't happen after just one touch. There is a price to pay each time you touch someone from the other side. It's called an exchange of matter, because you must give them a little piece of your soul and in return you must take on a little piece of their soul. It is said this is why it is so painful, because tearing a portion of one's soul is no simple task. If this exchange happens enough times, enough of your soul will be on the dark side and enough of their soul will be on our side, the light side. So, in essence, they will have enough power over you to take over your body. Meaning you will be trapped on the side of the dead and they will remain on the side of the living."

"So in order for Geneva to bring someone back from the dead, she has to die?" Remi asked incredulously.

"There must always be a balance. Nature requires it," replied Hollis solemnly.

"This power is useless!" Nova yelled. "Why would anyone want to be the Ponte Deorum if it means you have to die to bring someone back?"

"Precisely!" said Hollis.

"Precisely what? What do you mean Hollis?" Nova asked, unable to hide the anger in his voice.

Eja spoke up for the first time. He'd been sitting quietly, taking all of this in, but now he cleared his throat and stood.

"If I may?" he asked looking at me.

All I could manage was a stiff nod.

"I think what Hollis is saying, is that no one wants to be the Bridge of the Gods, but everyone wants control of it. If the Ravinori get ahold of Geneva, they can use her to contact the other side. They can force her to exchange matter with whomever they want."

"I won't do it," I said, fighting to keep my voice steady.

"You may not have a choice," Hollis said. "The Ravinori can be very persuasive. Especially Malakai. When he wants something he will stop at nothing to attain it. He'll implore despicable, ruthless ways to achieve his goals. He and the Ravinori have been known to implant visions that can deceive you into giving them what they want. If that doesn't work, they are particularly skilled at various torture techniques and they make it a habit to demonstrate this on your loved ones, until you give them what they want. Malakai is merciless. He's rumored to have killed his own wife. Make no mistake, he'll use whatever he can against you. If the Ravinori don't already know you're the Ponte

Deorum, you cannot afford to let them find out."

"Why are they after me if they don't know I'm the Ponte Deorum?" I asked.

"I believe they have given up hope that the Ponte Deorum exists. They may actually have another plan, which they need the Eva for, because she is a Pillar tracker and her blood will bind the ritual."

"What ritual?" I asked.

"I think they are trying to collect the four Pillars in order to try to create their own Bridge of the Gods. I suspect Malakai will imprison the Pillars and use them whenever he needs to contact the other side, perhaps even sacrificing them if it means bringing Ravin back."

CHAPTER LXVII

The mood in the room was somber after Hollis's speech. My legs were shaking as I sunk down into a nearby overstuffed chair.

I didn't know what to do next. Hollis's explanation of Ponte Deorum had knocked the wind out of my sails. Before the meeting I had been confident in our mission to return to the Troian Center to save the four Pillars, but now I felt hopeless. I was doing my best to put on a brave face for my friends. I didn't want to add to their worries.

"What do we do now?" Sparrow asked softly.

"Well, we can't go back to the Troian Center," Remi said. "Not now that we know they're waiting for us."

"We have to and we will," I said. "We can't just abandon our plan because of a new obstacle."

"A new obstacle?" Nova questioned. "Are you mad? Did you not just hear what Hollis told us? The Ravinori are hunting for you! They know you're coming. Malakai is expecting you."

"Yeah, and they're hunting for the four Pillars as well. We are the only ones who can save them and stop Malakai from bringing Ravin back. Besides, the Ravinori don't know I'm the Ponte Deorum yet.

We have to strike now before they figure it out."

"Hollis figured it out pretty quickly, so I doubt it'll take the Ravinori that long," Nova challenged.

"No, he didn't figure it out. Jemma ratted me out," I said glaring at my traitor of a sister across the room.

She returned my stare with a nasty look of her own, threatening to accost me again.

"What are you going to blame me for now?" she whined with an exaggerated eye roll.

"Haven't you caused me enough grief for one day Jemma?"

"You should really be thanking me. If I hadn't told Hollis about you, we wouldn't even know about Malakai or his plan. I probably just saved your pathetic life."

"Oh, get over yourself Jemma!" I hissed.

"Okay, let's go. You two need some time apart!" Nova said.

He plucked me up and threw me over his shoulder. I wiggled and kicked at first, but once outside the room, he set me down and I felt the fight drain out of me.

He looked deep into my eyes, his jaw set and his flawless lips turned down.

"Let's have that talk now," he said.

For once, I was too tired to protest. I followed Nova obediently. We walked down the dark winding hallway and finally through a tall, narrow red door. I could have sworn I tried that door earlier with Sparrow and it had been locked. But, under Nova's touch, it glided open smoothly.

Once inside the cozy room with the crackling fire, Nova grabbed my hand and pulled me into a fierce embrace. It caught me off guard, but in a good way. As he pressed my face to his chest, I drank in his intoxicating scent and it brought all my undeniable feelings for him rushing back to the surface.

Now was my chance to talk to Nova. I wanted to tell him how

I felt and get to the bottom of his feelings for me, especially if I was about to be used as a pawn in Malakai's chess game of domination. I wanted to know once and for all where Nova and I stood. No matter how many times I told myself my life was too complicated for a relationship or that I should just stay away from him, I knew that regardless of the legends, there was a magnetic connection that drew me back to Nova every time. Maybe it was because he was a Pillar, maybe it was more than that. But, either way, it was impossible for me to be away from him, even if sometimes being near him felt just as impossible. The threat of being so close to the Troian Center and having Malakai take everything away from me was spurring me to take action and giving me the courage to finally put these feelings to words.

"Nova," I started, but before I could finish, he pulled my face up to his and kissed me.

I lost myself in the pure joy and blissfulness of the moment. His molten lips, his smoldering stare. The desperate way in which he held me. It took everything in my power to pull away from him, but somehow I managed.

"We need to talk Nova!"

"I know, Tippy. I just… it's just we're not very good at talking. It always leads to yelling and fighting. But we're good at this," he said pulling my face towards his again.

"Nova! I'm serious."

He let go of me and sighed deeply as he turned to stare at the fire, running his hands through his hair in frustration.

"I don't know what you want from me Tippy!"

"I want the truth," I said.

"You want the truth!?" he asked incredulously whirling back to face me. "How about you be truthful with me for a change!"

"About what?" I yelled back at him. We were fighting already. Why was it so impossible to talk to him lately?

"You've been different since you fell into the cave. You've been so hot and cold, so .... closed off. One minute you're telling me you love me and the next I feel like you're avoiding me and I hate it. I know you're keeping something from me, but I just wish you would talk to me. You know you can tell me anything. I miss you Tippy. All I want to do is be there for you but you make it impossible."

"I make it impossible!? You make everything impossible! For someone who wants to be there for me, you sure spend an awful lot of time with my sister!"

"Tippy, she's your sister. Half the time I spend with her, I'm trying to fix your relationship with her... and - "

"And the other half you spend sleeping with her?"

"What are you talking about?!"

"Oh, who's keeping secrets now Nova!"

"Tippy, I honestly don't know what you are talking about."

Tears instantly welled up in my eyes. How could he stand there and lie to my face? It was breaking my heart all over again. I knew I'd seen them together. The image of their limbs intertwined, swaying sleepily in the hammock, had been burned into my mind. Why couldn't he just admit it? I'd made mistakes too, but I'd come with the intension to admit them and see if we could actually have a shot at love.

A deep sadness ripped through my heart. I thought Nova was different, I thought he actually cared about me, but he wasn't different. He was just a boy, a boy that I had foolishly fallen for. I suddenly felt so stupid for telling him that I loved him at the vine bridge. He had never said it back and he obviously didn't feel the same way.

I turned to run for the door, but he caught my arm and I felt that electricity, that spark that we've always had pulse through me. All of my effort was going to stopping myself from crying and I'd let my guard down and now I could feel Nova inside my head. He had promised not to read my mind, but apparently that was a lie too!

"Stop it!" I cried out, pulling away from him.

But, from the look on his face I could tell it was too late. He had seen it all. The color had drained from his cheeks and he backed away from me, as shock and disbelief washed over his beautiful face.

"You kissed him?" was all he managed.

"You promised you would stay out of my head," I whispered.

"It seems we're both liars."

"No, Nova -"

"Do you love him too?"

"It's not like that -"

"Then tell me what it's like!"

"He's my friend ... I ... I don't know!"

Pain contorted Nova's beautiful features as he stared at me.

"Nova…" I said starting towards him, but he backed away from me and it stopped me in my tracks.

We stood staring at each other for what seemed like forever. I knew we were at a crossroad and if I walked away now I might lose him forever, but in doing so, I might actually be saving him. It seemed like I ended up putting everyone I loved in jeopardy. Something Eja had read to me from the Book of Secrets popped into my head. 'The sun must give up the stars if the world is to go on.' Those words had a profound effect on me now as I stared at Nova, his beautiful features highlighted by the flickering light of the fireplace. He was my star and I wanted to be with him more than anything I'd ever wanted before, but I loved him enough to know I had to let him go. I could see the pain I had caused him in his deep emerald eyes. Hurting Nova felt worse than giving him up. I knew what I had to do.

"Nova, I think that whatever we are, whatever we thought we could be… it needs to be over."

He looked truly vulnerable for a moment, before I could see his wall go up as he steeled his face and said, "If that's what you want Tippy."

"It is," I said.

No two words ever tasted so bitter and so untrue, but I knew I was doing the right thing.

"And one more thing," I said.

"Yes?"

"Please stop calling me Tippy."

I could see this was the nail in the coffin for us. Even through Nova's tough exterior, I could see that this had wounded him. He had given me that nickname when we first met and it always seemed like our thing. Even after I'd learned my name and everyone started calling me Geneva, Nova didn't. To him, I'd always be his Tippy and I liked that. It made me feel special, but I needed to sever all ties with him if I was to spare hurting him any further. I needed to give up my star in order to save him.

There was a knock at the door and it made me jump. Eja's thin frame peeked in.

"Am I interrupting?" he asked timidly.

"No, come in Eja," I said.

"Are we done here Ge-ne-va?" Nova asked bitterly pronouncing each syllable of my name.

"Yes," I said hoarsely, swallowing back the hard knot in my throat.

"Very well," he said sternly and gave a sarcastic bow as he left the room in a hurry, slamming the door behind him.

Eja raised his eyebrows at me and I burst into tears, surprising him even further. I ran to the sofa next to the fireplace and collapsed, finally succumbing to the pain of my conversation with Nova. Eja stiffly tried to comfort me by patting my shoulders as I mourned the bitter remains of my broken heart.

"My Eva, what happened?" Eja asked, handing me a soft cloth to wipe my face with.

"I just ended things with Nova."

"May I ask why?"

"I don't want to talk about it Eja."

He nodded sympathetically. "May I say that I believe you are very wise in all of your decisions, my Eva? Have faith that what you decide is what is meant to be."

I forced a smile. Eja was starting to sound a lot like Jaka, but I feared this time he was wrong. Nothing felt right about hurting Nova. It was all too much. The pain of losing Talon, Jovi being a secret Pillar, the immense responsibility to be the Eva, and now this; hurting Nova. Losing him before I'd even had him. The dam finally broke. I dissolved to tears again and this time I told Eja everything.

When I was done I felt like a weight had been lifted off of my soul. Keeping secrets from all of my friends was such hard work. Now that I had finally let Eja in, I felt lighter; almost hollow inside.

He was silent the entire time I rambled on about Nova, Remi, Jemma, and what I'd discovered about Jovi. Now that I was done, I was waiting tensely for him to say something.

"I think you are very noble to give up the one you love in order to protect him."

"So you think it's the right decision?" I asked anxiously.

"I think all of your choices are the right ones for you."

"Eja, stop talking in riddles! What do you really think?"

"I think you are doing what you know how to do in order to protect the people you care about. But, I think you also need to focus on how to protect yourself or all of your efforts will be useless."

"How do I protect myself?" I asked.

"I can help you do that," he said.

CHAPTER LXVIII

It was late when I finally left the room with the fireplace and my head was fuzzy. Eja and I had talked for hours. We went over many different strategies and ways I could protect myself, but they were all risky and none of them seemed foolproof. We read and reread the legends in the Book of Secrets and other manuscripts that Eja had found in Hollis's library, until they all started to get jumbled together in my head. I remembered how, at first, I had loved the enchanting way the legends were written, but now I was frustrated by their riddles. They were vague and left so much room for interpretation. I wish they would just come out and say what was true! But, I guess they were good for something, because one particularly devious riddle dealing with deception, birthed a risky plan that seemed just crazy enough to work. We just needed to find a room with a reflective surface and keep our scheme from the others. The only slight complication, was that it involved Jemma, whom I wasn't speaking with.

We also discussed that we would have to revise our plan for when we reached the Troian Center. Now that I had told him about Jovi being one of the Pillars, he agreed it would be safer for her not to accompany us to the Troian Center. I sighed a breath of relief knowing she wouldn't be following us into the mouth of danger. At least one good thing had come of the civer ant attack, I thought. Without it, I never would have known Jovi was a Pillar and we would have unknowingly, delivered her right to Malakai.

Bringing Jovi so close to the Troian Center and Lux, only to send her away, wouldn't be an easy pill for her to swallow. I knew she'd be mad. She'd probably say how unfair it was that she'd come so close to visiting the places she longed to see. But, I would have to let her be hurt to do what was best for her.

Eja offered to stay behind with Jovi and have Hollis escort them back to the Beto tribe. The other tough decision I'd come to, was that Niv should stay with them as well. The Troian Center hadn't been safe for him before and since it seemed they were expecting us, I hoped the best way to protect the both of us, was to keep him away from me. At least if one of us was always safe, the other would have a chance at surviving since I'd tethered our souls. The last thing I wanted, was for Niv to become something Malakai could use against me. I'd been down that road before.

I hated how this was starting to become a continuing theme; giving up those I loved most to keep them safe. Eja promised to look after Jovi and Niv, and assured me that these decisions were for the best. I knew he was right, but that didn't make it any easier.

I sullenly wandered the winding halls, following Eja back to the main room, dreading the conversations ahead of me. I was still feeling raw from my last unpleasant discussion with Nova. I found myself wondering how long I could avoid these discussions. I could hear lively chatter coming from the kitchen where my friends were gathered around the worn table. There was a small spread of food on it, perhaps the last of the rations from Jovi's mom. I hesitated to enter the kitchen and disrupt such a normal scene. It was so rare to see everyone in one place, getting along, enjoying a meal; being kids, rather than soldiers in a mystical battle I had dragged them into. For a brief moment, I wondered if maybe I could spare them all by just slipping away into the night. I shivered, shaking the cowardly thought from my mind.

Those were the thoughts of a scared little girl, I scolded myself. *I'm their Eva, their leader. I got them into this mess and I'm going to do my best to get them out.*

After my internal pep talk, I breezed into the kitchen with renewed confidence.

Isby squawked his disapproval as I entered the room and all eyes turned to me.

"Hi Geneva!" Jovi said, bouncing over energetically. "Are you hungry? I saved you some sweet bread."

When I saw her smiling face, I knew it was now or never. If I waited any longer we'd be at the Troian Center and Jovi would find a way to weasel herself in with us if she had the chance to plead her case to the group. I had to talk to her now. Alone.

"Yes. I'd love some Jovi. Can you bring it out here? There's something I need to talk to you about."

"Sure!" she said, trotting away to grab some bread from the table.

I caught Nova's gaze for a moment while I was waiting for Jovi to return and I could feel his disdain for me as he dropped my stare and returned to his conversation with Journey. It was like a knife in the heart, but I took a deep breath and reminded myself it was for his own good.

"Here," Jovi said thrusting a cloth wrapped hunk of sweet bread into my hands, breaking my inner monologue.

"Thanks Jovi. I need to talk to you about something important."

"Am I in trouble?" she asked, eyes as big as saucers.

"No Jovi," I smiled. "But remember our secret?"

She silently nodded.

"Well, Eja knows about it and he's going to help us keep it."

"I didn't tell him Geneva, I swear!"

"I know Jovi. It's okay. I told him because we need his help. He's going to take you and Quin back to your mom and the Beto's."

"What?" she squeaked and I motioned for her to keep her voice down. "But I don't wanna go back! I wanna stay here and help you," she whined.

"I know, but I need to keep you and our secret safe. The best way for you to help me, is for you to stay with Eja."

"But…"

"Jovi. Let me finish. I need you to help me with something very important."

"What?" she pouted.

"I need you to take Niv with you."

"Your Niv?" she asked, confused.

"Yes. Niv and I are tethered. Do you know what tethering is?"

She nodded.

"Then you see why it's not safe for him to come with me?"

She nodded again.

"I'm trusting you to take good care of him for me, like the way you take care of Quin. I need you to keep him safe while I'm gone. It's a big responsibility, and I don't trust anyone else to do it but you. Will you do it for me?"

She nodded nervously.

"Do you promise?"

"I promise Geneva."

"Okay, good girl," I said pulling her close for a hug.

I could feel her tiny heart hammering against me. I prayed I was doing the right things to protect all those I loved.

"Alright, let's go tell the others our plan," I said letting go of her.

As I stood to walk away, she caught my hand and squeezed it. "Geneva, don't be sad. I'll take the best care of Niv, I promise. I won't let anything happen to him. I'll protect him. I can be brave like my brothers."

I squeezed back, fighting tears, "I know you will Jovi. I know you will."

Now if only telling Niv would go as smoothly I thought.

When Jovi and I went back into the kitchen, Eja was finishing up telling the others what we had been discussing regarding he and Jovi, and Niv and Quin, staying behind.

"Nice of you to consult us on your plans Geneva," Nova said sarcastically when I joined them around the table.

"Excuse me?"

"Oh that's right, you just do whatever you want and we have to be okay with that because you're the Eva."

"Nova, I'm doing what I think is best for all of us."

"Yeah, keep telling yourself that," he said as he stormed out of the room.

"What the heck was that about?" Sparrow asked.

"Never mind, it's fine" I said shaking it off. "Hollis estimates he can get us to the Troian Center by tomorrow. Our plan remains the same. We are still looking for the Pillars. We need to locate them and then get them out of there. Hollis will help us escape the Troian Center with the Pillars and any other Truiet orphans we can help when it's time. The only thing that has changed is that Eja and Jovi will be returning to the Beto tribe, along with Quin and Niv. It's not safe for them inside the Troian Center."

"How will we communicate with anyone outside of the Troian Center without Quin to carry our messages?" Jemma asked.

"Yeah, what if we need to get in touch with the Betos? And how will we get word to Hollis once we find the Pillars. If Malakai is truly expecting us, we need a backup plan," Journey argued.

"Hollis has been kind enough to help us with that. We will rely on Isby to communicate with them," I said reluctantly.

The irritable, old bird ruffled his feathers and cocked his head to the side when he heard his name. We narrowed eyes at each other, but the standoff ended when he squawked and tucked his long beak under his wing, unceremoniously.

I looked back at my friends who were all still staring expectantly at me. They all looked eager and optimistic. I wished I could join them in their hopefulness but quarreling with Nova was taking all the fight out of me.

"Everyone try and get some rest tonight. We're going to need it."

Everyone filed out of the kitchen and went to their sleeping quarters for the night. Hollis had been kind enough to have Isby prepare a room for the boys and one for the girls. As Journey brushed past me, he paused and put a comforting hand on my shoulder.

"You're doing the right thing leaving the kid here."

"Uh, thanks Journey."

He smiled and squeezed my shoulder with his usual overpowering strength and continued on his way.

Journey's comment had caught me off guard. It was out of character for him to be polite and encouraging, but it lifted my spirits a bit because he never wasted his breath. He must have truly felt I was making a good decision if he bothered to compliment me on it. I was so lost in thought, I almost missed Jemma breeze by me.

"Hey, Jemma wait. Can I talk to you for a minute?"

"Can it wait? I'm going to wash up for bed," she said with her hands on her hips in annoyance.

"No, it can't really wait. I need your help with something."

"Oh really? What could you possibly need my help for? Didn't you just tell me that you're the Eva and I'm not? It seems to me that you should be able to handle everything just fine on your own," she said turning briskly and sashaying away from me.

Oh why was she so impossible!?

I jogged after her and when I finally caught up I grabbed her hand and blurted out why I needed her before she could hiss out some other snide insult.

"I need your help so we can talk to Mom."

CHAPTER LXIX

I creaked open an old gold leafed door and peeked inside. Eja was waiting for us, just where he said he'd be. He was standing in the center of the room, next to a large stone fountain that was covered in layers of dust and cobwebs. It looked like it hadn't been used in a hundred years. But, it's still pool of water shimmered nonetheless; catching moonlight from the impossible skylight above. I walked in and motioned for Jemma to follow me. She'd soundlessly agreed to accompany me as soon as I mentioned our mother. She trailed me with a timidness that I wasn't used to seeing in her. Jemma's normally calculating eyes, were now large and doe-like as they darted around the dim grey room, as if she was expecting to see our mother already inside, waiting for us.

"You said we were going to talk to mom," she said with distrust when her eyes settled on Eja and the fountain.

"We are. Eja's going to help us."

"Why do you all of a sudden need me and Eja to help you get in contact with her? Haven't you been talking to her without me all along?" Jemma accused with the hint of her normal distaste for me returning to her voice.

"Jemma, if I may," Eja interrupted.

"I can see this is going to take a while," Jemma said rolling her eyes but waving to Eja to continue as she crossed her arms and plopped down into an old armchair, upholstered with blue and silver jacquard.

A little cloud of dust puffed out of the timeworn fabric. It caused Jemma to cough and sputter, scrunching up her pretty face, as she did her best to brush off the dust and her bruised ego.

"Geneva wants to extend an olive branch to you Jemma. She wants you to have an opportunity to speak to your mother before you all return to an uncertain future at the Troian Center tomorrow. This may be your last chance."

"Oh, you mean because we all might die on this stupid mission Geneva has thought up?"

"Jemma! I'm trying to be a decent sister. I want to put all of our issues behind us so that you can get a chance to talk to mom."

"How noble of you to be a good sister all of a sudden so you can clear you conscience before our suicide mission," she replied bitterly, but I could tell she was interested.

Her arms were still crossed but she was on the edge of her seat looking anxiously towards the fountain.

"Think what you want of me Jemma, but I want to let you talk to our mother if you will agree to help Eja and I make our trip to the Troian Center safer."

"I knew you had an ulterior motive. You lure me here with the promise of seeing my mother and you really just want something from me!" she said rising from her seat and starting to walk towards the door. "Forget it!"

"Isn't there anything you want from me?!" I yelled after her in desperation.

She stopped dead in her tracks and whirled around to look at me. Her expression was wild with anger and I could read her hatred for me on her face. Her anger and envy flashed in my mind in another one of my too enlightening visions and I knew that she wanted more than I could offer her.

I saw her jealousy that I was the Eva, that I had our mother's attention, our friends' loyalty, Nova's affection and our island's admiration. But worse than all of that, I saw how much she despised being my sister. It made me feel sick to the pit of my stomach, but I shook the feeling and tried to bait her with the only thing I had left. I knew it wasn't exactly what Eja and I had discussed, but I needed Jemma to help me and after what I'd just seen in her thoughts of me, I knew it would be the only way to get her to cooperate with the latest plan Eja and I had cooked up.

"I want you to take my powers away!" I whispered. "All of them."

A slow smile curved up her face when she realized I was serious and her intrigue was evident.

"I can do that?" she asked trying to suppress her smile.

"This wasn't the plan my Eva. This isn't what I meant. Jemma is just supposed to veil the Ponte Deorum power. And I'm not even sure it would work… ," Eja was saying trying to interrupt our discussion.

"Shhh…" I hissed at him as he tried to stop our hurried plans.

"You can veil them all Jemma. Then you'll have powers and I won't. You'll be more powerful than me."

"So you want me to take them all?" Jemma asked with a smile.

"Yes," I said confidently even though Eja was protesting in my ear.

"But, that would mean we can't talk to mom anymore?"

"Right. Not until we rescue the Pillars and it's safe for me to get my powers back. That's why tonight is our last chance to talk to her if you can do this for me."

Jemma was silent while she pondered this. She and I were standing on the cold stone floor next to the fountain, while Eja paced nervously behind us. He paused to whisper in my ear, but Jemma interrupted him.

"We'll be able to see her in there?" Jemma asked pointing to the fountain.

"Yes, Eja discovered a link between Ponte Deorum and my reflection since every instance where I've seen mom has been either a mirror or body of water where I could see myself. We're assuming any reflective surface should work."

"This wasn't what we discussed, my Eva." Eja interjected. "She was only going to veil the Ponte Deorum power so that the Ravinori wouldn't be able to make that connection if they were looking for it. The goal is to put you in less danger. But if she takes away all of your powers.... You won't be able to protect yourself or anyone else. I can't advise this."

"Eja, I don't doubt your concerns, but you need to trust me. This is the best way. If I don't have any powers no one will even suspect I'm the Eva and then all of you are no longer targets just by being associated with me. It keeps you all safe."

"Indeed my Eva, everyone is safe except for you," Eja said with an intense sadness as he held my gaze.

"I'll do it," Jemma said interrupting us and extending here hand.

"Let's get started," I said, clasping my sister's cold hand and hoping like hell I wasn't signing my own death sentence.

"Just tell me how it works again Eja," Jemma hissed. "How do I take away her powers?"

"You have to concentrate Jemma," Eja said with a deep sigh.

He was starting to get frustrated. We'd been at this for quite a while and Jemma kept trying to rush him through his explanations.

"You're not taking her powers, you're veiling them. You're a tracer which means you can find things and most tracers are also veilers, which is why they are often so untrustworthy."

I tried to stifle my snort of irony, over the fact that Jemma fit her stereotype so well.

"Anyway," Eja continued, "we're betting that you're also a veiler, which means you can hide things. We want you to hide Geneva's powers."

"That's what I said Eja."

"No. It's not. You said you were going to *take* them. That's completely different. You have to be very specific when veiling something Jemma. And you must know exactly where you put it or you'll never find it again."

"Fine, I get it," she said, rolling her eyes.

"Eva, I'm not comfortable with this. She's never even done it before."

"She can do it Eja. When we spoke earlier, you said it yourself; she'd be the only one with a shot to do this since she's my sister and we have such a strong connection."

"Yes, but that was when I thought she was just veiling the Ponte Deorum. This…" Eja shook his head uncertainly.

"This is no different. Jemma can do this. It's the only way to keep you all safe."

Eja took a deep, defeated breath and uttered, "As you wish, my Eva."

"Let's get to work," I said to them both.

CHAPTER LXX

After a grueling hour of preparation, we were ready. Eja had told us everything he knew about tracers and veilers. Jemma had successfully veiled and traced out small knickknacks we found in the room. But, even this didn't satisfy Eja. He drilled us on how the whole process worked over and over, still trying to discourage us from this risky move every chance he got. But, for once, Jemma and I agreed on something and we were effortlessly working together to convince Eja that this would work. It was strange how easy it was to work with Jemma when our goals aligned. Even though we were plotting a tricky move to strip me of my powers, it was the first time I really felt like she was being my sister. We were reading each other's minds without using powers, and finishing each other's sentences like we'd been doing it all our lives.

A chill actually ran up my spine when Jemma interrupted Eja's latest objection by saying, "Please don't doubt my sister. She has everyone's best interests at heart and I know she'll put everything she has into making this work. If ever there were two people meant to do this, it's us."

It was the first time I'd actually heard Jemma call me her sister without it sounding awkward or forced. She seemed so committed that it had me completely convinced this would work and apparently it convinced Eja too because he sighed, letting his shoulders slump in exhaustion.

"You're right," he conceded. "I've shared all the knowledge I have on the subject. You're as prepared as you can be. I still think we might benefit from sharing this plan with the others."

"Eja, we've been over this," I interrupted. "There isn't time and all that would do is cause confusion and distract us," I added, pushing back the images of my friends most likely overreacting to my latest plan to protect them. I knew Remi and Nova would never allow me to do it.

"Plus, we just had a long drawn out meeting with everyone going over our plan for when we reach the Troian Center tomorrow. This doesn't change anything, it just adds extra protection for everyone," Jemma added.

"Fine," Eja sighed. "Just remember what I said about having a safe talisman to store Gevena's powers," he warned Jemma.

"Yes, yes I know," Jemma said. "I already know exactly where I'm going to hide them."

"Jemma this is the most detrimental part of this plan. You must keep the location of the talisman a secret. You have to choose somewhere she won't be able to stumble upon and where none of us will think to look. And it's crucial that this is a safe place where no one else will find it, or her powers could be lost forever."

"Eja," I said laying my hand on his arm. "She knows. It's going to be okay. It's getting late and we still need to talk to my mother before Jemma does the veiling."

"I know," he said sadly, bowing his head apologetically. "I'll give you some privacy to speak to your mother."

The room seemed colder after Eja left. It was just me and Jemma now. I can't remember the last time the two of us were alone together.

It felt strange, yet natural all at once.

"Shall we?" Jemma said with a sincere smile, motioning for me to come kneel next to her by the fountain.

"Okay," I said after settling down next to Jemma and taking a deep breath. "Are you ready to talk to mom?"

"More than you know," she said fighting back tears.

"I know it's not fair but remember what Eja said, we can't touch her and we have to be quick. Each time I access the Ponte Deorum we risk attracting the Ravinori."

"I know," she nodded wiping back her tears and smoothing her jet black hair.

"You look perfect," I offered, squeezing her hand.

"Thanks," she smiled.

"I couldn't agree more," said another voice making us both jump.

"MOM!" Jemma screamed! "Oh Mom, is it really you?"

There she was, her ethereal reflection glowing back at us. I hadn't even done anything to my knowledge to call her, but she was here. Perhaps she truly did know when I needed her.

"Jemma, my beautiful girl, don't cry."

But Jemma was already blubbering. Tears were streaming down her face and her lips were pursed and trembled.

"Oh my darling daughters. You have no idea how my heart soars seeing you together, acting so bravely and kindly," Nesia said.

"Mom, thank you for coming to see us. As usual we don't have enough time with you, but we wanted to see you one last time."

"I know my darlings. I'm so proud of the way you are working together and how you are selflessly sacrificing to help your friends."

"So, you know that Jemma's going to veil my powers?" I asked timidly.

"Yes darling. I have been watching you and am so proud that you're working together to come up with a way to protect each other. I've regretted that I didn't get to spend enough time preparing you for the roles you were born into. I wish I could tell you more, but those on the other side are forbidden to interfere with the beings on your realm. Each time I visit you, it upsets the balance of our delicate realms. I've already taken too many risks to see you. I do my best to guide and encourage you when I can my darlings. There have been many times where I feel I have failed you, but I never doubted my brilliant daughters would have any trouble charting their own paths in this world."

"Mom, you *have* failed us! " Jemma cried, chastising our mother through her tears. "I have no real powers or role. I feel so insignificant. I'm not the Eva! I'm nothing!" she yelled before dissolving into a pile of shaking limbs and tears.

I was in shock. Jemma had been so desperate to see our mother and now that she had the chance, she was spending it scolding her and acting like a spoiled brat.

"Jemma, darling. I'm so sorry. You have every right to be angry with me right now. I know you feel abandoned and jaded, but I also know your strength and that you know you are not insignificant. You have the soul of a warrior and you are so important to me and all of this. Without you there is no Eva. She is the light and you are the dark. One cannot exist without the other. Please know this is true. You are an instrumental part of this. Geneva is moving down the right path, but she cannot get there without you. You need to protect and serve each other. In order to defeat the Ravinori you need to work together."

Jemma had stopped sniveling and was looking into the fountain now with a glimmer of hope in her eyes.

"You have to believe in yourself darling."

"I do," Jemma said bashfully.

"Jemma, I have complete faith in you. I know you will be able to veil Geneva's powers and keep her safe. Have you chosen your talisman?"

Jemma nodded and my mother's smile faded into sadness for a moment.

"Very well," was all she said.

"May I offer one word of advice to you before I must go? If you put each other's needs before your own, you will always succeed."

We both nodded at our mother's vague comment. But, I was hoping she'd continue, that there was something more she could tell us about how to find the Pillars or defeat the Ravinori or protect my friends, but she was already starting to drift away."

"Wait, mom!" I called and she paused.

I wanted to ask her so much, but the only thing that was consuming my thoughts in that moment was Nova. It seemed so trivial to be asking my mom for advice on my love life at a time like this, but she was my mom and I'd always been longing for motherly advice; some sort of affirmation that I was making the right decisions, that only a mother can offer.

"You've been watching us right? Am I making the right decisions when it comes to… " I paused not wanting to bear my soul in front of Jemma. "I just want to protect everyone I love."

"Eva, my dear one, you are very wise. Follow your heart."

"But my decisions are breaking my heart mom."

"Ah, the decisions that weigh heaviest on our hearts, are often the right ones. Follow your path Geneva," she said as she started drifting away from us again. "I must go my darlings. I love you."

"…but mom!"

"And, Geneva… stay away from Nova."

Her last words haunted me as she dissipated before our very eyes. So, my mother had known what I meant when I was asking for her advice on hiding my feelings for Nova in order to protect him. Yet, all her warning did was leave me asking more questions. Like, why she told me to stay away from him in such an ominous way? Were the legends true? Was Nova really like Kull? Or, was there something else

I wasn't seeing? I was aggravated that I didn't have time to explore all my queries.

Jemma was smiling at me, like she was a cat who'd just swallowed a canary.

"Well that was interesting," she said, all traces of sisterly affection gone.

I felt the hairs on my arms stand at attention as I picked up on a feeling I wasn't liking from Jemma. She was making me nervous. We had just spoken to our mother and she'd told us to work together. I had held up my end of the deal in letting her talk to our mother, but now I had a feeling that wasn't going to be enough to get Jemma to veil my powers, as she promised.

"We should get started," I said, moving over to the chairs by the unlit fireplace.

"Yes, I suppose we should," Jemma said, coming to sit in the chair across from me.

She pulled it much closer than I was comfortable with and stared at me. She was so close I could feel the warmth from her blood radiating towards me, in the cold room.

"I think there's one more thing I'm going to need before we do this."

"What else is there Jemma? Eja told you everything..."

"I don't need anything more from Eja. It's you that I want something from."

"What else could I possibly give you? You're taking all of my powers."

"*Veiling*. I'm *veiling* your powers." She said sarcastically quoting Eja.

"You know what I mean Jemma." I said trying to retain patience.

"Well it's really just a small thing, and after what our mother said, I can't see you'd have any use for him anyway."

The bottom dropped out of my stomach. She couldn't be asking what I thought she was, could she? Even for her this was too cruel. But as she gave me a slow, perfect smile, I knew before she even spoke the words, that I was wrong. I knew what she wanted. This was too steep a price and I already felt my broken heart shred further when she opened her mouth to say his name.

"Nova."

"No, Jemma. And he's not an object, and even if he were, he's not mine to give."

"Well you heard our mother. You're to stay away from Nova, so it's not like you have any use for him anyway. And, like you said, he's not yours, so you really can't do anything to keep me away from him. I would just rather not have you as a constant obstacle."

My blood was boiling, but she was right. What could I do? I had already decided I needed to stay away from Nova to protect him. Wasn't that why we'd gotten in that awful fight tonight? And now, after my mother's unexplained warning, on top of Jaka's and Vida's, it seemed I had made the right decision to distance myself from Nova. But, I hated being back into a corner like this. Jemma had given me an ultimatum, her help hinged on me agreeing to stay away from Nova so she could pursue him.

Thinking I couldn't be with Nova was more than my heart could bare, but thinking he would be with someone else wasn't even on my radar and it knocked the wind out of my lungs. But, what could I do? The only way to protect all of us was to get Jemma to help us. My heart was splintering into a million tiny pieces as I conceded to Jemma's wishes. Perhaps that meant it was the right choice I thought, as my mother's words echoed in my mind, *'the decisions that weigh heaviest on our hearts are often the right ones.'*

"Fine Jemma. You win. I won't get in your way."

"Thanks sister, I knew you'd see it my way," she gloated. "Besides, if you didn't agree to it, I'd just tell him that you kissed Remi. I figured that'd do the trick."

"Save it. I told him myself," I admitted, completely deflated.

I was so wounded that I didn't eve care enough to ask her how she knew about Remi and I. I doubted she'd give me a straight answer anyway.

"Huh, I didn't think you had it in ya," she mused. "Thanks for saving me the trouble. Nova seems like the type to shoot the messenger. Now let's veil your powers!"

CHAPTER LXXI

The veiling hadn't really taken any time at all. Jemma did it on her first attempt. It hadn't been brutal or grueling like when I shared all my powers with her previously. She'd felt no pain at all this time and neither had I. Just a faint warmth, and then nothing. Nothing at all.

I tested my powers by trying to case flames into the empty fireplace, but it didn't work. The fireplace remained dark and cold. I tried to hear Jemma's thoughts, or feel her emotions, but I couldn't. I couldn't bound or cast orbs, I couldn't dissolve into invisibility; nothing responded to me in an unnatural way. I was completely ordinary. The only difference I felt was that I was more tired than I'd ever remembered being. I didn't know if it was a result of being stripped of my powers or of the horrible night I'd had. Either way, I was relieved it was over. Despite all I had given up, I'd achieved my goal of protecting my friends.

Jemma and I walked back to our room. It was cold in the winding hallway, and I rubbed my bare arms to ease the chill I felt. I trailed Jemma, who seemed to have an extra lightness in her step. I could have sworn she was almost skipping at one point. No doubt due having veiled my powers, rendering me useless. And not to mention, her anticipation of pursuing Nova the first chance she got now that she had me out of the way.

She stopped just outside our door as if she was waiting for me. I tried to push past her, truly just wanting to get some rest, but she stopped me with a hand on my chest.

"Remember our deal Eva."

"I know Jemma. I plan on staying away from Nova."

"Good. And I just wanted to let you know that I added a little insurance policy to make sure you keep your word dear sister."

"What do you mean?" I asked, skin suddenly prickling with nervousness.

"I used Nova as the talisman for your powers!" she said, excitedly clapping her hands together with glee. "Brilliant isn't it?"

"Are you insane!?"

"Shh…" she murmured, holding a long, dainty finger up to her pouty lips. "Don't want to wake anyone do we?"

She went to turn the door knob, but I grabbed her hand, twisting it away from the door and behind her back. I shoved her against the wall, hard. Jemma was caught off guard for a moment and she gave a tiny gasp before shaking me off, regaining composure and smiling.

"Careful sister. I hold all the cards for a change," she warned.

"Jemma, how could you do this to him!? If you even cared for him half as much as I do you would never have done this! Can't you see this only puts him in more danger!? I was trying to protect him! To protect you! And everyone else. You ruined everything! He's already a Pillar, so that means he's a target for the Ravinori, but if they find out that he contains my powers and the Ponte Deorum, that's it. He'll be their number one objective. You might as well have painted a bull's-eye on his back!"

"Well," she hissed "if you stay away from him then no one will be any the wiser and your precious Nova will be safe. And I'm pretty sure this plan of mine ensures that you'll keep your word and stay away from him, so you can thank me later little sister."

"What's to stop me from telling him what you did right now?"

She laughed in my face. "Please, you wouldn't do that and you know it," she said patronizingly.

"Try me!" I said with trembling rage.

"Fine, go ahead, tell him. You know he'll only give you all your powers back the moment he finds out what you did and then we'll all be in danger again. Not to mention that I'm sure he'll be *so impressed* by this latest blunder of yours, *the great Eva*! He'll probably declare his love for you right on the spot and ask you to be his girlfriend," she said sarcastically.

She was right. How had I been so foolish to trust her? I'd not only ensured that any hopes I had of a relationship with Nova were gone for good, but I had put him in worse danger than he'd been in before. I was so worried about trying to protect him, that I hadn't seen I was actually endangering him. I couldn't win. He was doomed whether he was in my life or not.

I was so angry with myself for not anticipating Jemma's betrayal. When would I ever learn that I couldn't trust her? Tears welled in my eyes and my cheeks burned. It felt like my throat was on fire as I swallowed hard against the taste of treachery. Jemma just grinned, from ear to ear. She could tell I was coming to realize everything she said was true.

"Oh come now sister, it's not so bad. I'll take good care of him and he will be safe. We all will, and you'll get to be our hero. See, everyone wins this way. Just as long as you stick to your word and stay away from Nova."

"Just tell me how to avoid getting my powers back when I'm around him."

"Hmm, I'm not actually sure. I'm sure touching him probably isn't a good idea? Maybe you better just stay as far away from him as you can get and everything will be fine," she said with a devilish smirk.

It was obvious that she knew exactly how she'd veiled my powers and how I would get them back. There was no way someone as cruel and calculating as Jemma hadn't worked that into her master plan. But, it was also obvious that not telling me was half the fun, because she knew it insured I would treat Nova like the plague. I'd made it clear to him that whatever we were, was over. Unfortunately, it wasn't that simple. We still had to be around each other and work together to save the Pillars.

"Jemma what am I supposed to tell him? He's going to think something's up if I'm constantly dodging him."

"Not my problem," she shrugged.

She faked a dramatic yawn and said, "Well I'm beat. Veiling your powers was draining. I think it's time I get some sleep," and she slinked away through the door to our room.

I stood outside the door shell-shocked. I was exhausted but there was no way I could bring myself to walk through that door and sleep in the same room as my backstabbing sister. I wandered back through the hallway and managed to make it to the sitting room before collapsing onto the worn chesterfield. Niv came scurrying over to me and climbed into my lap. I was so happy to see him. I wrapped my arms around him, pulling him to my chest, letting his long whiskers tickle my face.

"Oh Niv. She's awful! How did I end up with the world's worst sister?" I sputtered, crying into his neck.

He wiggled his long nose, pushing it under my arm and cuddling in closer to me. This actually made me smile and dulled the pain in my heart for a fleeting second. I squeezed him tight and buried my face into his coarse dark fur, drinking in his sweet smell.

"At least I'll always have you buddy," I whispered into his fur. But as the words escaped my lips, I realized they weren't true. The realization that I had to leave Niv with Eja and Jovi tomorrow hit me with stinging force. I still had to break the news to Niv. But how could I? Everything was going wrong. I was losing everything I loved, while Jemma kept winning. It wasn't fair. I found myself wondering how many wars I could fight at once.

I reminded myself that this was all to protect the ones I loved and leaving Niv behind was the only way I could ensure I wouldn't be dragging my sweet, defenseless marmouse into harm's way at the Troian Center.

"Niv?" I said, trying to wipe away my tears enough to focus on his adorable twitchy face.

He looked up at me expectantly, his tawny eyebrows shifting from side to side like he was trying to figure out what had me so upset.

"I need to tell you something and you have to promise to listen to me and know that I'm doing this to protect us both, okay?"

Silence

"Oh no!" I cried, just realizing that with my powers veiled, I'd no longer be able to communicate with animals. "Okay," I said trying to regroup. "Just because I can't hear you doesn't mean you can't hear me, right?"

Niv nodded back to me, confirming my suspicions.

"Okay, good. Niv, I need you to stay here tomorrow when I go to the Troian Center. Eja and Jovi are going to take care of you while I'm gone. Hollis is going to take you all back to the forest so you can stay with the Betos where it's safe until we return."

Niv squeaked his disapproval and even without having my powers, I could tell he wasn't happy with me. But before I could try to reason with him, he jumped off my lap and scurried away.

"Niv!" I called after him. But, he was gone; disappearing into the shadows.

I couldn't take it anymore. I broke down into a fit of limb shuttering, crying. I slid down off the couch and sat hunched on the floor with my head between my knees, trying to catch my breath as

I felt my world crashing down around me. Out of the corner of my tearful vision, I saw my shoulder bag hanging on the back of a nearby chair. I crawled over to it and pulled it down, letting it slump on the floor as I rummaged around inside for my journal. When my hands connected with it, I instantly felt a tiny bit of relief. My journal had always offered me solace when I felt desperate. I pulled it out and ran my hands over its tattered cover. I opened it and muttered the charm, but nothing happened.

"Reveal," I said. "REVEAL!" Still nothing. Then the last few pieces of hope I'd been clinging to evaporated. Without my powers I couldn't even use my journal.

I let it fall from my hands and sobbed uncontrollably. Jemma had really won. I'd been such a fool to trust her. Even our mother's plea for us to work together couldn't get through to her. She stripped me of my powers and veiled them in Nova to keep me away from him. I couldn't tell him or anyone else where they were hidden, I couldn't escape into my journal, and now even Niv was mad at me.

"How could I have been so stupid?" I cried to myself. "I have no one now!"

"You still have me," came an unexpected voice and I froze when I felt his warm hands on my back.

"NO! Don't touch me!" I yelled jumping to my feet.

Remi stared at me with shock and hurt in his eyes.

"Geneva, what's wrong?"

"Oh thank god it's you!" I said, relief rushing through my tensed muscles. "I thought…. never mind."

I slumped back down onto the couch and Remi came to sit next to me.

"Who did you think I was?" Remi asked putting a comforting hand over my trembling ones.

"No one."

"Geneva?"

I glanced over at him and could tell from the serious focus in his kind brown eyes, that he wasn't going to drop it.

"I thought you were Nova," I whispered shamefully.

"What?" He was instantly on his feet. "What did he do to you Geneva? Did he hurt you?"

"No. Remi, it's nothing like that," I said pulling him back down next to me on the couch. I hadn't expected him to react that way, but I guess I should have known he would jump to defend me. He really was such a good friend.

"Then what?"

"Oh Remi," I cried, surprising myself and him when I burst into tears again.

I hated how I was such a wreck of emotions today. I couldn't remember the last time I'd cried so much in one day. I guess everything had finally come to a head and once I let the flood gates open, there was no stopping them.

Remi cradled me in his lap and let me cry and shake as I told him how I had allowed Jemma to veil my powers to protect everyone from being associated with the Eva. I mindfully left out that part that Jemma was blackmailing me by using Nova as the talisman. But otherwise, I filled Remi in on all the details, down to my mother's warnings and feeling foolish for being betrayed again by my sister. It felt better to get it all out there and off my chest. The situation was still as bleak, but I always felt better when I let Remi in. He offered me a familiar comfort, the way only a constant childhood friend could. I was relieved that he didn't judge me or tell me I was a fool. Remi always had my back. He just let me cry and pushed stray curls from my cheek while I caught my breath and drifted into sleep.

CHAPTER LXXII

I awoke to the smell of breakfast cooking and the voices of my friends. I opened my eyes slowly, as I let the fog of sleepy confusion lift. I wasn't quite sure where I was. I snapped quickly back to reality when I heard Remi's voice in my ear.

"Good morning sunshine," he crooned, stroking my hair out of my face.

My eyes flew wide open as I realized I was still lying on his lap, where I must have slept all night! I sat up immediately, wiping the drool self-consciously from my blushing cheeks.

"Remi, why didn't you wake me?" I hissed.

"You looked so peaceful," he smiled. "But now that you're awake, I say we get some of that breakfast before Journey eats it all!"

He stood up and stretched tall. His crumpled shirt lifted off his waist exposing his lean stomach and I blushed scarlet. What was wrong with me? We hadn't done anything wrong. I'd just fallen asleep next to him, like we'd done since we were old enough to crawl.

He's my best friend. Nothing to be ashamed of, I told myself.

I followed him into the warm, bustling kitchen, where the rest of our friends were gathered around the table piled full of food. But as soon as I walked into the room, I felt everyone's eyes on me, judging me and I wanted to shrink under the table when Journey whooped to Remi, trying to get a high-five that he thankfully ignored.

"Oh look who's up?" Jemma said cheerfully. "I made sure we saved you two some breakfast," she said as she handed us both plates. "You just looked so cute snuggled on the couch together this morning, I didn't have the heart to wake you."

"Thanks," Remi mumbled, taking our plates from her. "What are these?" Remi questioned, poking the flat dough patties on his plate.

"They're pancakes!" Jovi said. "Isby made them."

"An… dwr…gud," Journey mumbled between mouthfuls, giving a thumbs up.

"I'll take your word for it," Remi replied, while he finished piling sweet bread and berries onto our plates.

I hated that she was so chipper. No doubt still smug with her ability to veil my powers and continue her plan to steal Nova and ruin my life.

Nova was glaring at me, and Sparrow just looked confused. Everyone else was smirking and it was making my skin crawl.

"So you two must have been up late," Journey added sarcastically with a wink.

"We were just talking," I said defending myself.

"You must have had *a lot* to talk about," Jemma said with a giggle.

"We did, we talked a lot about you Jemma," Remi said, wiping the smirk off her face. "Do you want to tell everyone how you took advantage of Geneva or should I?"

The kitchen erupted once Remi told my friends that Jemma had veiled my powers. Everyone was yelling, accusations flying. I knew this would happen, but was hoping it wouldn't be quite so early in the day and I would've had a little food in my stomach first. I was not looking forward to another fight with my friends. I just wanted to get out of there! I had completely lost my appetite and took the opportunity to slip out while Journey was trying to voice his point of view over everyone else's arguments.

To my relief, no one seemed to even notice I was gone. I could still hear everyone's raised voices as I retreated to my room to change and pack up my belongings. I hadn't anticipated all the events of last night and hated that I felt rushed to try to get ready to depart Hollis for the Troian Center today. There was no telling when we would arrive, but I knew we'd probably be there sooner than I was ready for.

I finished packing my shoulder bag with what was left of my clothes and my useless journal. Then I set off to find Niv. We hadn't left last night on good terms and I wanted to make sure he was okay before leaving him with Eja and Jovi. I bumped into Sparrow in the hallway.

"Hey," Sparrow said, greeting me with less warmness than usual.

I brushed the strange feeling off, chalking it up to losing my powers. Everything felt strange without them.

"Have you seen Niv this morning?" I asked.

"Oh, no I haven't. Sorry."

"Can you help me look for him?"

"Sure, I guess," she said as she followed me wordlessly down the hall.

I kept getting the feeling that she wanted to say something. She was probably miffed that I'd been foolish enough to trust Jemma and give up my powers. I didn't have time for a lecture from Sparrow. I needed to find Niv, but since she really seemed to be following me like a lost cub, rather than helping me look for him, I finally confronted her.

"Out with it Sparrow! Just say whatever you want to say already."

"Well, I mean, I was just wondering what happened last night?"

"I screwed up! I know! Remi explained it already, didn't he? What part are you confused about? The fact that I have no powers or that my sister is a jerk?"

"No, I get that. I mean, I wish you didn't have to be so vulnerable without your powers, but I get why you did it and I really appreciate the sacrifices you make for all of us Geneva."

"Then what's confusing you?"

"I don't want you to be mad at me…"

"Sparrow! I won't be mad! Just tell me so we can get past it and you can help me find Niv!"

"Well, so are you with Remi now?"

"What?!" I squeaked. "No! Why would you think that?"

"Well I don't know? Maybe because when we woke up this morning we all walked past the two of you curled up on the couch together!"

"We were up late talking. I was really upset after getting in a fight with Jemma and he heard me crying and came out to talk to me and we fell asleep, that's it! Ah, why does everyone have to read so much into everything?"

"Well…."

"Well what?"

"Isn't that what you assumed when you saw Nova and Jemma sleeping in the hammock?"

"That's different Sparrow! Nova and I have… had something. Never mind. It doesn't matter anymore. Nova and I are over."

"I'm sorry," she said sheepishly. "I know how you feel about him. But, you also know how Remi feels about you and you shouldn't play with people's feelings."

"I'm not! Remi is my friend. I've already told him that I don't think of him any other way. He knows that."

"Even now that you're through with Nova?"

"Yes! Why are you pressing this Sparrow?"

"I just want to know what's going on. It's hard to keep everything straight around here. One minute you love Nova, the next you two are over. You kissed Remi, but you don't like him that way, but you cuddle on the couch all night with him. How do you not see that it's confusing to me?"

"Why do you care Sparrow?"

"Because maybe I'd like a chance to see if I could have a relationship someday and I don't want to step on your toes. I'm trying to be a good friend."

"You want to date him?" I asked incredulously.

"No! I don't know, maybe?"

"I really wish we could all stop focusing on this stupid stuff! Honestly, a boyfriend is the last thing that should be on our minds right now. I thought we all had more important things to concentrate on," I said bitterly.

"We do. I'm sorry I brought it up, I wasn't trying to fight with you," Sparrow said.

"It's fine," I sighed in frustration. "Just tell me if you see Niv, okay?"

"Sure," she nodded.

Journey was just rounding the corner.

"What's wrong?" he asked the moment he took note of Sparrow's crestfallen face. He rushed past me to her side.

I walked away from the two of them, shaking my head as Sparrow leaned into Journey's burly shoulder.

And she thought I was confusing? It was plain as day to me that poor Journey was in love with her and she seemed to be completely blind to it.

"Hypocrite," I muttered to myself

CHAPTER LXXIII

"This is where I leave you," Hollis bellowed.

We all crawled out of his protective shell and stretched in the warm breeze that bathed the edge of the rainforest. If I peered through the vines and vegetation, I could scarcely make out the ominous outline of the orphanage that had been my home. I knew this spot all too well and a prickling hint of nostalgia washed over me. This was where I'd first entered the forest with Nova and learned I had powers. Not too far from here we had rescued Niv, and buried his mother. We'd also fled through this area after we stole the Book of Secrets from the Troian Center. It filled me with a strange mix of emotions being back here.

Our voyage through the forest to get back to the Troian Center was harrowing, but I had a feeling today was the beginning of something much more difficult. Our quest to save the Pillars was immense and I was starting to realize that none of us were truly prepared for what lay ahead.

"Well here's to the first day of the rest of your life," Eja said as if reading my mind.

CHAPTER LXXIV

The rumble of thunder in the distance distracted the tall man from his plotting. He rose from his desk, smoothing back his long dark hair; unfurling his menacing black robes. He ascended the stone staircase, spiraling to the top of the open stone terrace above his office. From here he could see the barren landscape of Hullabee Island from every angle. When he stepped outside, a hot wind whipped his onyx mane from its neatly collected coif. For once, he didn't fix it. He let is lash at his face in an unruly way as he watched the darkening sky on the horizon.

Heavy, grey clouds gathered on the edge of the rainforest, like toiling ocean waves, giving warning to all, that a storm was brewing.

"And so it begins," he said, fighting the shiver that ran up his spine, while he smiled toward the forest.

He twisted the obsidian ring he wore on his left hand. It was something he did subconsciously when he was anxious. He polished it against his robes and then held his hand up to block out the intermittent rays of sun that snuck through the clouds. The inscription on the face of the stone blazed in the sunlight. MV – Malakai Venir.

CHAPTER LXXV

We gave Eja and Jovi tearful embraces and refused to say goodbye. It felt much too final. We said farewell instead as we watched them disappear back into Hollis's shell. We thanked him for granting us safe passage through the forest and he of course bowed and said he was honored to serve us. He promised to help Eja locate the Beto camp and safely deliver him and Jovi back to them. Quin would assist Hollis in tracking the tribe since much to my dismay, Isby was staying with us so he could convey messages back to Hollis and the Betos if need be.

I hadn't been able to find Niv. I knew he was hiding somewhere inside Hollis's maze of rooms. He was obviously still upset with me for leaving him behind and even though it hurt my heart to leave him without saying goodbye, I knew it was the right choice. Without my powers I couldn't protect him and I would never forgive myself if I put my sweet little marmouse in danger. I'd sworn to his mother that I would protect him and I intended to keep that promise. It reminded me of the oath I'd made to Jovi's mother too. I felt relieved that I'd upheld my word and that Jovi was now safely on her way back to her family. She had assured me that she'd find Niv and take care of him for me in a tearful goodbye.

We all watched Hollis lumber away until he was swallowed up by the forest. I was sad to see him go, but I felt better being outside in the fresh air. I think being cooped up in such close quarters with everyone had really gotten under my skin. Whatever magic made Hollis's impossible interior possible, had put us all on edge and I could tell instantly that we were all in better spirits now that we were out in the world again.

We gathered up our gear and fell into line as we silently walked the narrow path through the last few feet of forest. The thick vegetation fell away abruptly and before we knew it, we were all exposed, as we stood side by side, gazing across the sun scorched fields to the Troian Center, while thunder clouds gathered overhead, setting an ominous stage.

We stuck to the plan we'd come up with during our rotunda meeting. We were going to link hands and walk together towards the Troian Center under Remi's invisibility power. We had no idea what we were walking into or how we'd be welcomed. At least this way we could get close enough to get a better look.

We stood silently for a moment, waiting for Remi to give us the sign that his power had taken effect and we were all invisible. The wind picked up as the sun was swallowed up by the cloudy sky. My breath caught in the back of my throat as I realized this was it. This could potentially be the last time we were all together. We had no idea what was waiting for us, yet all of my friends were here, standing by my side, fighting my fight with me. Just then Remi squeezed my hand, letting me know he was ready. I knew there wasn't time to express how much I loved and appreciated every one of my friends in that final moment.

All I had time to say before we took our first official step towards our destiny was,

"Farewell."

SECRETS

The Geneva Project and Christina Benjamin are proud to be associated with the PASS IT ON! organization which was created to help promote reading in America and all countries around the world. When you buy a copy of The Geneva Project – Secrets, or any other book, we encourage you to Pass It On! to someone else when you have finished. There are many people in the world that cannot afford to buy books and with one small gesture you can help someone enjoy reading as much as you do. *Don't just put it on a shelf to collect dust, Pass It On!*

For more information on how you can
get involved in the PASS IT ON! program please visit

www.TheGenevaProjectBook.com

Made in the USA
Charleston, SC
22 September 2014